Second
You Sin

Second You Sin

SCOTT SHERMAN

KENSINGTON BOOKS
www.kensingtonbooks.com

KENSINGTON BOOKS are published by

Kensington Publishing Corp.
119 West 40th Street
New York, NY 10018

All Kensington titles, imprints, and distributed lines are available at special quantity discounts for bulk purchases for sales promotion, premiums, fund-raising, educational, or institutional use.

Special book excerpts or customized printings can also be created to fit specific needs. For details, write or phone the office of the Kensington Special Sales Manager: Kensington Publishing Corp., 119 West 40th Street, New York, NY 10018. Attn. Special Sales Department. Phone: 1-800-221-2647.

Kensington and the K logo Reg. U.S. Pat. & TM Off.

ISBN-13: 978-0-7582-6651-4
ISBN-10: 0-7582-6651-0

First Kensington Trade Paperback Printing: October 2011
10 9 8 7 6 5 4 3 2 1

Printed in the United States of America

*This book is dedicated to Marc, who helped me through a
very difficult time in my life with tremendous support, a
listening ear, and a loving heart. There will always be
traces of a song, places that belong to you.*

Thank you for joining Kevin and me for his second big adventure. We hope you enjoy the ride.

There are several shout-outs in *Second You Sin* to some of our favorite artists. Already heavily featured in Kevin's origin adventure, *First You Fall*, Barbra Streisand gets some love here, too. So do Ari Gold and Jay Brannan, two singer-songwriters from somewhat opposite sides of the musical spectrum but both of whom are great listens and lust-worthy on multiple levels.

Many thanks to fellow writers Josh Lanyon and Neil Plakcy for their help, encouragement, advice, inspiration, and wonderful stories.

This book wouldn't exist but for two great gentlemen who helped me get it into your hands—my literary agent, Matthew Carnicelli, and my editor at Kensington, John Scognamiglio. Thanks, guys, for believing in this story.

Two other fellows I have to acknowledge are my sons, Sasha and David. I love you boys bigger than the moon. By the time you're old enough to be reading this, you'll probably both be surly teenagers, but right now you're more precious than words could ever express. (BTW: I'll still love you when you're pain-in-the-ass adolescents, I promise.)

PS: There's a theme in the chapter titles to this book—can you figure out what it is? Send in your correct answer to the link on the home page at www.firstyoufall.com. On February 1, 2012, I'll pick a winner at random. If you're right, you'll have your choice between a signed copy of Second You Sin or the chance to have your name in print as a victim in one of Kevin's next adventures. Or, if you say something nice about the book, maybe both.

1

Wet

Despite my unconventional choice of profession, I tried to have a normal life. I really did.

So how come weird stuff kept happening to me?

I started my week in church, like the good boy I try to be.

By the time the week was over, I'd find myself covered in whipped cream, attending a party in my underwear, defending my mother against a monster, working for a man I considered a Nazi, losing my semi-boyfriend, and fighting for my life.

But I had to do it all.

As I was soon to find out, someone was murdering the most beautiful male prostitutes in New York.

And it was up to me to find out who.

As a male hustler working in New York City, I've done plenty of kinky things. I've been tied up, scrubbed down, and hosed out. I've played every role my young-looking features lent themselves to. I've been the naughty schoolboy sent to the principal's office for a paddling, the high school football hero treated for a pulled groin muscle by the horny coach, and the newspaper delivery boy who "accidentally" walks in on his customer in the nude. I've done it in the changing room of a major department store on Broadway, on a Thanksgiving float used in another store's popular parade, and in the DJ booth of the city's most popular dance club during an exclusive private party. With the DJ. I've been massaged, shaved, tickled, and wrapped in aluminum foil by some of New York's wealthiest and most powerful men. I've been with guys who wore everything from tutus to superhero costumes to scuba suits.

For the most part, I love my job. If you have an open mind, other people's kinks are fun and kind of sweet. I like that I give my clients a place to act out the desires they're afraid to show their boyfriends, partners, husbands, and wives. As long as the activity is safe, consensual, and semi-legal, I'm down with it.

I do have my limits, though. Anything involving urine or, God forbid, that other thing, is out of the question. No how, no way, no matter how much he's willing to pay. Not gonna happen.

Which brings me to the question of how I found myself, on this particular Sunday in November, being peed on by one Willem Patrick O'Reilly III, the golden stream arcing majestically to soak the entire front of my two hundred dollar John Varvatos hoodie.

"Pee!" Willem shouted happily. "I put my pee on you!"

Yeah, I let Willem pee on me. It wasn't so much that he was cute (though he was) or rich (well, his parents were) but the fact that he was three years old that let him get away with it.

"Sorry, Kevin, I should have warned you he's a soaker," Cindy, my co-teacher in the playroom, called out as she watched Willem hose me down. "Some boys are like that. The minute you get their pants off, they can't wait to celebrate."

Cindy was in her mid-sixties. She wore her long gray hair in a ponytail and dressed like a hippie-Wicca from Woodstock. She didn't seem to have a mean or sarcastic bone in her body.

"It's OK," I called back to her as she handed out more Play-Doh to the other kids in the class. "I'll consider it a baptism."

I looked down at Willem on the changing table, where he lay with a delighted grin.

"Good aim, kid."

Willem laughed. "I pee *all over* you."

"I'll notify the awards committee," I told him. "Now we both have to get changed."

Willem stuck out his lower lip. "I don't wanna get changed. I wanna play with Play-Doh!"

"Sorry, buddy," I said. I cleaned him with a baby wipe and put a fresh diaper on him. "Now that the missile's back in the silo, you want to get back to the other kids?"

Willem nodded enthusiastically.

I lifted him to the floor.

"How about next time," I said, "you try to make that pee-pee in the potty?"

Willem grimaced. "Potties are poopie," he explained.

"But," I said, "if you use the potty, you don't have to get changed and you'll have more time to play with the Play-Doh."

Willem looked thoughtful. "I scared of potty," he said quietly.

I knelt down. "Why are you scared of the potty, Willem?"

"My brudder said I fall in and go to poopie land."

"Your brother's just teasing you," I said, thinking I'd have to mention something to Willem's mother when she picked him up. "You can't fall down the toilet. I promise."

Willem took my hand. "If I go potty, you come with me?"

I gave him my most serious look. "I promise."

Willem kissed me on the cheek. "I wuv you, Kebbin." He ran back to the Play-Doh.

I love you, too, buddy, I thought. *I love you, too.*

The truth was, I pretty much loved all kids. If I weren't making such easy money as a hustler, I could see being a teacher. In the meantime, I satisfied my paternal yearnings here at the Sunday school program of The Metropolitan Unitarian Universalist Church of Manhattan.

I started coming to the church a few months ago, after a near-death experience that found me hanging naked from the ceiling of a serial killer's torture chamber. As said killer was choking me, I didn't see my life flashing before me, but I did, in a very Peggy Lee moment, think, *Is that all there is?*

Although I wound up being saved by my semi-boyfriend, the

incredibly beautiful and conflicted Officer Tony Rinaldi of the New York Police Department, I couldn't shake the feeling that there had to be more to existence than just getting by.

I might not have made it to heaven that night, but I got close enough that I wanted to make sure I knew the password.

I wasn't raised in a religion, so I asked friends about theirs. Eventually, I found out about Unitarian Universalism. It's a religion that has no dogma and no ritual. They don't tell you what to believe in or what to do. You're encouraged to live in a way that's honorable and respectful of the natural world and other living things. The UU principles value democracy and freedom. You don't even have to believe in God or Jesus to be a UU—although you're encouraged to be courteous to those who do.

UU churches are supportive religious communities that prize diversity and intellectual curiosity.

Plus, the reverend of my church is a brilliant, inspiring speaker, openly gay, and totally hot. Every week, I listen to his sermons and am simultaneously spiritually uplifted and turned on.

Sexy enlightenment? Works for me.

A couple of months ago, one of the Sunday school teachers called in sick. Reverend Jack asked if I could fill in. Although I had hoped that his first request of me would involve massage oil and nude wrestling, I would pretty much do anything he asked.

So, I helped out. Working in the preschool room reminded me just how much I enjoy being around children. When an ongoing position there opened up, I was happy to volunteer. Now, every Sunday, I attend the early sermon and help run the preschool for the second session. The kids are great, and my co-leader, Cindy, is funny and warm.

She's also been a teacher long enough to know just how uncomfortable working in a urine-soaked sweatshirt can be.

"Go see Shirley in the office," she told me. "She probably has some T-shirts left over from some church event or something."

Shirley-in-the-office was one of those women who seemed to work at every church in the world: somewhere between seventy and one hundred, hair pulled back in a tidy bun, harlequin glasses permanently perched on the tip of her patrician nose. She took a sniff as I walked into the room.

"Let me guess," she said in her hoarse rasp that proved that not everyone who smoked died young. "That's not juice."

"It was at one point," I offered.

Shirley gave a little shudder. "That is just *one* of the reasons I never had children. Filthy beasts." She waved her hand as if shooing something away.

"Listen," I said. "Cindy thought you might have something I could change into."

Shirley got up slowly. Her bones creaked like a door that hadn't been opened in years. I wanted to get her a can of oil.

"In here," she said, taking me into a small room behind her desk. Boxes were neatly stacked against the walls. She walked over to one and pulled out a white T-shirt that said "For Sale."

I didn't think Shirley knew what I did for a living, but the co-incidence was bizarre.

"We used these for the mannequins at the church bazaar," she explained. "But don't worry, wearing it won't make you look like a dummy." She snorted at her joke.

I waited for her to leave, but she stood there and stared.

"Uh, I'm gonna get changed now," I said.

"I'd imagine you would," Shirley answered. "You smell like a urinal."

"A little privacy?" I asked.

"Honey, look at me. If I were any older, they'd hang a plaque around my neck and declare me a historical site. It's not that often I get to see a cute young thing like you get half naked. Why do you suppose I watch those insipid soap operas—for the plots? If you think I'm missing this, you're crazy." She crossed her arms and nodded.

I sighed and pulled my damp hoodie over my head. Shirley whistled.

"Well, look at you. Strong little thing, ain't you?"

It's a reaction I often get. I'm a small guy. Just five foot three and a buck twenty-five. But thanks to years of gymnastics and weight training, what little there is of me is pretty well built.

Of course, for me, looking good is a job requirement. With my youthful features and blond unruly hair, I'm your typical boy next door. Assuming you live next door to an Abercrombie & Fitch.

I keep myself in the best shape I can—not too muscular, but slim, lean, and cut. In my clothing, I look like a skinny kid, but when I'm undressed, the results of my hard work are evident.

Shirley was getting a good show, as I had to struggle to get the T-shirt she'd given me over my head. I checked out the label. XXS.

"You have anything bigger?" I asked her.

"Sorry, that's all we have left," she rasped. "Keep working, it'll stretch." She looked down at her flattened chest. "Trust me, sooner or later everything does."

I continued to writhe. Eventually, I squeezed into it. If it were any tighter, I'd have died from strangulation. It clung to me like a second skin, the sleeves only covering the top inch of my biceps, and the bottom stopping an inch and a half above my belly button.

"Woo-eee, look at those abbydominals," Shirley observed. "You should dress like that all the time." She dropped her voice down to a whisper. "Although, not in church, honey. It's not really appropriate."

"Well, it's not as if I chose this. . . ." I began. "Oh, never mind."

Shirley-in-the-office watched as I left the room. "You should wear tighter pants, though," she offered. "Show off that cute butt of yours. Oh, yes, you'd fit right in on one of my shows."

As I walked back into the classroom, Cindy looked at me, blinked twice, and went back to reading the kids a story. When she was done, she pulled me out of earshot of the class and nodded toward my shirt. "Didn't they have anything in an adult size?"

I grimaced. "Shirley said this was all they had left."

"Well," she said, "at least it's better than walking around soaked in pee-pee."

"I look ridiculous, don't I?"

"Oh, no, you look fine," she lied. "I mean, at least you have the figure for it. Just don't walk past the middle school classes—those twelve-year-old girls will eat you alive."

2

New York State of Mind

After class was over, the parents came down to the classroom and picked up their kids. A few of them looked at me a little funny, but I tried not to make eye contact with anyone. My little talk with Willem's parents would probably go better when I wasn't dressed like the Whore of Babylon. A slap on my butt, though, got my attention.

"Look at you," said Nick, a darkly handsome guy in his late thirties who tended to be on the serious side. "Where have you been hiding all those muscles? And why bring them out to play today?"

"Hey," I said, giving him a quick hug. "Usual story. Changing a diaper, unexpected hose-down, had to grab whatever was handy."

"Yeah," Nick said. "Been there, hated that. Could have been worse, though. Getting painted with what comes out the other end's a real bitch."

Nick's partner, Paul, walked over with their son, Aaron, in his arms. He was a really adorable kid they'd adopted through foster care.

Aaron left one arm around Paul's neck while hooking the other around Nick. He pulled the three of them as close together as his little arms could.

"There's your Christmas-card photo right there," I said.

"Hey, Kevin," Paul said, giving me a peck on the cheek. Paul was about ten years younger than Nick, fairer, too, with a shy smile and cute, floppy hair. "You still have to come over for dinner one night. Aaron is dying to show you his action figure collection."

"I have Supahman and Ba-Man and Wonna Woman and 'Pider Man and . . ."

Paul bounced him in his arms. "Whoa, big man, save the whole list for later, OK? We want Kevin to be surprised."

"OK," Aaron whined.

"But really," Paul said, "you have to let Nick cook for you. He makes stuffed chicken breast to die for."

"Speaking of," Nick said, "check out those pecs on little Kevin, huh?"

Paul blushed, which was not unusual. He was definitely the sensitive type. He was also a pretty terrific painter. He was discovered by a gallery in LA a few years ago.

I knew their move to New York was paid for by his sales. I wasn't quite sure what Nick did, but I think he was in some kind of law enforcement. Maybe he'd get along with my semi-boyfriend, Tony. He was certainly butch enough—Tony wasn't comfortable around anyone too flamboyant, and Nick was definitely a man's man. He practically leaked testosterone.

Nick pulled Paul closer. "Don't worry, baby, you know I only have eyes for you."

"It's not your eyes I'm worried about."

Nick tousled Paul's shaggy hair.

"Will you call?" Paul asked me. "We really do owe you for taking such great care of Aaron."

"I will," I promised. "I'd love to come over sometime."

I meant it. They were a terrific family and I looked forward to getting to know them better.

"And wear that shirt," Nick called out, earning him a smack on the head from Paul.

"Don't hit, Papa," Aaron admonished.

"That's my boy," Nick said, pulling Aaron from Paul's arms and throwing him in the air. Aaron laughed with glee and Paul sighed the sigh of put-upon housewives the world over.

* * *

When class was over, I threw on my leather jacket and hurried out the door. Although it was unseasonably mild weather for mid-November, there was enough of a chill in the air that I wished I could have worn the sodden sweatshirt I carried in a plastic bag.

I kept myself warm by walking quickly through the streets of the West Village to the coffee shop where I was meeting my best friend, Freddy.

It was a lazy Sunday, with just a handful of people walking around and even fewer cars on the road. I love Manhattan when it's quiet and sleepy like this.

I've known Freddy since my freshman days at New York University, when I was an inexperienced freshman and he was the charismatic and dead-sexy student-president of the school's Gay/Straight Alliance. Thankfully, he fell into the first category of the group's name, and we quickly entered into a fast and thrilling affair. The sex was great—Freddy's one of the most sensual partners I've ever had—but it quickly became clear we made better friends than we did lovers.

Well, to be honest, it only became clear when I found out that he had slept with twelve of the fifteen guys who had joined the group that year, including two of the three straight ones. Freddy had the most voracious sexual appetite I've ever encountered, and when you consider my profession, that's saying a lot. Luckily for him, he's fantastically good-looking and has a body to die for, so getting laid is never a problem.

Relationships, however, don't come as easily. Freddy laughs off any suggestion that he might actually want to settle down with anyone—or any three or four, for that matter. It's a subject that's kind of awkward for me to pursue, because, despite the fact that we both act as if we're uninterested, there's an undeniably strong attraction between us. Which we've both been denying, that is.

I was pretty sure it could never work between us. We're better off as friends.

Freddy rose to greet me as I walked through the door. "Sweetheart!" he called.

The coffee shop where we met had just opened a few weeks before. It was called Drip. With its drop-dead gorgeous baristas and posters of sexy shirtless boys, it attracted a mostly male crowd. It was pretty packed on this Sunday morning, and the few diners in the shop who hadn't already noticed Freddy turned to look. As usual, the quick glances became gazes as they drank in Freddy's lusciousness.

"Hi," I said. We exchanged air kisses and I noticed a few patrons continued to stare. Some at me, I hoped.

Freddy had just come from the gym—his church—and he was wearing a snug long-sleeved Under Armor workout shirt and sweatpants. The white shirt hugged and accentuated every curve of his rounded biceps and prodigious chest, contrasting nicely with his chocolate brown skin. I could see why eyes bulged at the sight of him.

Forgetting that I was wearing the "For Sale" T-shirt, I slipped off my leather jacket. Freddy's mouth dropped.

Although I think it kind of titillated him, Freddy never really approved of my job. I winced, anticipating the drubbing about to come my way.

"Are we *really* that desperate for business?" he asked. "Have we taken to wearing promotional appeals on our chests? What's next, darling, a sandwich board that says 'Johns wanted, inquire within?' Shall we take out an ad in the *New York Times?* 'Cute young man available for hand jobs and light role-playing'?"

I noticed that the men at nearby tables had stopped talking as they hung on Freddy's every word.

"I mean, really," Freddy continued. He held up his hands in wonder. "Are times that bad? I know the economy is rough, but I thought sex was one of those commodities, like gas and toilet paper, that people are always willing to pay for."

One of the guys at the next table laughed so hard he spit coffee through his nose. Nice.

"It's not *my* shirt," I whispered. "And could you keep your voice down? People are looking at us."

"Consider it free advertising," he told me.

"You're horrible."

"I know. And I'm sure there's a fascinating story behind why you're dressed like such a whore today. Besides, of course, the fact that you *are* such a whore. You'll have to tell it to me one cold snowy night by the fire. But for now, how about I get you a coffee and a muffin or something. What do you ..." Freddy paused and took a sniff. Then another.

"Is that ... *pee* I smell?"

I blushed. "Oh, yikes. Really? Sorry."

Freddy put his hands to his face in mock horror. "Watersports? On top of everything else, now you're letting men *urinate* on you?"

Anyone who hadn't been looking at us before was definitely staring now. I willed myself invisible.

"All right," Freddy continued, "let me just get the coffee and something for us to eat. In the meantime," he stage-whispered, "maybe you could freshen up a bit."

Freddy got up and I tied the top of the shopping bag that held my Willem-soaked sweatshirt a little tighter. A middle-aged man who looked like the principal of my high school walked over and handed me his business card. "You sound like a lot of fun," he whispered into my ear. "Do you get into pig play, too?"

I didn't know what "pig play" was, but I suspected it wasn't for me. I grabbed my bag, Freddy's jacket, and pulled Freddy out of the coffee line. "We're leaving," I hissed at him.

"Why?" Freddy said. "Did you just make a sale?"

Freddy struggled to keep up as I race-walked down the street. Even with my shorter legs, I could make pretty good time when I was mad.

"Would you wait a goddamn minute?" he called. "What is this, *Chariots of Fire*?"

I stopped and turned to him. "I couldn't very well stay there after everyone heard you call me a big golden shower–loving prostitute!"

"I didn't say you *loved* golden showers," Freddy clarified. "A lot of people have jobs they don't like."

"Arrggh!" I threw up my hands.

Freddy tousled my hair. "I love how cute you are when you're embarrassed, do you know that?" He grabbed me in a great big bear hug. "It's not your fault that Auntie Freddy likes to tease, darling."

As always, I was surprised by just how strong and warm Freddy's hugs were.

"Whatever," I said, finding it hard to stay mad at him when his embrace felt so good.

"Actually," he began, stepping back, "I wanted to leave anyway. I slept with two guys there, and I was afraid there was going to be an awkward encounter."

I reminded Freddy that it wasn't unusual for him to run into at least two or three former lovers anyplace we went.

"I know," Freddy said. "But I slept with both of them *yesterday*. So, you can see where it could have gotten a little dicey. You know how some people are so touchy about every little thing."

"I cannot believe," I said, "that you call me a whore, when you have more sex in a week than I do in a month." I wasn't exactly sure my math was right, but I went with it anyway.

"But, darling," Freddy explained, "I do it for *love*. You do it for *money*. That's what makes me a 'free spirit' and you a 'whore.'"

"Love? I bet you didn't even know those guys' last names."

"Oh, I don't love *them*," Freddy said. "I love cock, darling. The guys are just what's attached."

Somewhere inside Freddy was a person yearning to love and be loved, thoroughly, with his whole heart and soul, and not just a frighteningly efficient sex machine.

At least, I hoped so.

We reached the door of another coffee house a block away. "Listen, Mr. Romance, why don't you peek in and make sure there isn't anyone inside you've fisted in the past twenty-four hours? Let me know if the coast is clear."

"Good idea," Freddy said, entering the door.

A moment after he disappeared from sight, I heard someone calling my name. I turned and saw Randy Bostivick, one of the city's most beautiful and popular male hustlers. Randy and I both worked for the same escort agency, run by the inimitable Mrs. Cherry.

Randy had been jogging. Although he was as big as a body builder, Randy kept himself lean through strenuous aerobics and liberal doses of crystal meth and steroids. While meth was usually a devil best avoided by anyone looking to live past the month, Randy tolerated it like he absorbed everything else life threw at him: with grace, a tremendous appetite, and no apparent bad effect. I suspected he might be the child of Norse gods.

As he waited for me to come over, he bounced on his heels, causing his massive pectoral muscles to bounce like happy puppies under his loose tank top. His skimpy nylon shorts were split up the sides to reveal thighs thicker than my waist.

"Hey, Rands," I said, walking over to him by the curb. He picked me up effortlessly, his hard biceps pressing into my back like . . . well, there's really nothing like an impressive bicep, is there? Warm and hard as a hot water pipe, yet still somehow pliant and inviting to the touch.

"How's my favorite little cupcake?" he asked, squeezing. I struggled to catch a breath.

"Good, but, BTW, you're killing me here."

"Sorry," he said, setting me back down. "Look at you. So sweet and scrumptious. I could eat you up right here."

Randy was a boy of simple pleasures, at least two of which, food and sex, he frequently confused. He was almost always in a good mood, except for the occasional 'roid rage, which, while intense, usually passed quickly.

"Let's see the goods," Randy said, his meaty paws unzipping my jacket. I loved the feeling of Randy's hands on me. We had gotten it on once, when we were both hired to perform at a gay bachelor party, and the experience was highly memorable.

"Whoa," he said. "'For Sale'? Putting it right out there on your T-shirt? That's really smart. I should do that."

"It's not what you think," I began.

"What's on the back?" Randy asked, turning me around. "A price list?"

I pulled my jacket closed again. "It's cold out here, bro."

Randy shifted from foot to foot, keeping his body in motion. "Not for me. Working up a sweat, baby." He took my hand and put it on his heaving wet chest, his nipple as hard as a pebble under my palm. "See?"

I snatched my damp hand back. "I'll never wash it again," I promised.

"Ha!" Randy laughed. "You're a funny kid. So cute and young. Like a lamb chop, you know, tender and sweet with mint jelly, just waiting to be bitten into. Goes down smooth as butter. Yum." Randy smiled with the memory of a meal or a screw long remembered. Who could tell with him?

"So," I said, "how have you been?"

"Great, but did you hear about Brooklyn Roy?"

Brooklyn Roy was another hustler, although as far as I knew, he was working legit now, having scored a role in the chorus of whatever musical Matthew Broderick was appearing in on Broadway.

Roy was a handsome guy, if a little bland. He had the kind of generic good looks that promised his eventual casting as the friendly, unthreatening neighbor on a TV series targeted at older women. Cute enough to bring home but not so much that you'd pine for him the next day. Randy and I had run into him a few times at the clubs.

"Yeah," I said, "he's in a show, right? Good for him. I don't remember the name."

"Dead."

"That's a horrible name for a musical," I said.

"No, Brooklyn Roy. Dead."

"What? How?"

"Mugging. Or gay-bashing. He was found a couple of weeks ago on Bleecker. His wallet was gone and his head was smashed in with a lead pipe. The police aren't calling it a hate crime, but I've been hanging out on Bleecker these past few nights hoping the bastards who hurt Roy come after me. I'll show them what a real bashing is." Randy balled his hands into fists and flushed red.

Anyone who'd go after Randy with anything less than a tank would have to be pretty stupid.

"Maybe I'll come with you," I said.

Randy grinned. "Let's do it, man. And afterward, I could take you back to my place and lay you out like an apple pie, sweet and sizzling from the oven, just waiting for me to take you in my mouth and . . ."

"I'm kind of seeing someone," I said.

"Then I'll just 'kind of' fuck you." Randy smirked.

I rolled my eyes.

"Speaking of fucking," Randy said. "I was watching TV and I saw, well, you'll never believe who I tricked with!"

"Who?" I said.

"First, I have to tell you, this guy had the biggest balls I've ever seen. Like two hard-boiled eggs. I wanted to dye them for Easter."

"And that's relevant because . . . ?"

"He's famous, dude. But he has such a straight-laced image. Meanwhile, he's a freak with a sac you could use to wreck buildings."

"OK," I said, "now I'm curious. Who is it?"

"It was . . ." Randy began. Then, a flash of metal and an explosive *bam* later, he was gone.

3

Like a Straw in the Wind

Out of nowhere, in the almost empty street, a car had raced by doing at least seventy miles an hour. It crashed into Randy head-on. I saw him fly up, do a 180 in the air, and land a hundred feet down the street. The whole thing happened in less than a heartbeat, but also in a weird kind of slow motion, where I could see every nuance of the look on Randy's face as he wondered what hit him.

Worse than the visual, though, was the sickening thud of the first impact, and the quieter *whomp* when Randy touched down half a block away.

"Kevin. Kevin!"

An impact like that must have killed him. So how was he calling my name?

I turned to answer, but it wasn't Randy at all.

"Earth to Kevin," Freddy said, annoyed. "I've been calling you for two minutes. It's safe to go in—there's only one guy in there I've even kissed, and that was just now, while we were waiting for our coffees."

I looked at him, open-mouthed.

Freddy cocked an eyebrow. "Are you OK? You look like you've just seen Elton John eating snatch."

"I . . . He . . . We were just . . ."

"What, Kevin?"

"Randy. We were . . . He's . . ." I pointed down the street.

Freddy looked at the body lying facedown in the middle of the road, and the small crowd that was beginning to circle it.

"Is that—holy shit, it's Randy!" Freddy grabbed my arm. "Come on."

He dragged my shell-shocked self to the scene.

Randy lay at impossible angles, arms going one way, legs another, his head almost completely turned around as if it couldn't bear to see what had happened to his beautiful body. His eyes were shut and a thin line of blood trickled from his ear to the ground.

I knelt down and a woman screamed at me. "Don't touch him! You could break something. I already called nine-one-one."

Really? I thought. *He's just been knocked half a block by a speeding car and I'm going to break something?* I resisted the urge to slap her.

I put my head on his chest. I listened for breathing but couldn't hear anything. "Randy?" I asked. "Randy?"

He was pale and shivering, so I took off my jacket and laid it over his chest.

"Hush." Freddy squatted next to me. "He can't hear you, honey."

I felt the blood drain from my face. "You think he's . . ."

"I don't see how he could have . . ." Freddy answered, unable to finish his sentence.

"Did you know him?" the annoying woman who had called 911 asked us. I'd guess she was in her fifties, with stylish gray hair and sharp, attractive features. She wore an elegant suit in the style of Chanel, with crisp white gloves.

"Yeah," I croaked.

"Poor thing," she sighed. "And look at him! So handsome. Like a movie star. Was he an actor?"

Freddy looked at her. "No, he was a prostitute."

I elbowed him. *"Freddy!"*

"What?" Freddy asked. "Like that's a bad thing?"

"It is *not* a bad thing," the annoying woman said. "Male prostitutes saved my marriage."

Freddy looked impressed. "You hire hookers?" he asked her.

"Heavens no." She waved her hand as if shooing away a fly. "My husband does. If he didn't have that small release, well, I don't know where we'd be today." She looked at my T-shirt. "Maybe you have a card?"

I was about to answer when something amazing happened.

Randy's eyes popped open.

"Freddy!" I cried. "Look!"

"Holy shit," Freddy said.

"Randy?" I asked again, leaning in to him as close as I could. "Randy, can you hear me?"

I quickly flashed on my favorite singer/actress/directress Barbra Streisand singing "Papa, Can You Hear Me?" and had to resist the urge to set my words to music.

Focus, Kevin, focus.

Randy coughed, the sound like a clogged pipe when the Drano begins to work.

I gently put my hand on his face. "Randy? You're OK, sweetheart. You're going to be fine." I felt as if I might start to cry. "Can you hear me?"

A tiny voice, a bird, slipped from his lips. "Dude," he said in the softest whisper I've ever heard. "What hit me?"

This time I did cry, a great sob of relief that I couldn't contain.

"Aw," Randy said, a little stronger. "Is that for me? I could eat you up like . . ." Then his eyes rolled back into his head and his whole body convulsed.

He was gone.

"Randy?" I called. "Randy!"

My words were drowned out by the sirens of the ambulance barreling its way toward us.

The doors of the ambulance exploded open as two paramedics rushed to Randy's side. One of them was a youngish guy with short hair and a slim build. His partner was a similarly fit-looking young woman.

For a second, it was like I was watching the scene on TV. It didn't seem real. I couldn't move. Freddy had to pull me out of the way. "Let them help," he said.

"Who can tell me what happened here?" the male paramedic shouted as he wrapped a blood pressure monitor around Randy's arm.

It took seconds to tell him: speeding car, sudden impact, flight.

"Does he have any medical conditions we should know about?" the paramedic asked. His nametag said he was Ross Vergood.

Do steroids and recreational drug use count in a situation like this?

"Nothing I know of," I answered.

"He's a prostitute," the annoying woman with the gay husband offered.

The paramedic cocked his head. "Huh. I can see that working out for him. Nice arms. Anything else?"

"He was conscious for a minute just now," I said. "But then something happened—it looked like some kind of seizure."

The female paramedic fished into Randy's shorts and pulled out a slim wallet. She held up a white card she found there. "He's epileptic," she called.

The rest happened in a flash. An IV was attached to Randy's arm and he was transferred to a stretcher that folded up and slid into the back of the ambulance. "Is anyone coming with him?" Ross asked.

"I am," I said, climbing into the back. Freddy was hot on my heels.

"Me, too," Freddy said.

"Sorry, just one," Ross said.

Freddy put a hand on Ross's arm. "What if I say *please?*" he asked, squeezing just enough that Ross could feel the strength and heat of Freddy's grip. Ross looked at him hungrily.

"Pretty please?" Freddy said, taking his hand away but not before letting it casually brush against Ross's chest.

"Fine," Ross said. "The more the merrier."

His partner gave him a dirty look. "Hey, it's just like that time at the women's basketball game, remember?" Ross said to her. "That player with the busted kneecap? Her *coach*?"

His partner blushed and nodded.

Freddy leaned over to me. "I bet paramedics get lots of tail," he whispered.

"I heard that," Ross said, as he watched Randy's vital signs.

"Let's go," his partner said, slamming the doors shut.

As she did, Chanel-lady called to me, "Hey, what about your card?"

4

Isn't It a Pity?

Two hours later, Freddy and I were in the hospital's cafeteria. Randy was in critical care. Unconscious, but stable. Other than the fact that he had a few broken bones and remained unconscious, he was in a lot better shape than you'd expect.

"He must have a thick skull," the ER doctor said.

Um, yeah.

A bored-looking pair of police officers took a statement from me. I described the car that hit Randy as best I could. I told them I didn't get much of a look at the driver, other than to notice he was a white male. Or a white woman with short hair. Or, for that matter, any other light-skinned race or ethnicity. I think he or she was wearing sunglasses, but I could be wrong. Something like sunglasses, anyway.

The officers obviously thought I was an idiot. They gave me their cards and told me to call them if I remembered anything else. They couldn't have seemed less interested.

Meanwhile, Freddy got Ross the paramedic's card. Ross couldn't have seemed *more* interested.

Funny world.

I absently picked at my salad while Freddy, with his characteristic relish for everything that's bad for you, dug into his chicken fingers and fries as if he hadn't eaten for days. He washed it back with a non-diet cola.

He always ate like this and you could still do your laundry on his six-pack.

I hated him.

The whole way down to the cafeteria we hadn't said a word, just walked side by side as old friends do. My mind was full of white noise. It felt good just to be quiet.

A loud clearing of Freddy's throat signaled the silence was about to be broken.

"So," he said to me, lifting one eyebrow in a sinister arch, "who do you think did it?"

"Did what?" I had to admit his fries looked good.

"Tried to kill Randy."

"What do you mean?"

"What do you mean, what do I mean?"

"I mean: What are you talking about?"

"Have you taken your medication today?" Freddy asked. He was referring to my Adderall, which I take twice a day to manage my attention deficit disorder. Without it, I tend to get fuzzy-headed, forgetful, and disorganized.

"My morning dose," I answered.

Freddy raised his hands in the universal gesture that means *see, I knew I was right.*

I fished out my keychain, to which I had attached a can of Mace and a small pill vial. I took one of the little pink pills and washed it down with my bottled water.

"Feeling better?" Freddy smirked.

I stuck my tongue out at him.

"Stop flirting," he cautioned. "And put that back."

I looked at my hand, which, all on its own, had snatched a French fry off his plate.

"Too late!" I said, jamming it into my mouth.

Freddy pulled his plate closer to him. "Seriously," he said, "you have any suspects?"

I thought about what Freddy was saying. "You think someone tried to kill Randy? On purpose?"

"*Naturellement!*" Freddy exclaimed. "It's elementary."

Freddy was very bright, but he often found himself a few steps behind. I could see he was proud of himself for having a theory about this before I did.

I wasn't into hearing his crackpot ideas right now, but the good news was he was so pleased with himself that he didn't object when I grabbed another fry off his plate. OK, a handful of fries. It had been a stressful day.

"What makes you think," I asked with my mouth full, "that Randy was run over on purpose?"

"Darling," Freddy said, "it was practically dawn on a Sunday morning." It was after noon, but Freddy was on gay time. "Where was the person rushing off to? No one in their right mind goes to church anymore—no offense, dear."

I sneered and took a long swig of his cola. Was there anything more delicious than carbonated sugar?

"The road was empty. All those open lanes and the driver's speeding right along the curb like that? Why?"

I had to admit that was weird.

"And you said the car just kept on going, right?" I nodded. "OK, I can see not stopping, that's why they call them 'hit and runs.' But to not even slow down? Not for a second? As if he"— Freddy stopped, remembered his political correctness—"or *she*, didn't even notice? How do you hit a person and not even notice? Especially one as dishy as Randy. Honey, you could spot those shoulders from an airplane."

"Hmmm," I said, as if deep in thought. I took a chicken finger off his plate.

"And you can't remember anything about the driver?"

"No," I said. "It was like I told the cops. The whole thing happened in an instant. The only thing I remember noticing, because it stood out, was he . . . I think it was a he, was wearing sunglasses. Except that's not right."

"What do you mean?"

"I don't know." I imagined my mind as a filing cabinet and I rifled through it, trying to find the right memory. "I remember thinking that it looked more like his eye was missing. Like there was darkness there."

"Oh my God," Freddy said. "Randy was run over by a Terminator. But one of the cool ones, not one of those stupid transformers from the shitty Christian Bale movie."

"Doubtful," I said, glad that Freddy was entertaining himself as I stole another fry. Or three.

"OK, so we have a speeding car where you'd never expect to find one, Randy hit as if the driver were aiming at him, and a cybernetic killer on the loose. It sounds pretty dodgy to me," Freddy summed up.

"Uh-huh."

"Plus, *you* were there," Freddy said.

That got my attention. "And?"

"Well, darling, isn't this your kind of thing?"

A few months ago, another friend of mine was killed under suspicious circumstances. Although the police called it a suicide, I suspected otherwise. After making a bit of a muck out of it, and chasing after a few wrong suspects, I actually solved the case. Well, kind of. It's a long story.

In any case, Freddy seemed to think I was now a magnet for murder.

"If it is," I said, taking a big hit of his soda while simultaneously reaching for another chicken finger, "don't you think you're in danger being here with me?"

Freddy slapped my hand away. "The only danger I'm in is of starvation," he snapped. "Eat that green stuff you got."

"But it's not as full of tasty goodness as your food," I whined. "Besides, stop acting like I'm Jamie Lee Curtis in *Halloween*. I'm not tripping over dead bodies every other minute."

"Not *every* minute," Freddy admitted. "What were you and Randy talking about, anyway?"

I told Freddy we had only been chatting for a few moments. "He was going to tell me about someone he tricked with," I remembered.

"Who?"

"We never got to it. It was just then that he was hit."

"Huh," Freddy said. "Do you boys talk about that kind of thing much? Who your clients are? Because I thought you took some kind of confidentiality pledge, like doctors and their Hypodermic Oath or something."

"Actually, no. It's not so much a pledge, though. It just gets boring after a while. I mean, we've slept with all kinds of people."

"Famous people?" Freddy asked.

"All the time. Can you imagine how hard it is for someone who's really well known to get some? Going out to a club is, like, impossible, and a Manhunt profile's going to get them into the *National Enquirer* real fast." I was thinking of a certain male singer from a popular reality show whose online escapades became national news. "Even openly gay celebrities want to be discrete."

Freddy leaned forward, suddenly more interested. He dangled a chicken finger temptingly. "Tell me about three famous guys you've boffed and you can have this," he purred.

My years of gymnastics training have made me limber and strong. I've also studied Krav Maga, the official self-defense system of the Israeli Defense Forces. I can strike silently, stealthily, and fast.

I had that chicken finger out of Freddy's hand before he even saw me move.

"Hey!" he said. "No fair using that kung fu stuff!"

"'The Force can have a strong influence on the weak-minded,'" I reminded him.

"Whatev." Freddy sighed. "If Randy was going to tell you about someone who hired him, it must have been pretty juicy."

"Probably," I admitted.

"Someone with a secret," Freddy continued.

"Possibly. But pretty much everyone who hires a rentboy wants to keep it secret."

"And maybe . . ." Freddy gave a dramatic pause, looked around as if afraid someone might be listening, and lowered his voice. "Maybe it was a secret worth killing for."

"We had one of those in our last murder," I reminded him.

"So?" Freddy asked.

"So," I said. "What are the odds?"

"In your case, darling? Always even money."

5

Can't Help Loving That Man

After Freddy got himself another plate of fries and a milkshake (I really, *really* hate him), we went back to the ICU. The nurse told us there was no change in Randy's condition. I was instructed to call the next day.

Freddy and I parted soon after.

"Remember, we have that thing tomorrow," I told him.

"Lamb chop, how could I forget? It only promises to be one of the most *fabulous* parties in New York," Freddy gushed. "It's engraved in my mind in letters of fire. I shall spend the entire day tomorrow fasting and bathing in champagne. I may even get a Brazilian."

"Ouch," I said. "Just shave."

Freddy smiled condescendingly at me. "Not *that* kind of a Brazilian, darling. I mean, an actual person from Brazil. This guy who works out at my gym. I may invite him over before we go to the party. Just to take the edge off."

"Be on time," I told him. We kissed and said good-bye.

I headed back to my one-bedroom apartment in Chelsea. My semi-boyfriend was coming over, and I needed to get ready. I didn't get that much time with him, and I tried to make the most out of every opportunity.

It was late in the afternoon and the air was getting colder. I shivered in my leather jacket and wondered if my sweatshirt was dry enough to wear yet. I decided that even if it was, wearing dried piss wasn't that much better than wearing it wet.

It was a ten-minute walk to my place; I strode briskly to stay warm.

Could Freddy be right? Could Randy's accident have been . . . not an accident? There were suspicious elements, but the whole thing seemed far-fetched. Freddy loved drama; this was probably a product of his overactive imagination.

Of course, that's what my semi-boyfriend said when I told him I thought my friend and patron, Allen Harrington, had been killed last summer. Turned out I was right.

Could Freddy be, too?

My head was spinning. Had I taken my medication this afternoon? Yeah.

Tony was my semi-boyfriend due to his total inability to commit to me. Worse, he was unable to commit to being gay. Since we both had dicks, that made being with me a problem for him.

Tony was my first love. We grew up together on the same street on Long Island, New York.

I always wanted him.

Tony was—is—absurdly handsome, with dark Italian skin, darker eyes, and the silky black hair of a pony. His strong cheekbones point the way to plump, kissable lips that any Hollywood starlet would endure endless Botox injections to have.

His body, which grew more muscular and defined with each passing year, was always lean, hard, and graceful. When we were kids, I remember being fascinated by the way he walked, bicycled, played stickball, and wielded a joystick.

Even his smell was a turn-on for me. I remember once, when I was twelve and he was fifteen, he was kicking a soccer ball around with some friends on a fall day that surprised us all by suddenly turning warmer.

"Would you hold this for me, Kev?" he asked, tossing me his denim jacket. It was redolent with Tony's scent—like just-mowed grass with a little musk—and I got a little dizzy inhaling his pheromones. I also got an erection so intense that I immediately understood something about myself that up till then I had just suspected.

Not that it was huge problem. I had grown up on MTV and around my mother's beauty shop, both of which were always full of gay men. Still, it's hard to be different, to know that you don't quite fit in. While the other boys were hanging up posters of Beyoncé, Shakira, and some girl from a Disney musical whose nude photos surfaced online, I had on my wall a signed eight by ten of Barbra Streisand from *A Star Is Born*.

OK, maybe it seems weird that my early crush on Tony is inextricably entwined with my love for Barbra. Like I grew up on Tony, I also was weaned on *La Streisand*. Literally. My mother told me that she'd often play Barbra's *Greatest Hits* while nursing.

(BTW, while that information may have helped me understand my obsession with Babs, I wish my mother kept it to herself. Any reference to the fact that I once suckled at her oversized breasts makes me a little dizzy.)

My mother was—is—a huge fan of Barbra's. In her shrill, piercing soprano, she constantly sang along to the soundtracks of *Hello, Dolly!* and *Yentl*.

When I sat down and watched my first Barbra movie, *Funny Girl*, at the impressionable age of eight, I immediately related to her. Barbra often played the smart, wisecracking girl who, despite her charm and offbeat appeal, was never good enough, or sufficiently pretty or, in one way or another, not quite *appropriate* for her leading man.

Yet, in the end, through her seductive manner and sheer force of will, Barbra took those men and she *made them* love her.

That's the power I wanted. I, too, grew up around boys and men I desired and couldn't have. Straight boys who dazzled me with their easy athleticism, broad shoulders, and confident strength. My seventh grade science teacher, Mr. Smith, with his carrot red hair and the pale blue eyes; Adam, who played soccer and lacrosse and who cut a swath through the neighborhood girls wider than the Lincoln Tunnel; Richard from the debate team, whose fierce intelligence and prematurely deep voice made me sign up for that club despite the fact that any kind of argument gave me a stomachache.

But at the top of my wish list was Tony Rinaldi, who lived just a few houses down the street. I sensed Tony had a thing for me, too. It was nothing I was certain of, and it wasn't enough to embolden me to take action, but sometimes I'd see Tony looking at me in a way that seemed kind of . . . hungry.

Take a bite, I'd think, but he never did.

Even though I was three years younger than him, he always let me hang out with him. I was a cute kid, but short and slight, and when the other kids would tease me, Tony would run to my defense. He'd rumple my hair or pat my butt, and I'd swear that his hand lingered a second longer than it should have. Sometimes, we'd play-wrestle, and I felt that if I shifted just so, if I only had the nerve, I could turn the hold into an embrace.

I was sixteen when I made my move. It was a hot summer day and we were hanging out in his room. Earlier, we had been swimming in the aboveground pool in his backyard, and we still wore our bathing suits. He was lying on his back, his hands behind his head. The position made his biceps look bigger, exposed his vulnerable armpits. I could smell his sweat mixed in with the scent of the cheap sunscreen his mother bought at CVS. We'd been baking in the sun and I felt heat rising from him, like the radiant warmth of a just-fired clay pot.

There was no seduction, no finesse. I didn't offer to rub his back or tell him a dirty story or suggest we find some porn on the Internet—all strategies I'd previously considered.

No, one minute he was asking me if I wanted a soda and the next I was lying on top of him, pressing my mouth to his while grinding myself against his crotch. I heard moans escape like smoke around my lips.

I wasn't sure if the sounds were his or mine.

I'd spent years trying to build up the nerve to do this, but when it happened, it took no thought or courage at all. It just happened. It felt inevitable, like fate, like falling, like giving in to gravity.

Soon, my hips were grinding against something hard in his shorts, something hot, and something that, at the time, seemed impossibly big and getting bigger by the second. I was on him for maybe a minute when I felt his strong arms wrap around me, flip me over, and then he was on top, humping me, holding me, making me crazy.

He growled like a bear and threw back his head. I felt a flash of fear—was he mad at me? Did he hate me now?

"I didn't," he began. "We shouldn't . . ." But even as his words tried to murder his feelings, he humped against me, his bigger body making me feel safe and surrounded, sexy but a little scared.

"Just this once," I panted beneath him. I wrapped my legs around his butt and pulled him closer, feeling wetness on my thigh where his excitement leaked on me. His eyes opened wider, and for a moment I saw he didn't know if he was going to pull away or dive in.

A small shift of my pelvis and my hands slipping into the back of his bathing suit seemed to make up his mind.

His head ducked to one of my nipples and he latched on, teaching me for the first time just how connected those brown nubs were to my crotch. It was my turn to growl, and when I did, Tony looked up at me and smiled. I knew he had never been with a guy before, but he'd had plenty of girls, and I think he was pleased to see that on this new playing field, all his old moves still worked.

"Please," I said, my voice small and weak and winded. "Please."

I didn't know what I asking for, but for the next three hours I got pretty much everything he had to give.

It was heaven.

We had a few unbelievably hot and passionate weeks together, in which it wasn't uncommon for us to sneak away three or four times a day for sex. It was all good until one day, after an explosive fuck that left us half dead and blissed-out in each other's arms, Tony told me he loved me. It was the happiest moment of my life, and had you asked me right then, I would have told you we'd be together forever.

I'd have made a lousy fortuneteller.

Not soon after that, I felt Tony pulling away. Two weeks later, I got an e-mail in which he told me it was over between us. We had to be "just friends."

If there are two more deadly words in the English language, I haven't heard them.

Plus, he broke up with me by e-mail, which is just wrong.

I spent the next few years getting on with my life. I finished high school, went to college, started hustling, dropped out of college, and never entertained the possibility of falling in love. The closest I came was Freddy, but that affair was doomed from the start. I built walls around my heart so high that not even Rapunzel's prince could have scaled them.

Tony came back into my life this summer, when he turned out to be the chief detective investigating the death of my friend, Allen Harrington. After insisting that he was married and not interested in me in "that way," we were sleeping together again within a week.

That was months ago and things hadn't progressed much since. Tony loved me but didn't know if he wanted the "lifestyle." He was fresh off a painful divorce and didn't think he was ready to make any commitments or major life decisions. He couldn't imagine a future without a wife, kids, and a house in the suburbs.

But he loved me. He did tell me that.

As much as I sometimes wished I didn't, I loved him, too.

At his insistence, we had an "open relationship." He told me he wasn't sure if he could ever give up sleeping with women, and I didn't want him to. I didn't really care where he stuck his dick when I didn't need it, as long as he was safe and came back to me in the end. So to speak.

I remember watching a documentary about a group of AIDS activists in the 1980s called Act Up. I fell in love with those boys and girls. Their energy, their commitment, their Doc Martens . . .

they were my heroes. I wished I'd been around to march alongside them.

In my heart, though, I wasn't really a political person. I didn't really want to Act Up. I wanted to Settle Down. With Tony. But every time I brought it up, he acted like I was proposing we restage the Stonewall riots.

Tony grew up in the same world I did, but he took the more conservative values a lot more seriously than I did. Hey, he became a cop, right?

Somewhere along the way, he learned the inherent contradiction some straight people maintain to justify their fear of homosexuality: Either they hate us because we're so different from them—shameless hedonists who just want to have kinky sex and take drugs—or they hate us because we dare to be like them, wanting legal unions and the right to raise children.

Damned if we screw and damned if we marry.

No wonder Tony was so confused.

We saw each other as often as Tony could get together. Which is to say, not enough. Tony's work as a homicide detective frequently called him away. That I understood.

There were lots of times, though, when I knew he wasn't working but he still couldn't see me. Sometimes, he'd mumble a halfhearted excuse; more often, he'd just avoid talking to me. I assumed he had dates those nights, with women, but that was part of our deal. So I dealt.

What else could I do?

Besides make myself irresistible, I thought. I got to work.

6

Love in the Afternoon

I got home, showered, shaved all the usual places (face, chest, balls, butt), liberally applied a handful of Aveda Rosemary Mint Body Lotion to my skin, and rubbed some Jonathon Product Dirt Texturizing Paste into my shaggy blond hair to give it a little body and shine. Not bad. I ran my fingers through my do to loosen it up a bit, so that it would, every few minutes, fall into my eyes.

I knew Tony liked brushing it away when it did that.

I finished with a splash of Tom Ford for Men behind each ear, a cologne I didn't really love, but Tom Ford was so crazy sexy that I felt better every time I wore it.

I threw on some low-slung 7 For All Mankind jeans and a tight old Abercrombie T-shirt. Tony was a total nipple man and I knew he'd like the way mine poked through the thin fabric of the worn cotton.

I also straightened up my bedroom. When Tony and I first got back together, my crazy mother was living with me after she left my father for *not* cheating on her (you had to be there). In one of the few ways that my mother *doesn't* resemble a vampire, she didn't need an invitation to enter my home . . . in fact, after conning the superintendent of my building into letting her in, she moved into my bedroom and displaced *me* to the couch.

Now that I had the place back to myself, Tony and I were no longer consigned to the sofa, with its thin mattress and creaky springs.

It was one of five thousand reasons I was glad my mother had reconciled with my dad.

I kept the TV on as I got dressed, more for the company than because I was watching any particular show. The LCD was tuned to *The Real Housewives of Boise* when the volume shot up violently. A commercial. Don't you hate the way they always play ads louder to get your attention? This one was particularly obnoxious.

The soundtrack was a children's chorus singing "God Bless America" over a shot of a Norman Rockwell family seated at dinner. A square-jawed dad, a pretty but medicated-looking wife, and two smiling children passed around a bowl of potatoes and chatted animatedly. Suddenly, the shot froze and the music stopped in a discordant screech. The picture of the perfect nuclear family ripped in two and a deep-voiced narrator began speaking.

"Homosexual activists want to redefine the American family." The shot of the "perfect family" was replaced by video of S and M revelers at a gay pride parade and bearded drag queens clinking martini glasses. The narrator continued. "But do we really want our children raised in a society that encourages every kind of behavior? Or do we still believe in the basic values of decency, morality, and faith?"

Cut to a tall, gray-haired Midwestern-looking gentleman in a blue suit and a red tie. He had the unremarkable good looks and slightly empty expression of a Sears underwear model. Which is to say, he resembled Mitt Romney.

"I believe in an America that tolerates everyone but that maintains its core values. Good people can get along without giving in. One woman, one man, one marriage, one family, one America. I'm Jacob Locke, and I approved this message."

The narrator came back on to intone, "This message was paid for by Locke for President."

It wasn't the first time I'd seen a Jacob Locke commercial, but I always felt compelled to watch. With his unthreatening attractiveness, flat Plains accent and mild-mannered approach, Locke was the kind of perfectly nice Nazi I was most afraid of. While no one thought this robo-bigot had a chance at obtaining the Republican nomination, his campaign was well financed by Evangelicals trying, at the least, to force the Republican party to the right.

I was glad Tony wasn't there to see the commercial. I had enough trouble getting him to commit without the help of craven politicians playing to their constituents' basest prejudices.

Tony arrived around six. Every time I unlocked the door to find him there, it was like opening the best Christmas present ever. He looked delicious, wearing dark blue jeans, black boots, a black turtleneck, and a black leather coat. Tony had a straight guy's sense of style (which is to say, bad) but he had an eye for the classics. Son of a bitch probably would look good in anything, though.

"Sorry," I said as a greeting. "I didn't order any incredibly handsome men today. Maybe next door?"

Tony grinned and kissed me. "How you doing, baby?" I stood at the door just to watch his confident stride as he walked into my apartment. He plopped himself down on my sofa and patted his lap. "C'mere."

I settled in like a cat. "You smell good," he told me. We kissed a little more and I felt him getting turned on.

"Mmm," I said, wiggling my butt. "That for me?"

"Maybe later," Tony said. He looked at me and narrowed his eyes. "What's going on?"

"What do you mean?"

"You've been crying," he said tenderly. He brushed a strand of hair from my face. "What's wrong?"

"It's a long story," I told him.

"All your stories are long, Kevvy," he answered.

"Smart guy. OK, you asked for it." I told him about my day, from Willem's peeing on me to Randy's accident to my trip to the hospital.

"Poor baby," Tony said, kissing me on the head. "Is Randy going to be OK?"

"They don't know," I answered. "He almost died." I wondered if I should share Freddy's theory but decided against it. I didn't want Tony to think I screamed "murder" every time someone around me got hurt.

"Why didn't you call me?" Tony asked. "Especially once the police got involved. I could have helped."

Because I don't get that much time with you, I wanted to say, *and I didn't want to waste what little I do on this.*

"I didn't want to bother you."

"It wouldn't have been a bother," Tony said. "Next time, call, OK?"

I nodded.

"So, how do you know this Randy?" Tony asked.

Tony's question wasn't as straightforward as it seemed. The first time I told him I hustled, he called me a whore and left me. He later grew more accepting, but it was still a sore topic. I was actually surprised he was as cool with it as he was.

As an accommodation to Tony, I promised him I wouldn't have insertive sex with any clients. That meant they couldn't fuck me and I couldn't blow them. Actually, this didn't hurt my business as much you might think. Most of the clients who come to me through my booker, Mrs. Cherry, have more ... elaborate fantasies.

I knew if I told Tony the truth, that Randy and I had met when we were hired as the raunchy entertainment at a private party, it would remind Tony of what I did for a living, which I always tried to avoid. On the other hand, I really don't like to lie. Plus, with my attention deficit disorder, I always forget what stories I've told to whom, which leads to nothing but heartache, trust me.

I decided to try and evade the question.

"I met him at a party," I said.

"What kind of party?"

"A bachelor party?"

"Who got married?"

"Two guys. You don't know them."

"Two guys can't get married."

"They can in some states," I lectured. "And in some countries, too. These guys had a ceremony in Vermont but the bachelor party here."

"What's a gay bachelor party like?" he asked.

"Probably like a straight one. A lot of booze and strippers."

Tony pulled me closer to his chest. "Did you like that?" Tony asked. "Were the strippers as cute as you?"

Considering that the strippers *were* me and Randy, I had to answer that one carefully. "They weren't as hot as you," I answered, truthfully.

Tony ran his hands over my belly. "Flatterer. Think you're smooth, huh?" His hands ran under my shirt and brushed my chest. "Mmm, you are smooth."

I moaned and rested my head on his shoulder. He ran his fingers over my nipples. I gasped.

"You like that?" he said, his voice husky. I felt him hard against me.

"Yeah," I whispered hotly in his ear.

He stood up and effortlessly took me with him, carrying me into the bedroom.

"Then you're gonna love this," he promised.

If I had to choose between the sex with Tony and the cuddling afterward, it would be hard to say which was better.

OK, there's one of those lies I hate to tell. The sex was better. But the cuddling was really special, too. I never felt as safe and loved as when I lay in Tony's arms.

In the afterglow, Tony brought up our earlier discussion. "Maybe two guys can get married," he said, "but what's the point? It's not like they can have kids."

"Of course they can have kids," I answered.

Tony's eyes widened comically. "They can? I thought you told me you were on the pill."

I punched his arm. A Nerf ball hitting hard steel. "I know lots of guys who are raising kids together."

"OK," Tony said. "I'm a cop in New York City. I know that. I see all kinds of families. But it's not really fair to the kids, is it?"

I looked at him like he was crazy. "Are you kidding? Kids need parents who love them. What difference does it make what gender they are? Studies show that adoptive parents are often better in a lot of ways than parents who have kids the old-fashioned way. When two guys overcome all the obstacles and stigmas of a hostile society to raise children together, you know it's because they really want to. It's not like they wound up as parents because of a drunken romp in the backseat of their car."

"All right, all right." Tony threw his hands up in surrender. "I didn't mean to start a debate. I just think a kid needs a mother and a father, that's all."

"I want to have kids someday," I told him.

"Yeah, right." Tony laughed. "Mr. Party Boy is going to become Mr. Mom."

In the few months that we had been together, Tony had come a long way in admitting what he wanted from me. Still, all this talk about children was too soon for him. Maybe it always would be. But it didn't seem like a smart fight to pick now. For one thing, I needed better ammunition.

"Well, at least I get my kid fix at Sunday school," I said, ready to change the topic.

"It's great that you do that." Tony kissed the back of my neck. "I'm real proud of you."

Tony was one of the few guys I've ever been with who I couldn't wrap around my finger, and I had to admit it was part of his appeal. He knew his own mind and he let me know, too. He was always honest with me, even when he knew I wouldn't like his answers. I loved that about him.

Tony flipped me onto my stomach. He straddled me, but sat high on his thighs, afraid to rest his full weight on me. "How about I get you nice and relaxed again?" Tony took the bottle of peppermint massage oil I strategically keep on the nightstand

and rubbed some oil into his palms. The scent of candy canes filled the air.

Tony's hands are strong and talented. I melted like butter beneath his touch. Which is why the next thing that happened sucked so much.

7

Mother

Tony's cell phone chirped three short beeps. I silently vowed to kill whoever was interrupting our moment with a text message. Tony stretched a muscled arm across me to retrieve the offending device. He flipped it open and read the message.

Tony scrunched one almond eye to show his displeasure. "Bad news, sport."

"You have to go?" I whined piteously.

Tony leaned over, gave me a quick kiss on the top of my head, and jumped out of bed. "I have to go. They just picked up someone I need to question."

"Can't he wait?"

"Maybe. But his lawyer can't."

I scowled. "I hate his lawyer."

Tony laughed. "Me, too. It's gonna be a long night. I'll give you a call when we can get back together. I know tomorrow's no good." Tony was just about to step into the bathroom for a quick shower.

"I have a date tomorrow, anyway," I told him. I loved telling Tony I had dates. He hated hearing about them. But, hey, he was the one who didn't want to commit. So, hah.

"Oh," Tony said, stopping for a moment in the doorway to the bathroom. The tips of his ears turned red, always a sure sign he was angry. He opened his mouth as if he was going to say something, then reconsidered, shook his head, and the next thing I heard was the creak of the shower door opening and the rush of water as Tony washed away the evidence of our love.

"So," Tony said, in an exaggeratedly cheery tone, as he dressed in one of the three business-appropriate suits he kept in my closet, "how about Tuesday night? Wanna get together?"

I got out of bed, still naked and a little sticky.

Tony was usually content to call whenever he was free and we could get together. I knew it was my mention of a date that had him booking a reservation.

"Sure," I said, happy to have rattled him. "That'd be great. How about I order in and we watch *Lost*?" Tony had never seen the show in its original run and I was watching it on DVD with him. Although he found it tedious at first ("I get enough sense-less mysteries at work, thank you."), now he was totally into it and we were halfway through season four.

I loved watching the show with him, despite his frequent ex-clamations that "Kate's hot!"

I'd always respond, "Yeah, and check out Sawyer's ass." That shut him up.

"Sounds like a plan," Tony answered. He was fully dressed now, just strapping on his holster.

I'd have hugged him good-bye if I weren't so greasy. Instead, I just waved and hopped in the shower when he left.

I was just drying off when the phone rang. Caller ID an-nounced it was my mother.

I loved my mother, but to say she was a handful would be like calling King Kong a cute little monkey.

I once asked my father how he put up with a woman who, not once to my knowledge, ever went a day without nagging him about something or reminding him of the six other mar-riage proposals she turned down in favor of his.

"Three little words," my father answered.

"'I love you'?" I asked.

" 'Yes, dear.' No matter what your mother says, I just say 'yes, dear.' "

"That's only two words."

"Well"—my father winked—"the third word I say to myself."

My father came from a reserved German family of some nobility. Every one of his relatives was blond, gorgeous, and looked like they stepped out of the pages of *Aryan People*. Family get-togethers resembled a casting call for *The Sound of Music*. If any of them ever had a pimple or a bad hair day, it wasn't around me.

How he came to marry Sophie Gerstein, a top-heavy Jewess from Flatbush, NY, who was voted "Most Likely Never to Shut Up" in her high school yearbook, was not only a mystery to everyone they met but, I think, to him, too.

In any case, as I had only too recently learned, ignoring my mother's calls was more perilous than dating Chris Brown.

"Hi, Mom."

"Darling," she said, "how are you?"

"I'm fine," I began. "I was . . ."

My mother cut me off. "That's wonderful, darling, I'm so happy for you. Now, ask me how I am."

"How are you?" I dutifully asked.

"Darling, I'm going to be a star! I'm going to be on *Yvonne!*"

Although I didn't watch her show, everyone knew who Yvonne was. Not quite an Oprah, but bigger than Tyra, Yvonne Rivera was the hot Latin American hostess of *That's Yvonne,* a daytime talk show about, well, Yvonne. No matter who the guest or what the topic, the center of the show's attention was always on Yvonne. Her full figure, throaty laugh, and often outrageous comments made her the favorite of housewives everywhere.

Yvonne's biggest claim to fame was her genuine niceness. She was incredibly warm and empathic, and whether she was sitting on the couch with Julia Roberts or a woman who sold crystal meth to preschoolers, you could tell Yvonne really cared.

The thought of my mother on *That's Yvonne* filled me with dread. What could the topic be? "Women Who Scare Their Kids to Death"? "Ten Ways to Make Your Children Neurotic"? "My Son's a Male Prostitute"? I shivered and wrapped the towel around me.

"That's, wow, that's just . . . So what are you going to be doing on the show?"

"Hair!" my mother enthused. "They're doing a series of makeovers for Yvonne and I've been chosen to give her one of my Mile High specials!"

My mother owned the, in my opinion, tastelessly named Sophie's Choice Tresses, one of Long Island's premier beauty parlors for women of a certain age who wanted hairstyles that have been out of favor for at least thirty years. Her Mile High special was an impossibly tall beehive that she was able to coax from even half-bald clients like Mrs. Shingles, my third grade teacher, who once said to me, "Your mother makes me feel like I'm ten feet tall!"

No, I wanted to tell her, *that's just your hair.*

The idea that someone like Yvonne would even want one of my mother's towering creations seemed preposterous. The only people who wore their hair like that were eighty-year-old women and drag queens. Either Yvonne was a lot older than she looked, or she had a cock. More likely, the selection had been made by a producer who hated her.

"That's great," I said. "You must be excited."

"You *have to* come to the taping," my mother said. "Promise me. I wanted Kara there, but she told me she'd bring the boys, and there's no way I'm having my TV debut ruined by those three little monsters."

I loved them to death, but my sister's triplets *were* infamously wild.

"When is it?" I asked.

"Tuesday! They're coming to the shop at eight in the morning to set up and *Yvonne*"—my mother whispered the name as if addressing a deity—"is coming around noon. Can you believe it! In just two days, I'm going to be a star!"

I expected that my mother had an exaggerated sense of what one appearance on *That's Yvonne* was going to do for her career, but she was never one to let reality distort her view of the world.

"That's seems like it came together pretty fast," I said.

"*I know,*" my mother squealed. "The producer I spoke to told me they had another stylist cancel on them and needed to make arrangements right away!"

My mother wouldn't normally settle for being anyone's second choice, but I guessed Yvonne was special.

"Dad must be excited," I said.

"Your father." My mother's voice was flat. "Your father." She paused and took a deep breath, as if gathering the strength to tell me some long-held secret that threatened to tear our family apart.

"Your father," she finally hissed, "didn't even know who Yvonne *is*. When I tried to explain that this could be my big break, he told me, 'Sophie, you're an old lady. The only big break you're going to get at this point is, God forbid, your hip.'"

I let a little laugh escape before clamping my hand over my mouth.

"Oh sure," my mother responded, "very funny. But you wait and see—Yvonne is probably going to ask me to be her personal stylist before the day is over."

"I bet she will."

"Oh," my mother added. "I almost forgot to tell you. That producer who called me? He said he knows you."

I didn't think I knew anyone who worked for America's third-rated talk show, but I asked his name.

"I wrote it down, hold on. Wait, here it is—Andrew Miller. Ring a bell?"

The bells were silent. "Nope."

"Nothing?" my mother asked.

I thought for a moment. "No, sorry."

"Could he have been someone you, oh, how do I put this delicately?" She hummed to herself in consideration. "Maybe one night, at a bar or a park . . ."

"Mom!"

"Or maybe the beach? On the subway? Well, not *on* the subway," she continued, as she couldn't see my pained expression, "but someone you *met* on the subway. Or in a men's room, like that Republican senator . . ."

"I'm going to hang up," I shouted. I had to speak up as I was holding the phone at arm's length from my ear.

"All right, all right," she said. "I don't know what you're so sensitive about, though. I'm a hairdresser, darling. I know what you people do."

"What 'you people'? I'm your son; I'm not from Mars."

"The gays, darling. I went to that PFLAG meeting once. I know the score."

"Listen," I said. "I've never had sex in a bar, or in a park or a bathroom or, for that matter, on the subway. Half the time, I can't even get a seat on the subway, let alone . . . oh, never mind." I was hoping she missed that I didn't deny the beach.

"Darling, it's the lifestyle. I understand these things. You forget your mother is a very sophisticated woman."

"Just because I'm gay doesn't mean I'm . . . easy," I pointed out petulantly.

"I'm not accusing you of anything." My mother attempted to be conciliatory. "There's nothing wrong with a little kink. Once, on the Long Island ferry, your father and I snuck into the . . ."

I hung up the phone, counted to ten, got a pen, and called her back. "Sorry, I hit the wrong button with my chin."

"That's all right, darling. I was just going to tell you about the time your father and I . . ."

I hit the phone with the pen. It made a satisfying clack.

"Damn," I said. "That's Tony on the other line. I have to take this."

"How is that handsome Tony?" my mother asked. Ever since

she caught sight of him bare-assed a few months ago, I think my
mother has had a bit of a crush on Tony. "Are you two still . . . ?"

I hit the phone again. Clack! "Sorry, I really do have to get
this, Mom. See you Tuesday."

"OK," my mother shouted. "Be there at noon! Bring Tony!"

I hung up and said a silent prayer for Yvonne, for whom I
suddenly felt a great rush of sympathy.

Now that Tony was gone, I wasn't sure what to do with my
evening. There was laundry to be done, and bills to be paid, but
my mind kept returning to Randy, lying in his hospital bed,
alone. I didn't know if he had any family or real friends. The
only person I could think of we were both close to was Mrs.
Cherry, the slightly demented but charming drag queen who ran
our escort service.

Mrs. Cherry! I had to tell her. She picked up the phone on the
first ring.

"My favorite boy," she greeted me. "To what do I owe the
great—no, the *orgasmic* pleasure—of this call?"

I told her what happened to Randy.

"Oh my dear," Mrs. Cherry said when I was done. "The
poor, poor lamb. I must call his clients and cancel their appointments. Would you be interested in perhaps picking up some
extra work? Oh, wait, that won't do, will it?"

Randy was the imposing muscle stud of legend; I was the cute
boy-next-door type. We didn't share the same clientele. "Probably not," I agreed.

Mrs. Cherry asked me the name of Randy's hospital and doctors.

"Don't you worry," she told me. "I'll make sure that Randy
has everything he needs. Momma will take care of the bills."

Mrs. Cherry always looked out for her boys, which is one of
the reasons many of the city's top hustlers worked with her.

I gave Mrs. Cherry all the information I had.

"You're such a dear," she said. "Now don't forget, tomorrow

afternoon, you have that client from West Eighty-second Street. That very nice, very rich one."

In Mrs. Cherry's eyes, I knew the two qualities were synonymous.

I told her I'd be there.

"You're perfection!" she exclaimed.

I ordered in Chinese food and channel surfed until I found *What's Up, Doc?* I watched the movie, ate my steamed chicken, and tried not to worry about Randy.

8

Send in the Clowns

The next morning, the phone awakened me at 6:30, which pissed me off until I saw who was calling. I hit "talk."

"Hey," I said sleepily. "What's up?"

"You still in bed?" Tony asked leeringly. "Nice picture in my head right now."

I sat up. "You're pretty chipper for a guy who just woke up."

"Never went to bed," Tony answered. "At the station all night. Driving home now to crash for a few hours."

He sounded tired.

"You should have stopped off here," I told him.

"Then I wouldn't be getting *any* sleep, would I?"

I had to admit that was true.

"Anyway, I just called to say I was sorry I had to run out on you last night. What did you wind up doing?"

I think he was trying to see if I went out. Tony was enjoying his freedom, but not mine. I told him I spent the night watching TV and went to bed early. A slight edge in his voice made me think he didn't believe me, but it might just have been his exhaustion.

We talked a little more until Tony told me he'd arrived home. "I could sleep for a week," he said.

"Old man," I teased him.

"I'll show you who's old—I'll call you soon, OK?"

Define soon, I thought.

"Yeah," I said. "Talk later."

"Over and out, Kevvy."

*   *   *

I went to the gym, had a protein drink and a shower there, and then headed to my volunteer job at The Stuff of Life. It was another warm-for-November day, and I wore baggy black Abercrombie & Fitch corduroy pants, a gray hoodie from Target, and my black leather jacket.

One of the best things about being a hustler is only having to work five or six hours a week. That left me plenty of time for my studies. Or it would if I were actually still in college. I dropped out early, but I'm going back.

When my friend Allen Harrington died, it turned out he left me a considerable inheritance. Unfortunately, due to the unusual circumstances of his demise, his will was held up in probate. When that money comes through, though, I'm returning to school.

Until then, I fill a lot of my free time volunteering at The Stuff of Life, where I supervise the lunch shift, making home delivery meals for people with AIDS.

On the walk over, I called Freddy and told him about my mom being on *Yvonne*.

"You're shitting me," Freddy said. "That girl does *not* know what she's getting into with your mother."

Every day, another church or community group came to help with meal preparation at The Stuff of Life. On Mondays, we were graced by the company of volunteers from the New York City Jewish Home for the Aged, or, as I like to call them, the Super Yentas. Depending on the particular week, and on what percentage of the group were having issues with their blood sugar, the Super Yentas were fifteen to twenty women in their seventies or eighties who shared the desire to do good works, moderate to severe hearing loss, osteoporosis, and very poor short-term memories.

"So," Mrs. Epstein asked, as she, along with the rest of her crew, stood at the long metal table where they passed to each other the brown paper bags that they loaded, assembly-line fashion, with today's lunch menu. "Have you found the right girl yet?"

"Not yet," I answered distractedly.

"I don't understand." Mrs. Fishmeyer turned to Mrs. Dreckeri. "Such a good-looking boy. What could be the problem?"

"It's these modern girls." Mrs. Dreckeri nodded wisely. She picked up a banana and put it in a bag. "They're all so busy with the working and the careers and the Pilates. Whatever that is. In my day, we didn't have all this nonsense. We knew what was what."

"What?" Mrs. Fishmeyer asked. She tapped her hearing aid. "I didn't get that."

"I said," Mrs. Dreckeri shouted, "we knew what was what."

"I knew a young woman who had Pilates once," Mrs. Goldmeister chimed in. "Such a terrible thing. She had to have a kidney removed." Believe it or not, Mrs. Goldmeister was just about the sharpest tool in this shed.

The ladies always talked like this. It took them twice as long to assemble the lunches as it should have. They were like the Golden Girls, but on crack.

"A shame." Mrs. Epstein shook her head. "How young was she?"

"I think in her sixties, early seventies. Just getting started."

Mrs. Dreckeri and Mrs. Epstein simultaneously said, "Oy."

Mrs. Epstein turned to me again. "So," she said, "have you found the right girl yet?"

Mrs. Goldmeister elbowed her. "Trudy! Enough with the 'right girl!' Don't you remember? He's *gay*."

"What was that?" Mrs. Fishmeyer said. "I didn't get that."

"A homosexual!" Mrs. Goldmeister shouted.

Mrs. Fishmeyer still looked puzzled.

"Like those boys on that show you watch, *Project Runaway* or some such," Mrs. Dreckeri helpfully offered.

"Oh, he's a *faygela!*" Mrs. Fishmeyer exclaimed.

Mrs. Epstein gave me a sympathetic smile. "Well, why didn't you just say so, dear?"

"Sorry," I told her, refilling their supplies of sandwiches and bagged carrots.

"He tells us every week," Mrs. Goldmeister chided Mrs. Epstein.

"Tells us what?" Mrs. Epstein asked.

"I think," Mrs. Fishmeyer said excitedly, "he tells us he's on that show. *Project Runaround.*"

"A star!" Mrs. Epstein beamed. "Girls, we're making lunch with a star!"

"Oy," said Mrs. Goldmeister.

The women had this conversation, or one very much like it, every week. I thought they were adorable.

I finished up with the ladies and helped the guys on the delivery crew load the large trays of bagged lunches into the delivery van. Then, I took a cab to the Upper West Side, where my client, Chase Landerpool, lived.

I hadn't bothered to change for our appointment, as it didn't matter what I was wearing. With Chase, I wouldn't be in it for long.

Chase lived in an exclusive co-op two blocks away from the brownstone in which he grew up. The Landerpool family was an institution in New York, renowned for their vast wealth and generous philanthropy. The city's third-largest cancer-specialty hospital was named after a Landerpool, as was a private school, a permanent exhibit at the Museum of Modern Art, and, I've read, a particularly pink and rare flower known as the Landerpool Lily.

The only thing that bears the honorific of anyone in my family is my mother's beauty parlor. And she had to buy that herself.

At the rate I'm going, the only thing I can imagine being named in *my* honor would be a venereal disease.

Not much of a legacy.

As you might expect, Chase grew up with every imaginable opportunity and indulgence. Top-notch schools, travel to the

world's greatest cities, the coolest toys, and the most fashion-
able clothing—Chase had it all. Still does.

Chase also has a predilection for an unusual kind of sex. The
kind of act that you're not likely to find on the "likes" list of
even the most progressive dating agency.

In fact, Chase's kink is so particular, so unusual, and so, well,
dirty, that, despite his youth (he's twenty-eight, according to the
society pages of the *New York Times*), aristocratic good looks,
and vast fortune, he still has to hire a sex worker to get his needs
met.

Which, at one thousand five hundred dollars a pop, works
out pretty well for me.

Chase's doorman let me into the building and walked me to
the elevator that only went to Chase's floor. He used his key to
open the door, and then pressed the button to take me to the
penthouse. The doorman, with whom Chase had arranged it all
beforehand, did all of this efficiently and wordlessly. I'm sure he
was well tipped for his discretion.

The elevator opened into a foyer that led to Chase's living
room. The apartment was a study in modernism and good taste.
Floor-to-ceiling windows along one wall gave a magnificent
view of Central Park. I took a moment to admire the Andy
Warhol silkscreen that hung over a white Eames chair before
proceeding to the large bedroom at the end of the hall.

As always, the room had been emptied of its furniture before
my arrival. Rubber mats covered the floor. The blinds were
drawn. Two rolling carts—one by the door, one by the window—held the supplies Chase needed to get off.

The outfit Chase wanted me to wear hung from a hook attached to the back of the door. I stripped naked and pulled on
the supplied tight pants, baggy shirt, and shoes.

I opened the closet. Inside, Chase had tucked a small vanity. I
sat on the tiny stool and applied the makeup as Chase had
taught me. First the foundation, then the rouge, and lastly the
lipstick. Bright red, ridiculously garish, but I knew that was
what Chase wanted.

Then the wig.

I looked in the mirror. I was almost unrecognizable. Even though I knew what was coming, and that Chase would not want his blows to hurt me, I still felt a little nervous.

I was studying myself in the mirror when—wham!—Chase hit me in the back of the head. I hadn't even heard him come in. I saw my own eyes widen in surprise.

I reached around to feel how much damage Chase had done. While most of the white cream was caught in my wig, I felt some drip down the back of my neck and trickle down my shirt, giving me the shivers. I wiped it away and brought my hand to my mouth.

Delicious.

"Hey," I shouted, "no fair!"

In one swift move, I leapt from the stool and turned to face my attacker. Years of gymnastics training had made me limber and quick on my feet. I crouched to defend myself.

"No one is safe from Socko the Magnificent!" Chase thundered. He stood at the doorway, tall and imposing. Well, as imposing as you can be in shoes that stuck out two feet, green pants, a rainbow-striped T-shirt, blue suspenders, white makeup, and a huge green Afro.

Not to mention the red bulb attached to his nose.

My outfit was similar.

The clown fight was *on*.

Chase—well, I suppose I should call him Socko when he's dressed like this—squeezed the bicycle horn hooked to his waist. "Come on, kids," he said in a trilling falsetto, "it's time to *get dirty!*"

He turned around to grab another of what must have been fifty pies off the cart by the door. I quickly headed over to the other cart and seized my own weapon. Just as Chase brought his arm back to pelt me with a plate of pecan-topped goodness, I caught him full in the face with the spray of an old-fashioned seltzer bottle.

"Take that." I laughed as he blinked and sputtered. He launched the pie at me, but, momentarily blinded, missed by a mile. I turned to grab a pie of my own, but as I reached to get it, Socko came up behind me and plopped one right on my head. *How does he move so fast in those stupid shoes?* I wondered.

I retaliated by dropping to my knees and hitting him with a plateful of Boston cream pie right in his crotch, using the bulging tube within as my target. Socko growled.

We were in constant movement, dodging and weaving. Both of us were laughing and panting as we ran around and fought to keep our balance on the increasingly slick floor. We called out silly taunts. We winged each other, hitting arms, legs, shoulders.

It was Socko who got in the next good shot, hitting me squarely in the face. My features were covered in whipped cream. A classic *Three Stooges* moment. I used my hands to wipe the sweet topping away from my eyes and licked my lips to clear my mouth.

Socko stood in front of me, breathing heavily. He stared glassy-eyed at my dessert-frosted face.

"God, you're beautiful," he moaned.

He pulled me toward him and kissed me hard. His tongue darted into my mouth. We both tasted Cool Whip. His strong arms pulled me closer. Then he ripped off my shirt.

For the next twenty minutes, we continued to pelt each other with pies and seltzer, but also tried to rip off each other's clothing, which, conveniently, was already strategically cut and loosely seamed. I don't know where Chase got tear-away clown clothing, or if he had it custom made (I'd love to hear how he explained *that* to his tailor), but even with our greasy hands, it wasn't long before we were down to our underwear and floppy shoes.

While I can't say that wet and messy clown sex is particularly my thing, Socko did look hot. His long and lean gym-toned muscles glistened from the various syrups and creams that covered him. He panted sexily from a combination of arousal and exertion. His shorts strained to contain what looked like a second bicycle horn, but I was willing to bet otherwise.

Finally, Socko grabbed me and held tight as he emptied a can of whipped cream right into my boxer briefs. My trying to get away (well, not really, but I squirmed enough to make it believable) only turned him on more, and soon I was down to just the floppy shoes while Socko diligently applied his tongue to the tough business of cleaning up the mess he'd made.

A short time later, after some extremely slippery frottage, Socko added his own special frosting to the mess already drying on my belly.

"God, I needed that." Socko, now Chase again, sighed as he rolled off me. His head landed in a pile of cherry filling.

"Always glad to help," I answered.

Chase pulled me toward him so that my head rested on his chest. "You're such a sweet kid." He stroked my hair, then, absently, started picking the larger pieces of piecrust from it. "So willing to play along with me. I hope you don't think I'm, I don't know, too weird or something."

Of course you're weird, I wanted to answer. *You get off on having pie fights while dressed as a clown. What isn't weird about that?*

But, who cares? If it turns you on, and doesn't hurt anyone, what's wrong with being a little weird? Most people never do anything that's particularly interesting. That's why they're unhappy and dull. Celebrate your messy, clowny weirdness, Socko! Let your freak flag fly!

I knew that wasn't what he wanted to hear, though. "I always have fun with you," I answered honestly. "And I think you're hot." I licked his nipple. Maple syrup, yum.

"I never know when I'm dating someone, when to tell them about"—he waved his hand around the now-wrecked room— "all this."

Right after you've told them you're worth a hundred million dollars, I thought.

"You're a great guy," I said. "But it's not the kind of thing you'd want to bring up on a first date. Do you also get into . . ." I wasn't sure how to put it. Normally, I'd have said "vanilla sex," but with Chase that had a double meaning.

"Regular lovemaking?" Chase asked. I nodded against his chest. "Oh sure," he continued. "But this for me is so much better, you know. So much more intense. It's not something I'd want to do every day but, but when I do, it's like . . ." This time, he couldn't find the words.

"The icing on the cake?" I offered.

Chase laughed and pulled me closer. "Yeah, that's it, little buddy. *The icing on the cake.*" He kissed the top of my head. "And you're the cherry."

"My advice? Wait till the fifth time you've slept with him. When it's clear you're both interested and you've already proved you can rock his world sans props. Then tell him, 'You know what I think would be fun to try?' And make it sound like a fantastic adventure, not a make-or-break demand.

"If he goes for it, great. If not, ask him again three months later. If he's interested in you, he'll get the message that it's something you really want to do. In the meantime, I'm always available for your sweet, sweet lovemaking."

Chase chuckled. "You know, that's not bad. Maybe I'll give it a try. Do you charge extra for the counseling?"

"I may take a pie with me," I answered. "That peach cobbler is delish."

After a quick shower in Chase's fabulous high-tech bathroom (which, BTW, was bigger than my entire one-bedroom apartment in Chelsea), I gave him a peck on the cheek on my way out the door.

"Here, take this," he said, pressing a wad of bills into my hand. I knew he paid the one thousand five hundred dollars for today's date online with Mrs. Cherry. This was a tip.

"Thanks," I said.

"And thanks for the advice." He grinned. "I promise not to wear these until at least the fifth date." He looked down at the oversized clown shoes still on his feet.

"Well, I don't know," I answered as the doors to his private elevator whooshed open. "They could work for you. You know, some guys think shoe size is directly related to . . ." I arched an eyebrow and entered the waiting lift.

Chase was still chuckling as the doors slid shut.

Always leave 'em laughing.

Especially the clowns.

I opened my palm and found five hundred-dollar bills curled together like contented lovers.

Sometimes I loved my job.

9

A Sleeping Bee

I needed to go home to get ready for the party I was attending with Freddy tonight, but first I decided to go by the hospital and see how Randy was doing. When I got there, I stopped at the gift shop and picked up a small white teddy bear holding a box of Hershey's Kisses. I didn't know if anyone had reached Randy's family yet, and the thought of him lying in an empty hospital room was too depressing.

Plus, if I knew Randy, he'd wake up hungry.

I went up to the intensive-care ward. The elevator opened to a large desk for visitors. A male nurse sat there making notes in someone's chart.

"Excuse me," I said.

The young man nodded. "One sec," he said. His short brown hair didn't do much to conceal his large ears, which stuck out like satellite dishes from his nicely rounded head. I noticed that, unlike most of the staff that works in hospitals, this guy actually seemed healthy. As he wrote in the chart, well-defined muscles in his upper back and shoulders did a lively little dance for me. He was slim, but wiry, not skin and bones. His neck looked smooth and strong.

"Sorry," he said, looking up. "Just had to get that down. Now what can I . . ."

He paused for a moment, and then smiled. I knew what he was thinking. *Hey, cutie.* I was thinking the same thing. He looked like he was about twenty-five years old. Fair skin, nice broad nose, and deep brown eyes. A pencil stuck behind his oversized ear made him look adorably geeky. He had a great smile. His ID card read "Cody Boyd." It sounded like a porn name.

He shook his head. "Sorry, lost my train of thought. Let me guess—you're here to see . . ." He looked at a clipboard on his desk. "Randy Bostivick."

I smiled back. "How'd you know?"

Cody considered his response. "Ummm, let's just say you look like you'd be a friend of his." He paused again, and then looked more serious. "Unless you two are, umm, a couple."

His blush was as appealing as the rest of him. "Nope," I said. "Just friends."

Cody broke into an inappropriately broad grin before dialing it back a little. "That's great!" he said. Embarrassed by his over-enthusiasm, he added, "It's great that Randy has another friend."

I'd have bet money that Cody was glad to hear that Randy wasn't taken, at least not by me. As snackable as I thought Cody was, he really wasn't my type, and I didn't get the sense he was interested in me, either.

"Another friend?" I asked. I didn't know who else would be visiting Randy. I remembered Freddy's suspicion that the car that hit Randy hadn't been an accident. Now, I wondered if whoever was behind the wheel hadn't come back to finish the job. I was about to tell Cody to check Randy's respirator when he continued.

"A Mrs. . . . *Berry?*" he asked.

"Mrs. Cherry," I corrected him, relieved. "We work for her."

Cody furrowed his brow. Cutely. "You do?" he asked. "She said she was his aunt."

"She is," I answered quickly. "She's his aunt *and* his boss. But she's just my boss. I'm not related to her. Them. We're just friends. Randy and I. And Mrs. Cherry, too. We're all friends. See? He works for his aunt." I was babbling. Had I taken my medication today?

Cody had a look on his face that told me he was trying to de-cide if I was adorably scattered or actually deranged. I gave him my best see-I'm-not-crazy smile. Cody decided to go with the first option.

"Got ya," he said. He pointed to a huge box of Godiva chocolates at the end of the desk. It had to cost over a hundred dollars. Shit was more expensive than steak. "She brought that. For the nursing staff." He winked. "Smart woman."

I held up my little white bear. "I brought something, too," I said, a little defensive comparing my pathetic offering next to Mrs. Cherry's extravagant indulgence.

"Bears are good," Cody said. He grinned. "Not as good as a fifty-pound box of chocolate, mind you, but still good."

"You can never have too much chocolate," I agreed.

"Yeah, that Mrs. Cherry really was a very nice woman," Cody continued. He stopped and looked at me to see just how honest he could be. "And when I say 'woman' . . ." He made air quotes.

Mrs. Cherry's drag couldn't fool a blind man, let alone a skilled medical professional like young Cody here, who, because he was cute, I wanted to imagine was a genius along the lines of Louis Pasteur.

"It's a hormonal thing," I offered.

Cody's "hmmm" indicated a certain degree of disbelief.

"Or it could be her testicles," I conceded.

"That'll do it," Cody responded.

At that we both smiled. I could have hung out longer with Cody, but I had to get going.

"So," I said, "I guess I should go see Randy. How's he doing?"

"Randy, right." Cody gave a brisk nod to indicate he was turning back to business. "Randy is . . ." He looked at his chart and grimaced. "Randy's about the same, I'm sorry to say. Still not conscious. But holding on."

I was hoping for better news. "Can I see him?"

Cody stepped out from behind the counter. "Come on, I'll take you in."

He signaled for another nurse to take over for him at the desk and walked me to see my friend.

"Whoa," I said. Randy's room was filled with flowers, balloons, and a huge pink stuffed bunny that sat in one of the two visitor's chairs. "Mrs. Cherry again?"

"She thought the place could use a little cheering up."

"The Macy's Christmas Parade isn't this cheered up," I said.

I went over to Randy. He lay motionless except for the slight rise and fall of his chest as a machine puffed life into his sleeping lungs. I brushed the hair off his forehead. The skin felt thin and cool.

He could have been sleeping. I wished he were.

Cody made himself busy checking the IV drip. "He's taking in a lot of fluids," he said.

"That good?"

"Yeah, it means things are working."

"Good," I agreed. "I never thought I'd see Randy looking so . . . weak."

"Yeah," Cody said, "he does have that Incredible Hulk thing going on, doesn't he?" Cody's admiring gaze made it clear that Randy's superhuman musculature worked for him.

"Maybe you should check him for exposure to cosmic rays," I suggested.

Cody corrected me. "Gamma rays. Cosmic rays are what gave the Fantastic Four their powers. Hulk was gamma rays."

"Nerd much?"

"I have a mind for useless trivia," he admitted.

"You like him," I teased.

"I treat all my patients equally, with compassion and no preference," he answered.

"Yeah," I said, "but you like him."

"I confess nothing," Cody said. "Although I may have paid his charge nurse fifty bucks to let me do his sponge bath."

I laughed. Even in a coma, Randy was the stuff of fantasy.

"I mean, does he live at the gym?" Randy continued.

"Not quite. But he'd appreciate knowing you think so."

Cody came over to me and looked me in the eyes. "I'm sorry your friend is hurt. Do you want to sit with him awhile?"

"Yeah," I said. "Do you think he can hear me?"

"I do. I think he'd really appreciate a little visit just about now."

As Cody was leaving I called out, "Thanks."

"No problem," said cute Cody.

So, I sat with Randy and told him about my visit with Socko the Clown, and asked his advice about how to ask Cody out for coffee without embarrassing the both of us by making it sound like a come-on. It's weird—hitting up a guy for sex is easy. Putting the move on a potential friend, though, gets awkward.

If Randy had an opinion, he kept it to himself.

"Besides," I told him, "I think he's into big boys like you. Tell you what, wake up right now and you can ride him into the night like a Harley."

Even that wasn't enough incentive to rouse him.

After a while I felt like Sandra Bullock in *While You Were Sleeping*. Only Randy was even better-looking than Peter Gallagher, and I wasn't in love with him.

But it did break my heart to see him like this.

As I was leaving, I asked one more question. "Listen, Randy, you're going to think this is crazy, and it probably is, but is it possible someone did this to you on purpose? The thing that has me wondering is, just before that car hit you, you were going to tell me about some trick. Who was that, Randy? What did you want me to know?"

I waited for a minute, but Randy wasn't telling.

As I was leaving Randy's room, Cody just happened to be walking by. Funny coincidence, huh?

"Hey," he said. "You OK?"

"Yeah, I'm fine. Wish I could say the same about Randy. Do you think . . ." I wasn't sure how to finish that sentence.

Cody put a hand on my arm. "I think he'll be fine. He seems like a strong guy. Hell, he seems like a friggin' gladiator."

I laughed. "He is pretty hunkalicious, isn't he?"

"You sure you two aren't . . ."

"No," I assured him, "we're just friends. I'm kind of involved with someone else these days."

"Good!" Cody's hand dropped off my arm. "Sorry, I just meant I was happy for you."

"What about you?" I said. "You seeing someone?"

"Me?" Cody frowned and shook his head. "I have bad luck with men."

I scrunched up my face. "You? A boy like you should be beating the guys off with sticks. And not just the ones who are into that kind of thing."

I meant it, too. He was smart, he seemed sweet, and you could just tell he'd be a snack and a half in bed. Plus, did I mention he was adorable in that lives-in-a-library way?

"I'd tell you about it if I wasn't afraid of boring you to death."

"I'm tougher than I look," I promised him. "Tell me everything."

Cody looked at the big clock on the wall. "I could take a break. You brave enough to eat cafeteria food?"

"Told you I'm tough," I answered.

Cody and I found a quiet table in the cafeteria. He sipped a coffee and tore into a tuna fish sandwich. I got a bottle of water and a croissant.

Cody was telling me about his man troubles. "Me, I'm kind of like that girl from *Twilight*. Bookish, pale, a little too thin. But a guy like Randy is all cheekbones and muscles and perfect blond hair. Guys like that don't notice guys like me."

The fact that Cody didn't know how hot he was only made him more attractive. "You're, like, totally luscious," I assured him.

"Oh please." He stuck out his tongue. "I'm just a regular guy. The only thing that makes me even a little special is . . ." He stopped and clamped a hand over his mouth. "Strike that last part," he said.

"What?" I asked.

"Nothing. I'm embarrassed. Just forget I said anything."

I swatted him on the head. "Come on, spill."

"It's embarrassing," he moaned.

I lowered my head and gave him my most threatening glare.

"OK," he said, "it's just that, some guys, they like me because . . . look, I'm don't want to sound like I'm bragging on myself. Can we just drop it?"

I pointed my croissant at him. "I have a baked good, Cody, and I'm not afraid to use it."

"OK, it's just that some guys like me because, at the gym and all, guys notice . . ." Cody blushed again.

"What? A third arm? Webbed feet? You're really a girl?"

"No, no, no." Cody took a deep breath. "I'm, well, let's just say my ears aren't the only part of me that's big."

"You mean you're embarrassed because you've got a big dick?"

"Well, not 'big' so much as 'huge.' It's kind of freakish."

"Oh, please," I said. "What's 'huge'?"

Cody put a finger down on the table and, about 10 inches away, laid down another.

"*No,*" I whispered.

"It's true. It's nice and all, but sometimes I think it's the only thing guys like about me."

I smacked him on the head again. "You idiot. I thought you were adorable way before I knew you had the Verrazano Bridge hiding in your shorts."

"Really?"

"I promise," I said. "Cross my heart, slap my thighs, stick a needle in my eyes."

Cody laughed.

"And if a guy can't see beyond that to notice what a really great guy you are, you're better off without him."

"Thanks. I appreciate that." Cody looked genuinely touched.

Then, because I was, at heart, a brat, I had to spoil the moment. "Of course, in their defense, it may be hard to see much beyond that. It must, I don't know, block the view. Being so big and all."

It was Cody's turn to smack me.

"And I thought you were a nice guy," he teased back. "But I see you're just rude, like that other friend of yours."

"What other friend? Mrs. Cherry?"

"Oh, that's right. You don't know. Another guy came by to visit Randy while you were in with him."

"I didn't see anyone."

"No, when I told him that Randy already had a visitor, he turned around and left."

I thought it might be one of our mutual friends. "Did you catch his name?"

"He didn't throw it. Just heard you were in there and high-tailed it away. Didn't say 'good-bye,' or 'thank you' or anything. Like I said, rude."

"What did he look like?"

"Gosh, I hardly noticed. He seemed all right, average height and build. Middle-aged. The only thing that caught my attention was his eye patch."

"Eye patch?"

"Yeah, on his . . . um . . . right eye."

Something about this bothered me. "What else?"

"I don't know—medium height. Brown hair. You know, now that I think about it, I was so caught off guard by his eye patch that I didn't notice much else. Weird."

The eye patch. It was making me think of something, but what?

Focus, Kevin, focus.

Where had I seen someone wearing an eye patch?

The guy who drove the car that hit Randy. There was something about his eye . . . I knew it wasn't sunglasses or, sorry, Freddy, a Terminator-like bionic enhancement, but I couldn't figure out what the black hole on his face was.

It was an eye patch.

Randy was run over by a pirate!

No, that didn't sound right.

But what were the odds that Randy would be hit by someone wearing an eye patch and then a similar cyclops shows up at his bedside?

The eye patch. Not really a disguise, but enough of a prop to distract you. It worked with Cody and me.

"Listen," I said, "this guy with the eye patch? I think he might have been up to no good."

"What do you mean?" Cody asked.

"I'll tell you in a minute. But first I have to call my semi-boyfriend."

Cody went back to his desk while I called Tony from the cafeteria. I told him about the strange appearance of Patchy at the hospital.

First, because he considers me to have somewhat of an over-active imagination, Tony told me to calm down. In his best policeman manner, he got me to admit that I hadn't really seen an eye patch on the driver. It could have been a shadow. He asked if this wasn't a case of my mind filling in the blanks. I admitted I couldn't be sure.

But he also said he'd relay my message to the officers who had taken my report on the accident. In the meantime, he suggested I have Cody call hospital security to be on the lookout for anyone fitting Patchy's description. Then he asked, "This Cody guy—the nurse—is he handsome?"

"Why, are you looking for a date?"

"No, I'm just wondering what you're doing with him on his coffee break. Does he provide this level of service to everyone who comes to visit?"

"He kind of looks like you. Only younger, hotter, and more muscular. And better hung." Does it count as kidding if one of those things was true?

"Ha-fucking-ha," Tony answered, 'cause he was classy like that. "Just tell him to keep his stethoscope in his pants, OK?"

"Yes, sir," I answered. I enjoyed Tony's jealousy too much to remind him that he was the one who wanted an open relationship.

"OK," he said. "Be good."

I went back to the intensive care unit and relayed Tony's message about alerting security. Cody said he would. He looked nervous. "You really think someone hit Randy on purpose?"

"I don't know," I said. "But watch out for him. And for yourself, too."

"I will," Cody assured me. "Thanks for the pep talk. You didn't have to say all those nice things."

"Listen," I said, "you need to get a mirror and realize that you have a lot more to offer than"—I nodded toward his crotch—"Old Faithful between your legs. Trust me, you're delicious."

This time, Cody's blush threatened to go nuclear. But if his dick really was as big as he said, he'd need a healthy blood flow, wouldn't he?

He was about to say something when a beep sounded from behind his desk. "I have to distribute meds now. But I'll keep an eye on Randy for you."

"Thanks. I'll see you later."

"No," he said, still blushing, "thank *you*."

10

Honey, Can I Put on Your Clothes?

I took a cab to my apartment in Chelsea. Once inside, I stripped off my clothes, set my iPhone's alarm to go off in two hours, and lay down on my bed. It was going to be a long night. A little disco nap would do me good. I thought I had too much on my mind to fall asleep, but the shocks of the past two days must have hit me harder than I realized. Within five minutes, I was out like a light.

I woke up to my iPhone's alarm playing an Ari Gold song. Not only is he a terrific singer, but he's crazy hot. My only regret was that he wasn't there to wake me in person. I decided to go back to sleep and dream of Ari when his sexy voice was interrupted by a ring tone. I picked up the phone to see who was calling.

"Hi, Freddy."

"*Darling,*" Freddy answered, "get out of bed and get dressed. I'll be there in an hour to pick you up."

"I'm not in bed," I said, getting out of bed.

"Of course you were. You're like an old man—you always nap before we go out."

"I hate you," I reminded him.

"Yes, yes. Have you opened Rueben's care package yet?"

I had totally forgotten. "No, how is it?"

"It's totally, totally hot," Freddy said. "Very butch. I look like a million bucks. We really get to keep this stuff?"

"It's a gift. As long as we wear it tonight, it's ours."

"Fagtastic," Freddy gushed. "This outfit probably costs more than my rent."

"What is it?" I asked.

"You'll have to see for yourself. Now, go open your little gifty and get yourself ready."

"Yes, Mom," I said, hanging up.

Rueben's package had arrived two days ago, dropped off by a private messenger. It was in a rectangular box about two by four feet long. On the top was scrawled "Do Not Open Until the Night of the Event," an instruction already hammered into me by Rueben the day before the box was delivered.

"Now, this party is very important to Ansell. He has everything planned to the smallest detail. You must promise me you'll wear exactly what we send," Rueben said.

"I promise."

"All of New York's fashion elite will be there, *Kevito.*"

"I get it."

Rueben was a former rentboy made good. About six months ago, he hooked up with Ansell Darling, one of New York's brightest up-and-coming young designers. It was love at first trick, and Rueben now lived in Ansell's fabulous SoHo loft. He was even pictured in a catty item on page six of the *New York Post* that asked "Is Darling's Darling Charging by the Hour?"

I hoped Ansell was good for Rueben. Rueben was a fantastically beautiful Puerto Rican guy of about my age. Skin the color of caramel and green eyes to die for. But he was also a bit of a party boy, and the last time Freddy and I saw him at a club—about a month before he started dating Ansell—Freddy took one look at the dark circles under Rueben's eyes and a telltale bruise on his arm and said "heroin."

I didn't know how Rueben was doing now, other than being anxious about the party.

"You, Freddy, a couple of my other best-looking friends, and all of Ansell's models are going to be wearing the actual designs from his latest collection. It's a whole back-to-the-seventies theme. It will be like a runway show, but you'll be interacting with the guests. Isn't it genius? It was Ansell's idea, but he's counting on me to help him pull it off. I really need this to work."

He sounded desperate. "Is everything all right between you and Ansell?"

"Let's just say, *mi hermano*, it's pretty crucial I come through for him on this."

I decided to let it drop. "Cross my heart, I'll follow your instructions to the letter."

"Oh, did I mention there were instructions? They're right on top of the box."

"I was kidding. Instructions? I know how to get dressed, Rueben. I may be blond, but I'm not *that* blond."

"Oh, it's a whole look you'll be putting together. I picked it out for you myself. I know you're going to love it. You'll be the hottest thing there. *Muy caliente, bambino.* You're not shy, are you?"

"What do you mean?"

"It's just . . . oh, there's Ansell now. I have to go. See you at the party!"

I opened Rueben's box, excited to see what was in there. As promised, right on top, were instructions, handwritten in Rueben's casual scrawl. The more I read, the worse it got.

He had to be kidding me. I tore away the paper in which my outfit was wrapped and discovered he wasn't.

Inside was the clothing and glass vial he described to me.

Oh my God.

I couldn't wear this.

I couldn't.

But I had to.

I'd promised.

And Rueben sounded really urgent that I show up exactly as he described.

Like his life depended on it.

"Love the coat," Freddy said, when I answered the door.

He was admiring the floor-length, gold-lamé down jacket

that Rueben had sent along with the rest of my clothing. I had to agree with him. It was a couture dream come true. A little retro but with futuristic detailing. The down was soft but the coat wasn't puffy. It felt as light as a feather and molded to my body as if custom made. It had to cost about two thousand dollars, and I was grateful to have received it.

Something I couldn't say for the rest of my outfit.

Freddy, meanwhile, really did look hot. His outfit seemed to take its inspiration from the costume worn by the construction worker from the Village People. Black, square-toed boots, tight jeans that were frayed in all the right places, a shirt with epaulets that looked like denim but, I could see, was really a midweight silk that draped perfectly over his prominent chest, and a matching faux-denim jacket that was actually blue-dyed leather. It sounds like a mess, but it was actually pretty cool. The mix of fabrics, cotton, silk, and leather, was very sexy and surprising. All the pieces made you take a second look at them.

"Wow," I said, "you look amazing." I grabbed him by the arm. "Let's go."

Freddy pushed me back. "Wait a minute," he said. "Let me see the rest of your ensemble, darling."

"It's nothing," I said, pulling his arm again. "Come on, I don't want to be late."

Freddy didn't budge. "What are you, retarded? Let me see."

"You'll see at the party." I tugged at him. "We have to leave. We might have trouble getting a cab."

Unfortunately, Freddy had about fifty pounds of muscle on me. "I am not moving," he announced regally, "until you open up that coat and let me see what Ansell made for you."

"OK," I said, "but you have to swear you're not going to tease me."

"Tease you, why would I tease you? You're wearing something by one of the hottest designers in the . . . Oh. My. God."

Freddy's jaw dropped as I opened my coat.

"Don't you say a word," I cautioned him.

Freddy used the palm of his hand to push his mouth closed.

"You swore you wouldn't tease me."

"Did not."

Damn. He was right.

"Well, you shouldn't tease, anyway. It's mean."

"You're, you're . . ." Freddy searched for the right word. "You're *golden*."

"Kind of."

"And naked."

"Not *naked*. Exactly."

"And you're so . . . bulgy."

It was true. If my clothing were any skimpier, I'd be arrested for indecent exposure. My entire outfit consisted of a pair of gold-lamé shorts. Short shorts. Low cut, high on the legs, and with a built-in pouch that lifted me in the front. I felt like my balls were wearing a push-up bra. The effect was more provocative than if I were nude.

The only other thing I wore were a pair of Ked sneakers, spray-painted gold to match.

Oh, I almost left out the contents of the vial Rueben sent me—gold body glitter, which he instructed me to apply liberally all over.

I looked like something that gets handed out at a kinky awards show.

My front door was still open—I prayed none of my neighbors would walk by and see me like this.

"Ugh," I said. "I can't go. I look like a freak."

"A freak? You look incredible! How come I didn't get an outfit like that?"

"I told you not to tease me."

"I'm not teasing." He pulled me toward him. "You have no idea how sexy you look in that, do you?" He ran his hand over the back of my shorts. "These are amazing. So smooth. The way they fit you. You look like an angel . . . a really raunchy angel." His voice was getting huskier and his crotch pressed a little more insistently. "Damn, boy."

Freddy felt really good against me. For a moment, I considered throwing him to the floor and showing him how easily the shorts slid off. *Just friends,* I told myself, *we're just friends, just friends, justfriendsjustfriendsjustfriends.* . . .

Problem was, my pants were rapidly getting bulgier by the moment and the only kind of temptation I was good at resisting was the kind that wasn't offered.

"Maybe we should . . ." I began.

"Right," Freddy said, pushing himself away. He cleared his throat. "We should. We should get going."

"Right," I agreed. I pulled my coat back closed.

There was a brief awkward silence, which Freddy mercifully broke. "You going to be OK at the party?"

"Yeah, I guess. I just wish I didn't feel like such a slut in this."

"Darling, please don't make me bite my tongue. I might need it later."

"You promise I don't look ridiculous?"

"You look fine. Come on, Oscar."

We left my apartment and headed for the elevator. Usually, there wasn't a quiet moment between us, but I think we both felt awkward about what we almost did in my apartment. Freddy pressed the down button and I tightened the belt on my coat. We watched the numbers over the elevator's door change as it neared us. Fascinating. Then a soft *ping* as it arrived on my floor. We hurried on with the zeal of thieves escaping a crime.

On the way down, Freddy said, "Listen, about what happened up there. It was just . . ."

"I know," I said.

"Because, we probably shouldn't . . ."

"It would be . . ."

"Just kind of . . ."

"Too . . ."

"Yeah."

"Right."

"Well," Freddy said, "I'm glad we can talk about it."

"Absolutely," I agreed. "Talking is good. Talking is our friend. It's one of the best ways to, you know, talk and . . ."

Freddy arched an eyebrow. "You're not about to start that babbling thing you do, are you?"

"No," I said. "Shutting up now."

Which was probably just as well. Otherwise, I might have told him that what I had been about to say when he was holding me upstairs was, "Maybe we should close the door."

11

The Main Event

The street in front of Ansell Darling's house was so crowded that we had the cab drop us off on the corner. A bus stop there had a large poster of Jacob Locke on its side. Someone had used a black marker to draw a Perez Hilton–style penis pointing at the conservative candidate's mouth.

"I hate that guy," Freddy muttered.

I was impressed. Freddy wasn't much for following politics. Porn and gossip were his major interests. "Me, too."

"His show is stupid, too."

"What show?"

"Isn't he the guy from that game show? *Wheel of Jeopardy* or something?" Freddy asked.

I was about to answer him when a small, attractive blond woman teetered past us on what looked like five-inch heels.

"Oh. My. God." Freddy was breathless. "That's Kelly Ripa!"

She he knew. Oy.

If I hadn't known better, I would have sworn that the door that led into Ansell Darling's three-story SoHo loft was a time machine transporting us back to a nightclub in 1978. Or to what I imagined a club in 1978 would have been like had I been born yet.

The space was dark and crowded. Everywhere I looked were strobe lights, smoke machines, and tambourines. Most of the furniture had been pushed to the sides, allowing for open dance floors, where an enthusiastic crowd gyrated wildly. A full bar with shirtless bartenders lined the back wall. Incredibly huge speakers played a mix of disco-era dance hits. There were even silver platforms on which beautiful boys and girls swayed with closed eyes and blank expressions.

"Jesus, Joseph, and Bianca Jagger," Freddy whispered to me as we walked in. "Did we just die and wake up in Studio 54?"

"If I really do die," I asked him, "could you please make sure I'm wearing something else?" The burly doorman had insisted I check my coat at the door, so I was pretty much naked. And golden.

Freddy and I inched our way through the crowd.

People stared at me.

Did I mention yet that I was golden?

A tall, skinny white girl with a silver tray and a huge black Afro roller-skated over to us. "Cute," she said to me. "And you're hot," she said to Freddy, putting her hand on his chest. "Straight?"

"Cher?" Freddy asked her.

"I guess that answers my question." She shrugged. "Can I get you something to drink?"

We told her maybe later and continued to work our way toward the bar. Most of the crowd was wearing contemporary outfits, but occasionally we'd see an attractive young guy or gal dressed in reworked retro like ours. We'd nod at each other and move on, trying to ignore that most of the other attendees were watching us, like we were part of the evening's entertainment. Since we were, in effect, modeling Ansell's new line, I guess we were.

It's tough when you don't know if it's you or your clothing getting cruised.

We were halfway across the dance floor when I felt someone grab me from behind.

"Kevito!" Rueben shouted, lifting me effortlessly.

He put me down and I turned to yell at him for sending me this ridiculous outfit. Instead, I just gaped. Rueben looked too ridiculously sexy to scold in his lime green pimp suit the likes of which have not been seen since Donna Summer's triumphant movie debut in *Thank God It's Friday*.

But instead of polyester, Rueben's suit was made of soft suede. The bell-bottom pants flared wide at the calf but fit snugly around his strong thighs. The wide-lapelled jacket draped like a second skin, revealing every sensuous curve of his sinewy shoulders and thick biceps. He didn't wear a shirt, but four gold chains around his neck drew your attention to his sculpted chest and tawny skin, which looked like caramel and probably tasted twice as sweet.

"You look *hawwwwwt*, baby," Rueben drawled, reaching out to tweak my left nipple. "And you, Frederico." He turned to my best friend. "How come I never see construction workers like you outside my apartment, *mi hermano?*" He kissed Freddy on the check.

Rueben looked back and forth at us. "Ah, *mi amigos caliente. Me gusta, muchachos.*" He cupped his crotch and licked his lips.

I took him by the arm and started pulling him off the dance floor. "Cut the Latin lover shit, '*muchacho,*'" I hissed. "We both know you grew up on the Upper West Side and went to Wharton."

"I'm just pimping, my brother." Rueben grinned. "Don't be hating on my mack-daddy style, now."

"Whateva," I said, rolling my eyes. "Let's just go somewhere we can talk. Come on, Freddy," I called, but Freddy was nowhere to be seen.

"There he is." Rueben pointed. Freddy was in the middle of the dance floor, dancing in perfect synchronization with a stunning slim Asian boy. They turned, dipped, and shimmied as one. A small crowd encircled them and applauded.

"What," I asked, "is that?"

"It's the Hustle." Rueben grinned again. "*Caliente,* no?"

"Where did he learn the Hustle?" I wondered.

"I don't know about him," Rueben answered, "but I learned it at Wharton."

*   *   *

Rueben took me upstairs to a locked room. He pulled a key from his back pocket and let us into a huge bedroom. The space was industrial chic. At the far end of the room was a huge bed half-hidden behind a folding silver screen. A flat-panel screen hung from the twenty-foot ceiling, all of its cables hidden in the steel tube that suspended it in midair.

By the door where we entered was a sitting area with a black leather couch and two red leather chairs. A Warhol *Marilyn* hung over the sofa.

He's got a whole friggin' living room in his bedroom, I marveled, and for a moment, I thought it might be nice to be Ansell Darling.

"What's the dilly-o?" Rueben complained as he settled onto the sofa. "Why you trying to kill my chill, homes?"

I gave him my best Joan Crawford don't-fuck-with-me-fellas stare. "Would you cut that out?"

"All right, all right," Rueben said in his perfectly unaccented prep school speaking voice. "I was just trying to get into character."

Rueben had been born to wealthy parents who owned about half of Puerto Rico's commercial real estate market. They did their best to Americanize him, but Rueben always yearned for a more authentically urban experience.

Which he got when, in his second year of college, he told his parents he was gay. They gave him an ultimatum—either repent and marry a girl of their choosing, or they'd cut him off for good.

I don't understand how parents can let the luck of the draw lead them to reject their own children. If being straight were the only requirement of good parenting, I'd hear a lot fewer stories like Rueben's.

Given a choice between being cut off from his parents or being true to his heart, Rueben chose freedom. Unfortunately, his subsequent decisions weren't as sound. He dropped out of school, started hustling, and dulled his pain with almost everything a person could inject, snort, or smoke.

The next two years for Rueben were filled with enough

drama and outrageous occurrences for five or six reality series on Bravo TV. I wasn't sure about the exact chronology, partially because the story changed a little every time Rueben and I talked. Maybe not all of it was true, but Rueben certainly had a tumultuous life.

Over the years, I've seen Rueben go up and down. When he was doing well and staying relatively clean, Rueben was gorgeous, sexy, and smart. A fun and funny guy who lit up the room.

Other times, he looked haggard and worn. Drugs and hard living took their toll. Some of the old Rueben would shine through, but it was dulled by addiction and depression.

The last time Freddy and I saw Rueben, he looked like shit. Beautiful shit, yes, but still shit.

Tonight, I was glad to see, he looked fantastic. Fit and healthy. Happy. I told him so.

"Thanks." He blushed. "It's Ansell. He's been really good to me. Took me in, dried me out. He's been incredible."

"Really?" I remembered how scared he sounded on the phone. "I thought, I don't know, I thought you two were having trouble or something."

"What? No. He's the greatest. It started with him as business, you know? He was a client. But one night, we got to talking, and we really connected. Then, I dropped out of the scene for a while." He looked away. "I went to Florida with a videographer for FratPackBoysOnline. You know it?"

I nodded. FratPackBoysOnline was an online "amateur" video site that featured "college boys." Supposedly, customers got twenty-four-hour access to a fraternity house's hidden cameras, where the "students," many of whom appeared to be in their thirties and semi-retarded, were frequently observed showering and having sex but, mysteriously, never doing anything that real students do, like attending classes, watching online porn themselves, or playing video games.

"At that point, I was doing meth pretty much twenty-four-seven," Rueben continued. "This video guy, he tells me he'll hook me up steady if I move into the FratPack, right? I was partying and doing group scenes all the time anyway, so I figured what the hell?

"What's the worst that could happen? Maybe someone would find my videos online and send them to my dad, and the old fuck would die of shock, right?" He smiled with one side of his mouth while the other half trembled as if he was about to cry.

"Maybe I'd send them to him." The half smile was gone now and his doe-like green eyes watered up.

I took his hand.

"I'm sorry," I said. "I didn't know."

"Please." Rueben blinked back the tears. "Please. I'm a big boy. I knew what I was doing. Stupid." He shook his head. "*Anyway*... some porn, I wouldn't mind doing, you know what I mean? If Johnny Hazzard wants to do a scene with me, baby, I'm there. I was a goddamn prostitute, Kevin. It's not like sex work scares me."

I noticed his use of the word "was."

This despite his mention of Johnny Hazzard, who I had to agree I'd do onscreen or off, too.

Rueben may have been a big drug addict, but he had good taste.

I was fondly recalling Johnny's, literally, seminal work in the genius productions of Miss Chi Chi LaRue when I realized I had stopped listening to Rueben.

Focus, Kevin, focus.

" . . . not too bad," Rueben was saying when I tuned back in. "But FratPack was a meat grinder. Boys coming and going, some ODing, some getting sick. Everyone treated like shit and encouraged to do as many drugs as possible so we wouldn't ask why we weren't getting paid. Pathetic."

"So, one night I go out in Miami with some of the other 'models' and there's Ansell. With his usual entourage of the rich and beautiful, right? Meanwhile, I'm looking like a truck rolled over me and probably smelling worse."

I knew Rueben run over by a truck would still look better than half the boys working the runway, but I didn't say anything.

"I'm thinking I better get out of there, because I didn't want Ansell to see me like this, right? But there's this other part of me thinking I *did* want him to see me, because maybe I could hit him up for some cash, you know? Maybe I could score some better-quality shit."

Rueben shook his head again. A tear rolled down his cheek. I squeezed his hand.

"While I'm making up my mind, one of Ansell's assistants sees me. He knows Ansell's type, so he points me out to him. Ansell comes over and soon we're talking like always, right? He says, 'Hey, let's get out of here, you can show me a good time.'

"I hesitate for a minute, because I'm wondering what I'd tell the guys I came with, when Ansell takes a couple of hundreds out of his pocket and presses them into my hand. 'A *real* good time,' he tells me. 'But we have to go now.'

"I liked Ansell well enough as a client, but I liked those hundreds a lot more. So I said, 'Sure,' and we go outside where there's this big stretch limo on the corner and, of course, it's his. I get in and it's the cleanest, quietest, most comfortable place I've been in weeks, man. I'm so relaxed I don't even realize it, and Ansell, who's looking at me real close now, says, 'Why don't you close your eyes for a minute?' and I do.

"The next thing I know I'm waking up in a padded white room. I thought I died and went to heaven. Then I saw lettering above the door that said 'The Gateway Clinic.' I was in a freaking psycho ward, man.

"I just about went crazy. But they're used to that there. I knew I couldn't be held against my will, so I started screaming to be let out. I could feel that scratchy hunger building. I wanted another hit. But the doctors showed me papers I signed saying they could keep me for seventy-two hours. I didn't remember signing anything. Still don't know that I did. But when you've got Ansell Darling's kind of money, you can make things happen.

"An hour after I woke up, Ansell showed up. I was cursing

him, screaming, but he had the doctors bring another bed into my room and that crazy-assed white boy stayed with me for the next three days. He held my head while I puked, he listened to my shit when I screamed, he even changed my sheets when I sweated them through, which was about every twenty minutes.

"Trouble with Ansell?" he asked. "I have no trouble with Ansell. Ansell's my angel. He got me clean."

"You still clean?" I asked.

Ansell held his arms out for inspection. "As mother's milk. I'm not going near that shit again. Not even a joint. Believe me."

I did.

"Ansell saved my life, Kevin. If not for him, I probably would have wound up like Sammy White Tee."

Sammy White Tee was another working boy who Rueben and I knew through that invisible network that links New York's most successful and exclusive male prostitutes. I don't know how we all got to know each other, but somehow we did. Sammy was one of the shyest of us—hence, his nickname. No one knew much about him except that he always wore blue jeans and a plain white T-shirt. In the fall, he added a dungaree jacket and in the winter its leather twin. In every season, he looked like James Dean at his most breathtaking and most innocent.

"Sammy White Tee?" I asked. "What happened to Sammy White Tee?"

"You didn't hear, *papi?*"

I shook my head.

"Sammy White Tee *es muerte, chico.* Dead."

12

Putting It Together

"Sammy White Tee is dead?" I asked. "What are you talking about?" I felt the blood drain from my face.

"*Sí,*" said Rueben. "Yes. I know, it's hard to believe."

Sammy had been such a sweet kid, so full of life. "What happened?"

"Died in the bath. They think he tripped on a bar of soap, hit his head on the side of the tub, and drowned. I heard about it from Corbin Fitzer, who told me *he* heard it from that boy who used to dance at Rumors. Dalon."

OK, the network between rentboys in this city may have been loose, but it wasn't unreliable. At least I didn't think so.

"Is it true?" I asked.

Rueben shrugged. "Yeah, I think so. Nobody's seen Sammy White Tee for weeks, so it makes sense. I heard he was high on something when it happened."

I shook my head.

"I know," Rueben said. "It's hard to believe."

"Actually," I said, standing up, "not so much. Come on, we have to find Freddy."

Freddy was still on the dance floor, sandwiched between a heavily muscled black guy who gyrated against him from behind and a Justin Timberlake look-alike who Freddy held in his arms. I've seen less explicit three-ways in pornos.

"Now, *that* is hot," Rueben observed.

"Not anymore," I said, grabbing Freddy by the arm and pulling him away.

"Are you crazy?" Freddy asked.

"Hey!" Justin Timberlake Boy cried.

"I saw him first," Muscle Head shouted.

I kept pulling. "Sorry, guys."

Freddy pulled back. "I want to go back to that place," he whined. "That was my happy place."

"We have to go," I said. "I need to talk to you."

"I'm sure you do, darling," Freddy said, twisting his arm away. "But I need to close the deal with those two highly motivated young men, so I'm afraid you'll just have to wait."

"It's *murder*," I hissed.

"Yes, darling, I know it's hard for you to wait, but I really do need to hump those boys some more. Maybe you should take one of your pills."

"Not that," I said, pressing myself against Freddy and whispering fiercely in his ear. "Someone is killing the most beautiful male prostitutes in New York. And I think it's up to us to find out who."

Rueben brought us back to Ansell's bedroom.

I filled Freddy in on what I'd just learned about Sammy White Tee. Then, I told Rueben what happened to Randy, and what Randy had told me about Brooklyn Roy.

"Holy hookers," Freddy said. "That's three."

Rueben looked as white as one of Sammy's trademark T-shirts. "You really think something's going on?" he asked. "I mean, it could just be coincidence, right?"

"Could be," I answered.

"Not likely," Freddy responded. "Kevin has a way of getting involved in murders."

"Freddy!"

"*Darling.*" Freddy turned to Rueben. "Let me tell you a little story." Freddy told Rueben about our role in investigating the death of my friend Allen Harrington, and how, in the process, we stumbled upon a particularly nasty homicide ring.

"We were like the Hardy Boys," Freddy explained. "Well, like a queer Hardy Boys. Or, young, beautiful Jessica Fletchers. Or . . ."

"Charlie's Angels!" Rueben enthused.

"Exactly," Freddy agreed. "We made the comparison ourselves, frequently. I was the glamorous, sexy poster-icon Farrah Fawcett-Majors (may God rest her soul), and Kevin was the brainy and plain Kate Jackson."

"Hey," I complained.

"Well," said Freddy, "you always need one on the team who's kind of ordinary. How else will the audience relate?"

I glared at him.

"Don't blame me," Freddy continued. "Go argue with Tori Spelling if you want."

"Tori was the daughter," I corrected. "Aaron Spelling was the creative genius behind *Charlie's Angels*."

"What did I tell you?" Freddy turned to Rueben. "Brainy."

"But wait," Rueben chimed in. "Weren't there always three Angels?"

"Of course," Freddy answered.

"Well, there you have it. You guys need me!"

Freddy and I looked at each other.

"Think about it," Rueben continued. "We'd be the most diverse Angels ever. Plain old white Kevin over there . . ."

"Hey!" I said again, as if anyone cared.

"The spectacular Nubian goddess La Frederista over here." Rueben put his hands together as in prayer and gave a Freddy a slight bow. Freddy nodded as if to say, *I accept your tribute.*

"And," Rueben continued, "now me, a midseason addition to the cast, an outrageous and curvaceous Latina spitfire always sure to elicit a guffaw and boner!"

Rueben leapt off his chair and shook his hips suggestively. "I am . . ." he intoned dramatically, "the third Angel! I must be on the team." He threw his arms in the air like a gymnast nailing the perfect dismount.

"There is," I said sternly, "no team."

"Oh, please." Freddy stood and put his arm around Rueben. "It's perfect! Right out of central casting. You're hired!"

"This is silly," I said.

"Don't be bitter just because you have to be the plain one," Freddy cautioned.

"Yes," said Rueben. "Even if you're not as pretty as we are, we still need you on the team to, I don't know, drive the car and defuse bombs and such."

"Guys . . ." I began.

"Enough," Freddy interrupted. "This is going to work. I just know it. Three is always better than two."

"Apparently," I said, remembering his little ménage on the dance floor.

"You know what they say," Freddy added. "The triangle is the strongest shape there is."

"Who says that?"

"Archeologists," Freddy asserted confidently.

"Architects?" I asked.

"Whatevaperon," Freddy said, tossing his head as if he had a Farrah-like mane instead of his shaved dome. He leaned into Rueben and mock-whispered, "I told you we need a smart one."

"Now," Rueben said, "we have to get back to the party before Ansell starts wondering where I am. And you guys are here to been seen. What say we all meet soon and start planning our investigation?"

"Sounds perfect," Freddy said.

I groaned.

"Ideally," Rueben continued, "I'd like to include some undercover work. Maybe we could join a college wrestling team or a roller derby or something."

"I don't see what . . ." I began.

"We'll work out the details at our meeting. Now let's see . . . I'm going to be busy all day tomorrow doing follow-up for tonight's event, but how about Wednesday? Can you guys come over around seven? I'll order in Thai."

"Marvelous," Freddy said. "I'll bring the speakerphone."

I rolled my eyes.

"But now"—Rueben dragged us with him toward the door—"it's time to get our party on. And I *must* introduce you to Ansell!"

Rueben hustled us through the loft. We squeezed by the dancers, slipped past couples of every persuasion making out, and avoided the waitrons wielding precariously balanced platters of drinks. Rueben knew where to find Ansell, in a roped-off area on a platform behind the dance floor.

The man had a VIP area in his own apartment. Unbelievable.

The tall, bald, and heavily muscled shirtless bodybuilder who guarded the velvet rope nodded at Rueben and let us pass. Freddy stopped on the way through. "Would you look at that?" he asked me. "That guy's more cut than a baby at a bris."

"Let's just get this over with," I whispered back. For some reason, despite Rueben's testimony to his character, I had a bad feeling about Ansell. When Rueben went to find him, I said as much to Freddy.

"Yeah, honey." Freddy patted my cheek. "I think that 'bad feeling' is envy. I mean, look at this place! Look at these people! It's like we died and went to homo heaven."

"Maybe," I said.

Rueben reappeared, with a reluctant-looking Ansell Darling in tow. Ansell wore an expression like he couldn't imagine who would be worth the trouble it took him to walk over here. Then he got a look at me and Freddy and his face brightened considerably.

"Well, *hello,*" he purred at Freddy, putting his hand on Freddy's prominent pec poking through his silk shirt. "This fits you like a second skin." He rubbed his hand up and down a little. "You don't mind, do you? It's just so rewarding to see my work worn so well."

Freddy rarely minded being felt up, and the fact that Ansell was rich and famous didn't hurt, either. Freddy was a true fashionista, and for him, being groped by Ansell Darling was like being touched by the hand of God. "It's an honor, Mr. Darling," Freddy gushed. "This stuff is beautiful. You're a genius."

Ansell chuckled. I took a moment to study him. Tall and thin with long black hair pulled into a ponytail. He had a strong nose and narrow lips, set off by pronounced cheekbones and elegantly arched eyebrows. His smooth, unlined skin seemed a little waxy. Was he wearing foundation? He wasn't handsome or well built, but he exuded confidence and control in a way I supposed was attractive.

"Seriously," Freddy said. "I've totally admired your stuff for years. That Ashton Kutcher spread in *Details* last spring? Like butter."

Ansell ran his hand down to Freddy's taut stomach. "You wear it better, you dazzling boy, you. You ever consider modeling?"

I turned from Ansell and looked at Rueben. His eyes narrowed to slits and his mouth set in a tight, thin line.

"And you." Ansell turned to me and beamed. "Just as I imagined. My golden boy." He reached out to grab me but I took a step back. Ansell covered by bringing his hands together in applause. "Just beautiful. Those shorts you're wearing? I plan on charging two thousand five hundred dollars a pair for them in my couture line. Less than a yard of fabric. Best of all, I can sell a cotton version for forty-five dollars through my Little Darlings line at Target and still make a boatload on them."

Ansell put his hands on Freddy and pulled my friend closer to me, so that we were standing shoulder to shoulder. "The two of you. Incredible. We have to make sure one of the photographers gets a shot of you two tonight." Ansell turned to Rueben.

As Ansell's head pivoted, Rueben rearranged his face into a generous smile. Only his eyes betrayed his tension. I don't think Ansell noticed. "My treasure," Ansell called to him. "Will you take care of that?"

Rueben nodded, fake smile in place.

Ansell blew him an air kiss. "You've really come through for me tonight." At that, Rueben's eyes relaxed and he released an audible sigh of relief. "All the boys you brought are delicious, but these two are perfection!"

Freddy beamed and I tried to look less annoyed than I felt.

Like I said, I was predisposed to dislike Ansell Darling, and his treating us like prime sides of beef didn't do much to change my opinion.

Ansell leaned into us and in a conspiratorial murmur muttered, "You working boys are the best."

Freddy's smile ratcheted down a notch. "Uh, Mr. Darling, I'm not a, you know . . ."

Ansell cocked his head to the side.

"I'm not a . . ." He searched for a polite term. This being his first attempt at tact, it didn't come easily.

"Freddy's not a 'professional,'" I stepped in. "He's actually the volunteer coordinator at an AIDS service agency."

Ansell's attention promptly fell from my friend. "Ah," he said, his olive eyes settling fully on me. "And what about you, my golden boy? Are you for hire?"

"For some people." I gave him a saccharine smile. "I have sex for money, if that's what you mean."

Ansell reached out for me again, and this time I let him rest his hands on my glittered hips. "Mmmm," Ansell said, leaning in to my ear. "You really are a tiny dream, aren't you, my dear." He ran his hands over my ass. "Yes, this fabric feels just as good as I thought."

He let go and reached into his pocket and took out a small, sterling silver case. "This is my card," he said, opening it and slipping a piece of paper into my back pocket. "My personal number is on the back. Why don't you give me a call and we'll see what we can work out? I'm sure I can make it worth your while."

Ansell, confident that I'd call, let me go. What working boy wouldn't want to score with a rich celebrity like him?

Freddy extended his hand for a card, too. Ansell ignored it and put the silver case back in his pants. Freddy's face dropped.

"So nice meeting you, too," Ansell said to him with a total lack of interest. Then, back to me, "Be sure you call."

Lastly, he turned to Rueben, whose face once again was stone. "You're too good to me," he said. "You get me everything I need, my sweet." He pulled Rueben into his arms and I saw clouds of anger, relief, appreciation, and disgust roll across Rueben's eyes. With Rueben's back to me, Ansell looked at me over Rueben's shoulder. His lips silently mouthed the word one more time. *"Call."*

He let go of Rueben and disappeared into the adoring crowd.

The moment Ansell was out of sight, I took the card from my pocket and held it out to Rueben.

"Here," I said, "I don't want this."

"No," Rueben said stoically, "you keep it, *bambino*. It's for you."

"Really," I said. "Take it. You're my friend, man. I wouldn't use it."

"No." Rueben was steel. "Ansell wants you to have it, so you keep it. Use it. Really, I won't mind. That's kind of my job around here. To get Ansell whatever he wants. Really. You'd be doing me a favor."

"Rueben," I began. "I couldn't do that to you . . ."

Rueben held up his hand. "No, stop. You wouldn't be doing anything other than helping me. Besides"—Rueben's lips trembled a little and he blinked hard—"Ansell will take good care of you."

I opened my mouth to respond, but Rueben put his finger to my lips. "Shhh. He will. Hasn't he taken good care of me?"

What could I do? I wrapped my arms around Rueben and hugged him. "I'm sor—" I began, but Rueben once again cut me off.

"No!" he barked. "Don't say that. Don't be sorry for me." He put his fake smile back on. "I'm fine, really. It's just the way it is. He's given me so much. It'd be selfish for me to expect fidelity, too."

He stepped back and gave a shudder, like a dog shaking water out of its fur. "We're still on for dinner, right?" He looked at Freddy and me. "Two nights from tonight, right?"

We nodded.

"Good." Rueben grinned, a little more steady now. "Good. Now, I have to go find my man. You two will be all right, yes?"

We nodded again.

"*Muchas gracias, muchachos.* I'll see you then. Angels unite!" He blew us air kisses and disappeared into the crowd.

Freddy put an arm around my shoulder. "This fun thing we're doing tonight? Not so much with the 'fun,' huh?"

"Not so much," I answered.

"Let's say we blow this joint, huh?"

"What are you talking about?" I asked. "I thought you were having a great time. Five minutes ago, you were calling this 'homo heaven.' "

"Yeah." Freddy squeezed me closer. "Now? Like I said, not so much."

Freddy and I sat in a diner down the street from Ansell's apartment. I kept my gratefully retrieved coat tied tightly around my waist. "Isn't it warm in here?" Freddy teased. "Sure you don't want to take that off?"

"*I'm fine,*" I growled, giving him what I hoped was a silencing squint.

"Do you have something in your eye?" Freddy asked.

I stuck my tongue out at him.

"Don't flirt," Freddy chided me. "So, your friend Rueben, what was that all about?"

"Pretty sad, huh?"

"I'd say. And what's with that Ansell Darling? That guy could have practically anyone he wants—actors, models, hell, I would have done him even though he's not that good-looking. I mean, he's Ansell Darling, right?"

I nodded.

"But, the minute he found out I wasn't a working boy, he lost all interest in me. Lost interest in *me!*" Freddy repeated, as if it were entirely unbelievable. "Is he only into sex if he has to pay for it? Is that what he's about?"

"It looked that way."

"Why? What would make a guy like him limit himself like that?"

"His parents never loved him enough, making him feel undeserving of anyone's affections. He went through school a skinny fag, with bad skin and an unflattering hairstyle, constantly rejected and hurt. As an adult, he's achieved a high level of fame as a designer, but really, his entire empire is built on ripping off other people's work. He feels like he doesn't merit his own success, and thus his self-image is fragile and suspect. Since he doesn't think he's actually earned anything, he doesn't trust anything that comes his way unless he's paying for it. The only love he can believe in is the love he can buy."

Freddy looked impressed. "Wow. Really? How do you know all this shit?"

"I don't," I said snarkily. "I just made that all up. Pretty convincing though, right?"

Freddy stood up and slapped me on the head.

"Ow. But, seriously, who knows? Most of us don't even understand our own motivations, let alone anyone else's. I spent this afternoon fooling around with a guy who only likes to have sex when he's dressed like a clown—having a thing for rentboys isn't even the weirdest kink I've seen *today*."

"You fucked a clown?" Freddy asked wide-eyed.

"That's beside the point," I said, instantly regretting opening that door. Freddy wasn't the type to let something like that pass unnoticed.

"It wasn't a group thing, was it? Like, you opened the door to his apartment expecting to find one clown there, but then a hundred tumbled out?"

I tried giving him another evil look.

"There goes that thing with your eye again. You really should see an orthodontist."

"Optometrist."

"Whatever. Or maybe you got some whipped cream in there. He didn't throw pies at you, did he?"

This was getting too close for comfort.

"Seriously," I said, "enough with the clowns. What about Rueben?"

"Yeah," Freddy said, looking down at his drink. "That was pretty sad. He seemed really upset at how blatantly Ansell put the moves on you. He treats Rueben likes he's staff."

"I agree. It's a bad scene. Rueben's trying to stay on the straight and narrow, and I can't believe his relationship with Ansell is helping."

"So what should we do?" Freddy asked.

"I don't know. We'll see him in two days, right? Maybe we can talk to him then."

"Great! We'll rescue our friend and solve the murders, too!" Freddy said. "I love this crime-fighting stuff."

"Yeah, well, last time you weren't the one who wound up tied up and tortured, were you?"

"Would you *please* stop talking about your job?" Freddy asked. I threw my napkin at him.

"Listen, before we go too far with this stuff, we don't even know that there were any murders," I reminded him. Sitting in the diner, the whole thing seemed a lot less likely than it did an hour ago. "Let's not let our imaginations run away with us."

"Yeah," Freddy said, "we really should stop *clowning* around."

"It's a shame your parents didn't have any human children," I said.

"Yeah, yeah, let's bounce. I'll walk you home." Just then, his phone buzzed in his pocket. Freddy flipped open the screen.

"Well, well," he said. He typed something into the keypad and hit "send."

"What's up?"

"That guy I was dancing with at the party. He just texted." Freddy showed me his phone. "Leaving now," the screen read, "want to finish what we started on the dance floor? J."

"J.," I said. "Which one was he?"

"Damned if I know." Freddy shrugged.

"How did you answer him?"

"Yes, of course."

"You don't even know who he is!"

"So what? They were all fine. Besides, why should you be the only one around here who gets to solve mysteries?"

Great, I thought, *Freddy in* The Case of the Unknown Trick.

"Unless," Freddy said, giving me the sexy stare that seduced half the eligible men in New York City, "you want to make me a better offer?"

"I'll pass," I said bitterly. Although what I had to be angry about, I couldn't have told you.

"Your loss," Freddy trilled, pursing his perfect lips in the manner that seduced the other half.

Is it? I asked myself, and not for the first time.

"Wait a minute," Freddy said as he was getting ready to leave. "Isn't tomorrow that thing with Yvonne and your mom?"

I had forgotten about that. I grimaced. "Yeah."

"Well, good luck with that, darling. Just remember, if the going gets tough, close your eyes and let warm thoughts of the man who loves you keep up your spirits."

"Tony?"

"No, darling. Bozo."

13

When You Wish Upon a Star

I didn't get home from Rueben's party until two in the morning. Four hours later, my phone rang, waking me from a deep and dreamless sleep.

The only person who'd call me this early was Tony, usually to say he was just getting off a late shift and wanted to drop by. Yum. As tired as I was, that thought was never unappealing.

I answered in a raspy morning voice. "Hey, sexy daddy."

"It's not Daddy, baby, it's your mother. And why are you calling your father 'sexy'?"

It was like waking up to a bucket of ice water poured on your head.

"I thought . . ."

"Never mind that," my mother interrupted. "Aren't you excited? I'm excited! Are you excited?"

I was until I realized it was you, I thought. "I'm so excited," I said, feeling very Pointer Sistersish. "What are we excited about, again?"

"*Yvonne,*" my mother said reverently. "You didn't forget, did you?"

"Of course not," I lied.

"Why aren't you here yet?"

I looked at the clock again. "It's six o'clock in the morning, Mom. You said to be there at noon."

"How could you sleep at a time like this?" my mother asked. "Aren't you excited?"

This is where I came in. "Listen," I said. "I'm really tired. I'll be there at noon, OK?"

"Can you make it by nine?"

"I'll try for eleven."

"Nine thirty," my mother countered.

"Ten thirty. That's my final offer."

"Fine," my mother said. "Just meet us at the shop. They set up the cameras and the lights yesterday. Isn't this exciting?"

My head was going to explode. "There are," I assured her, "no words."

"That's my darling boy," my mother enthused. "See you at ten!"

The car service got me to Sophie's Choice Tresses at 10:15, which seemed pretty reasonable, considering.

The place was a madhouse. Outside were two high-end steel gray trailers, with smoked windows and "Yvonne" decals applied to their sides. Thick bundles of cables ran from them into the propped-open door of my mother's beauty parlor. Various staffers, all wearing black *Yvonne* T-shirts, ran around carrying clipboards, cups of coffee, and thick rolls of silver tape. The air was dark and sooty from the idling trucks.

Meanwhile, about fifty neighborhood snoops stood outside, talking among themselves and peering through the shop windows. Two teenaged girls who really should have been in school held up a sign that read "We love you, Yvonne!" Mrs. Petroski, from the bakery down the street, was selling doughnuts to the crowd. She spotted me exiting the car.

"Kevin!" she cried, running over to me. She smelled like chocolate and powdered sugar. It was love at first sniff.

"Hi, Mrs. P.," I said.

She pinched my cheek. "Still such a cutie, you are. Isn't this exciting?"

Here we go again. "It's unbelievable," I answered, honestly.

"Your mother on *Yvonne*!" she gushed. "This is the most glamorous thing to happen to this neighborhood since Merv Griffin, now gone but not forgotten, at least not by me, almost choked to death on a piece of gefilte fish at Lenny's Deli on 167th Street. We really hit the big time then, sonny."

"That was something," I said.

"But this! It's quite a coup for your mother, I'll tell you. Everyone's going to want their hair cut at Sophie's now!"

"Let's hope," I answered.

Mrs. P. pulled a sheet of tissue paper from her apron and selected a jelly doughnut from her bag. "These were always your favorite, Kevin."

"Awww," I said, genuinely touched. Maybe there was something nice about coming home after all. "That's very sweet of you." I put out my hand.

Mrs. P. put out hers, too. "That'll be a buck twenty-five, dear."

The inside of my mother's shop had been transformed into the bastard love child of a beauty parlor and a television studio. Chairs had been pushed to the side, huge domed lights hung from alien-looking tripods, and cables and electrical cords snaked everywhere. Two huge television cameras captured my mother's workstation from both sides, while a third hung back at the best angle for the full-on capture of Yvonne's unfortunate transformation from sophisticated television star to tacky Long Island harridan.

Ironically, even though they were shooting in a beauty parlor, the producers set up a folding canvas chair, where my mother sat having powder applied by an extremely thin and fey looking African-American guy in his forties.

"Hi, Mom," I said, dodging various *Yvonne* staffers.

"Sweetheart," my mother said. "You're late."

"Am not." I leaned over to kiss her cheek.

"Nuh-huh," the haughty queen attending her admonished me, wagging his finger. "No touching the face, child. She's flawless."

I stepped back and put up my hands. "Sorry!"

Miss Thing puckered his lips. "No problem, sweetie. You're pretty flawless, too." He turned to my mother. "Is he taken?"

My mother, who always took any compliment to me as a personal credit to her, beamed. "He has a policeman boyfriend with commitment issues and a great ass," she answered.

I felt myself blushing. "Mom!"

"We're all friends here," my mother answered. Then, to the makeup artist, "Really. You could bounce a quarter off it."

Why, I wondered, and not for the first time in my mother's presence, doesn't the ground ever open and swallow you when you need it to?

The makeup artist gave my mother a sly smile. "You're going to look Tyra-iffic on the camera, dear. I'll leave you to chat with your boy."

I pulled up a chair and sat next to my mother. "So," I said, "how are you doing?"

Turns out, as she spent the next ten minutes explaining, she was pretty excited. Who knew? She might have kept talking until the cameras started rolling had she not gotten distracted by someone passing by.

"Andrew!" she shouted. "Get your little tush over here and say 'hello!'"

I turned and saw someone who could have been an underwear model for a Calvin Klein campaign saunter over with the natural grace of a born athlete. Six feet of lean and muscled bodyliciousness topped by a strong, angular face and sandy brown hair that fell into place like silk fringe on a really expensive shawl. He wore pressed khaki slacks and the ubiquitous *Yvonne* T-shirt, which fit him like the skin of grape. A really juicy grape.

"This is Andrew Miller," my mother said to me. "Remember I told you about him? Yvonne's producer? He says he knew you from high school."

Andrew had a mile-wide smile and I tried my best to place him. I couldn't imagine not noticing someone as good-looking as him.

"Hi," I said, a bit awkwardly. Andrew looked a few years older than me; I'd guess he was a senior the year I arrived in high school. Since upperclassmen rarely socialized with freshmen, I couldn't imagine when we would have met. Was he one of Tony's friends?

"Kevin." Andrew extended his hand, and his grip was strong and warm. "You probably don't remember me."

"You look familiar," I said, although I couldn't say from where. Maybe he'd done modeling. I couldn't imagine where else I'd have seen him.

"I was captain of the lacrosse team," Andrew said. "You came to a few games. I don't think we ever talked, but I remember seeing you around."

Oh. My. God. Andrew Miller? I had never known his name, but yes, I had attended a few games, mostly to ogle his incredibly fine form and the way the muscles in his arms moved whenever he swung his stick.

Swung his stick. Jesus. I remembered some of the fantasies I'd had about him and felt myself blushing again.

"Wow," I said. "I can't even believe you knew who I was. I was just another fan in the stands. Lacrosse fan," I added. I turned to my mother. "I love lacrosse. It's so . . . sticky, I mean, they play with really long sticks. Much bigger than baseball bats, you know."

I really needed to shut up.

"Funny," my mother observed, "I don't remember you ever expressing any interest at all in lacrosse. Or any other sports for that matter. A mother," she said to Andrew, "is always the last to know, though, isn't she?"

Andrew laughed. "Even people who don't like sports seem to enjoy lacrosse," he told her. "We always had great crowds for our games."

I bet, I thought.

My mother turned back to me. "And look at Andrew now. So young, and the producer of *Yvonne*."

"Well," Andrew said, cocking his head to the side, "I'm not *the* producer of *Yvonne*. He's in LA counting his money, I'm sure." Andrew winked at my mother and she laughed as if his joke was the funniest thing she'd ever heard.

"I'm just a segment producer," Andrew continued. "There are seven of us, and we rotate between episodes."

"Well, weren't we lucky that you got to produce *this* one," my mother gushed.

"Oh, luck had nothing to do with it." Andrew grinned. "I specifically request the episodes when we have beautiful women as our guests."

Another disproportionately loud laugh from my mother, this one accompanied by her well-manicured hand flying up to her ample bosom in a gesture that was meant to convey humility but instead shouted, *Hey, check out these babies!*

"Such a charmer," she purred. "And so successful at such a young age! Already a producer on *Yvonne*. While my dear Kevin . . ." Her voice trailed off and she threw up her hands in surrender at the thought of her useless progeny.

"Uh, standing right here," I said.

"Well, darling," my mother said. "I'm just saying that your friend Andrew here has one of the top positions on America's most popular talk show, whereas you, well, what is it you do anyway, dear?"

If we were really going to play Can You Top This, I could mention that last week I got seven hundred dollars to receive a scalp massage with a happy ending (don't ask) from the married author of the current number two book on the *New York Times* bestseller list, but I wasn't sure that would impress.

"You know what I do," I said. For years I'd been telling my family I worked freelance as a computer consultant.

"No, really," my mother persisted, "what exactly . . ."

Just then, another *Yvonne* staffer, a rather timid overweight young woman with purple hair and boxy square-framed glasses sidled over to my mother. *Why do they all look so frightened?* I asked myself.

"Mrs. Connor," she asked shakily. "We need to do a sound check." She looked at Andrew for approval. "Is that OK?"

"Check away," Andrew said, flashing his megawatt grin. I could have sworn the purple girl's glasses fogged up a little.

"Thank you, sir," she answered. "Right this way, Mrs. Connor."

"Please," my mother said, "call me Sophie. Mrs. Connor is my mother."

Actually, I thought, your mother is Mrs. Gerstein. But it didn't seem worth mentioning.

"Tell you what," Andrew Miller said as they walked away. "How about you come with me into the production trailer, and I give you a behind-the-scenes tour of what we do here?"

Step into my parlor, huh? As a working boy, I had a good instinct for when a guy was interested in me. I tried to tap into Andrew's vibe and got . . . nothing. He seemed a perfectly innocent jock extending a friendly and agenda-free invitation to an old classmate.

Damn.

14

He Touched Me

We walked into one of the long trailers that flanked my mother's shop. All kinds of monitors, control panels, and communications equipment ran along the walls. Andrew walked me to the back, where a bathroom took up one side and a narrow door marked "Producer" occupied the other.

Andrew opened that door and motioned for me to join him. The small space contained a computer station and various monitors showing live feeds from the cameras inside the salon. Andrew invited me to sit on the folding chair in the corner. He closed the door behind us and sat at the computer station, turning the wheeled task chair to face me.

"Well," he said.

"Huh," I answered.

"This is awkward," he said.

"It's cramped in here," I agreed.

"Seeing you again."

Sometimes, I didn't know if it was my ADD causing my confusion, or if the other person really wasn't making sense. Had I taken my medicine today? No. Crap.

"Well," I said, looking at the cluttered space where we sat almost knees-to-knees, "nice to see you, too."

Andrew frowned. "You know why I'm here, right?"

"To shoot my mother's segment," I answered.

"Well, yeah, but why do you think we chose your mother to be one of Yvonne's makeover artists?"

"Uh, I don't know, but I have to tell you, holding up my mother as any kind of 'artist' is only going to result in disappointment and pain. Just so you know."

"Your mom has a lot of personality and color. She's going to pop on the show, you wait and see. But why do you think, out of all the beauty parlors in all the world, we decided to shoot here?"

"Someone hates Yvonne and wants to make her look as bad as possible?"

"Well, that goes without saying." Andrew rolled his eyes. "But seriously, don't you get it?"

"I might get it," I said. "I mean, if I knew what 'it' was."

"You still haven't figured it out?"

We didn't have enough time to list all the things I haven't figured out. This was the least of them.

"I'm not much of a detective, Andrew."

"It's like this. We had this episode on the books for a while now—Yvonne gets made over at four regional beauty parlors. You know, a Midwest matronly kind of thing, the LA look, whatever. The New York segment was supposed to be at some high-class salon on Fifth Avenue—the glamour shot. But at the last minute the place backed out. They found out about Yvonne's reputation and realized they didn't want to deal with that level of drama—at least not on TV."

"Yvonne has a reputation?" I asked. Wasn't she called the Queen of Kindness or something? Hadn't she started an orphanage or a religion? Or was that Oprah?

Andrew rolled his eyes again. I seemed to have that effect on him. It was a little annoying, but he had really pretty green eyes that were nice to watch on their orbit.

"That's not the point. Anyway, when the Fifth Avenue place dropped out, we had to come up with something quick. We were going to reach out to another of those famous stylists when I remembered your mother's shop here in Long Island. I brought it up at our production meeting, and everyone loved the idea. A local neighborhood place with native New Yorkers—the kind of neighbors you have outside, with their signs and their doughnuts. You can't buy that kind of authenticity."

"You probably could," I told him. Although I couldn't imagine anyone wanting to. Growing up, I couldn't get away from this "authenticity" fast enough.

"Trust me," Andrew said. "This kind of stuff is golden. So, the executive producer is loving me because I found this great location, Yvonne is thrilled because she loves to pretend that she's one of the 'real people,' and I'm excited because I got what I wanted out of it."

"A good show?"

"No, you little jerk. The chance to see you again."

For a quick second, I turned around to see if there was someone standing behind me. "See *me* again?" I asked.

I didn't know he'd seen me the first time.

"Kevin, I've wanted you ever since senior year."

"Say what now?"

"I wanted you, Kevin. You think I didn't notice you in the stands, watching me? You think I wasn't incredibly aware of the cute kid sitting on the sidelines, eating me up with his eyes? You think I didn't look for you every time I went out on the field, that I wasn't disappointed when you weren't there?" Andrew rolled his chair closer to me and our knees touched. Electric currents ran from where we connected, up my legs, and into my crotch.

"You like guys?" I asked.

"I like you," Andrew answered. "You've always been so beautiful. Such a beautiful little guy. I used to fantasize you'd take a job as our towel boy. I'd come out of the shower, naked, dripping wet. 'Where's my towel?' I ask, and you'd run forward, dropping to your knees before me, rubbing the towel up my leg, along the inside of my thigh, finally brushing against my balls, getting me hard so fast, my big cock slapping wet and heavy against my flat belly." As he spoke, Andrew took his hands and ran them along the path he described, but on me, inside my thigh, up, up, until they stopped just below my tenders.

"I didn't," I began. "I mean, I shouldn't because . . . I'm kind of . . ." Andrew's hand rested firmly on my rapidly responding guy parts and squeezed. Released. Squeezed again. Had I been saying something?

"I have a semi—" *Boyfriend* I was about to say.

"I can feel," Andrew interrupted. "If this is the semi, I can't wait to feel it full on."

"No, I have a . . ."

"Kevin," his voice was raspy. "Kevin. I want you."

This was all moving a little fast. I put my hands on his knees and pushed him away. The task chair scooted a few inches back and Andrew pulled his hands back. He looked a little mystified, and I guessed he wasn't used to being turned down.

"Listen," I said, "you're a great-looking guy and don't take this wrong, but . . ."

I wasn't exactly sure what I was going to say, but it didn't matter. The door flew open and the doorway filled with a tall, gorgeous, and familiar figure.

"Damn it to hell, Andrew," Yvonne bellowed, "can't I turn around for one minute without you bringing your latest 'production assistant' into your office for a quick round of Hide the Chorizo?"

You know how, when you see people on TV or in the movies, you think that they're probably not as good-looking as they are onscreen? That the lighting and makeup and stagecraft cover a multitude of sins?

Well, as someone who's had sex with more than a few closeted celebrities, I can tell you you're right. Nine times out of ten, the people you see in movies or on shows are shorter, fatter, paler, and more pockmarked than you'd expect.

But to every rule there is the exception, and Yvonne was definitely Exception Girl. On her daily talkfest, she looks pretty but not amazingly so. There's an everyday averageness about her that puts the daytime audience at ease and makes her relatable.

In person, Yvonne was a knockout. More statuesque and shapely than I thought, with a bodacious figure that was all boobs and ass. Her heart-shaped face framed wide eyes, a perfect man-made nose (which matched the boobs in that respect), and full over-plumped lips. I'd guess she had a nip and tuck along the way; her skin was gorgeous but almost too smooth. She looked a little manufactured, yes, but still breathtaking, in the way that great architecture is magnificent.

Which is to say, the Eiffel Tower may be a thing of beauty forever, but I can't imagine anyone wanting to fuck it.

Yvonne, either. Maybe I'd warm up to her, but right now, she exuded all the charm of a bulldozer.

"Yvonne," Andrew said, rising from his chair. "I was just talking to Kevin, here, he's actually not a . . ."

Yvonne held up her hand. "Spare me," she hissed. Were her brow not paralyzed by Botox, I guessed it would have been furrowed in anger. "It's just that when I show up on set, I expect my segment producer to be waiting for me. It would be nice to know what the *fuck* I'm doing in wherever the *fuck* I am. Where am I, anyway? Is this Detroit? It smells like Detroit."

Andrew grabbed a clipboard off his desk. "You're a half hour early, Yvonne. We weren't expecting you yet."

Yvonne's mouth turned a millimeter lower and Andrew jumped in to interrupt the frown.

"Which is great, that you're here early. Just great. That's why you're the best!"

Apparently, the compliments worked, as Yvonne's lips returned to the neutral level where I assumed the collagen had settled.

"Let's go to your bus and get you comfortable, and I'll let you know what we're doing here today," Andrew said in his calmest voice.

"Fine," Yvonne said, still annoyed. She waved a hand at me. "And why isn't Flavor of the Week wearing one of my T-shirts?"

"Hi," I said, extending my hand, "I'm Kevin, and I don't actually . . ."

Yvonne looked at my hand as if it contained a steaming pile of shit. "I'm sorry," she said, "was I speaking to you?"

"Well, no, but I . . ."

She turned to Andrew again. "Would you please explain The Rules to him? Because I really can't bear every little peon who works here yammering at me all day."

OK, I take back my earlier comment. I don't want to offend any bulldozers.

Andrew put his hand on her back. "Let's just go to your bus and get you all ready," Andrew said in the manner of a kindergarten teacher taking sharp scissors away from a five-year-old.

"Listen, lady," I began, but Andrew turned his head around so quickly that I feared whiplash for him. His eyes opened as wide as they could and his mouth formed a long and soundless "Please." I knew anything I said would make him look bad so I suppressed my natural urge to tell Yvonne just where she could put her precious Rules.

"Why don't you wait here," Andrew said to me as he ushered Her Highness out the door. "I'll be back in a bit and show you how we monitor the show from here."

"I'm sure you'll show him a hell of a lot more than that." Yvonne snickered.

I've never been so happy to see a woman leave a room.

I gave Andrew and Cruella a few minutes to clear the decks, and then left the bus to check in with my mother. She was talking to one of what seemed like one hundred identically dressed *Yvonne* staffers. I heard her as I approached.

" . . . more surprised than I was," she was telling the thirty-something, short, plump young woman with purple streaks in her black hair and a tool belt around her waist. "I mean, my son dating a policeman! How incongruous! You should really have them on the show. Or, better yet, you could have *me* back, talking *about* them! Maybe I could be a regular, like that cute Nate Berkus on . . ."

"Mom," I said. "How's it going?"

My mother put an arm around me. "I was just talking with Margie here."

"I heard."

"Margie's a very important person on Yvonne's staff," my mother said. "I was giving her some show ideas."

"I hang the lights," Margie said in a deep voice, looking a little uncomfortable with her unexpected promotion.

"Well," I said, "it's nice to meet you. The lights look very, um, well hung."

"Thanks."

We stood looking at the lights for a moment.

"I have to go," Margie said.

My mother pulled her into an embrace. "Darling, thank you so much for your input. I'm sure we'll be working together again soon!"

Margie had that who-is-this-crazy-woman expression on her face that I'd come to know from a million other strangers unwillingly pulled into my mother's bizarre and scary universe.

"Yeah, bye," Margie said, scampering away faster than I thought a woman of her height and weight could move.

"Everyone's so *nice*," my mother effused. "I feel like Queen for a Day! Maybe I'll wind up as Yvonne's personal stylist out of all this!"

"If she's crazy," I muttered to myself.

"What's that?" my mother asked.

OK, maybe muttering wasn't my thing. I said, 'If she's crazy about the hairstyle, why not?' "

"This is so exciting! I'm going to be a star!"

"Well, brace yourself, because I just met Yvonne and, believe me, she's not the woman you see on TV."

"What do you mean?" My mother's eyes narrowed.

"I mean, she was kind of a bitch."

At that, my mother gasped. Yes, actually gasped. I thought for a second she was going to slap me.

"A bitch? *A bitch?* Do you have any idea how many children with AIDS she's had on her show? All the money she's raised for homeless veterans? The church she personally helped build in New Orleans?"

"I'm just saying . . ."

"Yvonne is a *saint*," my mother asserted. "She's like Mother Teresa, only she obviously follows a much more stringent skincare routine. Why, with all Mother Teresa's good works, no one ever offered that woman a bottle of sunscreen, I'll never know."

"Yeah, well, not everything is like how you see it on TV, Mom. I'm telling you, I just met Yvonne, and that woman is as evil as a box of bees. She's . . ."

"Here." I saw my mother's eyes widen as she gazed at something over my shoulder. "Oh my God, she's *here!*"

I turned and saw the woman I had just been describing as Hitler with breasts walking toward us with utter grace and serenity, flanked by Andrew, who followed two steps behind on her left. Yvonne ignored me as she approached my mother. She placed her hand on my mother's arm. I thought I saw my mother's knees buckle.

"I hear," Yvonne said, her voice pure silk and honey, "that you're going to be making me look beautiful today."

Had Jesus Christ himself just descended from the ceiling in a halo of sunlight and angels, I don't think my mother's expression could have been any more beatific. "Yvonne," my mother croaked, her voice betraying her awe, "God made you beautiful. I can only hope to gild the lily. The lily of you."

I threw up a little in the back of my mouth.

"Oh, dear." Yvonne threw back her head and laughed warmly. "If not for my makeup men and hairstylists, well, let's just say you wouldn't want to see me first thing in the morning."

Throw in some plastic surgeons and personal trainers, I thought, *and there might be some truth to that.* But I could see Yvonne had her Humility set to high.

"But look at you," Yvonne continued. She put a hand on my mother's cheek and I saw my mother resist the urge to kiss her palm. "I would kill for skin like this, dear. Now be honest—have you had a little work done?"

My mother shook her head, but not so vigorously as to dislodge Yvonne's hand. "It's all thanks to Mary Kay. We sell her full line of products here. I'll give you some before you leave today. Free."

I doubted Yvonne put anything on her skin that cost less than one hundred dollars an ounce, but she smiled as if she'd just won the lottery. "You are too kind. Well, I have to get ready for the show, but I did want to introduce myself to you before the cameras started rolling. I can tell you are going to be marvelous on the show, dear. Thank you so much for having us out here."

Yvonne was as lovely and gracious as could be. Had I not seen the scene in the bus, I'd have been in love with her, too.

"Thank *you*," my mother gushed. "Oh," she said, remembering me standing next to her. "Let me introduce you. This is . . ."

"Yes, we've already met," Yvonne said. She gave me a warm smile. "So good to see you again, dear. Now remember," she said sweetly, "next time I see you, I want you to be wearing one of my T-shirts, right?" She playfully wagged her finger at me. "Naughty boy. All right, I must go. See you all soon!" Yvonne floated away.

My mother stood star-struck for a few seconds.

"OK," I said, "I admit she seemed nice just then but . . ."

"Not. Another. Word." My mother was ice. "I don't know what you were thinking, but that woman is a saint."

"Or so you've said."

My mother looked at me as if I'd just spouted fangs. "You're not turning into one of those homosexuals who hate all women, are you?"

"Mom!"

"She even offered to give you a T-shirt."

"She thinks I work for her!"

"What?" my mother asked.

"Just . . . never mind." It was clear my mother was drunk on Yvonne's Kool-Aid, and I didn't have the antidote. No one could talk to my mother when she got like this, not even my . . .

"Hey"—that reminded me—"where's Dad?"

"Oh, your father?"

"Uh, yeah."

"Well, apparently," my mother said with a long-suffering sigh, "your father didn't want to be here today. He said something about how he didn't need to be around me when I get 'like this.'"

"Hmmm," I said. My father was a very smart man.

"I don't know what he meant, though. Do you?"

"No," I said, smiling and lying like a snake. "I can't imagine."

Hey, if Yvonne could succeed as a deceitful, insincere bitch, maybe it would work for me, too.

Another young woman in an *Yvonne* T-shirt ran over. "Mrs. Connor, we need you in makeup right now."

"Didn't they already do your makeup?" I asked.

"This will be the third time," my mother answered. "This is a strange business. But it keeps a lot of people employed, so that's good."

"This will be it," the young woman assured. "After this last touch up, we'll be doing a ten-minute interview with you about your little business here, and then it's time to bring out Yvonne!"

Normally, my mother would have been insulted by the reference to her "little business," but today she was too happy to object. Instead, she bounced a little on her heels and clapped her hands. "An interview? With me? Isn't this *exciting!*"

For what I hoped would be the last time, I agreed that this was, at the very least, the transcendent experience of a lifetime. "Good luck," I said, kissing her on the cheek as she was hustled away. "I love you." I waved.

"Love you, too," she called, waving back.

For some reason, I felt like an onlooker bidding farewell to a loved one as she boarded the *Titanic*.

15

Watch Closely Now

I was about to step outside for some air when I felt a strong hand clamp on my shoulder. "Come on," Andrew said, "let's go watch the show." He started walking toward the door.

"Shouldn't I stay in here?"

"You'd only be in the way. They'll be shooting for hours. We'll watch from the bus."

Andrew led me back to the mobile studio and ushered me into his makeshift office. He shut the door after us. "There will be some production assistants coming in and out during the taping," he explained, "but that shouldn't start for another few minutes. They may need me for something. But for the next little bit"—he put his hand on the back of my head—"we should have some privacy."

"Don't you have to be out there for the taping?"

"No," Andrew said. "Now that we're all set up, everything's taken over by the segment director. My job is basically done. But I do have to stick around in case something comes up. And," he added, "to do this."

He leaned down and pulled me toward him for a kiss.

"Hey." I pushed away. "Maybe you better pull into the slow lane for a while, Andrew. I don't remember the part where I told you I was interested."

"Uh, how about all those hours you spent staring at me at the those practices, Kevin? Or was that just your overwhelming interest in lacrosse?"

"OK," I said. "But that was a high school crush. I'm kind of involved right now."

"Oh." Andrew frowned. "Sorry. Anyone I know?"

Tony was in Andrew's graduating class. But since he was determined to keep us on the down low, I answered no. I hated having to lie about us.

"Lucky guy," Andrew said. "And I totally respect your relationship." He dropped a hand to his crotch and let it rest there. "But I'm not looking to get married, Kevin. I just thought we could maybe have a good time, you know?"

"I know, but . . ."

Andrew squeezed his crotch. "There aren't that many things in high school I wanted that I didn't get," he continued. "You're one of them."

I had to admit I was getting distracted by his hand, and the formidable bulge that was rising underneath.

"Thanks, but . . ."

"You know," he said, stepping a little closer to me, "if we got it on right now, it's not like you went out there looking for it. You'd just be wrapping up some unfinished business. Nothing wrong with that."

He took his hand from his crotch and used it to grab one of mine. "Right?" He put my hand where his had been. "You can feel I've really been looking forward to seeing you again."

Is that a lacrosse stick in your pocket, or are you just glad to see me?

If you had told me back in high school that I even had a chance with Andrew Miller, I would have called you nuts. Andrew was unattainable, a jock god. Saying no to him was going to be quite a challenge.

I squeezed my hand a little—just a little—to get a sense of what I was about to turn down. Andrew gave a low moan that didn't do much to strengthen my resolve.

After all, Tony was the one who didn't want to be in a committed relationship. So, what was my problem?

Andrew took advantage of my momentary weakness and

pulled me toward him. He bent his knees a bit so that our erec-tions ground against each other. *Our* erections? When had I gone hard? *Maybe I should be paying more attention,* I thought.

His lips moved toward my neck. He exhaled lustily and the hot shock of his breath on my skin was wickedly erotic.

"I knew you wanted this," he whispered lustfully into my ear.

I suppose I should have been glad one of us knew what I wanted, because I sure as hell didn't.

So, what made him so sure?

Suddenly, I saw Andrew not as the irresistible object of my helpless, hopeless teenaged crush, but as the arrogant star ath-lete who always got his way. Although that was the kind of boy I might have been attracted to back then—and who wasn't?—it didn't mean I liked him very much. I didn't even *know* him.

While Yvonne might have been an insufferable bitch, she might have been kind of right, too. How many other boys *had* Andrew brought into this little high-tech cubicle of seduction, confident that his ridiculous good looks and huskily whispered endearments would sweep them off their feet?

And, I thought, my anger gathering steam, *who cares that he wanted me all those years ago?* Did I really want to be just an-other item checked off his bucket list?

I pushed him away. "You know what, Andrew? You're right. I *did* want this. *In high school.* But that was a long time ago. I've grown up since then. How about you?"

Andrew eyes opened wide and he looked hurt. "Wow, I guess I misread you. No harm, no foul, OK?" He raised his hands like a cowboy surrendering a gunfight.

Now, of course, I felt badly for him. "OK," I said. "Listen, you know you're crazy hot, right? It's not that I'm not into you. It's just a little sudden for me. But we're cool. No offense taken."

"Cool." Andrew agreed. A few awkward seconds later, he added, "Sorry."

"Don't worry about it."

"I'm a jerk."

"No, you're not."

"No, I'm a jerk and I came on too strong and I'm really sorry."

"It's not a big deal."

"So, you don't hate me?"

"Of course I don't hate you. I don't . . . *anything* you, that's the whole point."

"So," Andrew said, dragging out the word and looking down at his feet, "would you maybe be interested?"

"Andrew . . ." I began.

"In getting to know me," he added. "I mean, would you be interested in getting to know me?"

"Sure," I said, although I had no idea where he would fit in my life. "That would be great."

"Great." Andrew smiled. "Can I apologize again?"

"No."

"All right then," Andrew said, opening the door of his office and flicking a switch that brought all the monitors on his wall to life, "let's watch the show."

It was weird seeing my mother from three different angles on the LCDs. She was standing by her styling station, busying herself with rollers, dyes, and hair sprays.

"They're shooting B roll now," Andrew said. "We'll use some of this footage behind narration, setting the scene."

My mother plugged something that looked like a torture device into an outlet and turned to one of the cameras.

"This is a curling iron," she explained. "I employ it in my efforts to impart wave and body to my customers' hair. Will I use it on Yvonne? We'll just have to wait and . . ."

The segment director's voice came from offscreen. "Mrs. Connor? For the third time, we really don't need you to say anything. Just act naturally and don't talk to the camera anymore, OK?"

"I thought maybe I could build some dramatic tension," my mother explained. "Keep everyone watching."

"How about," the disembodied voice responded a bit testily,

"I worry about keeping the audience's interest and you worry about doing as you're told."

"Well, how will the viewers know what I'm doing if I don't explain the tools of my trade?" my mother answered. "You'd be surprised just how interesting the job of a beautician can be. Every day, people ask me, 'How do you do it, Sophie?' And I tell them . . ."

I heard what sounded like a snarl coming from the director, but then a hush as everyone turned and looked toward the door.

"Yvonne," the director called. "We're all ready for you. You look wonderful."

Yvonne drifted into the scene and gave my mother a hug. "I'm so glad to see you again. We haven't scared you off yet, have we? Are you ready to make me over, my dear?" Her voice was pure honey.

"I'm honored," my mother said.

Yvonne turned to the director and, in a tone that was all gravel and demand, barked, "All right, Henry, where do you want me?"

"Let's get you walking in again, but this time, why don't you and Mrs. Connor act like you're meeting for the first time, OK?"

Yvonne put her hands on her hips. "Henry, if you have direction for me, could you please do me the favor of giving it to me *before* I come onto the set?"

"I couldn't give it to you until you got here," the director said, his manner long-suffering. "So, if you don't mind . . ."

Yvonne turned in a huff and walked away. "*Fine.* Let's try it again."

My mother turned to the director and shrugged. "That's show biz," she called out.

Everyone in the shop laughed. Andrew turned to me. "It looks like your mom's a bit of a ham."

"Oh, she's loving this," I assured him.

"Yvonne may have some competition on her hands."

Andrew and I continued to watch the monitors through Yvonne's reintroduction to my mother, her shampoo, and the beginning of her haircut. After the first few snips, the director called out, "that's a wrap for now. Mrs. Connor, why don't you just finish up the . . . whatever you're doing, then we'll shoot some footage when you're ready to apply Yvonne's color. We'll close with the big reveal, where Yvonne will finally get to see the results of your makeover. Mrs. Connor, how much longer do you need Yvonne in the chair before you're ready for the next step?"

"Oh, another twenty minutes at least," my mother answered. She leaned over to Yvonne. "I give all my customers this kind of treatment, not just the big stars like you."

Yvonne laughed at this, as did a few others in the shop. I had to say, Yvonne may have been nastier than herpes, but she and my mother did seem to be hitting it off.

"Great," the director said. "Let's all take twenty then and give these ladies their privacy."

Two of the three video screens above Andrew's desk went black, but one, which showed both my mother and Yvonne in a wide shot, remained on.

The walkie-talkie Andrew wore on his belt crackled to life. "Hey, Andy, Gabe didn't shut down camera three for the break. Do you want us to get it?"

"Naw, leave it running," Andrew said. "Thanks." He put the device back on his belt. "If I sent the cameraman back in to shut it down, Yvonne would notice and make me fire the poor guy."

"Why?"

"Oh, who knows? If she thinks someone's made a mistake, if she perceives any weakness at all, she goes for the kill. Blood in the water. She's like a shark, except sharks only kill what they eat, not for sport."

I smiled and looked at the monitor. My mother stood behind Yvonne, snipping away at her hair, but with a decidedly uncomfortable expression on her face. "Hey," I asked Andrew, "can we hear what they're saying?"

"Let's see if the mike is live," Andrew said. He leaned across the desk and turned a dial.

" . . . but they're all that way, right?" We picked up Yvonne midsentence. "I mean, this new kid, I'm never even seen him on set before, and my producer, Andrew, already has him in his office, ready to pounce."

I felt the heat coming off Andrew's face before I noticed how red he was getting.

"Hmmm," my mother said.

"Faggots can't control themselves," Yvonne continued. "Like animals. The only good thing about them is they don't have children or wives, so they make wonderful employees." Yvonne chuckled. "Totally devoted to their jobs, just the way I like them. I can't imagine what makes someone choose to be gay, though. Don't they want to be normal?"

My mother cleared her throat. "I hear," she said, her voice strained and thin, "that most people think they're born that way. I think I heard it on your show, in fact."

Yvonne smiled. "So, you *do* watch! Yes, I know, I have on all the experts and the scientists, and I talk the good PC game with the best of them, but really, Sophie, I can't believe God would make anyone like that, do you?"

"As a matter of fact . . ." my mother began.

Yvonne cut her off. "What is it about a hairdresser that makes us open up like this, Sophie? You should have been a therapist!"

My mother's smile was as thin as a razor and only slightly less dangerous-looking. "Thank you, but . . ."

"Just between us girls"—Yvonne winked—"you know what it is I think makes these boys go the wrong way?"

My mother croaked out a "What?"

"Their mothers, of course. Imagine having a mother so awful that she turns you off all women forever. I've never met a mother of one of these so-called 'gays' who wasn't a shrew."

A sound like glass grinding came from my mother's throat. She reached over to a table out of the camera's sight and came back with the biggest pair of scissors I'd ever seen.

"Uh," I began, "maybe we better get in there."

"Why, do you have a gun she could use instead?" Andrew asked.

"You're laughing now," I told him, "but if she kills Yvonne, you're out of a job."

"*So* worth it," Andrew said.

"Well," my mother said, "just a few more snips and we'll be ready for your color." I heard the strain in her voice as she sought to retain her composure.

Truth to tell, I was a little disappointed that she didn't slit Yvonne like a stoolie in an episode of *The Sopranos*. It would have been nice to see her stand up for me, and herself, a little. But I guess it wasn't worth blowing her chance to be on *Yvonne*.

"Of course," Yvonne said, "if you want to be in show business, you better learn to work with the fags. They're everywhere. The only thing worse than them are . . . what did you say your last name was again, darling?"

"Connor," my mother answered.

"Good. As I was saying, the only people worse than the fags are the Jews. They run everything in Hollywood. Between the kikes and the queers, I don't know how I take it."

Even in the wide shot, you could see my mother's fingers whiten as she squeezed the scissors ever more tightly in her hands. Too bad Yvonne didn't know my mother's maiden name was Gerstein.

"Do it," I heard Andrew whisper to my mother's image on the monitor. "Do it, do it, do it."

"You know," my mother began, her face clenched even tighter than her fingers. "I think . . ."

"Oh!" Yvonne interrupted. "I just realized—that new kid on the set I told you my producer was putting the moves on? You met him. He was that little blond piece of ass you were talking to when I walked in. Cute, but what a little queen! Imagine what *his* mother must be like!"

"Would you excuse me for a minute," my mother said. "I just need to get something."

My mother walked out the camera's range and Andrew and I watched with a kind of morbid fascination as Yvonne leaned closer into the mirror and examined her face with the rapt attention of an astrophysicist studying the surface of Jupiter for microscopic evidence of life. She pulled her skin tight behind her ears, released it, pulled it back again.

"If she has one more facelift," Andrew said, "her eyes are going to be behind her head."

My mother came back into view with a glass bowl halfway filled with a viscous-looking brown gloop. "I have your color mixed," she said cheerily.

"Isn't that kind of dark?" Yvonne asked. "You know I want to stay blond, right?"

My mother smiled. "It gets lighter when I put it in your hair. Don't worry, sweetheart. I've never met a woman who's more blond than you."

Yvonne smiled back. "Darling Sophie," she said. "It's always such a pleasure to meet someone like you, someone I can really open up to. Most people are so stupid. Take my audience—a bigger bunch of morons you've never seen. I want to throw up every time I have to stand in front of those idiots and losers. But you! You've been so helpful. I guess it's part of your being a service person. I feel you're genuinely interested in taking care of me."

"Oh," my mother said, her smile growing even wider. "I'm going to take care of you, all right."

16

The Best Thing You've Ever Done

My mother told the director that she was ready to dye Yvonne's hair. He started the cameras rolling again. All three monitors above Andrew's desk came back to life.

As you might imagine, Yvonne steered the conversation to much safer shores, and my mother chatted along as if she didn't have a care in the world. My mother combed the dye through Yvonne's hair and massaged it into her roots. She wrapped the wet strands in a towel and placed a shower cap over Yvonne's head.

"We just need to let it sit for ten minutes," my mother cooed, "and then it's time for your big unveiling!"

The director's voice came from offscreen again. "While you're sitting, Yvonne, why don't we shoot some interview drop-ins with Mrs. Connor?"

"Marvelous," Yvonne cooed. "Are we set?" The director answered yes. "So tell me, Sophie, how did you get into the beauty shop business?"

"It's an interesting story," my mother began, which was always a sure sign that it would be just the opposite. I took this as an opportunity to chat some more with Andrew.

"I'm kind of disappointed," I told him. "I thought my mother would defend me a little more. Hell, I thought she'd defend herself."

"Don't be too hard on her. Celebrities have that effect on normal folk. I've seen Yvonne be a lot ruder than that to some of our guests during the commercial breaks, but when the cameras start to roll again, everyone's still there smiling and chatting away. Nobody stands up to people like Yvonne. Even people who've had to eat her shit for years keep coming back for more. Exhibit A: Yours truly."

"I'm sorry," I said.

"Everyone's got to make a living. And I can always hope that one day her key light falls on her head. At least I have that to look forward to. Who knows, maybe one day I'll get the chance to start a show of my own."

"She's ready," my mother chirped, and Yvonne settled back at my mother's station. The shower cap around her head ensured that not a single lock of her new hair color revealed itself. The director moved the cameras around a bit to make sure they captured the look on Yvonne's face as she saw the results of her dye job.

Yvonne wiggled her shoulders excitedly. "I can't wait to see what you've done, Sophie. Will I be terribly, terribly glamorous?"

"You'll feel like you're in *The King and I*," my mother promised. She eased off the shower cap, revealing the tightly wrapped towel beneath.

"I've always loved Deborah Kerr in that movie," Yvonne whispered. "So elegant!"

"Dear, dear, Yvonne," my mother answered, pulling away the towel, "I meant the *other* star . . ."

My mother enjoyed the shocked silence for a moment before finishing her sentence. ". . . Yul Brynner, darling."

Gasps and one short yelp came from the production staff in the salon.

Yvonne couldn't seem to catch her breath. "I'm . . . I'm . . . I'm . . ."

"A bitch?" my mother offered. "An insufferable, homophobic, anti-Semitic poser with bad implants and a worse attitude?"

Yvonne's eyes narrowed into slits. Her faced flushed a radioactive shade of red. "I . . . You . . ."

"What is it, dear?" my mother asked sweetly. "I'm just trying to help. You know how we 'service people' are."

"I'm *bald!*" Yvonne screamed.

Andrew and I ran from the bus into my mother's shop. Every face in the room was white—even the African-American ones. Nobody knew what to do or say.

"Don't you hear me?" Yvonne's screamed again. "I'm bald! Somebody do something."

"We offer a full selection of wigs," my mother said pleasantly. "Perhaps something in the style of Eva Braun? You can wear it with your swastika."

Out of the crew's shocked silence, one woman, I think it was Margie the light hanger, let slip a low chuckle that grew into a palms-over-the-mouth giggle and finally erupted in a loud and hearty guffaw. That set off the woman next her, then the queeny beautician, and soon half the room was cracking up.

"You, you, you." Yvonne couldn't find the words. She ran her hands over her smooth head. "You all . . . *suck!* I hate you all!"

That got everyone laughing, finally free to put in her place the tyrant who had oppressed and terrorized them for years.

"They're all laughing at me!" Yvonne wailed, like Sissy Spacek in *Carrie*. Only, Sissy was the hero of that piece.

I made my way through the crowd to my mother's side. "You OK?" I asked her.

"Never better," my mother said. "You ask me, she deserved a lot worse. She's lucky she didn't come in for a bikini wax."

I kissed her cheek. "My hero."

Yvonne looked at us. "You two . . . you two know each other?"

"Oh!" my mother said. "Let me introduce my son, Kevin. You had such kind things to say about him. And me."

Yvonne stared at the two of us, open-mouthed. I suspected it was the first time in years she'd been speechless.

"I know the trim I gave you may be a tad extreme," my mother continued. "But once I saw your true nature, Yvonne, I couldn't resist making the outside you match the beauty within."

"You, you *cunt!*" Yvonne cried.

My mother put her hands to her cheeks in mock outrage. "Such language! In front of my child, no less."

"You vicious, kike *cunt!*"

"Yeah, yeah," my mother said. "Fuck you, Kojak." She triumphantly turned her back to Yvonne and took my arm. "Let's go, my darling, faggot son."

Walking her to the door, I ran into Andrew.

"Are you going to be all right?" I asked him.

"Peachy," he answered. "She'll probably fire me for this." His face was lit with joy.

"And that's a good thing?"

"Sure is. Watching Yvonne today, I realized just how miserable I am working for her. There has to be something better I can do with my life than work for that nightmare." He turned to my mother. "Thanks, Mrs. C. I owe you."

"Darling." My mother threw her arms around him. "I'm so sorry if I got you into trouble with that terrible woman."

"No, really," Andrew said, "it's a good thing. I need to move on."

"Such a good boy," my mother said, still pressing Andrew against her ample bosom. "If Kevin wasn't so hung up on his conflicted bisexual boyfriend, you'd be perfect for him."

"Hmmm," Andrew replied to my mother, but smirked at me over her head, "Kevin didn't give me all that detail when he said he was involved with someone."

"Well, Kevin's like that," my mother answered. "Always afraid to show his vulnerability. Even when he was a little boy, when he'd wet the bed, he'd take the sheets and . . ."

"Maybe we could save the humiliating walks down memory lane for another time," I suggested.

"See?" my mother said to Andrew.

Andrew disentangled himself from my mother. "Sorry it didn't work out for you being on the show."

"Oh." My mother sounded surprised. "You don't think they're going to air this?"

"Uh, no," Andrew said. "Of course not."

"Huh," my mother said. "I think it would make for a very exciting episode. I could see it playing to a broad range of demographics across a wide spectrum of households sampled by the Nielsen ratings."

I looked at her with a WTF expression.

"What?" my mother asked, as if she always talked like that. "I took a book out of the library about television programming. I thought if I was going to be getting into the business, as it were, I might as well learn a little about it."

I considered telling her that one appearance on *Yvonne* didn't exactly put her on a level with Brandon Tartikoff, but I knew I'd be wasting my breath. I turned to Andrew instead. "So, you're going to be OK?"

"Yeah," he said. "I'll find something. Or maybe even start my own thing."

He gave me a hug and whispered in my ear, "Listen, if things don't work out with Ambivalent Man, give me a call, OK?" He took one of his business cards out of his pocket and pressed it into my palm. I put it in my wallet.

"I will," I said.

Just then, Yvonne's screaming voice cried out "Andrew!" only spread out over several seconds, so it was more like "Annnnndddrewwwwwww!!!"

"Sounds like they're playing my song," he said cheerily.

"Maybe Yvonne's song should be 'I'm Gonna Wash That Man Right Outta My Hair,'" my mother suggested. "Oh, I guess she can't really sing that anymore, can she?" My mother laughed at her own joke.

Andrew chuckled and walked away.

I took my mother's hand and we headed for the door.

"You know," my mother said, "I hope I did the right thing. Do you think I went too far?"

It was reassuring to hear her ask. Till that moment, my mother had never shown any sign that she even understood the concept of "too far." Or, at least, that it could apply to her.

"You kidding? She's probably needed someone to tell her off

for years. I was proud of you! But making her bald? That took courage."

"Oh, that? Please. Her hair had been treated, colored, and straightened so many times that it was two or three blow-dries away from falling out on its own. I just hurried the process along a little. Trust me, I've cooked spaghetti that was in better shape than her hair."

Behind us, we heard Yvonne continuing to scream, Andrew raising his voice to be heard above the roar, and the director making calming noises while more than a few staffers whispered and snickered among themselves.

"They really don't like her very much, do they?" my mother asked.

"Apparently not."

"I can't imagine what that must be like," my mother said. "Everyone at Sophie's Choice Tresses loves me, you know."

"I know, Mom."

"I'm a very good boss."

"The best."

We'd reached the front door. My mother warily regarded the crowd that had gathered outside to watch the taping through the window. They were still there but stood stock-silent, the "We Love Yvonne" signs hanging limply by their sides.

"Would you describe them," my mother asked, "as an angry mob? Because, if so, maybe we should wait awhile before going out."

"They look more stunned than angry," I said.

"Yvonne is quite beloved," my mother observed. "Maybe I shouldn't have depilatorized her. That could have been a mistake, ratings-wise."

"You don't have any ratings," I reminded her. "Yvonne is the one with a show, not you."

My mother continued to study the crowd. "We all have ratings, dearheart. In one way or another."

"In that case, let's go face your critics." I put my hand on the door handle.

"I don't know about this. Do people still get lynched? I have a very sensitive neck."

"I don't know," I said, opening the door and pushing my mother outside, "let's see."

The crowd stepped back a bit as we emerged. They surrounded us in a half circle and openly gawked at us, as if waiting to see what horrors my mother might commit next. We were like twin Frankenstein monsters being eyed by torch-bearing villagers.

Then, from somewhere to the left, I heard someone slapping something, then the same sound to my right, then from everywhere, the noise swelling and rising until I realized it wasn't slapping but *clapping*.

"Way to go, Sophie!" someone called.

"You got her!"

"That bald bitch better not show her face around here again!" That was from Mrs. P., the doughnut lady.

My mother brought her hands to her bosom. "You're not all mad at me?"

"Mad at you?" a gray-haired woman with one of my mother's signature beehives asked. "Why would we be mad at you? That stuck-up Hollywood cooze thinks she can come here to Hauppauge and insult one of our own? You gave her what she deserved!"

"You could hear us?" my mother asked.

"We didn't have to," Mrs. P. said, coming over to put an arm around my mother. "We could see everything through the window. We know you, Sophie. For you to do a thing like that, that woman must have . . ." She finished her sentence in a long string of Yiddish that meant nothing to me but got half the crowd laughing.

"You're good people," another woman offered.

"We love you, Sophie," one of the young girls with the "We Love You, Yvonne" sign shouted, proving just how fickle a teenage girl's affection can be.

My mother was choking up. "You're all so kind to me," she croaked. Mrs. P. wrapped her up in a comforting hug.

"You know what I'm going to do?" Mrs. P. asked. "Tonight, when I close the store, I'm going to stop by your house with a chocolate layer cake. You know, that one you love with the red and pink roses on top? I make those by hand, you know, not from a mold. It's an art."

My mother nodded into Mrs. P.'s fleshy shoulder.

"You deserve a treat tonight, after what that woman did to you," Mrs. P. told her.

I had to say the whole thing made me see my old neighborhood in a new light. Everyone there had seen what my mother had done to Yvonne. None of them had the slightest idea what, if anything, Yvonne did to deserve such a fate. But they all stood behind my mother and supported her, for no other reason than she was one of their own.

It was pretty cool.

Soon, almost everyone in the crowd was lined up behind Mrs. P., waiting to give my mother a hug, a handshake, or just their best wishes.

My mother, who spent her entire life believing she was a star even when no one else was paying attention, lapped up the attention like a kitten devouring a saucer of milk.

It was kind of touching to see my mother finally enjoying in real life the applause she previously only heard in her head.

Mrs. P. came over to give me a hug, too. "You're a good boy, Kevin."

"Thanks."

She pressed her cheek against mine and her lips to my ear. "That'll be twenty-two fifty for the cake. I'll take it now if you don't mind, sweetheart."

17

All I Ask of You

"Bald?" Tony asked me for the thirty-third time. "Completely bald?"

It was almost midnight. After a day spent with my mother deforesting one of America's most beloved personalities and a dinner in which she alternately compared herself with Golda Meir and Martin Luther King Jr. ("Someone had to take a stand for those who have no voice," my mother congratulated herself, to which my father responded, "Why couldn't it be your mother who has no voice?"), I was glad that Tony came over as promised.

"Total cue ball," I said. "Professor X with fake boobs and overinflated lips."

We were lying in bed, which was pretty much our favorite place. Truth to tell, it was pretty much the *only* place we spent any time together. Being with a guy in the closet made it easy to plan your dates.

"Wow." Tony whistled. "Remind me not to piss off your mother anytime soon." He ran his fingers through his own thick locks. "I've kind of gotten attached to this."

I put my hand between his legs. "She's not the one you need to worry about," I said. I squeezed his balls. "Screw with me and you'll lose a lot worse than your hair."

"Oh, a tough guy, huh?"

I squeezed him again. "Scared yet?"

"Mmmm," Tony moaned. "Terrified."

A stirring tower under the sheet made it clear fear wasn't the only thing he was feeling. "You like it rough, Rinaldi?" I pulled his balls tighter. He moaned again. I pulled harder.

"Fuck," he hissed.

I took my other hand and wrapped it around his cock, tugging in the other direction. *Like a taffy pull,* I thought.

Precome leaked onto my hand and I used it to slick my palm's slide to the base of his cock, getting it slippery and wet. I worked my hands in synchronicity, sliding up his shaft with one while pulling his balls with the other. The sweet slithery sensation on his dick competed with the aching pressure from his overstretched sac. I tormented him, up and down, back and forth, pain and pleasure, teasing and torture. He arched his back and threw back his head.

"What are you doing to me?" he rasped.

"Everything," I said, throwing a leg over his pelvis and straddling his waist. I bent over and took a nipple into my mouth. Bit it with a bit more vigor than usual. "I'm going to do everything to you."

I sucked his nipple hard, and when it was at its most distended, bit down again.

Tony grabbed my head and groaned. "I don't like pain," he croaked. His achingly hard cock told me he didn't mind a little discomfort, though.

"It's not pain," I said. "It's love."

Tony bucked into my hands. "How do I know the difference?"

I looked at this man who was always so willing to join me in bed but so unready to be anywhere else with me. He looked so hot like this, his eyes rolled back in pleasure, the well-defined muscles of his chest and arms straining with the pressure of holding back and letting me run the show. He was so perfect in so many ways.

But was he perfect for *me?*

"I don't know," I said. There was a catch in my voice that probably sounded like passion to him. "Maybe there is none." Then I bent over to kiss him and tried not to think so much.

*   *   *

"Come on," I said, "please?"

"No," Tony said, his tone resolute.

"Pretty please," I pleaded.

"No way."

"Pretty please with sugar on top and the dessert topping of your choice spread over your body and licked off by yours truly."

Tony tilted his head. "Tempting. But no."

We were sitting on the leather couch in my living room. Unusually, our lovemaking left us restless rather than wiped out, and we were eating leftover ordered-in Chinese food out of its paper cartons.

I'm not exactly the domestic type.

I was trying to talk him into seeing *Super Rangers,* the new movie based on a superhero cartoon popular when I was eight years old. I always loved the Super Rangers, a team of five intrepid teenage boys who, one day, came across a mysterious glowing meteor in the woods. They touched it to see what it was made of, and were enveloped in a cocoon of brightly shining green energy. Even as an eight-year-old, I thought they were pretty stupid to be touching a strangely luminescent space rock. Had they never heard of radioactivity?

Luckily, instead of radiation poisoning, the light gave them the powers of the Super Rangers. Each of the boys received different powers and abilities, as well as his own totally styling costume. In what must have been a bit of foreshadowing, my favorite Ranger was Rainbow Lad, whose colored beams each had a different effect: red for heat rays, blue for cold, yellow for concussive shots, and amazingly, pink for healing.

Rainbow Lad was the gayest hero ever, and I loved him with all my prepubescent heart.

While Rainbow Lad might have been my favorite, I worshipped all the Super Rangers. I watched the show every day and amassed a ridiculously large collection of their action figures, comic books, and lunch boxes.

To this day, I can't walk in the woods, not even Central Park, without keeping an eye out for brightly glowing meteors. You never know.

Now, after a year of leaked photos and teaser ads, *Super Rangers: The Motion Picture* was playing at a screen near me, and I'd be damned if I was going to miss it. It had already been out for three weeks, and I was desperate to go.

"All right," I said, "what do I have to do to get you to see this movie with me?"

"Try getting a time machine and sending me back twenty years," Tony mumbled through a mouthful of moo shu pork. "It's a kid's movie. I'm a little old for it."

"Come on," I said. "It'll be fun."

Tony looked unmoved.

"Tell you what," I pleaded. "You see *Super Rangers* with me and I'll . . . watch football or something."

Tony kissed my forehead. "I wouldn't want you to hurt yourself. Get Freddy to see it with you."

"Freddy's already seen it. Twice."

"I'm sure you could find someone. Maybe you could take your mom. She could fantasize about shaving their heads."

"Did I mention dessert toppings?" I asked. "Because that includes syrups, and those can take forever to lick off."

"Forget it." Tony finished off his beer.

I wished I could change his mind, but I could see it was a lost cause.

"Why did I have to fall for an old man like you?"

Tony looked over at my bedroom, where the disheveled, stained sheets provided evidence of the most obvious reason. "For my sparkling personality, clearly."

"Uh, that would be no."

"Well, if it's my fortune you're after, I have bad news for you."

"That story you told me about being Donald Trump's secret love child isn't true?"

"Sorry."

I climbed into his lap. "I'm sure there's something I like about you, but I just can't put my finger on it." Instead, I rested my whole hand there.

Tony put his hand on my head. "Maybe there's something else you can put on it."

I felt him coming to life beneath me. Tony had recuperative powers Wolverine would envy.

"Hmmm, any ideas?"

The pressure on my head increased. "That depends. Have you had enough to eat?"

"I could probably go for a little something more."

"A *little* something? I'm insulted."

"Tell you what," I said. "You swallow your pride . . ."

"And you'll swallow something else?"

"Deal."

He pushed a little more and my head wound up where it would do him the most good.

"OK," I admitted, mouthing him through his sweatpants, "maybe not *that* little."

"That's my boy," Tony said. "You like that, huh?"

I would have answered him, but it's rude to talk with your mouth full.

Later, back in bed, I asked Tony if he'd do me a favor. "What's that?" he asked.

"I got a dinner invitation and I'd like you to come with me."

"It's not at your parents', is it? Because I may be a tough-guy cop, but you know your mother scares the shit out of me, right?"

"No, it's at some friends' house."

"'Some friends'?" Tony asked. "What kind of friends?"

"What do you mean, 'what kind of friends?' Friendly friends."

"You know what I mean."

"Another couple."

"What kind of couple?"

He was really pissing me off. "A nice couple, Tony. Good

people. I think you'd like them. Does it really make a difference?"

Tony stroked my hair. "Kevvy, you know how I feel about you. But I'm not signing up to a join a movement, here. I just want to be with you."

"It isn't a recruitment session, Tony. It's just dinner. If you don't want to go, fine. I'll go alone." I rolled over onto my side, as far from him as I could get without falling off. Under my breath, I muttered, "I guess I better get used to going places alone, huh?"

Tony rolled over and wrapped me in his arms. "If I wanted you to be alone, Kevvy, I wouldn't be here."

"Right," I said.

"I just . . . I'm just not as used to all this as you are."

I pushed his arms away. "Don't worry about it."

"Kevvy," he began. He scooted closer. I edged farther away.

Unfortunately, I ran out of mattress before I ran out of hurt feelings.

"Ouch," I said, falling onto the floor. A sharp pain ran from my hip to my shoulder. "Fuck."

"Hey," Tony said, throwing his legs over the bed and crouching next to me. "Are you OK?"

"Fine," I snapped. "Just dandy."

"'Dandy'?"

"I'm fine, Tony. No big deal. Let's just go back to bed."

"OK," he said, lifting me up and laying me down.

Tony was so strong in so many ways.

"Why don't you go ahead and let your friends know we'll be there for dinner."

"Really?" I said. "This isn't just a pity yes?"

"Maybe a little. I just don't want to hurt you."

I rubbed my sore back. For a guy who didn't want to hurt me, Tony sure had a habit of getting the job done.

How do you know if it's love or pain?

"They're really nice guys," I promised. "You'll like them."

Tony took over the rubbing of my back. "No problem," he said, grinning. "I'm sure it'll be 'dandy.'"

18

Soon It's Gonna Rain

At six AM, the alarm clock on Tony's phone rang. I think we had gotten about three hours sleep. The more time I spent with people who had one, the less appealing a "real job" seemed.

Bad thing for me was that the slightest noise wakes me up, and once I'm awake, I can't get back to sleep. Not so Tony, who continued to snore quietly. I called his name. I poked him with my elbow. Shook his shoulder. Nothing.

I thought about biting him, but that would be mean. Likewise, dousing him with a glass of ice water. I put my mouth close to his ear. "Crap," I said in a normal tone. "My mother just walked in."

Tony jumped to his feet, his hand reaching reflexively for his gun. "Where?"

"Where what?" I asked innocently.

"I thought you just said . . ."

I got out of bed and kissed his cheek. "You must have been dreaming. Go grab a shower; I'll put up some coffee."

"Huh," Tony said groggily, stretching. Michelangelo would have loved to sculpt him like this. My thoughts ran to the less artistic.

I didn't drink coffee, but I liked making it for my man.

Tony came into the kitchen wearing only a towel and the smell of Irish Spring on his still-damp skin. His freshly shaven face was red and smooth.

"Do you want some eggs," I asked.

He shook his head.

"Bacon? Pancakes?"

"You don't have any of those things, Kevvy." He poured himself a cup of black coffee and took a sip. A pained look crossed his face. He put the cup in the sink.

"How's the coffee?" I asked.

"Same as usual. Tastes like shit."

I held up the can. "I don't understand. I follow the recipe."

"That's not a recipe, babe. It's just instructions."

"Well, whatever it is, I follow it. It's not my fault I don't have a round spoon."

Tony took the can from me. "It's a 'rounded' spoonful."

"Isn't that what I said?"

Tony sighed and kissed my forehead. "I'm going to get dressed now. Try to stay out of the kitchen until I get back. I wouldn't want you to get hurt."

"I could make you some toast," I offered.

"Do you have bread?" Tony asked as he walked back into the bedroom.

"Uh, no."

"Key ingredient."

I looked in the refrigerator. Take-out containers from various Asian restaurants within my delivery area, milk, protein powder, two containers of low fat yogurt, a couple of bottles of water, and an unwrapped slice of spinach pizza. At least, I hoped that's what it was. I took it out and sniffed. OK, that was *so* not spinach. I threw it away before whatever was growing there developed independent motor skills.

If I was really going to make a play for Tony, I realized, I might need to ramp up my housekeeping. He was used to a wife. I was more like a fraternity brother.

I kissed Tony good-bye at the door. "See you tonight?" I asked.

"Uh, not tonight," Tony said. "Tomorrow maybe?"

I waited a minute to see if he'd offer an excuse, but he didn't. Oh well, I'd agreed to no strings, right?

Which was good, because if there were any, I'd probably use them to strangle him.

"Give me a call," I said, trying to sound casual and upbeat, like someone scheduling a racquetball date at the gym.

Tony winked and was gone.

After Tony left I sat at a stool in the kitchen and felt sorry for myself. Very satisfying.

One of the most helpful things for people like me with attention deficit disorder is to make lists. I wrote one in my head as I wallowed:

Things Tony Wasn't Willing to Give Up to Be with Me:

- His identity as a straight guy
- The approval of his family, friends, the church, and God
- The chance to have and raise children
- His job as a police officer (not that he couldn't be a gay cop; he didn't *think* he could be a gay cop)
- Sex with women

It seemed like a long list.

My pity-party was interrupted when my iPhone buzzed to alert me to a text message.

Freddy: "You up?"

I hit the "call back" button.

"Darling," he answered. "I just wanted to . . . hold on." There was a smacking sound. "Sorry, I just wanted to make sure you—" He sucked on something and said, "Damn, one second," and I endured some more wet slurps.

"What are you doing there?" I asked. "Or should I ask 'who are you doing?'"

"You should have asked me that last night, darling. Now, I'm trying to get rid of these damn pubic hairs I have caught in my teeth. I swear, that boy was part monkey. But a sexy monkey with long hair. Like Hugh Jackman."

"Could you spare me the details of your sordid sex life?"

"Darling, it's nature's dental floss. All natural. It's certainly a lot more green than those ridiculous queens at the local market who act like they're saving the planet because they're slowing down the line with their reusable grocery bags. The other day, the cashier asked me if I wanted paper or plastic, and I said plastic, and this skinny boy in line behind me with long hair and wearing some kind of sandals asked, 'Do you know how many dolphins get strangled every year in those bags when they wash out to sea?' and I told him, 'No, but I know a dizzy twink who's about to get strangled right here right now if he doesn't mind his own goddamn business.' I mean, I'm trying to buy some eggs and lube here, I'm not looking to save the whales or anything."

"Is there a point to this call?"

"Like you never ramble."

"I'm sorry, I'm just a little cranky about things with Tony."

"Things not going well in Pleasantville?"

"It's complicated."

"I have time."

"I'll tell you later. I'm just trying to figure out if what I want is any good for me."

"Men are like snack foods. The ones you want are *never* good for you."

"OK, that's too deep for this early in the morning. Can we pick it up again later?"

"Fine. I just wanted to make sure you didn't forget about tonight."

"Forget what?"

"Dinner with Rueben. Remember? The third Angel? The sassy Latina spitfire along the lines of a young Jennifer Lopez."

I really needed to remember to write things down. "Of course I didn't forget," I lied reflexively. "I'll see you there."

"Perfect. Just remember your place on the team, darling. Wear something plain and unassuming. Nothing says big brains like a dowdy pantsuit in a bad synthetic. Something that the mother on *Beverly Hills, 90210* would wear, but from the original series, darling, not that horrible remake."

"Any other advice?"

"Sensible shoes, darling. You might want to check out Payless."

"You," I reminded him, "are a cruel bitch."

"I'm a delicious chocolate treat with a creamy white filling," Freddy said. "Of course I'm no good for you."

After I hung up with Freddy I opened the calendar program on my iPhone and put in the meeting with Rueben. I also saw that I had a one o'clock with a steady client who had a few kinks that his wife wasn't equipped to handle.

But first, it was time for some career development. I grabbed a shower and headed for the gym. My body is my business and keeping in shape is a job requirement. I suffered through a grueling ninety-minute workout with my personal trainer, whose most recent employment, I suspected, was a stint at Guantanamo Bay.

I went home, showered again, and slugged back a protein drink and an Adderall.

I was all set to go when I remembered I had a phone call to make. Tony had agreed to go meet some of my friends for dinner and I had a specific couple in mind. I called them up and told them what I needed and why. They were only too happy to help out. We made a date for tomorrow night.

I texted Tony and he said he was free. I put dinner in my calendar, too.

I got dressed and was off to visit The Dentist.

I hailed a cab outside my building and inched forward through traffic to SoHo. I think I could have walked faster. Why was there so much traffic in the middle of a weekday? There were definitely too many people living and working in New York City.

My iPhone buzzed with a text message from Mrs. Cherry.

"Don't forget your one o'clock, lamb chop!" Mrs. Cherry knew how scatterbrained I could be, and reminding me of my appointments was just good business. I typed back a message assuring her I was on my way.

By 1:10 I was sitting in The Dentist's chair listening to the Muzak version of "Single Ladies (Put a Ring on It)."

"So, Kevin, how have you been?"

"My toof kine of hurrz," I said, as The Dentist ran his latex gloved hands inside my mouth. "I fink I haff a caffity."

"Oh dear," The Dentist said, "you have a very big cavity indeed, dear boy." His facemask hid his expression but his eyebrows arched suggestively.

The Dentist is a fifty-something man with salt-and-pepper hair and a trim little body. Definitely a DILF. Not that I'd have the opportunity to.

The Dentist brought the inhaler to my face. "Now, this is just a little nitrous oxide, son. It will make you feel drowsy, and a little light-headed, and you won't remember anything when I'm all done. Is that OK?"

"No pobbem," I answered, as the inhaler settled over my mouth and nose.

"Now, breathe deeply son."

I did as instructed, catching what I'd guess was a hint of chamomile from the fine piece of china The Dentist held over my face.

Yeah, the inhaler was a teacup, and the dental office was really his living room, and The Dentist was a married Broadway actor who's appeared on some soap operas and commercials.

When I first met The Dentist, he explained the origins of his fantasy to me. When he was a young teen, struggling with his sexuality, he had a big crush on *his* dentist, Dr. Delaware. He'd always get turned on when the dentist would put him under with laughing gas. His fantasy was that the dentist would seduce him while he was drugged.

"In my mind," he told me, in his deep actor's voice, "it was the perfect opportunity for me to have sex with another man without having to take responsibility for it. I was, after all, under the influence of a narcotic. Who could blame me?"

Somehow, the scenario got turned around, and The Dentist liked to role-play that I was the innocent teen at his groping hands. Like a lot of guys with kinks, The Dentist had a part of his libido stuck like a needle in a record. He kept repeating the same song.

If society didn't teach young people to be ashamed of their sexuality, there wouldn't be so many traumatized adults running around with the compulsion to act out their repressed adolescent fantasies.

So, in a strange way, it's the people who are most interested in repressing sexuality who create the conditions that lead to the freakiest kinks.

Which is good for *my* business, so I say, go Team Shame!

Speaking of business, my monthly visits with The Dentist were definitely one of my easier gigs. I just had to lie there pretending to be in a stupor while The Dentist felt me up and masturbated himself to orgasm.

Over time, I learned that he most enjoyed himself if I pretended to retain some consciousness. At first, I would just issue the occasional moan, noticing how it made his breath race. Then I started saying things, like "oh yeah," or "more," which really got him going.

After a few visits, I added more elaborate non sequiturs in my best stoner voice, like, "Oh yeah, Mary Sue, touch me there," or, "Dude, I'm not kidding, you better stop tickling me or I'm gonna wet myself."

Today, I threw all kinds of shit out there, but since whatever I said only increased his passion, it was all good.

"Hey, get back in your sleeping bag, man . . . Do these jeans fit me right? They feel so tight . . . Not here, Laura, not in science class." The Dentist reached his climax as he ran his hands over my nipples and I said, "Oh my God, Principal Jones, you're making me feel all funny in my private places!"

Excited enough to forget his usual impeccable aim, The Dentist ejaculated all over my two hundred fifty dollar For All Mankind jeans. *That's gonna cost you extra,* I wanted to say, but that would be mean.

Like a lot of guys with a kink, The Dentist's anticipation and execution of his fantasy were so exciting that the logical part of his mind shut down while enacting his fetish. But the second he came, rationality returned, and he felt a little sad and ridiculous.

A hooker in my easy chair while I wear a paper mask and wave around a fake drill, The Dentist was probably thinking. *Really? Has it come to this?*

Some guys I've known who work in the quote-unquote sex industry think their clients' kinks are pathetic. When the session is over, they act insulted, patronizing, or appalled. Where's the fun in that?

I think part of the reason I'm successful with clients like The Dentist is because I totally get what they're going through. The Dentist has his pretend laughing gas and silly little teacup and I have Tony. We're all stuck on *something.* Who am I to feel superior?

So, I understood how The Dentist felt, and I made it my job to make his landing as soft as possible.

"That was fun," I told him, taking the paper towel bib off my neck.

"Really?"

"Yeah, and look at that load you shot. Pretty hot. You must have been storing it up for days."

The Dentist smiled. "Sorry about your trousers."

"It'll wash out," I assured him.

The Dentist tousled my hair. "You're such a good kid. Let me get my wallet."

In the elevator going to the lobby, I took the cash The Dentist gave me from my pocket. A two hundred dollar tip. Nice. Kindness, I was glad to see, has its rewards.

Freddy and I weren't supposed to go to Rueben's until later that night, but I had a pocket full of cash, a pants leg damp with another man's jizz, and a song in my heart. Or something like that.

Rueben's apartment, well, actually Ansell's apartment, wasn't far from The Dentist's, and I didn't feel like schlepping all the way up to my place just to come back here later. I decided to walk over and see if he was available.

Although Freddy and Rueben's idea of the three of us as a male crime-fighting team was pretty lamebrained, I was looking forward to hanging out with them.

Maybe it would distract me from the fact that Tony wasn't available tonight.

Again.

Not that I was dwelling on it.

After all, it wasn't my fault he was . . .

OK, maybe I was dwelling on it.

Focus, Kevin, focus.

Friends of mine were dying or getting hurt.

But were Freddy and Rueben right—was there even a crime to fight?

The more I thought about it, the less likely it seemed that Randy's accident and the deaths of Sammy White Tee and Brooklyn Roy were related. Sure, they were all sex workers, but so was I and about a thousand other guys in this city. Other than their hustling, what did they have in common? I thought about them and me and Rueben and realized: not much.

Maybe Tony was right. Just because I had stumbled onto one murder ring a few months ago didn't mean I had to start seeing intrigue everywhere I went.

In a few minutes, I was at Ansell's door. I rang the doorbell and waited. Nothing. I rang again. All right, maybe dropping by early wasn't such a good idea. Did I have Rueben's number? I fished my iPhone out of my pocket and, just for good measure, rang the doorbell one more time.

"What is it?" Ansell Darling flung open the door. "What do you want?"

Ansell looked terrible. His normally pale face was whiter than usual. Exhaustion ringed his red, wet eyes.

Still not recovered from the party? Or had the reviews not gone his way?

"Sorry to drop by like this. I'm Kevin. Rueben's friend. We met at your party here the other night."

Ansell looked at me like he didn't understand a word I said.

"I had a date with Rueben tonight. Well, not a 'date' date. We're just friends."

Ansell still didn't get where I was going with this.

"Anyway, I'm early, I got off work early, I suppose, and I thought I'd come over to see if he was around."

Nothing. Was he even hearing me?

"So"—I figured if I was very direct maybe I'd cut through whatever haze surrounded him—"is Rueben home?"

"Is Rueben home?" Ansell asked.

"Um, yeah."

"Is Rueben home? Is Rueben home?"

His flat voice and buggy stare made me think of Paula Prentiss in *The Stepford Wives,* in which she plays the android neighbor of Katharine What-Ever-Happened-to-Her Ross.

In a climactic scene, Katharine stabs Paula in the belly with a kitchen knife, and a short-circuited, brain-dead Paula paces the kitchen in circles, saying, "I thought we were friends . . . I thought we were friends . . . I thought we were friends. . . ."

Ansell had that same zoned-out robotic glaze.

It's not a trick question, I wanted to say, but Ansell didn't seem like someone up for a joke. So I just waited.

"No," Ansell finally said, bitterly. "Rueben isn't *home.* Rueben is *dead.*"

19

Crying Time

"Rueben's dead."

I figured Ansell meant it metaphorically. Like, "Ruben's dead wrong on this one; *Buffy* was clearly a better show than *Serenity*," or, "Ever since he had that affair with the Republican fundraiser, Rueben's been dead to me."

I mean, Rueben couldn't be "dead" dead, right?

"I'm sorry," I said pleasantly, "what was that again?"

"Oh, God," Ansell said, gasping and putting a hand to his chest. "Rueben's dead. He's dead!"

I took a step closer to Ansell where he stood in the doorway. "Ansell, I . . ."

Ansell's face crumpled before me. He gave one great, explosive sob, and the tears came. "Oh God, oh God, oh God," Ansell cried. "Rueben's dead and I killed him!"

Ansell a murderer? He looked like he barely had enough energy to hold the door open, let alone kill someone.

What he meant, I supposed, was that he'd killed his *relationship* with Rueben.

What could he have done?

"Ansell," I said, "why don't we go inside and . . ."

Hysterical now, Ansell clasped one hand over his mouth. He pushed me to the side, ran to the street, and promptly threw up in the gutter.

I had no idea what the hell was going on.

* * *

Ten minutes later, I was sitting next to Ansell on a long, modern sofa in the cavernous lower level of his tony, chic loft.

The only other time I had been there was the night of his big fashion show. Then, the space had been reconfigured for the party and was filled with hundreds of people. The dancehall-sized living room seemed glamorous and enviable.

Today, the furniture was back in what I assumed was its usual configuration. I was struck by how huge and bare the space was. With its high ceilings and minimalist furnishings, the room felt cold and empty. Out of scale for a place in which actual human beings lived. Like a mausoleum.

I put my hand on Ansell's back as he continued to cry. I looked around to see if Rueben was around. If so, I didn't see him.

I patted Ansell gently. "Shhh, shhh," I said, hoping to calm him enough so he could talk.

Ansell wiped his face with the sleeve of his silk shirt. "I'm sorry," he said. "I'm sorry. I don't even know . . ."

He stood up suddenly, throwing my arm off him. He regarded me blankly through bloodred eyes. "I'm sorry, I don't know who you are."

His voice was polite and apologetic, as if he'd just forgotten my name at a society fund-raiser. Was he on something?

I reminded him of who I was and how we met at his party.

"Right," Ansell said, pacing the room. "I remember you now. You were here with your black friend, right? You two were a real hot number."

"That's right," I said, in the tone I usually reserved for the toddlers at Sunday school. "That was me."

"You were Rueben's friend," he continued.

"Yes."

"Rueben didn't have too many friends."

"What happened, Ansell?"

Ansell's legs started to buckle. I got up and quickly walked him back to the sofa. "Sit down," I told him. "Do you need some water?"

"I don't know," Ansell said.

"Listen," I said. "I don't know what's going on here, but you're clearly pretty upset. You shouldn't be alone. Is there someone I can call?"

Ansell gave a bitter little laugh. "I don't have too many friends, either."

"Are you kidding me? I was here two nights ago and this place was filled with people. There has to be someone who could come sit with you."

"Those people? Half of them were there to see how much money I was going to make for them, and the other half were hoping to see me fall flat on my face."

Not knowing what to say, I said nothing.

Ansell's face changed from angry to sad. "Were you really Rueben's friend?" His voice broke on the last word.

I took his hands in mine and looked him directly in the eyes. "Yes, Ansell, I am."

"Well, *you're* here," Ansell said, the tears falling again. "Can you stay a bit?"

Ansell cried for a while longer, too upset to talk. I held and rocked him in my arms.

I didn't know Ansell, not even a little, but I was used to touching people I didn't know. I've had clients who broke down like this, because of fear or relief or whatever. When he calmed down a little, I went to his high-tech kitchen and got a cool, wet cloth for him and glasses of water for both of us.

I gave him the towel and he buried his face in it. I put the water on the table in front of us. "Do you want to tell me what happened, Ansell?"

Ansell sat up straighter. "It was the night of the party. It was late, I don't know, three or four in the morning. You know the party was like a runway show for me, right?"

I nodded.

"My brilliant idea. Or maybe Rueben's. I don't know. A new way to unveil my next line. A party. It'd be fun.

"And it was. It was exciting and glamorous and . . . it was magic." Ansell took a deep breath, willed himself to go on.

"I wasn't born Ansell Darling, you know. I mean, no one names their kid 'Ansell Darling.' I grew up in Cleveland, Ohio, as Henry Cohen. A skinny, pale kid with a sketchpad under his arm and a kick-me sign permanently stuck to my backside. Might as well have been."

Ansell gave another bitter snort, and I thought, *This is definitely a guy with anger issues.*

"All my life, this is what I wanted. This house in New York City, the riches, the fame, the glittering parties, all of it. This is what I wanted.

"Fabulous, right? I wanted to be fabulous. And I am.

"But fabulous takes money, and in the fashion business, you're only worth as much as your next line. Oh, maybe not if you're Michael Kors or Donna Karan, but for me, I'm only one season's sales away from being on the first bus back to Cleveland.

"OK, so back to the night of the party. Like I said, it's late. I'm all hopped up. The energy of the evening was off the scale, the models looked great, everyone was having a brilliant time. Then my business manager comes over.

"'This is a disaster,' he tells me. I ask him what he means. He says that he spoke to the buyers from the most important stores. He said they were all having a wonderful time, but they had no idea what they were looking at. They said they couldn't tell the difference between my designs and what anyone else was wearing that night. Worse, they certainly couldn't place orders based on what they'd seen. 'Maybe,' one of them told him, 'Ansell needs to spend a little more time at the design table and a little less time at the clubs.'

"I thought he was exaggerating. I was about to tell him so when the buyer from Bergdorf's comes over. 'Sweetheart,' she told me, 'you really must think of changing professions. Forget design, Ansell, you should be planning parties for a living. This is marvelous!'

"'I'm glad you had a good time,' I answered. 'How do you think the line is going to do in your stores?'

"'Oh, who knows?' she told me. 'I'm just having such a good

time. I didn't really notice the clothing. But let's get together soon.'

"And she was gone."

Ansell wiped tears from his eyes. "You have to understand, I was out of my mind. I imagined everything I'd worked so hard on, everything I'd fought and scratched for, gone. I know it showed on my face, because even though he hadn't been close enough to hear what happened, Rueben walked over and put his arm around me. 'That's OK, *papi*,' he told me, 'it'll be fine.'

"I just . . . blew up at him. I started screaming that this was all his fault, his stupid idea, and why had I listened to him, why had I trusted a stupid hustler like him in the first place, why had I let him into my home, my business, my life?"

I felt the blood drain from my face as I remembered my conversation with Rueben from that night. *Ansell is everything to me,* he'd told me.

"I called him stupid. I called him a stupid junkie whore who ruined me." Ansell exploded into another shuddering series of sobs, his shoulders shaking violently as he buried his face in his hands. "Funny thing is, he was so tired of the sex trade, even if we broke up, I knew he'd never return to hustling. One day, we were watching TV, and some guy who hired him comes on the screen. 'Biggest hypocrite ever,' Rueben said to me. 'I'm never going back to that again.' "

I knew I should have said something comforting to him, but thinking about how much he must have hurt my friend, I couldn't bring myself to do it.

"He left," Ansell said once the flow of tears slowed to a trickle. "He went out the door with nothing in his pockets and I let him. I knew what I said was wrong, but I just let him go."

As I suspected, when Ansell said Rueben was dead, he meant "dead to him."

"Ansell," I told him, "you have to pull yourself together. You can still make this work. Rueben has a heart as big as the world, and I know he really loves you. This doesn't have to be the end."

Ansell looked at me gravely. "Kevin, the next day two policemen showed up at my door. They found Rueben in the alley half a block down. He overdosed on heroin, Kevin.

"Rueben is dead."

It was my turn to cry.

20

Hands Off the Man

"It's just like when Farrah Fawcett's character, Jill Munroe, left the Angels," Freddy said, his voice soft and sad. "Only, she left to become a race car driver. Not because she was dead or anything."

I nodded. After spending another hour with Ansell Darling, I called Freddy and told him to meet me at our favorite restaurant, Foodboys. He assumed I'd be here with Rueben. When he arrived, I told him what happened.

"Of course, when Jill left," Freddy continued, "she was replaced by her sister, Kris, played by perky ingénue Cheryl Ladd. Because the producers knew there always had to be *three* Angels." Freddy looked down at his uneaten plate of pasta, absently twirling it into abstract patterns, like those people who rake Zen sand gardens on their desks.

"Yeah," I said. "I remember."

"So my question to you is"—Freddy looked up from his plate, his deep brown eyes damp—"who's going to be *our* third Angel? Because I was all set for Rueben to join our little team, and now he's, well, he's not coming back, is he?"

I shook my head. I didn't trust myself to say anything just then.

"Fuck." Freddy went back to spinning his spaghetti. "At least when Farrah left the show, she had a good reason. She had to get on with her movie career. OK, maybe that didn't turn out so well, but that's not the point. At least she was moving *toward* something. Something positive. But this . . ."

He lifted a fork full of food halfway to his mouth, let it drop again, the silver banging noisily against the plate.

"I thought you said he was *clean*, Kevin." Freddy's voice was about twice as loud as anyone else's in the place. "I thought you said he was *done* with that shit."

By this time, a few other patrons were stealing glances at us. We were becoming The Angry Fighting Couple That Everyone Stares at in the Restaurant. Only we weren't a couple and we weren't angry. At least, not with each other.

"I know," I told him, pitching my voice low in an effort to quiet him down. Although I felt like screaming, too. "That's what he told me. And Ansell, too. He had us all convinced."

"Then what *happened?*" Freddy asked loudly, rendering moot my efforts to calm him.

"I don't *know*," I answered, a little overemphatically myself.

Two guys at the next table looked at us and whispered. The older one was classic bear, full beard, fuller belly. He had the heavy build of a Colt model, as solid as a soldier from *300*. He looked angry.

His younger, cuter, multiply pierced companion seemed to be laughing him off. The big guy, who reminded me of Smokey the Bear, only not as likable, shook his head. Congruent with his assigned role, he growled.

"Goddamn it," Freddy cried, hitting our table with his fist. Every glass, plate, and utensil lifted a few inches and noisily fell to its new place.

"Hey, Salt and Pepper"—Smokey turned to us—"could you two keep it down a little? We're trying to have dinner here."

I decided to ignore the racial slur in hope of avoiding a scene. "Sorry," I said. "It's just a bad time . . . we lost a friend today."

Piercey Boy looked about to offer a sympathetic comment but he was beaten to the mike by Smokey. "Yeah, well, the way you two act, I'm surprised you didn't lose *all* your friends." Smokey chortled.

Freddy tensed his jaw. I could see he was holding himself back. Probably a good idea.

Piercey Boy hit his companion on the arm. "Their friend is *dead*, man. Show some respect." *Hmm, I thought, take the metal out of Piercey's eyebrows, ears, and whatever that area between your nostrils is called, and he'd be a real honey.*

"Like they showed us respect when they started their little show at the table next to ours? I didn't come to this place to be insulted by twinks like Blondie and his pet monkey here."

I knew Freddy was thinking exactly what I was: that Smokey deserved to be taken down hard for his obnoxious attitude. But tonight was not the night for it.

I think we would have stuck with that plan had Smokey not taken it to the next level.

"And you," Smokey said, grabbing Piercey Boy's forearm in his beefy paws, "better learn not to hit me. Or correct me. Especially in public."

Piercey Boy tried to squirm out of Smokey's grip. "I'm sorry," he whined. "I didn't mean it."

Whatever trip these two were on didn't look like a whole lot of fun. At least not to me. But who knows what they were into?

How do you tell the difference between love and pain?

Smokey glowered. "You're just getting yourself into more trouble, boy. Shut up."

Piercey tried harder to pull his arm away. "Come on, man, you're hurting me. This isn't what I signed up for."

A vein in Freddy's forehead throbbed steadily in a way I'd never noticed before.

Smokey twisted Piercey's arm a little. Piercey gasped in pain.

"All right," I said, "that's enough. I'm sorry if we bothered you. Let's just forget it."

"Fuck you," Smokey barked at me. He gave another quarter turn to Piercey's arm. Piercey moaned.

I looked at Piercey. "Is this what you two do? I mean, I don't want to get in the middle of—whatever it is you have going—but it looks like he's really hurting you."

Piercey's eyes were wide with alarm. "I . . ."

Smokey let go of Piercey's arm and stood up. He leaned over our table. His face was inches from mine. "You little shit. Who the fuck do you think you are, talking to my boy?"

Freddy stood up, too, his chair falling back with a crash. I took a quick look around—yup, we had everyone's attention now. Waiters whispered to each other with a what-do-we-do-now urgency.

"I got this," I told Freddy. I stood up, too.

Hey, let's make it a standing party.

My head was a few inches south of Smokey's chest. Hard as it was to be intimidating at this angle, I figured I'd give it a try.

"Listen, buddy," I said, "I said we were sorry, OK? So, let's just go back to our dinners and move on."

Smokey grabbed the front of my shirt in his huge hand. "Oh yeah, little man? Who's gonna make me?"

Freddy stepped forward but I put up my hand. "I said I got this.

"All right, Kong," I said, "your friend may think it's fun being pushed around by you, but you have five seconds to get your grubby hand off of me."

"Or what?" Smokey snickered. "You gonna call your mommy on me?"

Smokey may be a bad guy, but I didn't hate him that much.

"Or," I said sweetly, "I'm going to break off your arm and beat you to death with it."

Smokey brought his hand up to smack me. "I am really going to enjoy slapping the smart out of you, boy." He pulled me toward him.

I was always a little guy. Blond, cute, boyish. The kind of kid who couldn't put up a fight if you paid him to.

A few years ago, I was in a near-empty subway except for some guys who decided I was a little gay-looking for their tastes. Two hours later, I was in the hospital with no wallet, multiple bruises, and a cracked rib.

I don't remember anything that happened between the time those guys started walking toward me on the E train and when I woke up in my hospital bed.

But I do remember how I felt when I woke up. I remember the pain and the humiliation and the decision I made never to be a victim again.

Little as I was, I needed an edge. I was already strong and limber from years of gymnastics, but that wasn't enough to protect me. So, I took some self-defense courses at the Gay and Lesbian Community Center. I followed them up with advanced training in one of the principles they taught at the center, Krav Maga.

Krav Maga is a fighting technique initially developed for self-defense in World War Two by Jews in Czechoslovakia who were harassed by Nazi youth. It was later refined and expanded upon by the Haganah, an Israeli defense force.

Let me give you a piece of advice: Don't fuck with the Israelis.

Krav Maga isn't a sport like karate or an art like Judo. Krav Maga is about survival. It's about doing whatever is necessary to neutralize your opponent and take him down fast. It teaches you how to move quickly from defense to offense, to employ the aid of any available objects in your vicinity, and to go for your attacker's most vulnerable areas first.

It's not pretty and it's not fair.

But it works.

Smokey wanted to pull me closer? Fine. I went with it, not only allowing myself to be pulled toward him but actively moving in. It caught Smokey off guard; he expected me to pull away. I felt him stiffen in surprise. Good.

We all have hard and soft parts. It was time to introduce some of Smokey's squishy bits to some of my hard ones.

I brought my knee up to meet his balls. The air whooshed out of him. "Fuck," he cried, instinctively bending over at the waist. "You little . . ."

But I was denied the pleasure of hearing whatever Smokey was about to say because as he was leaning down, I was jumping up. The top of my skull is hard, what's inside his mouth, not so much. Which is why it must have hurt like a motherfucker when I hit his jaw with my head and he almost bit off his own tongue.

Now, he didn't know which way to bend. He let go of me and stepped back. One hand went to cradle his balls, the other flew to his mouth.

I checked out Piercey. Was he going to rush to his boyfriend's defense? Apparently not. In fact, he was smiling. I smiled back.

Smokey noticed I was looking away and decided to make his move. He bent forward to rush me. Too bad for him, he was slow. Whether naturally or because his testicles had swollen to the size of ostrich eggs, I couldn't say.

You know what really hurts? Getting hit in the kidney. Now, Smokey knew, too. He doubled over again.

Time for my hard elbow to meet the back of his exposed neck. I brought it down decisively. Smokey crumpled to his knees.

I brought my leg back enough to let him see how well positioned I was to kick him in the head. "Enough?" I asked.

He nodded. Gently, as if getting ready for a nap, he lowered himself to the ground, curled into a fetal position, and whimpered. I was pretty sure he wasn't playing possum, but I kept my eyes on him, anyway.

It wasn't the first time I've taken down a big guy. As much as I hated to admit it, it never stopped being fun. I felt better than I had all day.

There was a murmur of voices as everyone went back to their meals. That's New York for you. When the show's over, it's over.

"Why is it," Freddy asked, "that I love seeing you do that so much?"

"Me, too!" Piercey gushed. "That was *awesome*."

Freddy looked at him. "So, what's the deal with you two? You going to take him home and kiss his boo-boos?"

"You kidding?" Piercey asked. "It was a first date. Last date, as it turns out. We met on BearTrap.com. I like a bit of rough, but this guy's just plain rude."

"There's never an excuse for rudeness," Freddy agreed. "Good manners are important even in S and M. *Especially* in S and M, now that I think of it."

Piercey squeezed Freddy's prodigious bicep. "What about you, stud? You like it rough?"

Freddy put an arm around Piercey. "I throw it down like it's going out of town," he asserted.

I didn't even know what that meant.

This was usually the point of the evening where Freddy made his excuses and walked off with the flavor of the hour.

I was still watching Smokey, but I felt Freddy's eyes on me.

"But not tonight," he told Piercey. "Tonight my friend needs me."

Well, that was a pleasant surprise. I smiled.

"But that's just tonight," Freddy said. "Give me your number because tomorrow I might need *you*, baby."

That's my Freddy.

21

I Got Plenty of Nothing

Ten minutes later, Freddy and I were at The Scoop, a local ice cream shop that makes its own New York–inspired flavors. Since our dinner had been rudely interrupted, it was only logical we skip right to dessert. At least it seemed that way to us. Tomorrow, I'd pay for it on the treadmill.

The Scoop had a laid-back, downtown vibe that perfectly suited our mood. The lights were dim and the music was mellow jazz. We took a quiet banquette in the corner so we could talk.

Freddy enjoyed a Broadway Banana Split, with once scoop each of Chelsea Chocolate, Lickin' Center, and All That Razz. I had a Subway Sundae with Verrazano Vanilla and Whip Me Cream.

"Maybe Rueben's overdose wasn't accidental," Freddy said.

"Ansell told me he had enough heroin in him to kill three people," I answered.

"Exactly. But Rueben was an experienced user, right? He would have known how much he could take."

"You think he killed himself on purpose?"

"You knew him better than I did." Freddy might not have eaten his pasta earlier, but he attacked his ice cream with a single-minded ferociousness not seen since *Jaws*.

I thought for a moment. Rueben had been through a lot. He was a pretty tough customer. Yeah, he'd come to depend on Ansell, but so much so that he'd commit suicide over a single spat? I could see him storming out of Ansell's apartment, but only to intentionally overdose half a block away?

"It's a stretch," I admitted.

"So, if he didn't kill *himself*, whether accidently or on purpose . . ."

"He was murdered?"

"Maybe Ansell was madder at Rueben than he led you to believe," said Freddy, through a mouthful of cold heaven. "He could have killed Rueben."

"Possible," I said. "Or maybe Rueben's death is related to the others."

Freddy put down his spoon. Anytime he did that during dessert, I knew that meant he was about to say Something Important.

"That's it"—he pointed his finger at me—"you're getting out of the business *now*."

"Rueben wasn't killed on the job, Freddy."

"No, but how many dead boys have to pile up before you figure out that you're not exactly in the safest of professions?"

"People die all the time, Freddy. And we don't even know that Rueben's death is related to the others. Or that any of them are related at all."

Freddy's jaw moved back and forth, but he didn't say anything. I could see he was furious.

"Why the sudden freak out, anyway?" I asked. "You already knew about Brooklyn Roy and Sammy White Tee. Not to mention Randy. What makes Rueben's death such a big deal for you?"

"Because I *knew* him, you idiot. I was just talking to him two days ago. This is all getting too close to home, Kevin. If anything happened to you . . ."

"Nothing's going to—"

"I couldn't take it, OK? If anything happened to you, I . . ." Freddy's voice trailed off and he shook his head. "You're the most important person in my life, you stupid asshole." Freddy picked up his spoon and jabbed it angrily into his ice cream. But he didn't eat.

I felt myself tearing up. Freddy wasn't exactly the type to talk about his feelings. The flame between us burned out a long time ago, but the embers still burned hot. We may not have been lovers, not anymore, but there was still a lot of love between us.

Perhaps Freddy and I were going to spend the rest of our lives in some in-between state. Not quite lovers but more than friends. We needed a word for it. Frovers. Lends.

Maybe once we finally have equal marriage rights, we'll call our spouses "husbands" or "wives" and reserve the word "partners" for couples like me and Freddy. 'Cause that's what we felt like. Partners in crime.

Or was that all?

I slid next to him on the banquette and put my head on his shoulder. He put an arm around me and stroked my hair. We sat like that for a few minutes. Then he took his arm away and started eating again. Whatever crisis or opportunity we might have awkwardly been heading toward had been averted. I scooted back to my bowl.

"OK, so we're back to square one," Freddy said. "If we're going to save your sorry ass, we better figure out if someone's really offing these boys."

"All righty then," I said, happy to have the business of murder take our minds off the business of our questionable relationship. "Tony tells me the first rule in any case is to ask 'who benefits?' "

"From killing male hookers?"

I nodded.

"OK, I'll play. Let's see . . . a pervert. Some homo Jack the Ripper. He gets off on killing pretty boys."

"Maybe," I said. "But wouldn't you think he'd kill them during sex or something? If it's a pervy thing, I mean."

"What, I'm the expert on sex crimes now? I don't know. Ask your boyfriend."

I was pretty sure if I told Tony I thought someone was killing male sex workers, he'd handcuff me to my bed. But not in the fun I'm-putting-a-blindfold-on-you-and-you-have-to-guess-where-my-lips-are-going-to-land-next kind of way. More like the you're-not-leaving-this-house-until-you-promise-me-you'll-never-hustle-again way.

No sense getting him worried just yet.

"Let me think about that," I said. "Who else benefits from the death of working boys?"

"A closeted client who doesn't want word to get out about his extracurricular activities? He hires a hooker, then offs him. It's a one hundred percent guarantee of confidentiality, right?"

"Most of my clients are closeted," I said. "None of them have tried to kill me."

"Yet," Freddy added reassuringly.

"It seems thin," I told him.

"Maybe someone famous," Freddy offered. "Someone in the public eye with a lot to lose."

"Being caught with a hooker doesn't end your career. Just look at Hugh Grant."

"No, I said someone *famous*." Freddy drew out the word like I didn't know what it meant.

"Hugh Grant is famous."

"He is? Who is he?"

"A British actor."

"Darling, the only British actor I care about is Robert Pattinson. He can suck on my neck any day. Oh, and that guy who plays James Bond."

"Daniel Craig."

"*Daniel Craig*," Freddy sighed. "Now, there's an English muffin I'd like to toast and butter. Talk about your nooks and crannies. Whoever managed to write cock and ball torture into a mainstream film like *Casino Royale* deserves an Academy Award."

"We're getting off track."

"Right. Fine, so what do we have so far?"

"Jack the Ripper and Hugh Grant."

"Hmmmm . . ." Freddy tilted his bowl to his mouth and slurped the last of his ice cream. I wondered if finishing mine could really be made up for by forty-five minutes of aerobics.

"I know!" Freddy jumped in his seat like an excited third-grader with the right answer. "You!"

"Me?"

"Yeah, you benefit. So do all the other hustlers, right? Kill off your competition and whoever's left standing gets to charge whatever he wants. It's the law of supplies and Depends."

"That's 'demands,' not 'Depends.' Depends are a brand of adult diaper."

"Like you never had a client who was into that." Freddy sneered.

I considered Freddy's suggestion. It didn't strike me as much of a business model. "I don't think we're ever going to run out of boys who'll peddle their papayas for a couple of hundred bucks."

"Well, maybe it's a war between pimps? Or some mob shake-down thing?"

That didn't seem entirely impossible. But Randy worked for Mrs. Cherry, like I did. If she thought there was any real danger, she'd tell me. Wouldn't she?

This was all getting to be too much for me to think about. Fuck my body-fat ratio. I took another spoonful of dessert. "This is giving me a headache," I admitted.

"That's just a brain freeze from your ice cream," Freddy said. He reached over and grabbed my bowl. "Luckily, I'm immune. Let me finish it for you, darling. Wouldn't want you to suffer."

Great. An hour of brainstorming and still no leads. And now, I didn't even get to finish my ice cream. This was shaping up to be a very depressing investigation.

22

Remembering

After Freddy and I finished our servings of sugar and fat, I went home and crashed. I woke up the next morning feeling tired and bloated.

Even though Freddy stole half my ice cream last night, I still had to pay the price for eating the other half. So, despite being sore from yesterday's torture session with the Marquis de Personal Training, I hit the gym and did forty-five excruciating minutes on the StairMaster. Not my favorite exercise machine, but it burns calories like a forest fire and gives you an ass you can bounce a quarter off of. Which is about the most you can do with a quarter these days, anyway.

Then it was back to my place for a protein drink, an Adderall, and a shower. I threw on a pair of baggy khaki pants, a tight long-sleeved Transformers T-shirt, and my white Keds. I wore a Levi's jean jacket over the whole mess.

It was a volunteer day for me at The Stuff of Life. I got there a little early for my shift, so I stopped off to say hi to my friend Vicki, the volunteer coordinator there. Vicki was a smokin' little dykette, with the looks and slicked-back pompadour of a pretty Elvis Presley. In her tight Lee jeans and untucked cowboy shirt, Vicki had the hot swagger of the sexy town mechanic who wipes the grease from her hands on her pants before she feels you up.

I always had to remind myself around her that I liked boys.

"Hey, cutie," she said. "I like the T-shirt. 'More than meets the eye,' huh?"

"I hope so," I answered. "How're things here?"

"Business as usual. Money's a little tight, but more people are coming in to volunteer. I guess they give how they can."

"Who's my crew today?"

Vicki checked a roster on her desk. "OK, this one may be a little tricky."

"Shoot."

"Work release candidates."

Work release candidates were guys incarcerated for non-violent crimes at one of the city's many prisons. They were eligible to work nine-to-five jobs outside of the jail, but first they had to prove themselves under supervised conditions, like here.

This wouldn't be my first time working with one of these groups.

"I can handle it," I said.

"You with a bunch of guys locked up with only their right hands and each other for comfort on those dark and lonely nights? You're gonna be like chum in the water, cupcake."

"Naw, they're mostly white-collar criminals or first-time drug offenders. It's not like *Oz*."

"The Wizard of?"

"The HBO adults-only series. It's a soap opera about male rape in prison. Stayed on the air for six years, so I guess there's a bigger audience for situational homosexuality than you'd think."

"Please, don't all straight boys want to be held down and fucked 'against their will'? I've pegged enough guys in college to know what I'm talking about."

"'Pegged'? Is that some lesbian thing?"

"You don't know what 'pegging' is?" I shook my head. "It's when a girl wears a strap-on and fucks a guy up the ass. It's hot."

"You fuck guys?"

"I've been known to dabble. Equal opportunity penetrator, if you know what I mean. But don't spread it around. The Lesbo Police get kind of uppity about that kind of thing. I could lose my membership card. You've never been pegged?"

"Well," I said, blushing, "I've never needed to. I mean, the guys I'm with don't really need the strap-on, right?"

"I'd peg you right here, right now." Vicki winked. "Cute little thing like you. Bet I could give it to you better than half the guys you're with."

"OK, ewww," I said. "No offense."

I actually thought it could be kind of hot, but my life was complicated enough, thank you.

Vicki was too cool and confident to even acknowledge the rejection. "That show *Oz*, it sounds like *Bad Girls*. You know it?"

"No."

"It's an English show about a women's prison. Same basic thing, lots of wild prison action, but without the blokes. 'Blokes.' That's English for 'guys,' you know."

"I've heard."

"Heh. And they say you can't learn anything from watching TV."

"That where you learned about pegging?"

"No, I learned about that on Dan Savage's podcast. And, boy, am I grateful to him."

My lunch shift with the work release candidates went smooth and easy. They were an amiable group, just happy to be out of prison. No flirting whatsoever, but some of the guys locked up on drug charges were cute in a stoner kind of way.

BTW, it freaks me out that we imprison bright young people with their whole lives ahead of them for smoking weed. Really? What's wrong with this country?

After my shift, I headed to the hospital to check on Randy. Cody was back at his desk, and he smiled from one jumbo ear to the other.

"Hey, Kevin," he called. "It's good to see you again." An

elaborate basket of fresh fruit sat at the nurses' station courtesy of Mrs. Cherry.

"I see Mama's been good to your crew again." I pointed to the basket.

"She's making sure we're keeping a sharp eye on your friend," he said. "Not that we wouldn't anyway. Practically every nurse here is a straight woman or a gay guy. I couldn't keep them out of Randy's room with barbed wire. He sure is a fine-looking fellow."

"That he is." I grinned back. "It's nice to see Mrs. Cherry watching out for him, though. And how about you? Any hot dates?"

"You kidding?" he said. "There are a million incredible-looking men in New York. Sure, someone like you has a boyfriend. . . ."

"Semi-boyfriend," I corrected.

"I'm sure your friend Randy has them lined up like bad singers at an *American Idol* audition. Me? Not hardly."

"Don't put yourself down," I said.

"Plus, when would I meet someone, anyway? I work about a million hours a week."

"So? I thought you said there were a bunch of gay male nurses here."

"No, I said *all* the male nurses here were gay. There's only five. And they're all in their fifties or older, not to mention married—two of them to each other."

"So, go out after work."

"What, so I can be ignored there, too? Please, I get enough rejection from credit card companies; I don't need any more. I think it's cool that you're encouraging me, but I'm not exactly hot stuff."

We were going to have to do something about Cody's self-esteem problem. I thought I had an idea. "Excuse me," I said to him. I sent a quick text message.

I decided to change the subject. "Any more visits from Patchy?"

"No, not that I've seen, and there's a note on the nurses' station warning everyone to watch out for him."

"Good. Now, let's go see the object of everyone's desire."

Randy looked better. He had some color in his face and his eyes were open. I said hello but he didn't respond.

"We think he hears you," Cody said. "That's why we leave the TV on." He pointed to the wall, where a soap opera played on a flat-panel screen. Speakers on either side of Randy's bed relayed the audio to him, but it was only barely audible from where Cody and I stood. "The stimulation might do him good."

"He looks a little more alive," I told Cody.

"Yeah, he's definitely on the mend. Being in such great shape helped him. He had a lot of hard padding to cushion the impact. There's no sign of permanent brain damage, either. All in all, he was lucky."

He's probably indestructible, I thought. *After the bomb falls, it's going to be the cockroaches and Randy left.*

Cody turned to the TV. "Hey, check that out."

I looked at the screen. Two boys, one an adorable boyish blond and the other an equally cute brunette, were passionately making out.

"Wait a minute," I said. "Is this pay per view? Because this is not my mother's daytime TV."

Cody laughed. "No, this is a totally mainstream soap opera, believe it or not. That's Luke and Noah; the show is *As the World Turns.*"

The dark-haired guy looked kind of like Cody. "Why didn't they have this on when I was thirteen?" I asked. "I would never have gone to school."

"That's why." Cody laughed again. "They were looking out for your education."

"Scope that," I said, pointing out the screen to Randy. "Those two cuties are going at it like they just invented hot." Randy remained unfazed.

"Well, if he's not responding to this," I said to Cody, "we're screwed."

"He may not be talking, but that doesn't mean he isn't responding. Look." Cody arched his eyebrows and nodded toward the prodigious and slowly rising tent under Randy's sheet.

"You think?"

"It could be a coincidence. But maybe not. If he's an especially sexual person, that scene could be reaching some part of his brain that's particularly responsive to stimuli."

That sounded about right.

"Maybe," I said, "you should reach under and give him a hand with that? Don't you have a responsibility to serve your patient's needs? Maybe it'd wake him up."

Cody scowled playfully. "I have professional ethics to uphold," he said. "But I could leave you two alone if you'd like."

"Naw, stay around. With my luck, I'd kill him."

Luke and Noah's romantic kiss ended and the scene faded to black.

"You have rewind on that thing?" I asked.

"Sorry," Cody said.

Even through the tinny sound of Randy's bedside speaker, I heard the familiar sound of a children's choir singing "God Bless America." *Oh no,* I thought, *another Jacob Locke commercial.*

"I hate this tool," Cody said.

"Who doesn't?" I agreed.

The droning narrator ran through his string of dull clichés and the now-familiar image of Jacob Locke stepped onscreen. "I believe in an America that tolerates everyone, but that maintains its core values. Good people can get along without giving in. One woman, one man, one marriage . . ."

Cody stuck a finger down his throat and pretended to gag. Then he said, "Hey, that's him."

How was he talking with a finger down his throat?

"That's who?" Cody asked me.

"I didn't say anything. I thought that was you."

We turned around. Randy was sitting up, his eyes not just open but *seeing,* and he was looking at Jacob Locke.

"That's the guy I was telling you about, Kevin," Randy said. "The guy with the hard-boiled eggs!"

I couldn't believe Randy was talking. Cody's mouth was open.

He looked pretty good that way. Cody really was adorable. I bet he . . .

Focus, Kevin, focus.

I ran to Randy's side.

"Randy!" I said. "You're talking!"

"Of course I'm talking," Randy said. Then he looked around. "Hey, where am I? Weren't we just . . ." His eyes rolled back in his head and he fell back onto the pillow.

"Press that," Cody told me, indicating a button by the side of Randy's bed. I did.

"The doctor will be here soon," he said. "Don't worry, this is a good thing."

"But he didn't stay awake," I said, concerned.

"People don't come out of comas all at once. This is typical. He's getting better."

I felt relieved but still concerned.

"And it's perfectly normal that he wasn't making sense," Cody added. "What did he say? That Jacob Locke gave him eggs?"

If Randy meant what I thought he did, what he said might have been true. I was about to explain it to Cody when the door slammed open. I turned, expecting to see the doctor, but it was the other person I'd called in to consult.

"Hey," Freddy said, "what's the emergency? Your text said I had to get here right away and . . ."

Freddy saw Cody and stopped in his tracks. "Well, hell-loooo."

"Cody," I said, "my friend, Freddy. Freddy, Cody. Cody's the emergency."

"What?" Cody said.

"Is he on fire?" Freddy asked lasciviously. " 'Cause I got just the hose to put it out."

"OK," I said, "that's gross."

Cody beamed. "I don't mind."

Freddy slipped an arm around him. "I hope not."

I was about to explain Cody's crisis of self-esteem when the real doctor came through the door. Cody quickly slipped out of Freddy's grasp. "How about you two wait outside while I fill the doctor in on what happened?" Cody asked. "I'll be out in a few."

"I will *definitely* be waiting," Freddy said.

Cody blushed again.

I couldn't wait to get outside and tell Freddy what Randy woke up to say.

23

Just Leave Everything to Me

Seated in a waiting area outside Randy's room, I told Freddy about Randy's recognition of Jacob Locke.

"Wow," Freddy said, "and I care about that why? Let's talk about Cody. Is he available? Is he as edible as he looks?"

"Can we hold off on that for one minute, Sluttyanna? Remember your theory—that maybe the boys who've been attacked had a closeted client in common? Someone with a lot to lose? Now we know that Randy, for one, was with Jacob Locke—a conservative presidential candidate whose campaign would not be helped by revelations that's he's been screwing with male prostitutes."

"Again," Freddy replied, "topic for later. Did you see those ears on Cody? Like Dumbo. You know, sometimes big ears on a guy correspond with . . ."

"They do in this case, but that's not the point right now, you oversexed horror show—"

Freddy cut me off. "How do you know he's hung? Are you doing him? Did you bring me here to boast? Because that's really immature, Kevin."

"Oh my God, would you stop making this about Cody?"

"I thought you called me here to meet Cody."

"I did, but that was *before* Randy revealed the Big Bad."

"Yeah, and what I want to know is when Cody revealed *his* 'big bad' to you!"

At least Freddy's pissiness about this topic made it clear he was interested in Cody, which had been my plan all along.

"It came up in conversation," I assured him. "Totally innocent."

Freddy gave me a disbelieving look.

"It's a long story, but I promise you, I haven't touched the boy. He's my gift to you, all right?"

Freddy wiped a mock tear from his eye. "It's the nicest thing anyone's ever done for me. But, if I may approach the bench, why?"

I told him that I really liked Cody, but that Cody had self-esteem lower than the success rate of abstinence-only programs (Hi, Bristol!).

"I thought that if a guy like you showed interest, he might feel better about himself."

"And what made you so sure I'd be interested?" Freddy asked, deciding whether or not to be insulted.

I gave him my best you-have-got-to-be-shitting-me look. "Do you really want me to answer that?"

"I don't, thank you for asking." Freddy put his hands over his heart. "I accept this award on behalf of the Academy. And all the little people. Like you, darling."

"OK, now that we have that out of the way, can we get back to topic number one?"

"Absolutely," Freddy said. "You're right, there's way more important stuff to discuss. So, how big *exactly* did Cody say he was? Are we talking *Eight Is Enough, Deep Space Nine, Ten Little Indians,* or, God help us, *Ocean's Eleven*?"

I shook my head at his relentlessness.

"*No,*" Freddy whispered. "*Cheaper by the Dozen*?"

"I didn't ask for exact measurements. Can we please discuss the life-or-death issues, now?"

"Believe me," Freddy said, "*Cheaper by the Dozen is* a life-or-death issue. Have you never heard of a punctured colon?"

"I'm gonna puncture your head if you don't . . ."

"OK, OK," Freddy said. "Angels mode it is. So, Randy wakes up to tell us he tricked with Jacob Locke, right?"

I nodded.

"Only, who knows if Randy was telling the truth? He's not exactly sane in the membrane yet, is he?"

I conceded that could be correct.

"And even if he was, we have nothing to connect the other boys to Locke."

"True."

"So, we're going to have to investigate. You know I love to investigate, right?"

"I think I have an idea where to start."

"Good. What do you have in—" Freddy stopped mid-sentence as Cody walked over.

"So, good news," Cody said, sitting next to me. Freddy scowled. "The doctor says that Randy is definitely more responsive. His vitals are stronger, too. The doctor expects we'll see more moments of lucidity like this as time goes on. Your friend's going to be fine."

"That's great," Freddy said. "Now, if I may ask you, in your medical opinion, what are the odds of me taking you out to dinner tonight?"

"Really?" Cody's voice cracked like a twelve-year-old's.

"Well, yeah," Freddy replied.

"But you're like, I mean, I'm just . . ." Cody turned from Freddy and looked at me with wide eyes.

"What's with you?" Cody asked me. "First, Randy, who comes in all banged up but still looking like Michelangelo's *David* come to life, and now this guy shows up with all these muscles and that face and . . . are all your friends this ridiculously attractive? Because, if so, I do not fit in with this crowd. You're all like boys in magazines and I'm just this ordinary . . ."

I thought I could ramble. God knows how long Cody might have gone on had Freddy not gotten up, pulled Cody into his arms, and laid a kiss on him that got me turned on, and I was just watching.

By the time Freddy let him go, Cody was breathless and even more flushed than before.

"I'm sorry," Freddy told him. "But I really had to shut you up right then."

Cody pulled down his gauzy white nurse's shirt, trying unsuccessfully to cover his reaction to Freddy's unexpected advance.

And, yes, from the size of the bulge in his pants, he hadn't been lying. He was going to need a much longer shirt.

"Here's the deal," Freddy told him. "If you really think you're 'ordinary,' you either need a couple of years of therapy, a really, really long look in a mirror, or shock treatment. Because you are one of the five sweetest things I've laid eyes on all year, and we're already in November.

"Or, you could save yourself some time, come out with me for dinner, and we'll see if that leads to some opportunities for me to show you just how special you are.

"Your choice."

"Are you really interested in me? This isn't some kind of fraternity prank, is it? I'm not on *Punk'd* or anything, am I?"

Freddy gave him a look that would have silenced a volcano. "You put yourself down one more time, and I *will* slap you."

Cody looked around, this was his place of work after all, and seeing the coast clear, leaned over and gave Freddy a quick kiss on the lips. "I would love to go to dinner with you," Cody said. "And thank you." A beeper he wore on his hip buzzed loudly.

"I have to go check on a patient," he said. "But this has been . . .wow."

Freddy handed him a card. "I'm an expert at 'wow.' Call me later and we'll work out where to meet."

Cody grabbed the card like a drowning man going for the life preserver. "Thanks again."

"Thank me later," Freddy said. "And remember: Actions speak louder than words."

24

All in Love Is Fair

Freddy and I parted ways at the hospital, he anticipating an evening of boosting Cody's confidence with what I could only assume would be a variety of prurient and possibly back-breaking acrobatics, and I looking forward to a less playful, but hopefully more productive and educational dinner with Tony and friends.

What can I say—I'm a giver?

I got home in time to make myself presentable for my semi-boyfriend. But first, I had a phone call to make. "I need to know if someone's a client of yours," I began.

"My dearest boy," Mrs. Cherry gushed. "No, 'How are you, oh Queen of all that is Dark, Dirty, and Mysterious?' No, 'Oh, how I pine for the luscious scent of your satin panties?' No, 'You drive even a one hundred percent gay boy like me to dream of the infinite pleasure I'd find munching the fresh grass that blooms between your spread and generous thighs?' Where are your manners, Kevin? You wound me."

"Sorry," I said. "This is serious. I need to know if someone's a client of yours."

"Darling, hundreds of men hire dates through me. It's what keeps Mama off the streets and up to her elbows in pearls."

"I need to know about one client in particular."

"Well, I'm sorry, my dear, but you know Mother holds her secrets in the strictest of confidence. Even you don't know the names of some of your longest-term clients—well, not their real names, anyway. Only I know that, and Mrs. Cherry's lips are sealed."

"I wouldn't ask you if it wasn't important." I told Mrs. Cherry about the string of coincidences that resulted in the deaths of Sammy White Tee, Brooklyn Roy, and Rueben, as well as the possible attempt on Randy's life. "I think they may have had a client in common, someone important."

"You have someone in mind?" Mrs. Cherry asked. I think it was the most direct sentence I'd ever heard her utter.

"Yeah," I said. "Jacob Locke."

Mrs. Cherry laughed heartily. "That horrible man from the television? The one who thinks he's going to run a presidential campaign on a platform of Get the Gays? Oh, darling, Mrs. Cherry may insist my boys wear condoms, but that doesn't mean I do business with scumbags."

"So, you're sure he's never been a client of yours?"

Mrs. Cherry paused. "Well . . ." she began.

"'Well'?"

"The answer is no. But to be perfectly honest, someone of his stature, well, they don't rent boys under their own names. They usually have an assistant or associate take care of that for them. There's no paper trail that way. More than once I've arranged for a date with someone who sounded perfectly average only to have my boy report back to me that he just fucked a CNN newscaster or a sitcom star.

"So, if I had to be honest, which I never, never am, darling, but I'll make an exception in this case, I'd have to say that just because I don't remember having ever done business with Mr. Jacob Locke doesn't mean he's never availed himself of my services. It's unlikely, but not impossible."

Just on a whim, I thought I'd run another name past her.

"Ansell Darling?" she answered. "Well, let's just say if I awarded frequent flyer miles, Mr. Darling would be traveling first class for the rest of his life. I don't know how much money he could possibly make with those awful rags he peddles at cut-rate department stores, but he certainly spends enough to maintain me in designer muumuus and caftans. You know Mama's a plus-sized girl with a heart of gold, darling."

"OK," I said, feeling more confused than when I'd started. I'd better take another Adderall before my date with Tony tonight. "Thanks for being honest with me."

"Anything for you, dearest. But tell me, are you really worried? Because if I thought for one instant that my boys were in any danger, I'd pull you all off the job tomorrow."

"No," I said. "Maybe I'm paranoid. It could be nothing. I'm not sure."

"Well, keep me informed. Now, kiss Auntie Cherry good night."

I blew her a kiss into the phone and hopped into the shower.

Tony arrived at my place right on time, looking every inch the straight boy in his pressed chinos, white collared shirt, and navy V-neck sweater. Oh yeah, there were loafers, too.

Still, a more delicious straight boy you never saw.

I was wearing black, straight-leg AX jeans and an oversized baby blue merino wool sweater that matched my eyes and made me look more boyish than usual. The sleeves came to my knuckles and the waist just above my ass. The sweater's deep scoop called attention to the soft skin on my shoulders and upper chest.

I wasn't entirely sure how tonight would go, and I figured reminding Tony of some of the things he liked about me wasn't entirely a bad idea.

Tony looked as nervous as a teenager on a first date. Usually, he ravished me with hungry kisses as soon as I opened the door; tonight, he looked down at his dumb loafers and shuffled his feet. "You ready to go?"

I grabbed my denim jacket, keys, and wallet. I put my arm through his. "You're not headed to your execution, you know."

"What?"

"You look kind of glum."

"Oh." Tony gave me a quick peck on the cheek as we walked

to the elevator. "You know me. I'm just not that social a guy. I get uncomfortable meeting new people. That's all."

New gay people, I thought. "You'll like them," I assured him. "And they'll like you. It's just dinner. We never ask you to sign the recruitment papers at the first meal."

Tony stopped walking and looked at me.

"Kidding," I told him.

"I know that," he said, with one of those fake laughs where the person actually enunciates "ha-ha."

"It's just dinner," I repeated. "No agenda. I promise."

But of course, I was lying. Agenda was actually the main course at this meal, as I was hoping to strike off the list at least one of the things Tony thought he was going to have to give up to be with me.

We drove Tony's car across town and arrived at a beautiful townhouse in the West Village. "Nice digs," Tony said, as we nabbed an illegal parking space in front of their house. Tony put his shield on the dashboard to prevent a ticket.

"They're nice people," I told him. I got out of the car and waited for Tony to join me on the street. It seemed like he took an extra few minutes to extract himself from his seat belt.

He really was nervous.

"Would you come on?" I urged him. "If you don't hurry up, we're going to miss our turn in the sling before the appetizers are served."

Tony froze again.

"I'm still kidding."

"I know that," Tony said. "You know, it's not like this is my first dinner with gay people. Sheesh." He ran his hands through my hair. "I'm not a rube. I know the sling doesn't usually come out till dessert."

Did he just make a joke? "Wow," I said. "I'm really proud of you."

"And I am really sorry I'm being such a dick about all this. You're right; I should meet your friends. Maybe it's not going to be so bad to be at a dinner with you where I don't have to be afraid to do this." Tony took me in his arms and planted a kiss on me so scorching that I worried for a moment if hair gel was flammable.

"I think I forgot to do that when I first saw you tonight," he said. "Forgive me?"

"Absolutely not," I said. "You think one kiss is gonna do it?"

On the second one, I think I actually felt my lips start to blister.

"OK," I said, pushing away, "you're forgiven. But you kiss me like that in there, and this really will turn into a gay orgy."

Tony took my hand in his. "Let's go meet your friends."

Nick opened the door on our first ring. In his dark denims and white button-down shirt, he looked like he could be Tony's brother. He kissed me hello.

"And this must be Tony," he said, giving Tony a naturally butch handshake that immediately put my semi-boyfriend at ease. "You know, we're pretty crazy about Kevin in this household. You treating him right?"

Tony put an arm around me. "I try to watch out for him."

"Well, then, welcome. Can I get you a beer?"

"What have you got?"

"I'm not too fancy about that stuff, I'm afraid. I'm a Bud man. That OK?"

"That's perfect," Tony said, and I could hear the relief in his voice. I think he expected a pink daiquiri or something.

We walked though the hallway into the living room. Paul was coming toward us with a red cocktail in each hand. As always, his long floppy hair fell over his forehead and he shook it out of his eyes. Obviously the chef tonight, Paul was barefoot, in faded denims, a black, long-sleeved tee, and an apron that read, "I cook, you clean. Deal?"

"Here," he said, handing me a Cosmo. "Unless you're drinking diesel oil like the real boys tonight."

I kissed him on the cheek. "This is great, thanks. And this," I said, feeling very proud of my handsome and so far socially acceptable semi-boyfriend, "is Tony."

Paul wiped his hand on his apron before shaking Tony's. I watched Tony's face, and apparently Paul's grip was strong enough to earn a smile from him. "Really nice to meet you," Paul said. "Kevin's been single for too long."

"I'm sorry," I said, "did I leave the room?"

"Nice meeting you, too," Tony said. "This place is great. Thanks for inviting us."

"Don't thank us yet," Nick said. "You haven't eaten his cooking."

Paul smacked Nick on the head.

Tony smiled again.

See, I thought at him, *they're just like real people. You can do this.*

"I'm sure it'll be great," Tony said.

Nick rolled his eyes. "You must like to live dangerously."

"I'm a cop," Tony said. "I'm used to walking on the wild side."

Wow. For Tony to share that so soon meant he really was feeling comfortable.

"You are?" Nick asked. "No shit. I used to be on the job, too."

"No shit?" Tony said.

"No shit," Nick answered.

Paul looked at me, his expression saying, *See how well the boys are playing together?* I smiled back.

"So what are you doing now?"

"I'm a PI," Nick said.

I didn't even know that. These two really were getting along like two houses on fire.

Maybe I should be worried.

"Hey, come in the kitchen with me and grab that beer. We can trade war stories."

"All right," Tony said, "and maybe after the second beer, I'll tell you about the time I saved Kevin's ass."

Nick and Paul looked at me.

"It was nothing," I said. "A friendly little murder scheme I happened to stumble onto. It could happen to anyone."

"Why," Nick asked, "do I doubt that?"

"Wow, I guess you really do know him, huh?" Tony teased.

When your friends pick on you the first time they meet, it's always a good sign.

It looked like my plan was going to work.

"Hey," Tony said, stepping on something. He picked it up. "Oh, sorry, man, it looks like I crushed your . . . Superman action figure? Aren't you two a little old for this kind of thing?"

"Oh, that's Aaron's," Paul said.

"Aaron's?" Tony frowned for a moment, and I think he was wondering if this nice couple he was starting to like was really living in some freaky three-way arrangement. If so, his question was answered by the sound of little feet running down the hall.

"Kebbin!" Four-year-old Aaron threw himself into my arms. "You came!"

"You are supposed to be in bed young man," Paul said.

"Aw, but . . ." Aaron whined.

"Hey," I said. "How about I tuck the little tiger in? Would you like that, Aaron?"

"Yeah!"

"OK," I said, "but first you have to say hello to my friend, Tony."

Tony tickled Aaron's belly. "Hey, little man. You're lucky. 'Kebbin's' the best tucker-inner in the tri-state area."

"Are you his husband?" Aaron asked.

Tony blanched. "Ah, no, we're just friends."

I gave Tony a death glare.

"Special friends," he amended.

"Come on," Aaron said, losing interest in Tony as soon as he figured out where he fit in. "You can tell me a story."

As I carried Aaron to his room, I heard Tony asking, "So, is that your nephew or something?"

Nick laughed. "Didn't Kevin tell you? Aaron's our son. He didn't mention we were dads?"

"Ah, no, he didn't," Tony said. You could feel the temperature in the room drop a few degrees.

"That's funny," Nick said cluelessly. "I wonder why he didn't say anything."

"Yeah," Tony said, his voice tight. "Wonder why?"

Paul, being the more sensitive of the two, knew Nick was jumping on thin ice. He tried to lighten the mood. "Surprise!" he said, throwing up jazz hands.

Oh no, I thought, *not the jazz hands.*

"Yeah," said Tony, "big surprise."

25

Being at War with Each Other

"What I don't understand," Tony snapped at me as we walked into my apartment, "is what were you *thinking?*"

"I was thinking they were a nice couple and we'd have a good time," I answered innocently.

We'd driven back from dinner in a tense silence.

"Did you really imagine," Tony asked incredulously, "that I wouldn't see what you were up to? I mean, of all your friends, you invite me to dinner with the poster family for gay daddies? Was that even their kid, or did you rent him for the evening to prove how 'normal' they were?"

"They are normal."

"That is not normal, Kevin. Kids need a mom and a dad."

"OK, well, tell that to the ten million kids being raised by single parents in this country and see what they say." I totally made that number up, but I didn't think Tony would take the time to Wiki it.

"It's not the same," Tony barked.

"No, it's *better,* Tony. Aaron has two parents who love him and take care of him. He's surrounded by friends and an extended family that spoil him rotten. What's the problem?"

"The *problem*"—Tony over-enunciated in that way that always told me he was really, really mad—"is that poor kid is going to go through life teased and miserable because he has two dads."

"So what? I went through school getting picked on because I

was short, kids made fun of Vinny Bartucci because of that lisp he had, and Melinda Ninetrees got beat up because her *mother* was fat. Bobbie Pickney went through three years of junior high school being called 'Booger Pickme' because he got caught with his finger up his nose in science class. Kids get teased all the time."

"My point exactly! Why make life even harder for them?"

"The world is what makes life hard, Tony. Parents are the people who teach you how to deal with it."

"Again, why ask for more problems?"

"Because we don't conquer bigotry by painting everyone white, and we don't cater to idiots by all pretending to be stupid. The world needs more kids being raised by devoted parents who really love them, no matter what genders they are."

"Kids need a mom and dad," Tony repeated.

"Right, because we know how fabulous Adolf Hitler and Ted Bundy and, I don't know, Attilla the fucking Hun turned out. It's like cake mix—add a penis and vagina, throw in a kid, cook for eighteen years, and it's all perfect."

"See," Tony yelled, slamming his fist against the wall. "This is why I didn't want to do this. This is why I want it to just be us. I don't want to be part of your movement, or join a crusade, or spend my life battling social injustice. I just want us . . ." His voice trailed off and he fell onto the couch. He put his elbows on his knees and his head in his hands.

I felt myself choke up and asked the question I was afraid to ask. "You want *what,* Tony?"

"I just don't want to do this. I don't want to fight the world and I don't want to fight with you, either." He lifted his head and I sat next to him, close enough to touch but not touching.

"Tony . . ."

"Because whether we fight the world or each other, Kevin, we're going to lose. Either way, we both lose."

"Couldn't we both win?" I asked.

Even though I was trying to be totally in the moment and responsive to Tony's needs, I suddenly realized I was repeating a line from a Barbra Streisand movie.

Babs is a funky left-wing Jewish activist, trying to convince her play-it-safe WASP boyfriend (Robert Redford, BTW) that, despite their differences, their relationship is worth fighting for.

It didn't end well in the movie.

Oh. My. God. I was living *The Way We Were.*

Tony reached over and pushed my bangs out of my eyes. I scooted a little closer to him. He put an arm around me and I nestled in.

"I'm sorry," he said. "I'm just going through a lot right now. There are things I can't talk about with you. I didn't mean to take it out on you like that."

"I know," I said, resting my head against his strong chest.

We sat like that for a few minutes and Tony kissed the top of my head. "I have to go," he said.

"You're not staying the night?" I pulled away.

"No, I really do have a ton of crap I have to get to."

"OK," I said coldly.

Tony pulled me back to him. "I'm not leaving because I'm mad, I promise. I'm just on overload. I'll call you tomorrow."

"OK," I answered, a little thawed out.

Tony kissed me on the lips then, a good kiss, like he meant it, and I hoped it might lead to something more. "They really did seem like a nice couple," Tony said. "I liked them." He kissed me again. "I like you."

"I like you, too," I said, very butch and very serious. I gave him a manly punch on the arm.

"You're a nut," he said, getting up. "I'll call you tomorrow."

"Sure," I said, seeing him to the door. "Tomorrow. But, Tony?"

"Yeah?"

"What you said before, about things you couldn't talk to me about. You can, you know. You can talk to me about anything."

"What?" He screwed up his face. "I didn't say that."

"Yes, you did. Just before. You said you were dealing with things you couldn't share with me."

"Huh," Tony said, his expression innocent. "If you say so."

Like I was the crazy one.

Tony never lied to me.

Right?

He gave me one last kiss and was gone.

OK, so maybe introducing him to Nick, Paul, and Aaron wasn't quite as good an idea as I hoped it would be. But it didn't end too badly, did it?

Was I pushing too hard? Not hard enough?

Why don't relationships come with an FAQ?

What was it that he was so busy with lately? What couldn't he discuss with me?

I hoped there wasn't something else I needed to add to the List of Things Tony Wasn't Willing to Give Up to Be with Me.

My iPhone rang, announcing it was my mother. Well, I could use a distraction.

"Hey, Mom," I answered.

"Bitch!" my mother yelled.

"Nice to talk to you, too."

"That horrible, horrible bitch," she continued.

"And we're talking about . . . ?"

"Yvonne!" my mother screamed. "Guess who just left my front door?"

"Um, Yvonne?"

"No," my mother said, sounding all annoyed with me. "Why would Yvonne be at my front door? We didn't exactly part as friends."

"I'm confused," I admitted.

"Her lawyers came here. Or someone from her law firm or some such. They gave me papers!"

"Papers?"

"Papers! In an envelope!"

"What do they say?"

"How should I know?"

"Didn't you open them?"

"No, why would I open them?"

"To see the words inside?"

"I don't need to see the words. The men who dropped them off, and she sent two, the bitch, she must be scared of me, told me Yvonne was suing me!"

"Suing you?"

"Suing me!"

"Why is she suing you?"

"She says I permanently damaged her scalp and now half her hair won't grow back in."

"Ouch."

"She was half bald when she walked in, the bitch! I told you, I've seen healthier hair on chemo patients. She's just being spiteful. You know what she wants?"

"What?"

"She wants my *shop*. My shop! That *bitch!* She could buy one hundred Sophie's Choice Tresses if she wanted to. Not that there isn't a lot of value in the business, mind you. It was voted the third-most popular beauty parlor by the readers of *Hauppauge Today*, if you remember."

"I have the article framed," I said. I had been too tense during dinner to eat anything. I opened my refrigerator. Nothing. I needed a wife.

"And we would have been number two if it wasn't for Hair-Cuttery. How am I supposed to compete with twelve-dollar haircuts, I ask you?"

I found a Clif Bar in the cutlery drawer. Good enough. "What are you going to do?"

My mother heaved a beleaguered sigh. "I don't know. Your father said Yvonne could probably tie us up in court so long that we'd lose everything anyway, even if she doesn't win. You don't think she can win, can she?"

"No," I lied. What world did my mother live in? Yvonne was one of television's most beloved personalities. My mother was a crazy Long Island harridan who scarred her head with caustic chemicals in a premeditated attack. It sounded like an open and shut case to me, and not in my mother's favor.

This was bad news. What if my parents really did lose the

shop? Or, for that matter, their life savings? Where would they live? My sister had a husband and three kids in a two-bedroom house—no way they'd go there.

I looked around my apartment and put the Clif Bar back in the drawer. I'd lost my appetite.

"Maybe you could settle," I suggested. "She doesn't need your money. Maybe she just wants an apology."

"An apology? From me? I'd sooner chew glass than apologize to that bleached hussy. The words would choke in my throat like poison. My lungs would fill with blood and collapse. My heart would explode like a—"

"All right, all right, I get it. But, you know, some fights aren't worth having. Not if you can't win." I experienced a moment of déjà vu. Huh.

"It's always worth fighting for what you believe in. Have I taught you nothing?"

Huh.

"No," I said, "you're right. Without your principles . . ."

" . . . You're nothing. I'm not afraid of a fight, Kevin."

She may be a crazy woman, but my mother sometimes makes me proud.

"So, you're OK?" I asked.

"What are you, *meshugana*? I'm a wreck! I'm being sued by a rich witch who can take everything I've worked for over the years and flush it down the toilet without a moment's thought. I'm terrified."

"I thought you weren't afraid of a fight."

"I'm not afraid of a *fight*," my mother insisted. "It's just the possibility of *losing* that scares the you-know-what out of me."

"Listen," I said. "We'll figure this out. I'm not going to let that woman hurt you." I had an idea.

"My Kevin," my mother said.

"And this place is much too small to share with you and Dad, anyway."

"Kevin?"

I hadn't meant to say that last bit aloud. "Nothing. Just listen to me: We'll figure something out. We always do."

"You're right," my mother said. "Thank you. I feel better. There's no way that Hollywood hag is going to take down the woman who built the third-most popular beauty parlor in Long Island!"

Well, really the third-most popular beauty parlor *in her town* in Long Island, but this didn't seem like the time to correct her.

"That's the spirit! Should I say hello to Dad?"

"It's not a good time. He's locked himself in the bathroom. He may be throwing up. It's hard to tell over the sobs."

"OK, well, I'll call you later."

"I love you."

"I love you, too."

I had to share the news from Crazy Town with someone. I called Freddy.

"Yo, ho," he answered.

"Funny."

"I thought so. Why are you bothering me? It's my date night with Cody, remember?"

I did now. "Sorry. I'll let you boys get back to . . . whatever."

"No, it's cool. He's not here."

"Oh, sorry about that." Guess I wasn't as good a matchmaker as I thought. "It didn't go well?"

"No, it was great. He's great."

"I don't understand. If he's great, why isn't he there? Was he not into you?"

Freddy laughed. "'Was he not into you?' That's a good one, sweetie."

"I know how you work, Fredster. If you liked him, and he liked you, you two should be banging like explosions in a Michael Bay movie by now. What are you not telling me?"

"Nothing. We had dinner. We really enjoyed each other. I walked him home, we hung out for a while in his apartment, and then I left."

"That was quick. Was he bad in bed? Because he looked like he'd be smoking, but sometimes you can get fooled. Again, sorry."

"Listen, dummy, we didn't have sex, all right? We just made out for a while and then I decided to . . ." Freddy's voice trailed off.

I gave him a minute. "Freddy?"

"I can't think of the word . . ."

"Leave?"

"No."

"Shower?"

"No."

"Run to the corner store for some lube and an enema kit?"

"No!"

"What?"

"Wait!" Freddy triumphantly exclaimed.

"Wait for what?"

"No, that's the word. I decided to *wait!*"

"What? You decided to wait? You don't wait. You're not a waiter. If you want a guy, you take him. There. Then. End of story."

"I know," Freddy said, laughing. "It's insane! But I like him. He's sweet and tender like a part of your body that's been covered by a bandage for a while. You know how you peel it off, and the skin underneath is all soft and clean and new? Only he's like that all over. I wanted to drill him like Sarah Palin wants to drill the Alaskan wilderness, but I just decided to . . . wait."

I was speechless. "Wow."

"I know."

"You going to see him again?"

"We have a date this weekend."

"Holy shit. You're dating!"

"Am not!"

"Are, too!"

"I don't 'date.' "

"You sure about that?"

Freddy paused. He whispered, "I think I want to date him."

"Aaahhh!" I screamed, but it was a happy scream.

"I know! Aaahhhhh!" Freddy screamed back.

Now we were two screaming queens on the phone.

"I'm really glad for you," I said.

"I'm glad for me, too. Thanks for introducing us."

"My pleasure, Fredmeister."

"Why does it seem like all the best things in my life somehow connect back to you?"

"You are so going to regret saying that at some point, aren't you?"

"That point would be *already*."

"OK," I said, "can we get to my drama now?"

"Shoot."

I filled Freddy in on what had happened with Tony and with my mom.

"So, you didn't tell Tony about Jacob Locke or anything else?" he asked.

"No, I don't think I can. Tony barely tolerates my work as it is. If I give him even a little more reason for concern, he'll break my legs to keep me off the job."

"Seeing as how most of your work is done on your back, why would that slow you down?" Freddy asked.

"Wow," I said. "Ever since you started 'dating,' you've become so catty."

"Like you can talk, whore."

"Hussy."

"Tramp," Freddy countered.

I played my ultimate card. *"Dater."*

"Oh, Jane," Freddy groaned. "You wouldn't be able to do these awful things to me if I weren't in this wheelchair."

"But you are, Blanche," I volleyed back. "But you are!"

26

Who Are You Now?

The next day was Friday, and at four in the morning, I gave up on my fitful quest for sleep. My head was too full of Tony, Freddy, Cody, Rueben, and, mostly, Jacob Locke.

Too many men in my bed.

Never thought I'd say that.

Jacob Locke. So, he was The Eggman. I should have seen that coming.

Other than his odious gay-baiting commercials, I didn't know much about him. Who was he?

I got up from bed and opened the refrigerator. Hmmm . . . nothing had magically appeared since last night.

I really had to go shopping.

Then I remembered—the cutlery drawer! I opened it gleefully and found the Clif Bar I'd put there last night. I grabbed a bottle of water and headed for the computer.

Sitting in the dark, eating my chalky breakfast bar, I had to wonder: Could my life be any more fucking glamorous?

Sigh.

I booted up my Mac and opened Safari. On the Google home page, I entered "Jacob Locke."

Five million four hundred thousand results came up for the conservative candidate. That seemed a little unwieldy, so I tried to narrow it down. "Jacob Locke gay." Why not? Maybe someone had outed him along the way.

Somehow, that only brought the number of hits down to two

million four hundred sixty thousand. A quick perusal of the headlines didn't reveal anything juicy about him personally. Although, it was pretty clear he had gays on his mind quite a lot, not to mention on his tongue. Well, not literally. At least, not that I could prove.

What I could prove was that he talked an awful lot about homosexuals.

I decided to see what wisdom he had to share on this matter to which he was so obviously drawn. Here are some of his choicer quotes:

"On the subject of homosexuality, I'm more inclined to believe the teachings of Moses from the Mount than the boys from *Brokeback Mountain.*"

Moses taught about homosexuality? Really? Where—in the book of Leviticus/Club Remix version?

"Homosexuality is an aberrant, unhealthy, and sinful lifestyle that we have to tolerate but are under no obligation to accept."

This struck me as what they call "kinder" conservatism. What the hell is the difference between tolerating and accepting us? Why do either if we're so irredeemably twisted? It's just a bunch of words thrown together to simultaneously appeal to his rabid religious base while not totally alienating the moderate voters in the middle. If a patient in a mental hospital said this, they'd up his medication.

"So-called gay rights have about as much in common with real civil rights as gay marriage has in common with normal marriage."

I kind of agree with him on this one, but that logic leads me to the opposite conclusion. Move on.

"America cannot continue to build the family of nations around the world if we allow the collapse of the family here at home."

Yes, because we all know how equal marriage rights for gay people will cause every heterosexual union to immediately splinter and fail.

"America's culture is based on the fact that we are a religious people. If we recognize God in our Declaration of Independence and our currency, shouldn't we be willing to recognize him in our bedrooms, as well?"

Hey, I've slept with a lot of guys, but I was still pretty sure if God showed up in my bedroom, I'd recognize him. Bet he'd be hot.

"They say 'go gay'? I say 'no way!' "

Way!

I could go on, but I think you get the point.

What makes someone like Jacob Locke? I read his bio. Born in Utah to a religious fireman father and a stay-at-home mom who only made it though the sixth grade. He was home-schooled, thus ensuring no new ideas could enter his tiny little head. His father was a strict disciplinarian.

"My dad would lay out the hose at work and smack us with his hose at home," he told Barbara Walters in 2001. Boy, did I wish Babs had a better ear for a double entendre.

Despite being taught through high school by an academically limited mother, Locke attended and graduated, with C's, from Brother's Baptist University before going on to St. Simon's Seminary in Austin, TX.

Although headed for a life in the clergy, Locke apparently decided that God's true plan for him led to show business: Locke dropped out of seminary with one year to go to take a job in Christian broadcasting. His *Ask Father Jacob* show became an instant hit, despite the fact that he was only a "father" at that time to his first-born daughter.

From a *People* magazine article in 2002: "Jacob Locke is not your typical talk show host. Mixing folksy common sense advice with Biblically inspired teachings, Locke's humor, humanism, and down-home charm have even non-believers tuning in daily."

Unhelpfully, the article didn't specifically address whether he takes it up the ass.

Locke's need for attention (still looking for Daddy's hose, buddy?) wasn't satisfied by the pulpit or the radio show. By 2004, he was the star of *Father Jacob Speaks the Truth,* a strange little show on the second-most popular conservative cable news channel. Here, he interviewed many world leaders and celebrities, lecturing each on how God would want them to behave.

Like all narcissists, however, Locke craved more and bigger mirrors. In 2008, he began building a political operation, and now, he was launching his first presidential campaign.

When asked why voters would support a presidential candidate with no previous elective experience, Locke replied, "Well, when you buy a bar of soap, you don't want one that's covered with slime, do you? I'm here to clean up our country. The fact that I'm not part of the current mess makes me *more* qualified for the job, not less."

Who knew that "folksy wisdom" was synonymous with "bat-shit crazy"? But the truth was, millions of people were buying his shtick. While no one considered his bid for the presidential nomination particularly serious, he was definitely up to something. Setting himself up for a more credible run in the future? Building up his donor database? Who knew? He had some kind of plan.

My guess was it was for something bad.

I was still on the computer when the sun rose. I hadn't turned up anything scandalous or useful.

But I did have an idea.

According to Locke's site, his campaign headquarters were in New York City, near the Times Square area. It seemed incongruous—shouldn't a conservative candidate with his credentials be running his campaign from Arkansas or Mississippi or somewhere else they taught creationism in the public schools? His Web site addressed the issue:

"We've chosen to establish our beachhead in New York City for a reason—to show that good, God-fearing people who want this country to return to its core principles are everywhere. The beating heart of America's financial and media empires mustn't be left to the liberal elite. Father Jacob's messages of faith, fidelity, and family values are for all Americans to hear. But we need your help! Click below to make a contribution of time or money to help us take back America."

Below were links to "Contribute" or "Volunteer."

I clicked on the latter. The linked page explained that perspective volunteers should feel free to come by the office any weekday, from nine to six, to fill out an application.

Sounded like a plan to me.

27

Ordinary Miracles

At seven, I headed out to the gym and punished myself through a heavy back and legs routine, followed by thirty minutes on the elliptical. I picked up a protein drink and drank it on the way home. On my corner, I stopped at the local deli to get some milk, bananas, and bread.

"Hey, Kevin," I heard from behind me. I turned around and saw a face I never expected to see in my neighborhood grocery.

Or anywhere else, for that matter.

"Marc!" I said, giving him a big hug. "I can't believe you're here!"

Marc looked down sheepishly. "Ta-da."

Marc Wilgus was a former client of mine. Handsome, charming and supersmart, Marc was a computer genius. His specialty was hacking. But he was no crook. Marc could break into any computer system anywhere in the world. Companies and governments paid him hundreds of thousands of dollars to identify the holes in their networks and develop the tools to patch them.

You'd never think anyone with his looks and money would need the services of a professional sex worker such as myself except for one small problem—he was a total agoraphobic.

Marc lived his whole life in his spacious, high-tech apartment where his every need was either met online or delivered to his door. Like I used to be.

I really liked Marc. So much so that, after Marc helped save my life a few months ago, I had to stop working for him. It was pretty obvious he was developing feelings for me, and likewise, me for him.

I was honest with him. I told him that what was growing between us was more than a business relationship, and that we had to figure out what we wanted to do about that. Marc admitted he was falling for me and that he thought it was best we stop seeing each other.

After one last fling in the sack, and a somewhat teary goodbye, I thought I'd never see him again.

"What are you doing"—I couldn't think of a polite way to put it, so I just said—"out?"

Marc looked a little pale and wide-eyed. "Pretty amazing, huh?"

I couldn't help but hug him again. "I'm so proud of you."

Marc hugged me back. Tightly. I could feel his heart pounding. "You still like that chai tea?"

"Live off the stuff."

"How about I take you to that Starbucks down the street and tell you about it?" He blushed furiously. "Unless you have somewhere else you need to be? I'm not sure what the protocol here is. . . . It's not like I run into a lot of people in my apartment."

"No," I said, remembering I had nothing on my calendar until a nooner with a podiatrist on Sixth Avenue. "I'm totally free. Let's go grab a cup."

At the coffee shop, I got a better look at him. Marc was still as good-looking as ever, tall and thin, with a prominent nose and strong cheekbones. But there was tension in his body language that I wasn't used to. He was nervous.

"So," Marc said after a little small talk, as we sat across from each other in a small booth. "After you and I had our talk, you know, 'the' talk . . ."

I nodded.

"I realized it was time I ran a few diagnostics on myself. Turns out, not leaving your apartment for five years isn't normal." He gave a little sideways grin that made me want to kiss him. I sipped my too-hot tea to burn off the impulse.

"Who knew?" I offered.

"I had . . . issues, Kevin. Fears. There are reasons why I am the way I am, but they're not important.

"What was important is that when you walked out that door the last time, I wanted to run after you. I really did.

"I made it as far as the lobby of my building before collapsing to the floor. A full-blown anxiety attack. I'd never had one before. I thought I was going to die.

"The doorman found me hyperventilating in a fetal position and called an ambulance. By the time it arrived, I was already back in my apartment, trying to catch my breath by breathing into a paper bag."

"Marc," I said, "I'm so sorry. I didn't know. I would have been there."

"It wasn't your fault. It wasn't so bad. I didn't have to go to the hospital or anything. I explained to the paramedics what happened, they took my readings, gave me a Valium, and suggested I get some help.

"So I did. It took five weeks before I was able to find a psychiatrist who was willing to see me in my apartment. But that's what I needed. Baby steps. Then, bigger steps. Then the first steps out the door. Now, I take two or three walks a day, always different paths, each one a little longer than the day before."

Marc was drinking black coffee. He twirled the cup restlessly. "God, when I tell you this, it all sounds so crazy. You must think I'm really fucked up."

"Can I be honest with you, Marc? I don't know if it's because of my line of work, or because of my family, but I think *most* people are really fucked up." I reached across the table and took his non-coffee-twirling hand in mine. "Thing is, *you're* actually doing something about it. Do you know how few people ever admit to their demons, let alone face them down?

"I think you're pretty amazing."

Marc squeezed my hand. "Wow. I can't believe how much I'm feeling right now. That's one of the things about my . . . condition. I pretty much controlled everything. Nothing arrived in my world unless I sent out for it. I didn't have to worry about feeling surprised, or scared, or hurt.

"I didn't have to feel anything, really.

"Out here"—he looked around the Starbucks as if it was an alien world he'd just discovered—"it's so much more frightening. So many possibilities. When I write code, I create a world. I control the world. Here . . . anything can happen. For so long, that seemed like a risk I couldn't afford, you know?"

He chewed his lower lip in another move that made me want to kiss him.

"But right now, running into you like this," he continued, "I realize . . . OK, let me tell it to you like this: One day, when I was trying to describe to my therapist all the things I was afraid could happen to me in the 'real world,' he asked, 'Did it ever occur to you that something *good* could happen, too?'

"It hadn't. It really never occurred to me that something good could happen out here. But, look. Today, I ran into a friend in the street. A friend I really missed.

"Something happened that I didn't program or order and it was great. It made me happy."

Marc blushed again. "OK, I know you're not really my friend, I get that, we had a business relationship, but I think of you as a friend, Kevin, I do, and I'm happy." A tear rolled down his cheek.

That was it. I stood up, leaned across the table, and kissed him on the lips. At first, he straightened as if to pull away. I didn't know if it was because he was shocked, or afraid to kiss another man in a public place, or what, but I was relentless.

After a few moments, he started kissing back, and it was so sweet and good that it made me remember why I had to stop seeing him.

I sat back down.

"Wow," he said. "This leaving-the-house stuff really pays off, doesn't it?"

"Listen," I said to him. "I know this is all kind of Strange New World for you, and I don't want to lay too much truth on you at once, but let's get one thing straight—I *am* your friend, OK? If I wasn't, if I didn't have genuine feelings for you, I'd be happy to still make five hundred bucks off your ass every two weeks or so, right?"

Marc blushed and laughed again. He ran a nervous hand through his thick curly hair. "I guess."

Marc was such an incredible catch. I used to think, *If he'd only go out, I'd be going out with him.*

Now, my head was so full of Tony, I knew there was no room for Marc in there.

Seeing how vulnerable and raw Marc was, I knew the worst thing I could do would be to start something with him that I couldn't finish.

But I was really, really tempted. Because if he thought that kiss was a good reward, my apartment was less than a half block from here, and I could bring him home and show him just how pleasant running into an old friend *really* could be. I could take him to my bed and . . . no!

Focus, Kevin, focus.

"So," Marc said, trying his best to sound casual. "Are you still seeing that cop?"

"Yeah," I said. "We're kind of serious."

Marc nodded and tried not to look disappointed. "That's great. And are you still . . . hustling?"

"Yeah, gotta pay the rent."

"How does that work? I mean, you do what you do, which is kind of illegal, right? But he's a cop, pretty straight-laced from what you told me, so how do you make that work?"

Wow. Marc was kind of perceptive. "It's not easy," I said. "We don't talk about it. But it's there, and it's a problem."

"Doesn't he bug you to quit?"

"We've fought about it, but I'm not about to be forced out of doing something I love and make good money at just because Tony doesn't like it."

"You know," Marc said, "when I'm coding a program, I can write a million lines and everything's going great when, all of a sudden, the whole thing comes crashing down. So, I have to go back, over every line, every value, until I find that one wrong phrase or bit of bad code that brings the entire system to its knees."

"OK," I said. I wasn't sure what we talking about anymore. I wondered how much medication it took to get Marc out of the house.

"You don't get it, do you?"

"Something about computers?"

"Something about *you*, Kevin. Listen, if things had gone differently between us, if I had been a little bit less crazy a little sooner, maybe we could have had something, right?"

"I know," I said. "I kind of wish things had gone differently, too. But the chips fell where they did and . . ."

Marc held out his hand "Stop. That's not where I was going with this. Just listen, OK."

I took another sip of tea.

"If I had been saner faster, maybe it'd be me dating you, Kevin, not him. But that's not what happened and I don't want you to walk away thinking, 'Oh, that was about poor pathetic Marc trying to get back with me,' because it's not. No, what I want to tell you is this: If I were your boyfriend, there's no fucking way I'd let you stay out there and have sex with other men, let alone hustle."

"It's barely sex," I said. "Sometimes I don't even take my clothes off. My last client just wanted to give me pretend laughing gas while he takes advantage of me in my stupor."

"See," Marc said. "That's what I'm talking about. He says he's giving you something perfectly safe, and you still wind up in a stupor. Who knows what you're breathing in?"

"I'm not actually breathing in anything. Well, other than air. He just puts a teacup over my nose." Marc looked at me as if I were speaking Esperanto. "OK, it sounds strange, but to each his own, right? The point is, I'm not really at any risk. It's easy money. I have another customer who, once a month, just like to watch me take a shower and smell my wet hair. Then there's Mr. Tickle who, well, you can probably figure out that one on your own."

"Jesus," Marc said, "we just used to make out and screw. Maybe I was missing out on something." He arched his eyebrows suggestively.

"Don't worry," I said. "Maybe if you're real good, I'll let you put a teacup on my nose one day, too." Marc laughed. "No, but seriously, these guys have harmless kinks. I really feel like I'm helping them. What's the big deal?"

"I still wouldn't let you do it, Kevin. I'm sorry. I just couldn't take the idea of you being out there, putting yourself at risk. And, I have to admit, it would probably drive me crazy with jealousy."

"Listen, wait till you get to know me better. My being a sex worker is one of my least annoying qualities, believe me."

Marc grinned. "I doubt that. But it's not the point. I'm a liberal-bordering-on-treasonous computer hacker and I couldn't date you if you continued to hustle. Your boyfriend Tony's a hard-ass conservative New York Cop. Why isn't he insisting you stop?"

Holy shit. Had I spent so much time working on my List of Things Tony Wasn't Willing to Give Up to Be with Me that I forgot to take a look at what *I* wasn't willing to give up for *him?*

I waited for Marc to ask me the obvious question: "If you really love Tony, why don't you stop doing the thing you know he can't accept?"

Which is why I was surprised when he said, "If he's willing to put up with you hustling, I wonder what secrets *he's* keeping."

"Saywhanow?"

"I figure it's a trade-off. He doesn't push you on your job, because there's something he doesn't want you to push him on. Right?"

There are things I can't talk about with you.

"No," I said. "That's not it. He just doesn't want to force me to quit something I want to do."

"Because he's so easygoing?"

"I wouldn't exactly describe him as 'easygoing.'"

"So, why do *you* think he doesn't make you quit?"

Truth to tell, since it worked out conveniently for me, it wasn't a question I'd ever asked. "I don't know. Because he loves me?"

Marc reached over and mussed my hair. "I'm sure he does, Kevin. And it's none of my business. Look at me: A few months of therapy and I'm giving relationship advice." He chuckled. "Sorry about that."

I smiled, hoping it didn't look as shaky as it felt. "No probs."

"It's the hacker in me. Always looking for the flaws in the system. Sorry to get all Dr. Phil on you. What else are you up to?"

To get us both off the topic of Tony, I told Marc about Randy's accident, the other deaths, and what led me to suspect Jacob Locke.

"I thought that maybe if I volunteered at his campaign office," I wrapped up, "I might be able to get close to him. Maybe I'd get a vibe from him, or stumble across something."

Marc narrowed his eyes and frowned. "It sounds dangerous."

"I'm not looking to make a citizen's arrest. I just want to get a feel for him. But, talking it through with you now, it sounds kind of unlikely. I mean, even if I went there, I'd probably never get close to him. The guy's a lightning rod—I'm sure they screen who gets to meet him."

"You promise you're not going to put yourself in any danger?"

I crossed my heart. "Scout's honor. Why?"

"If you're determined to do this, we can probably get you right next to him. It just calls for some social engineering."

It wasn't a phrase I was familiar with. "We're going to build something?"

"Kind of," Marc said. "We're gonna build a new you."

28

Don't Rain on My Parade

After Marc told me what he had in mind, we said good-bye to get started on his plans.

I went back to my apartment, sent him some JPEGs he asked for, and quickly showered and changed for my meeting with Dr. Franklin Mitnick, a podiatrist with a foot fetish. After he noisily shot while buffing my left sole with a pumice stone, I had to ask him a question that'd been bothering me since our first session.

"Don't your 'interests' make your job kind of hard?"

Dr. Mitnick wiped his spooge up from the floor. "How do you mean?" He was a fifty-something man who, with his pink skin, shapeless body, and bald head, reminded me of a boiled and peeled shrimp. He put the wet paper towels to his side.

"Aren't you, like, in a state of constant excitement working around feet all day?"

"Oh dear, no." Dr. Mitnick waved his hand to say *pshaw*. He reached for a bottle of lotion and started rubbing some into my feet. "By the way, do you mind if I do this? You mustn't exfoliate without adequate hydration afterward."

It felt like a dream come true. "No, hydrate away." The bracing scent of lime drifted up to me.

"Marvelous. As to your previous query"—Dr. Mitnick had a precise way with language that always made me think he should have a British accent instead of his flat Upstate New York twang—"the feet I see here are calloused and injured and old. But these"—he dug his fingers into my heel—"these are perfection. So smooth, so delicious, so clean." He licked his lips and began to breathe a little heavier.

What he was doing felt so good that I normally would have let him continue. But I had places to go.

"Thanks, doc," I said, pulling my foot away. He gave a little whimper. Sorry, dude. "Can you hand me my sock?"

"I'll get it for you," he said, rolling the sock over my toes with the care and reverence of an archeologist sliding a rare and precious find into a specimen bag. "My pleasure."

I went back to my place and checked my e-mail. There it was: A note from Marc telling me the deed was done. Boy worked fast. I checked out a few links Marc included in his note and was amazed at what he was able to achieve.

Mad genius, indeed.

A lot of people think that because I'm a male hustler I have to dress provocatively all the time. It's pretty much the opposite. I meet most of my clients at their apartment buildings or hotel rooms, and they usually appreciate if I arrive looking as conservative as possible. Strangely enough, most men don't want a young guy whose outfit screams "gay whore" showing up at their door. Go figure.

So, I have a large selection of what I call my "young Republican" drag. For my first trip to Jacob Locke's headquarters, I selected khaki Banana Republic slacks, a white Nordstrom brand button-down shirt, and a blue Brooks Brothers blazer. Brown Oxfords and a brown belt completed my transformation into someone who wouldn't look out of place at Liberty University. I laid everything out on the bed and was about to get changed when I realized I needed navy socks, too. Alas, a thorough review of my sock drawer made it clear I didn't have any clean ones.

I went to my overflowing laundry basket and started looking for the least raunchy worn ones. Sniffing each carefully (Dr. Mitnick would have been in heaven), I found two that matched and didn't smell too bad.

OK, but it was definitely time to get my clothes washed. I usually brought my laundry to the cleaners on the corner. After losing an iPod, a watch, and God knows how much cash, though, I learned to check my pockets first.

Since I figured I'd drop off the laundry on my way to Locke's office, I went through it, finding a ten-dollar bill in the pocket of a pair of sweatpants and my ATM card in my gym shorts. Sweet.

At the bottom of the pile were Tony's jeans. Aw, I was his laundry-whore. How romantic.

I didn't mind. In my head, I played my favorite song for doing domestic chores: "Housewife," by the super-talented and cute Jay Brannan, a folksinger I had a bit of a crush on.

Did I want to be Tony's wife? Well, duh. I mean, a wife with a cleaning woman and a personal chef, please, but still, *yes*.

Which made me think of Marc's remarks from earlier this morning. Did Tony refrain from nagging me about *my* work because he didn't want me looking too closely at what *he* was up to?

Naw, not Tony. He was ambivalent and conflicted, but he wasn't a cheat. He told me he wasn't ready for a commitment and we had a somewhat (on my part) begrudgingly open relationship. So, what could there be to hide?

I checked his jeans. Maybe I'd make a buck. No such luck. Just some string, a Dentyne wrapper, and a movie ticket. Had we gone to see something recently? Not that I remembered. I checked the stub.

Super Rangers.

The movie I had asked—begged—him to see with me. The one he told me he'd *never* go to, because it was for kids. A waste of his time.

But someone got him to go. I checked the date on the ticket stub. A Saturday afternoon two weeks ago. I remembered that day. We usually spent Saturdays together, but he'd told me he had to work.

He lied to me.

I wonder what secrets he's keeping? Marc had said.

I'd dismissed him, but maybe he was smarter than I knew.

If Tony wasn't lying to me about wanting to sleep with women, why would he hide something as insignificant as having seen a movie?

Why do we tell small lies? To distract from the big ones.

Tony was seeing someone else. I knew that was a possibility. But I could never imagine he'd take that person—a boy?, a girl?—to something he knew I wanted to do, and then lie to me about it.

Unless the person was important to him.

How do you know if it's love or pain?

I still had Jay's "Housewife" playing in my head, but this time, the closing verse: "We haven't met yet." It reminded me that, even in song, the housewife fantasy isn't always meant to be.

Had I not met my soul mate yet, either? Would things never be right for Tony and me?

Fuck it, I thought. *Regrets are for losers.* I'd figure out Tony's Big Lie later.

Now, I had a job to do. I had someone else to be. It was show time.

29

New York State of Mind

Not only was John Locke's campaign headquarters in New York, but it was in Times Square, the dark heart of the city's carnal excesses. Despite various attempts to clean it up, Times Square still felt seedy and wild. I lived off Eighth Avenue, and on my thirty-block walk uptown to Locke's office, I passed about twenty-five adult boutiques, X-rated video stores, and peep shows.

I guess the efforts to neuter Times Square were as successful as every other attempt to suppress human sexuality, which is to say, a total bust.

My nice-boy Oxfords weren't the greatest walking shoes, but I hoped the long hike would take my mind off Tony.

To further distract myself, I played The Pedestrian Game, in which I pick a person walking twenty feet ahead of me and hurry to catch up. Once I pull alongside him, I pick another target and chase her, and so on, constantly challenging myself to reach the next goal.

Because the streets of New York are always so crowded, it's not just a matter of walking fast—you have to weave in and out of the foot traffic, dodging, sidestepping, and slipping between wherever possible. Speed isn't enough; you have to be crafty.

It takes a lot of concentration to play The Pedestrian Game. It's a good workout, too. By the time I reached the storefront that served as Locke Central, I was a little sweaty, had put Tony out of my mind, and was looking forward to not being Kevin Connor for a while.

* * *

The former retail space occupied by Locke for President wasn't fancy, but it was festive. Everywhere you looked hung red, white, and blue posters with the phrase, "For our country, for our families, for our future—Locke now!"

Desks with phones and computers were somewhat haphazardly placed wherever an electrical outlet or phone jack allowed. A large map on one wall was dotted with pushpins. Another wall had an oversized calendar with events penciled in. Omnipresent were photos of Locke himself, sometimes kindly, sometimes stern, always looking at you with the direct gaze of a particularly earnest salesman.

I wouldn't describe the place as busy. More than half the desks were empty. While every other campaign office I ever visited was filled with ringing phones and young people, Locke's space was quiet and staffed mostly by senior citizens. I noticed a few people dressed in clerical garb collating papers and stuffing envelopes. At the far end of the room, outside a closed office door, a guy who looked to be in his forties, young for the room, typed furiously. The whole scene was a little depressing.

"Can I help you?" asked a woman at the bridge table that had been set up by the door. She put down the book she'd been reading and smiled at me. Fifty-something, I guessed, with a round face and pale smooth skin that spoke of a lifetime of avoiding cigarettes, alcohol, and the sun. She wore a dark blue cashmere turtleneck with a string of simple pearls. I noticed the book she put aside was *The Holy Spirit: Activating God's Power in Your Life*, by Billy Graham. She wore a nametag: Lucille.

"Hi," I answered, giving her my best Sunday school smile. "I'm here to volunteer on the campaign."

"Well, bless your heart," she answered, her voice musical. "We can certainly use more young folk around here. Come along." I thought I detected a bit of a Southern accent in her lilt and I wondered if she came to New York just to work on the campaign.

She led me to a long folding table against the wall facing her desk. She selected some papers from a hanging rack, like the kind that hold magazines at a dental office, and handed them to me. "Now, why don't you fill these out and bring them back to me. Someone from the campaign will go over them, see where you'd do the most good, and get back to you in a couple of days."

"OK," I said. "Although I really am anxious to start."

"Well, you know what they say. 'Those who are patient inherit what has been promised,'" she trilled.

Actually, I didn't know anyone who ever said anything remotely like that.

"Yes, ma'am," I answered equally cheerily. "Good things come to those who wait!"

Lucille beamed.

"Oh!" she said sharply, a sudden frown crossing her face. Had I already done something to blow my cover? "I didn't give you a pen! Let me fetch you one."

I reached into my jacket and pulled out an expensive Montblanc that had been given to me by my late friend Allen Harrington. "I brought my own."

"Handsome *and* clever," Lucille chirped. "I bet the girls are all over you."

Not exactly. What would the proper Christian response be? "I'm saving myself for marriage"? Probably too much. I decided to just smile.

Lucille smiled back.

Now, we were both smiling at each other. I waited for her to say something, or leave, but she just kept smiling. Is this what nice people did? I guessed she really *wasn't* from New York.

"OK," I said, trying to sound even more chipper than before, "I better get to work!" I waved my pen to remind her what I was supposed to be doing.

"You just give me a shout if you need anything, honey."

I waited till Lucille's happy ass was seated back at her desk and surreptitiously slipped my iPhone from my pocket. I crooked my arm to hide it from view.

I opened up the e-mail Marc sent me earlier today and copied the information from it onto the volunteer application. As I wrote, I looked around. Not too much, though—the pace of the geezers who were working there was pretty glacial, and I didn't want to startle them with any quick movements. I saw Lucille talking to the guy I noticed earlier in the back, then watched as she drifted back to her desk.

"All finished," I announced, as I handed her my forms. "I hope I hear from you soon."

Lucille (shocker alert!) smiled even more broadly than she had earlier. "You're a lucky boy today"—she looked at my sheet—"Kevin Johnson!"

Marc had suggested I not use my real last name.

"I am?"

"Why, yes, you are! Remember how I told you it takes a few days for us to get back to you? Usually, newcomers have to wait until our volunteer coordinators review their applications. But today, Mr. Jason Carter, our very own chief of staff, the man closest to the man himself, has offered to meet with you." Her awed voice and wide-open eyes let me know his was an honor far beyond anything I could have imagined.

"Wow," I said. "Lucky me." I wasn't particularly looking forward to meeting whatever creep would serve as Locke's right-hand man.

"Come on then." She grabbed my hand. "You don't keep a man like Jason Carter waiting!"

Maybe you don't keep Jason Carter waiting, but the reverse isn't true. At least it wasn't that day, as Lucille and I stood by his desk for five minutes while he talked on the phone and ignored us. His head was down as he listened and spoke intently into the handset.

"No, no . . . we'll have to see. Right. Uh-huh. We can do it on the ninth, but only if Locke gets to speak before the senator. Right, *before*. Uh-huh, uh-huh, I know, I know, but he has to go first. Why? Because I want the audience *awake* for him, Roger. You know as well as I that Senator Franklin puts a crowd to sleep faster than a stallion takes to a mare. Uh-huh, yeah, well, I've seen the senator's polling and I think we do him more good than he does us at this stage, so that's the way it has to be. I surely would appreciate if you could make that happen. You can? That's great. We'll see you on the ninth then, Roger. Good job."

As Jason talked, I studied his work area. Messy, but in a way that looked productive, as if he didn't have time to be fastidious. On the credenza behind him, a photo of his wife and two children, a family so perfect they looked like the picture you get when you buy the frame.

Jason hung up the phone and shook his head, chuckling to himself. Lucille cleared her throat. "Mr. Carter?"

Jason looked up. My first impression was surprise—he looked even younger than from across the room. I'd put him at around thirty-five. He had bright red hair in a military buzz and a red-head's fair complexion. Blue eyes and freckles made him look even younger. He had a medium build, neither heavy nor particularly slim. It certainly wasn't a gym body, but he looked healthy and in good proportion.

His poly-cotton white shirt was wrinkled, with a coffee stain on the left sleeve. A red tie was loosely knotted around his neck. I couldn't see his slacks behind the desk, but I'd bet even money they were Dockers. I noticed the wedding ring on his left hand.

Jason wasn't traditionally handsome, but he had an appeal, and when he saw us and smiled to reveal white even teeth and an unexpected dimple, he went up a grade or two. His slight Southern accent was also pretty charming.

"Miss Lucille," he chided, "I've done told you, 'Mr. Carter' is my Pa. You can call me Jason."

"Now, you're in charge around these here parts, Mr. Carter, and you don't go around calling the boss by his first name. It ain't proper."

For a quick second, I had the surreal feeling that I was watching Aunt Bee lecture Opie on *The Andy Griffith Show.*

"Fine, fine," Jason relented. "Thank you very much, Miss Lucille. I'll take it from here."

Lucille squeezed my arm. "Good luck, honey." She handed Jason my volunteer forms and floated away.

Jason gestured to a chair facing his desk. "All right, chief, take a load off. Kevin, right?"

"That's right," I said, extending my hand. "Kevin Johnson. It's a pleasure to meet you, Mr. Carter."

"Tell you what," he said, leaning forward and resting his hand on his chin. "I'll make ya a deal. You call me 'Jason' and you're hired."

"OK, Jason," I answered.

Jason grinned and let out a sigh of release. "My Lord, I do miss hearing my first name around here. I'll be frank with you, Kevin, the average age of the person who walks through those doors"—he pointed to the front of the room—"is somewhere between fifty and death. When Miss Lucille told me you were here to help out, I figured I better grab ya before you leave, thinking you wandered into one of them senior citizen homes by mistake."

I grinned, too. I kind of expected to hate everyone here, but Jason didn't seem too bad. "Well," I said, "I left my walker and colostomy bag at home today."

Jason threw back his head and roared with laughter. You could see he didn't get much chance to cut loose much around here. A few heads turned toward us, their attention drawn by the unusual outburst.

Jason leaned back toward me. "That was a good one, chief. I needed that." He darted his eyes around the room. "Some of the folks around here," he whispered, "seem to think they're in church. That's why it's so darned quiet around here all the time. My Lord, I've been to funerals more lively than this place."

It was my turn to laugh.

Jason looked down at my volunteer form. "Now, let's see, Kevin Johnson. I know you can make me laugh. But who are you, really?"

30

Don't Believe
Everything You Read

Watching Jason read over my application was a little like listening to his phone call. "Uh-huh," he mused to himself. "OK. Well, well. Look at that. You don't say . . . huh."

None of the comments were directed toward me, but they were about me. Well, not about *me*, exactly. Kevin Johnson may have had my face and my first name, but after that, the similarities ended. Kevin Johnson was the brainchild of my friend and former client, Marc Wilgus, who created him out of imagination, technology, and a strong desire to discover the truth about Jacob Locke.

"You know I'm a hacker," Marc had explained to me earlier that day at the coffee shop, "so you probably think what I do has a lot to do with computers, right?"

I nodded.

"And it does. But you know what the most vulnerable part of any system is, Kevin?"

"The Internet connection?" I guessed.

"The people. A big part of my job isn't finding the holes in the software, it's finding the vulnerabilities and desires of the people who operate it."

Huh, I thought. *Kind of like my job.*

"Have you ever heard of 'social engineering'?" Marc asked.

"Nope."

"Social engineering is the act, well, the art really, of manipulating people into doing things that divulge personal or sensitive information about themselves or the companies they work for. It's a kind of con game, a way of establishing confidence with your target and exploiting his weaknesses for personal gain.

"Computer programs have bugs, right? So do people. In the biz, we call them 'cognitive biases.' People are programmed to respond to certain things in certain ways.

"Let me give you an example. Let's say you take a group of people and put them in an art gallery. You show them a canvas of some red splotches of paint and ask them to rate it. Most would say it's terrible, that it looks like something a child would do.

"But what if, just before you ask them for their opinions, you arrange for them to 'accidently' overhear an art critic describe it as a work of great value. Now, the same people who dismissed the painting as a piece of junk rate it much higher. That's called the 'authority bias.' People unconsciously allow their own common sense and perception of the world to be altered by a perceived authority on a topic.

"Here's another example of cognitive bias. Let's say I flip a coin five times and it comes up heads. What are the odds that the next flip will turn up tails?"

"Math isn't really my strong suit. Do you have any questions about fellatio?"

Marc gave me a stern look.

"OK," I said, "well, since the last five times were heads, let's say six to one you'll get tails."

"Nope." Marc smirked. "It's still fifty-fifty. You're assuming that future probabilities are altered by past events, but they're not. The coin doesn't know it's 'due' to be tails. You just exhibited what we call 'the gambler's fallacy.' "

"Told you I wasn't good at math." I pouted.

"OK, so we know that people have flaws, right? Well, social engineering exploits those flaws. For example, let's say I want to get into the computer systems at a local bank, OK?"

I nodded.

"So, I get a phone directory and start calling people randomly. Whenever I get someone on the line, I tell them that I'm calling from technical support about the ticket they sent in. Ninety-nine percent are going to say they didn't submit anything, right? But eventually, I'll find someone who says, 'Oh yeah, thanks for calling back.' The game is on.

"I ask them to tell me what the trouble is, and then tell them to connect to a Web site I've set up with a file that will fix their machine. Of course, the file they download and install isn't a fix at all—it's really a keystroke capturer that records everything they do on their computers and sends it to me. Or, it's a virus or malware or some other destructive program. In any case, it's the person who was to blame, not the software. Make sense?"

"Perfect."

"So, we're going to social engineer the Locke campaign. We know what they want, right? A bright young guy with solid conservative experience and credentials. That's going to be you."

"How?"

"I do this kind of thing all the time, Kevin. Just give me some information, send me a picture or two of yourself, and I'll e-mail you your new identity in a few hours."

After a few more minutes reviewing my paperwork, Jason looked at me with love in his eyes. Not the kind of love I'm used to getting from a man, mind you, which usually involves a desire to get me naked as quickly as possible, but with genuine respect, curiosity, and admiration for my intellectual achievements.

It was a nice to be looked at that way for a change.

"Wow, you certainly are an impressive young man. President of the Student Republican Club at your college? An article in the *Philadelphia Bee* on 'The Tyranny of Political Correctness'?"

I tried to look humble.

"It says here you started a Facebook group called Generation Sane: Young People to Protect the Sanctity of Marriage. Do you really have over one thousand five hundred followers signed up there?"

"Check it out," I said.

"I think I will," Jason said, setting his fingers on the keyboard. A minute later, he was on what looked like an official Facebook page, complete with friends, comments, and events. My picture was in the corner, along with a biography that conformed to the information I'd put on my application. If he clicked on something, it would take him to a similarly realistic link that made the whole thing appear on the up-and-up.

Similarly, if he Googled Kevin Johnson's article on political correctness, it would lead to a reprint of an article Marc had found somewhere, replacing the real byline with Kevin Johnson's.

In his note to me, Marc explained that he created fake identities for himself all the time. He had completely convincing Web sites for schools that didn't exist (like the one where I was the leader of budding conservatives), newspapers that were never printed (the *Philadelphia Bee*?), and pages on social networking sites for all kinds of people who existed only in cyberspace. He just plugged "Kevin Johnson's" information into one of his dummy sites and, all of a sudden, I had a virtual identity that was every bit as convincing as a real one.

Social engineering. Find out what someone wants and give it to him. Play into his insecurities and biases. Be endorsed by authorities—if Kevin Johnson was good enough to be published by the *Philadelphia Bee* and had one thousand five hundred followers on Facebook, he must be a pretty smart kid, right?

While I watched, Jason read through some of the incredibly supportive comments on "my" Facebook page and clicked through to read Kevin Johnson's thoughts on why we needed to return to the traditional values that made this nation great.

If Jason looked in love before, he was now ready to marry me. "You should have *my* job," he said. "You, young man, are the kind of person this campaign needs to reach. Smart, articulate, and committed to the issues."

I blushed. Even though the person who so impressed Jason wasn't really me, I felt absurdly flattered by this attractive, sincere man.

"And you know what I like?" Jason continued. "There's none of that 'us versus them' in your writing. Those people who go on about a 'culture war.' I hate that kind of talk. Who are we at war with? Our neighbors? The guy at the gas station? I have a sister who's a lesbian; am I supposed to hate her? It's like the left hand fighting with the right. It's crazy. We're all people. We just have to get along."

If ever there was a speech I didn't expect to hear from Jacob Locke's chief of staff, that was it. I must have looked surprised, because Jason started to chuckle again.

"Now, don't get all skittish on me, boy. I'm not saying there's no 'right' and 'wrong.' I'm just saying it ain't the same as good versus bad. We're all God's children. I love my sister, and I wish her the best, but I don't want to have to explain to my kids that Auntie Bess and Auntie Mimi got married. I love children, but I don't want my tax dollars teaching sixth graders how to use condoms. I love my country, but . . . Aw, why am I telling you all this? You could probably say it better than me."

I was blushing again. OK, I didn't agree with everything Jason Carter said, but he wasn't the awful bigot I'd expected.

"That's the thing that gets to me." Jason slumped his chair, looking exhausted. "Here we are, in New York City, trying to build bridges, but everyone around here treats us like we're hateful zealots. They act like all we do is sow discord and fight, but Jacob Locke's message is really one of love and healing. Maybe we don't do such a good job putting it out there, but, Lordy, why else would we be here? We go on the Sunday talk shows, and we want to talk about Locke's positive vision for our country, but they only want to focus on the most divisive issues. Get that sound bite. It's like we keep getting tricked, and I don't know why."

As someone pulling one of those tricks even as he spoke, I was starting to feel guilty.

"You've done campus organizing—you must know how those of us who support traditional values are always being tarred and feathered. How did you do it?"

"I just put myself in His hands and do whatever the man

wants from me." I was describing what I did in my real job, but they say it's always best to speak from experience.

Jason looked at me intently. Studying. Then he jabbed his finger at me. "You have to meet him."

"Who?"

"Jacob Locke, of course. He needs to see there are young people like you, supporting him, believing in him. You know, it's always the lead horse who has to suffer the burden of the herd, and Locke's burdens are heavy, indeed. You want to help the campaign? Meet Jacob Locke and tell him what you just told me."

"Wow," I said. "Sure. I mean, that's great. I'd love to meet Mr. Locke. It's why I'm here." This was going better than I'd hoped. I owed Marc big.

"Great. He'll be in the office tomorrow. Can you come by around noon?"

"Absolutely."

"He's going to be pleased as a pig in poop to meet you, chief." I bet.

"I can't tell you," Jason said, looking genuinely relieved, "what a pleasure it has been to make your acquaintance. In a town where we've had such a harsh welcome, to meet a young man like you, well, it's pretty much restored my faith for the day, it has."

If I felt any lower, I could play handball off the gutter.

I came here looking for something that would expose Jacob Locke as a murderer. Now, the whole thing seemed like a ridiculous fantasy and I was the one feeling like a criminal. Jason seemed like a really nice guy; it was hard to believe he'd be associated with the monster I imagined Locke to be.

"Now, I'm just about to take this stack of media requests"— he pointed to a large pile on his desk—"and go through them to see what our man should be doing. You seem pretty savvy. How about you sit with me and we take a look at them? I'd like to hear your thoughts."

"I'd love to," I said.

Strange thing is, I wasn't lying.

31

What Are You Doing the Rest of Your Life?

I stayed at Locke's office for another couple of hours, helping Jason with the media requests and getting to know him better. At seven, he asked if I wanted to grab a bite with him, but I'd figured I'd done enough sleeping with the enemy for one day. I told him I had to go and decided to walk home, even in my uncomfortable shoes.

I needed to think.

It was a perfect fall night, the air crisp and clean. Leaves and litter crunched under my feet.

As much as I hated to admit it, I really enjoyed working with Jason. It made me feel good.

I liked him. He was a totally decent guy who came up to New York because he sincerely believed Jacob Locke was a good man who could lead our country to a better place.

Jason had a sweet sense of humor, worked eighteen hours a day for a cause he passionately believed in, and was committed to making a positive difference in this world.

He inspired me.

OK, maybe the specifics of his vision were different from mine, but at least he had one.

What did I have?

When Jason was reviewing "my" application, and praising "my" accomplishments, I couldn't help but feel proud, even if it was all a lie. To be admired by a good man like Jason felt affirming.

The funny thing, men admire me every day. But it's my tight ass, or my eight-pack, or the way my blond bangs fall over my eyes they applaud. My mind, my ideas, my achievements . . . not so much.

When was the last time someone genuinely appreciated something I did fully dressed?

If I were filling out an application for a real job, for a cause in which *I* believed, what could I put on it? Good role-playing skills and the ability to maintain an erection even with men I'm not attracted to? Kind to animals and tricks? Tight, gym-toned body with a nice-sized dick? Not exactly a Nobel Peace Prize–winning resume.

I wasn't ashamed of what I did. I just wasn't sure if it was enough. Yeah, volunteering at The Stuff of Life was a good deed, but was I capable of contributing more to the universe than supervising the assembly of boxed lunches and facilitating the erotic fantasies of strangers?

Or, for that matter, hanging on to Tony, a man who identified as straight and lied to me about his dates?

What was I *doing* with my life?

All these questions.

I needed some answers.

Focus, Kevin, focus.

I needed to figure out what I was going to do with the next sixty years. But, first, I needed to decide what I was going to do *next*.

I made a to-do list in my head:

1. Meet Jacob Locke tomorrow and see what I could find out.

2. Confront Tony. Maybe.

3. Check in with Freddy to see how things had gone with Cody.

There was something else I had to do. . . . What was it? Something wacky, I remember. Totally nuts. Who was the craziest person I knew?

Oh, yeah. *Her.*

I stopped at the next corner and stepped into the lobby of one of the nice hotels near Locke's office. Dressed as I was, I got nothing but smiles from the doorman and everyone in the lobby. Money loves money.

I fished a card out of my wallet and called the mobile phone number on it.

It was time once again for me to parent my mother.

Bats and Balls was a sports bar on Thirty-third and Ninth, and like many of the neighborhood's joints, it was mixed straight and gay. The person I called on behalf of my mother told me he was there with friends, and, since it was on the way home, I asked if I could meet him there.

Considering how strongly he'd come on to me the last time we met, I was surprised at his unenthusiastic, "Yeah, sure, whatever." Either he'd gotten over me real quick, or he was playing hard to get.

Turns out, it was neither.

Even from across the room, as I walked to the table where he sat with two guys and girl I recognized from the other day, I could see Andrew Miller looked exhausted and ill. Three days ago, at my mother's disastrous encounter with Yvonne, Andrew was the picture of vitality and strength. Now, he was as pale and drawn as Robert Pattinson in the *Twilight* movies, except without the sexy vampiric brooding and crazy hair.

No, Andrew's unhappiness looked all too human, and I had the terrible feeling my mother was to blame.

"Hey," I said, reaching his table. The bar was crowded and dark, the music low and thumping. LCD screens on the walls showed various sporting events from around the world, but no one seemed to be watching them. Certainly not anyone at Andrew's table, who all looked down at their beers as if something really interesting was about to emerge from them.

"Hey," Andrew said weakly. He gave me a sickly half smile and took a swig of his drink. "Guys," he said to his table mates,

"I'm going to catch up with Kevin for a little bit. Hold my seat, OK?"

His friends grunted their assent. None of them said hello to me or even met my glance. This was not going to go well.

Andrew stood up and, without another word, walked to an empty booth at the far corner of the room. I followed obediently.

"So," I said, sitting across from him, "what's going on?"

Andrew took another long slug from his bottle of beer, shook it to ascertain it was empty, and set it down with a bang. "Let's just say the last few days have pretty much been the worst of my life."

"Oh my God, I am so sorry," I said, meaning it. "She's my mother and I take full responsibility for . . ."

Andrew put up his hand. "Stop. It's not your fault, Kevin. Obviously. It's just a really bad situation."

"I know, but still . . ." I was about to apologize again, but a glare from Andrew convinced me otherwise. "What happened? Last time we talked, you said you didn't care what came next. Either Yvonne was going to fire you or you'd quit. You sounded like you were glad to have an excuse to get out of there. What changed?"

Andrew's forehead furrowed in anger and he scowled. "It wasn't that easy. Yvonne blamed me for the whole thing. But she told me she wasn't going to fire me. She wanted to keep me around to make me as miserable as I'd made her.

"I figured that was OK, I'd just quit. Then the executive producers of her show called me. They made it clear how connected and powerful they were. They said it was their job to keep Yvonne happy. If having me there for her to kick around did that, that's what was going to happen.

"They made it clear that if I quit, I'd never work in the industry again. They'd tell everyone how badly I fucked up. I mean, let's face it, I booked her with a guest who assaulted her!"

"Well, I wouldn't call it assault, exactly," I offered.

If looks could kill, Andrew's would have been guilty of first-degree murder.

"Yeah, well, the producers *would* call it assault. Let's be honest here, Kevin, so would most people. If someone didn't know what Yvonne did to provoke your mother, it would just look like your mother was a crazy person who I put in a position to attack the princess of talk TV. Some producer I am, right? It's my job to screen our guests. Who'd hire me now?"

"I guess Yvonne thinks most people would consider it assault, too," I admitted. I told Andrew about Yvonne's plan to sue my mother for everything she had. All of which probably wouldn't be enough to pay Yvonne's monthly dry-cleaning bills.

"She's so fucking evil." Andrew banged his fist on the table. "I can't tell you how horrible it's been to work with her these past few days. She openly insults me in front of everyone, calls me stupid or 'faggot' or, when she's really riled up, 'maricón.' She has me run some ridiculous errand for her, like fetching her a café latte and, when I bring it to her, throws it in my face, insisting she asked for a café mocha. It's so fucking humiliating.

"The worst part is, I'm completely trapped. My life is ruined and it sounds like she's going after your mother, too. I'm the one who's sorry, Kevin; I should never have dragged you and your family into this."

Andrew rubbed at his eyes. I couldn't tell if he had tears there or if he was just exhausted. He gave a bitter little laugh. "All because I wanted to see you again, Kevin. 'Cause I wanted to get into your pants. Maybe Yvonne is right. I do think with my dick."

"Listen," I said to him. "The only thing Yvonne is right about is not letting you quit. Because you're probably the best producer she'll ever have. You think that show is a hit because of her? No way. It's how you package and present her that works. Making that nasty skank into America's sweetheart takes a special kind of magic, Andrew, and you're the guy who makes it happen. I bet she knows that on some level, and that's the real reason she won't let you go."

Something related to a smile, maybe a third cousin, struggled across Andrew's lips. I think my little pep talk helped. But I wasn't done.

"About everything else," I continued, "Yvonne is dead wrong. And you know what her biggest mistake was? Fucking with my friends and family. I've spent my whole life standing up to bigger bullies than her. That bitch is going down."

Now, the smile on Andrew's face was halfway there. "Little tough guy, huh? Nice fantasy, Kevin. But she's rich, powerful, and protected. How are you going to fight back against someone like her?"

"Actually," I said, "I have an idea."

Andrew listened to me intently. As I explained my plan, he got increasing agitated, nodding and, eventually, smiling for real. It was nice to see.

"That just might work, Kevin. Holy shit. We might have her."

I grinned and pointed to my head. "Pretty *and* smart."

Andrew jumped out of his seat and slid next to me. He acted like his old self—athletic, graceful, and quick. Welcome back, buddy.

He threw an arm around my shoulder and pulled me toward him. His body felt warm and strong. I remembered just how muscular he was.

"You are a genius, Connor. I am totally, hopelessly, and forever in love with you. You *have* to come home with me right now. I'm going to screw you so hard you're going to see stars."

OK, maybe Yvonne was right about one more thing: Andrew really *did* think with his dick. If we stayed in contact when this was all over, I was going to have to work on that with him.

"You could do that," I said. "Or you could check out my idea and see if it'll work."

"Arrghh," Andrew said. "Decisions, decisions." But I could see he was dying to find out if I'd just handed him a Get Out of Hell Free card.

I kissed him on the cheek. "Go do what you need to do, Miller. You know how to find me."

"And we can get it on then?"

I was pretty sure the answer was no, but, I figured, let him live in hope. I gave him the answer I use on the toddlers in Sunday school whenever they make an unreasonable request. "We'll see."

"I'll take that as a yes!" Andrew said triumphantly. Yeah, the three-year-olds take it as yes, too. Ah, kids. Then, he added, "Unless you're still stuck on that screwed-up cop your mother told me about."

Not for the first time that week, I thought, *Thanks, Mom.* "He's not screwed up. He's just not up to a commitment right now. We have an open relationship."

Andrew pumped his fist. "You guys have an arrangement? Score one for the home team!" he shouted. I saw a few of the other customers look at him questioningly. We were in a sports bar after all. What game was he watching?

Andrew leapt up from the table again, full of energy and enthusiasm. He took my face in his hands and planted a long, hard kiss on my lips.

What the hell, I kissed him back. When he pulled away, I gave him a little push. "What are you waiting for, boy? Go!"

Andrew looked at me for a moment, and I think it was the first time he saw me as something other than a receptacle for his cock. He looked at me like a friend. "Thank you," he said.

He ran to his friends at the other table. "Guys, we have to call Gabe. Anyone have his number?"

32

Some Good Things Never Last

I walked home feeling pretty good. I couldn't exactly put it on my resume, but helping Andrew reminded me I have talents that don't involve the emission of bodily fluids.

Even if my plan didn't pan out, at least Andrew wasn't moping around like the living dead anymore.

I didn't know what I was going to do about Tony. It was clear he'd been keeping something from me for a while now. But I didn't want to confront him about it. Our relationship was tentative and fragile as it was. I was pretty sure that if insisted on a truth he wasn't ready to share, whatever we had would fall apart.

I wasn't ready to lose him.

I resolved not to say a word about the movie ticket I'd found. Tony'd tell me the truth when he was ready. I could wait.

What had Lucille from Locke's office said? *Those who are patient inherit what has been promised.*

Well, no one had promised Tony to me, but I intended to collect anyway.

Speak of the devil.

When I got to my door, Tony was waiting outside, looking all kinds of gorgeous in his brown corduroys and beige turtleneck. "Hey, kiddo," he said, "I was just about to give up on you."

"Why didn't you call?"

"I was in the neighborhood. I've only been here five minutes. Figured I'd see if I could surprise you."

"OK," I said. I looked at him standing there, six feet two inches of Italian pony boy whom I've loved from the moment I laid my eyes on him.

Such a good man, he was. A cop, for God's sake. Struggling with his sexuality not because he hated gay people, but because he didn't want to disappoint his family and friends. Because he wanted to "be good."

But why did being good have to preclude being mine? Did he think of me as a bad thing?

For the first time I could remember, I didn't want to touch him. As solid and strong as he was, I felt like my embrace would make him disintegrate like a ghost.

Tony noticed my standoffishness. "So, um, happy to see me?"

"Why did you lie to me?" I asked.

Wow. I didn't expect to say that. In fact, I had just resolved *not* to say that.

But as my friend JoAnne used to tell me, if it's on my lung, it's on my tongue. For better or worse, I can't keep my feelings bottled up. They spill.

A cloud passed over Tony's face. "What are you talking about?"

"About seeing *Super Rangers*. You told me you'd never see that movie. But I found a ticket stub in your pocket. So, why did you lie to me, Tony?"

"That? That was nothing." Tony walked toward me and started to put his arms around me. "Come on, let's talk about it upstairs."

"No," I said, pushing him away, suddenly furious. "Let's talk about it here, Rinaldi. 'Cause the thing about it is"—I felt myself start to choke up and I swallowed hard—"you're the person who *doesn't* lie to me. You're the person I trust, Tony. So, why?"

"Kevin." Tony tried stepping closer and I backed away.

"Why?"

"It's nothing."

But he wouldn't look at me when he said it, and I knew what that meant. "You're still lying, aren't you?"

"Can we have this discussion in your apartment, please?"

For some reason, the last thing I wanted was to talk about this inside. I had a feeling something very toxic was about to be released, and I didn't want it in my home. This needed to be aired out here, in the fresh evening breeze, where there was a chance it could blow away.

"No."

Tony's lips set in a straight line, becoming thinner and more strained as they did. His eyes narrowed and appeared darker. "All right," he said. "I lied, OK. I saw that stupid movie. Big fucking deal, Kevin. Can we get on with our lives now?"

Why do we tell small lies? I remembered thinking earlier. *To distract from the big ones.*

"Who did you see it with, Tony?"

"Kevin, we agreed not to talk about . . ."

"Who the *fuck* did you see the movie with, Tony?" The voice that came out me didn't sound like mine.

"It doesn't matter, Kevin."

The evening wasn't cold, but a chill ran through me. I felt the blood drain from my face. "There's someone else, isn't there?"

Tony's eyes widened and he sucked in his breath. He looked at me with the face of a stranger. "Yes, Kevin. There's someone else."

"Huh." I felt myself starting to tear up. I didn't want to say what I said next, but I felt like I'd come down with a sudden case of Tourette's, and I knew there was no stopping me now. "It's serious, isn't it?"

Tony worked his jaw from side to side. "Yeah, it's serious, Kevin."

"Serious in a way that means we can't be together?"

"I don't know. I'm trying to figure that out."

"And when were you planning on telling me that, Tony?"

"Kevin, you know I don't want to hurt you. . . ."

"Oh my God," I yelled. "Do you get paid every time you say that? Because that's always your excuse for holding back, for not being honest, for leaving! For a guy who doesn't want to hurt me . . ."

I guess to be a cop, you had to be quick, because before I even knew what was happening Tony had taken the three steps toward me and had me in his arms. "Don't say it," he said in my ear, his cheek pressed hotly against my forehead. "Please." I felt tears running down my face and realized, with a shock, that they were his.

We stood like that for a while, Tony shaking in my arms.

How do you know if it's love or pain?

"I love you so much," Tony said into my hair. "So much."

"I know," I said, stroking his hair.

Slowly, as if through some strange magic, I felt as if the power in our relationship was transferring from him to me. I ran my hands over his back and tried to soothe him. "It's OK, it's OK," I comforted him.

Tony was a good man. One lie, even a big one, didn't make him otherwise. Despite his tears, I knew he was a strong man, too. In one way or another, he was always going to be there for me.

What he wasn't, though, was *ready*. Whether he wasn't ready to be with another man, or ready to commit to me specifically, or ready to give up his dreams of a perfect suburban family, or ready to stand up for our love, I didn't know.

And you know what? It didn't matter. The bottom line was, he just wasn't ready.

If I had to be honest with myself, and this seemed like as good a time as any to start, this whole open relationship thing he wanted wasn't working for me, either.

It wasn't about the sex. If Tony wanted, or needed, to screw someone else every once in a while, I couldn't care less. Maybe we'd even have merry threesomes one day. As long as I got my share, he could do with his dick as he pleased.

But Tony's heart? *That,* I wanted. I wanted all of it. *Damn it,* I thought, *I've earned it.* I've certainly waited long enough.

I wanted to share my life with Tony. Not a few guilty evenings a week.

Tony's trying to keep me in his life was killing him. It was making him into someone he didn't want to be. He didn't want to lie to me, and he didn't want to hurt me. But here he was, keeping secrets and breaking my heart into a hundred million pieces.

Maybe someday we'd *both* be ready.

But not today.

Truth was, I'm the one thing Tony couldn't be strong about. I guess it was my turn to man up.

I let go of him. "You need to work some things out, Tony. You need to figure out where you want to go. But, you're never going to find your path if I'm standing in your way. So . . ." I pointed to my front door. "I'm going to go. And you're going to decide what you want."

Tony cocked his head to the side. His eyes were wet and red. "Kevin . . ." he began.

"No," I said, "I'm fine with it. I understand." I put a hand on his cheek, because I knew what I was about to say was going to hurt him.

"But I'm done. No more halfway, Tony. If you come back, I want all of you. No reservations, no ambivalence, no 'someone elses.' No secrets. Not from me. Not from anyone. That's the deal, Rinaldi.

"There are some things in life you have to pay a price for, Tony. I'm one of them. You can't have it both ways forever. You have to choose."

"I can't imagine not seeing you."

"I know the feeling."

"The worst part is," Tony said, his voice trembling, "I know you're right. I'm cheating you out of so much that you deserve. And I want to give it to you. It's just . . ."

I put my finger to his lips. "If it's right, Tony, if it's real, I'll be here. When you're ready."

A single tear spilled down his cheek. "What if you're not, Kevin? What if, by the time I figure out all the . . . moving pieces in my head and heart, what if you're not here anymore? What if you've moved on?"

I tried my best to smile. "Well, don't drag it out, Tony."

He chuckled through his tears. "Kevin, I know it's not perfect between us, and I know I have my issues, but I can't, I can't just leave."

Man up, Connor.

"I know," I said. "But I can."

And I did.

The short walk to the front door of my apartment building felt like a hundred-year march. At every step, I had to force myself not to turn around. Not to look back.

Never in my life have I had to so consciously will my legs to move. *Walk,* I commanded them. *One step in front of the other. Now another. Another. One more.*

As I reached the door, I thought I heard Tony call my name, but it might have been the wind or my own sad heart beating the sound of his voice.

I didn't look back.

I made it to my apartment just in time to explosively throw up in the kitchen sink. I don't know why they call the pain of a breakup "heartache." It always hits me in the gut.

As I was cleaning up, the phone rang. Tony? Already? For a moment, I was filled with joy.

I looked at the caller ID. It was Andrew.

I figured he must be calling to let me know if my plan worked.

It was pretty simple, really. I remembered that on the day of my mother's taping, Andrew and I were able to watch the incident between her and Yvonne on a monitor because the cameraman—Gabe, as Andrew had reminded me—had accidently left his camera running during a break. If Gabe still had that film, Andrew could use it to get the producers to back off him—and my mom.

They couldn't take him to court with that in his back pocket.

Anxious as I was to hear Gabe's answer, I couldn't talk to Andrew right now. I leaned against the counter until my iPhone beeped to let me know I had a voice mail. I hit "play."

"Hey, babe," Andrew said. He definitely sounded better than when I first saw him this evening, but not ecstatic. "Bad news. Gabe didn't keep the digital videotape. But it was worth a shot. And it got me out of my funk, man. Maybe we'll come up with something else. And don't forget—my other offer still stands. Call me if the ambivalent cop isn't meeting *all* your needs, sexy."

Ugh. I was about to throw my phone against the wall when an alert came that I'd received an e-mail from Jason Carter. I gave him a fake e-mail on my application, part of Marc Wilgus's new identity for me, but Marc set it to forward to my regular account. I figured I'd better check what Jason had to say:

"Wanted to let you know that it looks like the meeting between you and Jacob Locke is going to have to be put off for a while. He got a great opportunity to speak at a Christians for a Brighter Future fund-raiser in DC tomorrow, and he'll be flying out in the morning. He's on the road for two weeks after that, but I'm still planning on getting you two together when he gets back, sometime in December. I hope you still can come by around noon tomorrow, though. We could really use your help. And I could use the laughs. (p.s.: Feel free to wear the colostomy bag, if you need to, Gramps. I promise not to tell. Smile.) J. C."

Great. A few hours ago, I had a semi-boyfriend, a great idea I was sure would rescue my mother, and an opportunity to personally scope out the man I thought might be killing my friends.

Now, I was painfully single, my mother was going to lose everything she (we) owned, and it was going to be weeks before I got a chance to take my investigation of Jacob Locke any further.

Not to mention my realization today that while I'd spent the past few years earning a good living and making a lot of men happy, I hadn't exactly been building a sustainable career path.

What did I have left? Apparently, my best option was a future as a conservative political operative. If, that is, I was comfortable pretending to be Kevin Johnson for the rest of my life and betraying every principle in which I believed.

My stomach gave another lurch and I felt the second return of lunch rising in my throat. This time, at least, I made it to the toilet.

Gee, things are looking up already, I thought snarkily. Then I hurled again.

33

Gotta Move

It hadn't been my greatest night ever. I considered going for a walk, watching TV, calling Freddy, maybe even taking Andrew Miller up on his offer to screw my brains out. I certainly had no use for them.

Instead, I put on *The Owl and the Pussycat,* a movie that never failed to make me laugh.

It failed.

I picked up my iPhone ten times to call Tony and tell him to come back, that I'd made a mistake. But I knew that would be *so* the wrong thing to do. Instead, I just stared at it, willing him to call me, but that didn't work, either.

I tried to fall asleep, but I failed at that, too.

Finally, at four AM, I took an Ambien so I could get at least a few hours of rest. As I held the bottle in my hand, for one moment, I had the fleeting thought, *Why not take them all?*

Whoa. I'd never considered suicide in my life. Truth to tell, I wasn't considering it then, either.

But I did, for the second that thought flittered across my consciousness, understand why someone would.

Yeah, it was bad losing Tony, losing the chance to get that videotape, and losing the opportunity to meet Jacob Locke.

Really, really bad.

Especially that first part.

But it was losing hope that kills you. That I had to hold on to.

I took one of the sleeping pills with a slug of water from the sink.

I lay down again and tried to make a list of things to be hopeful about in my head.

If I came up with any, I didn't remember them when I woke at eleven the next morning.

I've benched 180 at the gym with less effort than it took to get my eyelids open the next morning. My bedroom was uncharacteristically dark for so late in the day. I looked out the window; the sky was as gray and gloomy as my prospects. Perfect. I thought about Tony.

I should go to the gym, but there was no way that was going to happen. Since I started dating Tony, I kept my weekends free of clients, so I was open for the day with nothing to do but mope. Great.

I stumbled to the kitchen and found an amazing assortment of nothing. I checked my phone, no messages.

My stomach growled. I growled back.

I threw on a pair of sweats and a hoodie and ran to the deli on the corner. I picked up a quart of plain low-fat yogurt, some bananas, a loaf of whole wheat bread, peanut butter and jelly, skim milk, a box of Total high-protein cereal, and a half-gallon of bottled water.

Since I'd decided not to kill myself, I might as well not die of starvation, either.

I had a bowl of cereal with a banana sliced in it. I thought about Tony. I swallowed my Adderall with a glass of milk. I took a long, hot shower and thought about Tony some more and since my tears were indistinguishable from the water washing down my face, I figured that didn't count as wallowing.

I had to stop thinking about Tony.

Still wet and naked from the shower, I called Andrew Miller. He needed a friend right now, and since it was my mother who got him into this jam, I figured it should be me.

By the time I called him it was just after noon. I woke him up. I apologized. He told me not to worry and we chatted for a bit.

"I'm really sorry your friend Gabe didn't keep his tape," I said. "I thought we had her for sure."

"I know, it's a bitch. After he did the standard upload, he just recorded over it, which erases whatever was there before."

"Upload?"

"Yeah, we shoot digital. When the camera operator gets back to the office, he or she uploads the video onto the central server. Then we use the tapes again."

"You keep everything that gets shot?"

"Well, I don't, but the production company does. It's all cataloged and retained. You never know when some old footage might come in handy."

"So, there *is* a copy of the tape?" I felt my pulse quicken.

"Yeah, but I can't get to it. Neither can Gabe. Once it's uploaded, it's stored in these massive data banks somewhere. I don't have access and can't get any. Believe me, I wish I could."

"But it's on a computer?"

"Somewhere. Why?"

"Can I put you on a hold for a couple of minutes?"

"Hey, I'm still in bed. Hold away. I'll just imagine you're here."

He got points for relentlessness. "Great. Hold on."

I hit "conference" on my phone and dialed Marc Wilgus. Until I pressed the button again, Andrew would be on hold.

"Kevin," Marc said, happy to hear me. "I'm glad you called. I was thinking about you yesterday. Did you make it over to Jacob Locke's office? Did they believe you?"

I told Marc it all went perfectly and thanked him effusively for his assistance. "But now I need another favor," I confessed.

"What's up?"

I told Marc, in the most condensed manner possible, about my mother's run-in with Yvonne and the subsequent fallout. I explained what I needed him to do. "Can you help?"

"Probably," Marc said. "I'd need to know more about the specifics, but it doesn't sound too hard."

"I have the guy I was telling you about, Andrew, on the other line. If you're willing, I could conference you in. Would you talk to him?"

"When exactly," Marc asked, "did I become Alfred to your Batman?"

"I'm sorry," I said. "You're right. I'm taking advantage of our friendship. Don't worry, I'll figure out something else—"

Marc interrupted me. "You kidding? I *love* playing Alfred to your Batman. No, scratch that. Can I be Batman to your Robin?"

"Help me out on this, and you can be anything you want."

"You know I can't say no to you, Kevin. Put him on."

Andrew told Marc everything he knew about the systems on which the video was stored, and Marc sounded pretty confident he could get the files within a few hours.

"Can you e-mail them to me?" Andrew asked.

"You don't want that," Marc said. "The last thing you need is an electronic trail linking you to the files. Let me get your address and I'll have a DVD messengered to you."

Andrew gave him the information, and they exchanged e-mails and telephone numbers.

Marc hung up to get to work.

Andrew asked me, "You really think he can do this?"

"You kidding?" I answered. "He's the fucking Batman."

It was 12:35 by the time we finished talking.

I tried to sound more confident with Andrew than I felt. Although I had great faith in Marc's ability, the way my luck had been, I was sure something would go wrong.

I checked my e-mail on my phone and saw that Jason Carter had written five minutes ago: "What's the matter, old man? Your arthritis acting up again? Please don't leave me alone here with the seniors and the holy rollers. I need you! J. C."

Jason's message made me smile and I headed to my bedroom to pick out something appropriate to wear to the campaign office.

I was just through the doorway when I said aloud, "What the hell am I doing?"

I didn't usually talk to myself, but this seemed like a good time to start. Because, obviously, I was insane.

Why was I going back to Locke's office? After all, there was no chance The Man Himself would be there. As touched as I was by Jason's commitment and sincerity, I wasn't about to become an anti–equal marriage, pro-life zealot.

Was it just about wanting Jason's approval, the attention of an attractive, interesting man? Was I really that shallow? That desperate?

Apparently so.

God, my life sucked.

All I wanted to do was go back to bed.

I was about to write back to Jason with an excuse, but decided not to bother. Maybe I'd just let Kevin Johnson disappear into the same virtual never-world from which he sprang.

I, unfortunately, was stuck in this world. That being the case, as I still had to make a living, I decided to force myself to go to the gym.

No reason for me to look as bad as I felt.

I threw on the sweats I wore to the deli this morning and opened my coat closet to grab my gym bag.

That's when I saw it.

Floating on its hanger like a ghost, like an unsaid accusation.

The gold lamé Ansell Darling coat that Rueben had sent me just a few days before his death.

Rueben.

I took the coat off its hanger and brought it to the couch. It was soft and plush. I cradled it like a security blanket, like a child, like a lover, and let the sadness wash over me.

Rueben. Brooklyn Roy. Sammy White Tee. Maybe some others, too, whose names I didn't even know. All gone, forever.

Randy, still in a coma, who knew how he'd emerge from it?

I thought *I* had problems?

What was *wrong* with me?

Had I really just thought I was *stuck* in this world? Even with the semi-boyfriend, crazy mother, and thin resume, I was *lucky* to be in this world. What wouldn't Rueben or any of the others have given for another chance? Who was I to waste even a moment of mine?

It was half past closing time at my self-pity party. It was time to get to work.

OK, so Jacob Locke wasn't going to be at his campaign office today, but that was no reason to give up. Maybe I could still snoop around, figure *something* out.

How could I do anything less?

The sweats came off again. What does a young Republican activist looking to make a good impression wear on the weekend?

I chose a pair of navy Banana Republic chinos, one of their trim-fit white button-down shirts, and a zippered navy cardigan. I threw a J. Crew corduroy blazer over it and, satisfied that I looked like, well, Kevin Johnson, headed out the door.

But first, I replied to Jason Carter:

"On my way back now."

And, you know what?

I was.

34

Doing the Reactionary

"He's sick," Jason whispered in my ear as he shook my hand, and, with his other arm, pulled me in for a bro hug.

Five minutes earlier, I saw Jason's smile light up from across the room as I walked in the door, shaking off the rain that had drenched me when the already gray skies decided to let loose.

The super-cheery Lucille greeted me, uh, cheerily. "Back again? I'd have thought you'd be with your lady friend on a beautiful day like this."

Beautiful? I guessed every day on Planet Lucille was all sunshine and lollipops. This was also the second mention she'd made of me having a "lady" in my life. Either she suspected I was gay, or she was planning to pounce on me herself. Maybe she could start her own group: Concerned Christian Cougars of America.

"I'm here to see Jason," I replied by nonanswer. "May I?" I pointed to a tissue box on Lucille's desk.

"Absolutely." Lucille beamed, handing the box to me. I grabbed a handful of them and mopped whatever water I could off my head.

As I did, I looked around the office. I was surprised it was slower on a Saturday than on a Friday. Usually, most volunteers were working people, or students who had classes to attend. Which meant most campaigns were bustling on the weekend.

Locke's base of retirees and clergy weren't bound by the restrictions of the workweek. Three-quarters empty, the haphazardly organized office space felt like a set from *I Am Legend*.

The general gloom wasn't improved by the volunteers themselves, mostly elderly, who moved though the office with the shuffling gait, outdated clothing, and pale pallor of recently risen zombies.

Apparently, Locke's pro-life position didn't apply to his staff.

"Thanks," I told Lucille, handing the box back to her. "Guess the weather kept a lot of people away today, huh?"

"Mercy, no." Lucille put a hand to her heart. "This is a good turnout for us! Last weekend, it was just me, Jason, and Mr. Bishop." She pointed to a man who appeared to be in eighties. He was sitting at a desk in the middle of the room, slumped in a chair, his eyes closed. He snored lightly.

"He's really very sweet," Lucille said. "Except the first day he came in, Lord save me, I saw him sitting there like that and thought he'd died! Scared me half to pieces!"

They all scared me there, including Lucille, with her too-big smile and Minnie Pearl wardrobe.

"And what about you?" I asked her. "You work on the weekend, too? Even on a, uh, nice day like today?"

"I'm here whenever they need me," Lucille said. "I believe the Lord has put me here to help Mr. Jacob Locke take back America. There's *nothing* I wouldn't do for that man."

Thanking her again, I gathered my courage and crossed through the office to see Jason. For some reason, I found myself thinking, *Yea, though I walk through the valley of death . . .*

I was rewarded for my courage by Jason's quick, macho hug and his whispered proclamation.

"Who's sick?" I whispered back.

"Locke," Jason said, settling back in his chair. He waved for me to sit, too.

"Oh, I'm sorry to hear it."

"No, Kevin, it's *good* news. He decided to cancel his DC trip and the rest of the week's travel, too. He's coming into the office today. You'll get to meet him if you can stick around."

That *was* good news. My smile was genuine. "Great! I've really been looking forward to meeting him." Then, remembering my role, I added, "I hope he's not *too* sick."

"Naw, just a head cold. But last time he flew with a cold, he wound up getting a sinus infection and was down for two weeks. So, he's real cautious now."

"Better safe than sorry," I said. Sticking to the dullest possible clichés was part of my strategy for success here.

"Yup, ya don't want to run your prize horse too hard before the big race. Gotta keep our boy on his feet, ya know." He winked at me and I felt a flush of attraction. I really wanted to hate this guy, but he was just too damn lickable. I meant, likable. I bet he smelled like hay and had a light dusting of scarlet hair across his tummy that got narrower and finer until you reached his . . .

Focus, Kevin, focus.

"Too bad he's not going to be able to participate at the conference tonight," I offered.

"Good news there, too, chief. He's going to appear via a video feed. They're coming to set up around six and he speaks at seven. If ya don't mind me asking"—Jason cocked his head to the side bashfully—"I was kinda hoping you could help me out with his remarks. I have a draft, but I think they could use some punching up. Can you take a look at them?"

Oh, God, no. "Sure."

"Great. Do you think you can stay for the taping? We could always use another hand."

Since I always reserved Saturday nights for Tony, I had nothing else to do. "Sure."

"You wouldn't happen to have any TV production experience, would you?"

Not exactly, I thought, *but my mother just completed a fabulous guest-starring role on* Yvonne *as an insane hairdresser.* "Sorry."

"Don't worry about it, chief," Jason said. "Just figured maybe you had. Seems like you've done everything else a boy could do."

If only you knew.

Jason set me up at a desk with a computer a few feet from his. He handed me a copy of the speech he'd written on a USB stick.

Jason's talking points were pretty good for a load of conservative horseshit. They seemed like the same things Jacob Locke said everywhere else, so I don't know what he needed my help with. Maybe he was just insecure.

I thought about what Jason had shared about himself the day before. Small-town boy, grew up on a farm. Hence his adorable aw-shucksness. Not a family of any means, worked to put himself through school, blah-blah-blah. Split major in political science and theology. Worked as an aide to a US senator for a few years, then as an independent political consultant.

Three years ago, when Jacob Locke was still just a television preacher, Jason was watching him and had an epiphany. Here was a man (or so Jason thought) who combined a love of scripture with practical understanding of the world around him. He approached Locke for a job and Locke hired him.

It was Jason who convinced Locke to enter politics, seeing in him a populist appeal that Jason thought would cut through the noise of other politicians.

I looked over at Jason. He was on a conference call with the state directors of Locke's campaign. He was leaning back in his chair, his legs on the desk. He absently chewed on a pencil while listening to the reports from the field.

I wondered just what it was about Jason that appealed so much to Locke. Watching his long, lean body as his lips worried that pencil, I thought I might know.

Not that I thought there was anything sexual between them. I pretty much made a living with my Gaydar, and it was telling me that Jason was one hundred percent straight. I believed he had great personal integrity as well. I couldn't see him doing anything physical with Locke.

From his humble beginnings, Jason ascended to the role of chief of staff to a rising Republican star. Watching him at work, it seemed to me like he knew what he was doing. But I could see why he might feel unconfident. It's hard to overcome the insecurities of childhood.

I made some tweaks to his remarks. Inserted a few topical references, took out some of the hoariest clichés, added a joke, and changed a line that read, "we have to work harder to protect *our* families," to, "we have to work harder to protect *all* families."

I knew I was taking a risk on that last one, but I couldn't stop myself.

I felt my iPhone buzz in my pocket. A text from Freddy. "Call me!" I wrote back, "Busy right now, ring you later."

Knowing Freddy, I turned the phone off. He'd call or write one hundred times until I got back to him, and I didn't want to be distracted from what was happening here.

By the time I was done, it was 5:15. I saved my revision to the speech and e-mailed it back to Jason. He had long been done with his conference call.

I watched surreptitiously as he opened the document and read my changes, gratified to see him nodding and chuckling where appropriate. As he started to look up, I ducked my head back down and pretended to be absorbed by the *Drudge Report* on my screen, required reading, I imagined, for all young conservatives.

Jason walked behind me and clapped me on the back. "Great stuff, chief. Top notch. Jacob's going to love this."

Once again, I gritted my teeth at how gratified I was by Jason's praise.

"What say," Jason began, "I order us in some grub and we hang out till the TV folks get here? Sound good?"

"Great. I'm starving."

"Pizza OK?"

"Pizza's *essential.*"

Jason laughed and dialed for delivery.

When he hung up the phone, he walked over to Lucille, the only other person still in the office. "That does it for the day," he told her. "Why don't you go on home?"

"But you and Kevin are still here," she observed with a little whine in her voice. "I don't mind staying."

"Now, darlin'," Jason said, taking her coat from a stand by the front door and holding it out for her. "You have done more than your duty for the week. Y'all get outta here while the gettin's good."

Lucille reluctantly stood up. "You sure you two boys are going to be all right on your own?"

Jason walked over with her coat and practically forced her arms into it. "We're gonna be fine, Miss Lucille. Now, skedaddle."

"All right then," Lucille said, her smile a little tremulous. "If you insist."

"Thank you for your service this week, Miss Lucille," Jason said, opening the door for her. "I don't know how we'd get by without you."

At this, Lucille beamed again. "Oh, Mr. Carter," she gushed. "I bet you talk to all the girls like this." Coquettishness didn't go very well with her plus-sized appearance, but I gave her points for trying.

"Only the pretty ones," Jason said with a wink. Lucille giggled as he led her out the door.

The moment it closed behind her, Jason turned the deadbolt, locking the door. He turned to me. "At last! I thought we'd never be alone."

Was I wrong about Jason? I was pretty convinced he was as straight as his resume, wedding ring, and the picture of his wife and children would suggest. Not that those were guarantees against liking to fool around with guys. The majority of my client list was married, as was Jacob Locke. I just didn't get a sexual vibe off of Jason.

Not that I'd mind being wrong. Plus, I rationalized, if he was attracted to me, I bet he'd be more forthcoming in my investigation of Locke. I figured I'd give him an opening. So to speak.

"You certainly seemed pretty eager to get rid of her," I said, walking over to him. I flung back my bangs and licked my lower lip. "What was that about?"

"Isn't it obvious?" Jason said, moving closer to me.

I matched him with another step forward. We were close enough to kiss. "Maybe I need you to spell it out for me." I looked up at him expectantly.

"Well, duh." Jason rolled his eyes. "I only ordered *one* pizza. With Miss Lucille around, we'd be lucky if she left us the cardboard box to eat." He punched me in the arm. "Now, come on, slugger. Let's proofread those remarks one more time and print 'em out." Jason walked around me back to his desk.

Guess I had it right the first time. Damn.

Five minutes after our pizza arrived, so did Jacob Locke.

"Sir!" Jason sprang to his feet when Locke walked in. "Let me get your coat." He started to sprint over.

Locke waved him away. "Now, don't be getting up, boy. Eat. I can take my own fool coat off."

Jason walked over anyway and took the coat from Locke anyway. "I'll hang it up, sir." He looked at the door and squinted. "How did you get in, sir?"

Locke pursed his lips. "I have a key, Jason." He reached over and took his coat back from Jason. He put his hand in one of the pockets and pulled out a silver key on a cross-shaped ring. "See?"

"Of course, sir. I thought you had told me you lost it."

"No." Locke laughed. "I told you I lost the five copies you'd given me previously. This one I've managed to keep."

Jason laughed, too. "I'm proud of you, sir. Fund-raising is going well, but I don't think we can afford to keep getting the locks changed."

Locke put his hands on his hips in a way that looked surprisingly . . . fey. He pursed his lips and rolled his eyes. "Brat." He pretended to look annoyed but chuckled. He slipped his key back into his coat, which Jason hung on a rack by the door.

Locke threw his arm good-naturedly around Jason and they walked to where I was sitting. I could see they had a good rapport going. Jason was deferential and respectful to Locke, but they could joke around, too.

On television, Locke had the bland good looks of a local news anchor in a medium-sized market. In person, he was more distinctive. Probably about six foot two, fit for his age, silver hair sprayed into place like the model in an ad for men's hairspray. Bright hazel eyes and a strong nose were the first things you noticed about his face, but the rest of it was fine, too. His skin was ruddy with a healthy glow that stopped a little too abruptly at his neck. I suspected bronzer.

He was dressed conservatively in a navy suit with a red tie and white shirt. Not a particularly original color scheme for a politician, but he wore our flag's hues well.

Everything about him, from the carefully styled hair to the *just so* cut of his suit to his just-shined shoes, was perfectly in place and polished. He looked good, but the deliberateness of it all spoke of a certain vanity. Almost a prissiness. He came over to where we were sitting and pulled up a chair.

"And who," he asked, his voice musical, "is this fine young specimen?"

Jason blushed a little. "This is the young man I was telling you about," he answered. "The kind of bright, young thing we need around here. Kevin Johnson, this is Jacob Locke."

I stood up and extended my hand. "It's an honor to meet you, sir."

Locke remained seated, his eyes pointed directly at my crotch. "Can't say I'm sorry to make your acquaintance, either, son." He put his hand in mine, limply, and let it rest there. The uniform length and perfection of his nails displayed a recent manicure.

It was kind of awkward. It reminded me of how the Queen of England gives you her hand. What are you supposed to do, again? Oh yeah, kneel and kiss it.

Locke looked up at me, a sly smile appearing on his face. I had a feeling he was thinking the same thing.

"You look like *just* the kind of thing we need around here," Locke said to my dick.

Remember what I said about making a living with my Gaydar? Despite the fact that I momentarily had my doubts about Jason when he kicked Lucille out of the office, usually it was pretty reliable.

What was my Gaydar telling me about Jacob Locke? Let's put it this way—if it was measured on a scale of one (Kris Allen) to ten (Adam Lambert), Locke was registering a fifty-five.

The fact that Locke probably liked to play with boys came as no surprise to me. After all, what brought me here was the knowledge that he'd had sex with at least one of my friends.

What shocked me, though, was what a big old queen he was.

I remember something an older friend of mine who had attended a year of seminary told me. Most of the clergy-in-training were gay. Although many of them chose to abstain from sex, dormitory life was like bunking with the touring company of *A Chorus Line*. The young men and their instructors camped it up wildly, lip-syncing to Judy Garland records and trading dialogue from *All About Eve*.

When it was time to take the pulpit, though, they reeled it in. You'd never know they'd spent the previous evening conjecturing which cast member of *The Real World* had the biggest cock.

Finally, Locke gave my palm a soft and sustained squeeze, and let it slide slowly through his fingers. Talk about a hand job.

I stood there uncomfortably for a moment when Jason cut in. "How about a piece?" he asked.

That was direct, I thought. Then I realized he was talking about the pizza, the box of which he extended to Locke.

"No, thank you, son," Locke said, still facing my crotch. "I'm not in the mood to eat . . . pizza."

I could see why he needed someone to write his speeches for him. I sat down before he decided to take a bite out of me.

"We have your remarks ready, sir," Jason said, handing the printed copy to Locke. "Perhaps you'd like to review them?"

"You're too good," Locke said to Jason, looking at me.

"Actually, Kevin here was helpful in putting them together," Jason said. "He's a really bright kid."

Locke took the papers from Jason. "Then he should come in while I look at them." Now he turned to Jason. "Has he seen the inner sanctum yet?" he asked in a teasing whisper.

Jason shook his head. "No, sir."

"Then you must allow me to give him the tour." He stood and gestured for me to follow. "Come into my web . . ." he crooned, arching his eyebrows.

It was so obviously suggestive that Jason flinched.

I followed.

35

Who's Afraid of the Big Bad Wolf?

Locke ushered me through the closed door beside Jason's desk, which led to his private office.

While the rest of the campaign space was haphazardly organized and messy, Locke's office was grand and expensively decorated. Plush new carpeting, wood-paneled walls, cherry furniture, and original oil paintings. At one end of the office was Locke's desk, an imposing piece of furniture, with a black leather pad and marble and gold letter trays and penholders. A plush executive chair with gold studs sat behind it. Two nice but simpler chairs faced the other side of the desk.

In the middle of the room was a small conference table with seating for six and a speakerphone placed in its center.

On the far side of the room was a formal-looking black leather sofa, faced by two matching chairs with a coffee table between them. A forty-inch LCD hung from the wall over the sofa. Wires led to a cable box and a DVD player installed on a shelf to the left. A wooden credenza in the corner of the room held two file drawers.

As we walked in, Locke threw an arm around my shoulder. "Come along, I'll give you the nickel tour." He left the door open, for which I was thankful.

Locke guided me around the periphery of the room, where pictures of himself with famous people hung anywhere there was space. We looked at him with each of the past five presidents, a bevy of politicians from both parties, two popes, and celebrities of every kind.

Every few pictures, Locke would tell an amusing or educational story about whom he was with and what they were doing. He'd throw in personal details wherever he could, like, "I might not have agreed with Bill on everything he did, but I'd have to say he was the most charismatic president I've ever met. That man could charm a snake right out of his skin." Or, "Standing on that stage with Bono, I could feel the goodness of his soul shining on me like the sun. The only other person I ever felt that way around was Mother Teresa, God rest her soul."

Although he kept his arm around me for the entire fifteen-minute travelogue, he was a very different man from the one I'd met outside. His voice was deeper, the timbre more somber, and he displayed no trace of his earlier campiness. He was articulate, authoritative, and smooth, revealing just enough details to make me feel like an insider while, at the same time, establishing just how connected, caring, and successful he was.

It was a calculated presentation. I imagined he'd given this tour to many others, from contributors to reporters to other dignitaries. It was the Jacob Locke Show, carefully orchestrated to entertain and impress. He was on script now, and he delivered his lines well.

The last picture he led me to showed him standing in a sandy locale, a sea of young black children surrounding him, cheering.

"This was in South Africa," he recalled, "on one of my missions to an orphanage I founded to help children whose parents died of AIDS." He let out a heavy sigh. "Sadly, many of the young people themselves are infected by that terrible, terrible plague. This is the work I feel the Lord calling me to, making the lives of young people like these all over the world safer and healthier. Giving them a shot to survive, to thrive, because doesn't the Good Book teach us that every life is precious? Even the unborn ones. It's why I'm out there every day, fighting the good fight, enduring the attacks from the liberal media and the lies of the unsaved. Those who want to bring not just me down, but our American way of life, the Judeo-Christian principles that make our country not just strong, but uniquely blessed and held above all others. That's why I need your help."

How we got from children with AIDS in Africa to a pro-life pitch and an attack on the liberal elite was beyond me, but I admired the way Locke pulled in these and other conservative/religious hot buttons to close his tour on a moving call to action. All he needed was a string choir playing "America the Beautiful" in the background and it was enough to inspire a contributor to write a check or bring a congregation to its knees.

Which is where I thought, for a moment, he was trying to bring me, as the pressure on my shoulders suddenly increased as he started to push down.

But, no, he wasn't forcing me into Blow Job Position #1.

"Make yourself comfortable," he said, directing me to one of the chairs facing his desk. He sat on the other side and picked up the remarks Jason printed out for him.

"Let's take a look at what you're trying to"—dramatic pause—"put into my mouth." He winked, I nodded blankly as if I didn't get the joke. He began reading.

"Why that boy doesn't print these out bigger, I'll never know," Locke said. He opened a drawer and pulled out a pair of glasses. "Bothersome astigmatism. Another of the blessings of aging. Now, I need reading glasses like some old coot. Can't say I like that much. The doc has me on a training program that's supposed to be helping, but I haven't seen any improvement. Guess I'll just have to pray on it some more. But would you make sure Jason gives me the large-type version for the taping?"

"Yes, sir," I answered.

Locke looked down at the paper, then at me, then at the paper, then at me again. "All right, Bright Young Thing, you better get on out of here or I'm not going to get a lick of work done." He put the emphasis on the word "lick" in that last sentence.

"Yes, sir," I said, getting up. The whole reason I had come here was to scope out Locke; now I couldn't wait to get away.

"Later," Locke said, "I want to hear all about *you*. I have a couple of ideas how a boy like you can be a real asset to this campaign. To me. I can see you're ambitious. Stick with me, and you could go far. Jason tells me you have a lot of potential. You know how it is in politics, though. One hand washes the other. You have to do what it takes to get ahead. You willing to do what it takes, boy?" He dropped a hand in his lap.

Apparently, it wasn't just his political speeches that were a mess of clichés. This guy was about as subtle as a colonoscopy, only less pleasant.

"It would be an honor to talk with you again," I said, continuing in my role as the naive young innocent.

Locke grinned like the Big Bad Wolf, only hungrier. I turned and beat a hasty retreat. I felt his eyes on my ass as I left.

As I exited Locke's office, Jason looked at me expectantly. "Y'all do OK in there, chief?"

"Right as rain," I said, wondering what the hell that expression meant, anyway.

"Good on ya," Jason said. "He like his speech?"

"He's still reading it. Oh yeah, he wants you to print him another copy in a bigger font."

Jason rolled his eyes upward. "Lord, Jesus." He sighed. "If I gave him the large-print version first, he'd be complaining that I treat him like an old man."

"Ah," I said. "Vanity."

"No man is perfect," Jason agreed. "He's doing these exercises the doctor said would improve his vision, but I think Doc's just shining him on. At least he's doesn't dye his hair."

Locke actually looked very sexy with his silver mane, but I didn't think Jason would appreciate my saying so.

The doorbell rang and Jason went over to let in the crew that would set up the video feed. "Would you let Father Locke know they're here?"

I knocked on Locke's open door and did as Jason asked.

"Mahvelous," Locke said, extending his hands in a divalike pose. "I'm ready for my close-up, Mr. DeMille."

As Jason would say, *Lord Jesus.*

* * *

While the camera crew set up in his office, Locke transformed again. Gone was the preening queen as well as the polished politician. Locke took one look at the brawny blue-collar videographers and went into full all-American-guy mode. He joked with them about football and "the old ball and chain."

As they laughed and chatted amiably, you could tell they thought he was a great guy. I heard one of them say, "Most of these political types are real dickwads, but this one's a stand-up guy, you know?"

When it was time for the actual taping, Locke gazed into the camera with an intense concern and delivered his lines with conviction and strength. I looked around the room and saw the video crew nodding along. When he was done, they gave him a standing ovation. Locke accepted their applause modestly. The video crew packed up and got out of there in less than ten minutes; they didn't want to be working on a Saturday night any more than I did.

After Jason walked them out, Locke emerged from his office. "Jason, it's been a long day for me, and I better get to bed if I'm going to beat this cold."

Strange, I thought. I remembered that he'd canceled his travel due to illness, but he didn't seem sick at all.

"Yes, sir," Jacob said. "I'll call your car."

"Good man," Locke answered. When Jason went to his desk, Locke gave me another wolfish grin. "And you, Bright Young Thing? Have you thought about what I said?"

"Yes, sir," I answered, eyes wide. "I'm here to serve in any way you need me to, sir. All you have to do is ask." My words could have been perfectly innocent, but I tried to make them open to just enough interpretation to keep him interested.

Locke cleared his throat. "I have a feeling we're going to get along fine, boy."

I bit my lower lip. "I certainly hope so, sir. I'm willing to do what it takes to get ahead." I looked up at him adoringly. "You're a hero to me, sir." I looked down and, sure enough, the front of Locke's pants were fuller than before.

Locke leaned in toward me and looked around to see if any-one was watching us. Sure enough, Jason was hanging up the phone and heading over. I don't know what Locke was about to say or do, but he looked disappointed. He leaned back.

"Jason," Locke barked, a little pissed. "When am I back in the office?"

"Monday, sir."

Locke turned to me. "Will you be here?"

"Yes, sir," I answered.

"Excellent. Jason, did you call my car?"

"He was just down the street, sir. It should be here now."

Locke put his hand out again. I placed my hand in his and, as before, he held on long past the normal handshake. "You stay good now, you hear?"

"Yes, sir. Good night, sir."

"And I'll see you Monday?"

"Yes, sir."

Locke smiled. "I need a moment with Jason. Would you ex-cuse us?"

"Of course," I said.

Locke went into his office with Jason and shut the door. I looked around for a glass, a stethoscope, anything I could use as a listening device, but no such luck. Instead I made myself useful getting something I knew Locke would need.

They were in Locke's office for less than five minutes. When they came out, Locke had his arm around Jason again and looked pleased.

"Sir," I said, "if I may?" I held out the coat I'd retrieved for him.

"What service," Locke observed, as he slid his arms in. "I'm telling you, Jason, this one's a keeper."

"I hope, sir," Jason answered. "He's already been a big help around here."

Jason walked Locke out to his car. When he got back, he asked me if Locke had said anything.

"About what?" I asked.

"I don't know," Jason answered. "For a bit there, when you

two were talking, he seemed in a foul mood." He was referring to the moment when he'd interrupted as Locke was leaning toward me ready to . . . I'm not sure what. Whatever it was, it was enough to give him a woody.

"Did something come up toward the end?" Jason asked.

Other than his dick? "If it did, it must have been something small. He seemed OK to me. He was probably just tired, being sick and all."

"Yeah, that's probably it," Jason agreed, relieved. "So, what did you think of him?"

"Amazing," I said. "Everything I expected and more."

"I told you he is an amazing man. He's just so good and so loving, well, sometimes people misinterpret his kindness, is all."

"What do you mean?"

Jason looked at the wall about five inches to my left. Whatever he had on his mind, he didn't want to be saying it. "Just, you know, how friendly he is. We live in such a cynical time. People aren't always used to someone who's so open with his feelings."

I wondered if there'd been any sexual harassment allegations against Locke. I'd have to remember to check Michael Roger's BlogActive when I got home; he always had the scoop on closeted, hypocritical politicians.

If I didn't like Jason so much, I would have pressed further. But it was clear this topic made him uncomfortable. "No, everything was fine," I assured him. "I'm really glad to have met him."

Jason looked grateful to be done with our conversation. "That's great, Kevin. Now, I got some stuff to finish up tonight, but you go and get out of here."

After thanking him again and saying good night, I did. Jason locked the door behind me.

36

Fight

I was about to walk home when I realized I needed to talk to someone about my big day of crazy. I took my iPhone from my pocket to call Tony. Crap. Forgot that wasn't an option.

Freddy, then. I remembered he was trying to contact me when I turned the phone off. I restarted the phone and it buzzed wildly in my hand. Twenty-two unread texts from Freddy, four from Andrew Miller, and voice mails from Freddy, Andrew, and my mother.

Apparently it was the end of the world and I'd missed it. Everyone was trying to reach me.

Everyone but Tony, that was.

Fucker. I hoped his balls shrivel and fall off.

Not that I was bitter.

I skipped the messages and texts and called Freddy back. "What's up?" I asked.

"Where the fuck have you been?" Freddy barked.

"Nice to talk to you, too."

"I'm serious. I've been trying to reach you."

"I know, I had the phone turned off. What's the emergency?"

"Where are you?" he asked. I told him.

"Fine," Freddy said. "I'm at Tea and Strumpets. Come meet me."

Tea and Strumpets was a local coffee bar/tea house/Internet café that was a popular hangout in my neighborhood. It was a fifteen-minute walk from Locke's offices. I started downtown.

"Let me go home and change first," I said. I didn't want to show up there in my Young Republican drag. Tea and Strumpets was the kind of place where you wanted to look hot, not like you were recruiting for the Mormons.

"No time," Freddy said. "Get your lily white ass here yesterday, Kevin."

"All right, all right," I said, stepping up my pace. "What is this all about?"

Freddy asked, "Do you really not know?"

"No," I said, suddenly anxious. "Can you just tell me what's going on?"

"Baby," Freddy said, "you get over here and I'm going to *show* you what's going on. This, you're going to have to see to believe."

"You know I hate suspense," I told him. "Would you just spill?"

"If you're talking," Freddy said, "you're walking. If I were you, I'd be *running* down here. Toodles, doll." He hung up.

I'm wearing the wrong shoes for this, I thought as I started jogging.

As always, Tea and Strumpets was crowded. I saw Freddy at a table in the back. "Hey." I waved.

Freddy beckoned me over. As I walked back, I saw two guys I knew from my gym. I nodded at them and brushed past, intent on getting to Freddy.

"Dude," one of them said, grabbing my arm. His name might have been Ralph. Or Roger. I'd spotted him on the bench once, and rejected his advances in the steam room shortly afterward. He and his friends were a bit of a clique, harmless enough, but more in love with themselves than was strictly necessary. They were big boys, with the kind of heavy gym muscles that looked good, if a bit overdone. I'd bet money that at least some of that bulk was built by steroids.

I didn't really go for show muscles like theirs. Sure, they looked impressive, but ask them to help you on moving day and you could be sure they'd be claiming a bad back.

He was at Tea and Strumpets with another guy I recognized from the gym. They weren't hot enough for the amount of attitude they carried, but such is the Chelsea boy's burden. They wore the kind of hip, stylish clothing that announced good incomes and bad taste.

Ralph/Roger waved his hand up and down at my outfit. "What happened? Did a JCPenney throw up on you?"

I smiled and tried to pull away.

"Naw," his buddy said, "I think he's just seen the softer side of Sears." I looked at him and realized I'd shot him down once, too, right in this very café. On this night, he was wearing a distressed T-shirt that read "9.5." Probably meant to be a reference to his dick size.

Having seen him in the showers, I knew he was rounding up. By five.

I looked at him and his friend. Their glassy, diluted eyes told me they were on something that might promote them from harmless annoyances to genuine irritations.

Ralph/Roger grabbed my ass. "Well, the packaging may be different, but the fruit's just as ripe. Mmmm, sweet. Wouldn't mind splitting those melons."

Oh, please. Helen Keller could have pegged this demented faggot as a total bottom. "Hey, it was nice seeing you guys, but I have to . . ."

Ralph/Roger—or maybe it was Ron—pulled me closer. My face mashed against his hard chest. "What do you say I take you home and we get you out of all that polyester, baby?"

Mr. Doubles-His-Size moved behind me and pressed against my rear. "Or, I could come over, too, and we could have a real party."

Great, I thought. *A meatless sandwich.*

"All right, boys," I said, my voice sounding weaker than I would have liked, muffled as it was against What's-His-Name's prodigious pecs. "I really have to go."

"I don't think so," he said. "I think you want to play with us. You just need a little convincing."

I really wanted to end this before it turned into a scene from *The Accused.*

"Listen," I said, "I'm trying to be nice about this, but . . ."

"Fucking little tease," his friend said from behind me.

That tore it. I stepped into What's-His-Name's embrace and brought my heel down on his instep. "Ow!" He stepped back, giving me enough room to pull my arm forward and back, driving my elbow into Multiply-By-Two Boy's solar plexus. He stepped back, too, grabbing his chest and wheezing for air.

I slipped out from between them. "Nice seeing you boys," I said.

Unable to put his weight back on the foot I'd stamped on, an unsteady What's-His-Name reached out to grab me again.

I caught his hand and bent his fingers back. His eyes widened with pain. "You put one hand on me again," I said sweetly, "and I'll shove it so far up your ass that you'll be able to jerk off your boyfriend *while* he's fucking you. You feeling me, Chesty?"

He nodded vigorously. His friend looked at me terrified. "And you," I advised, "should really lose that T-shirt before you're sued for false advertising."

If anyone observed our little scene, they didn't say anything, except, of course, for Freddy. "Ah, darling," he greeted me as I reached his table. "Always making friends, I see."

"Some help you were," I harrumphed.

"Like you needed any," he answered. "Anyway, I might break a nail." Truth is, Freddy could have taken those two and half the other guys in here, too.

I saw two drinks at Freddy's table, one of which he held. Nice of him to order for me. I sat down and grabbed the other cup.

"Uh-uh-uh," Freddy said, waving his finger at me. "Swiper, no swiping."

"What are you, drinking for two?"

"It's for him," Freddy said, pointing his chin to the pastry counter, where Cody was walking over with a tray of pastries and another cup.

"Hi, Kevin," Cody said. "Freddy said you like this." He put a chai tea in front of me and placed the snackage in the middle of the table.

"Hey, Codes," I said, getting up and giving him a big hug. He sat down next to Freddy, who put a hand on his thigh.

They looked cute together.

Freddy studied the pastries as if they might reveal the secrets of the universe. His hands hovered over the tray like the pointer on a Ouija board before settling on his unlucky victim.

"So," I said, "enough suspense already. What's going on?"

Freddy mumbled something, his mouth full.

"What?" I asked.

"Cannoli here," Freddy said, pointing at his pastry. "Priorities, darling."

"I just ran down here from—"

"OK, OK." Freddy threw up his arms. "Don't whine! I surrender." He turned to Cody. "Shall we show him?

Cody wrinkled his brows in concern. "Maybe we better tell him, first, Freddy. I mean . . ."

Freddy put a finger to Cody's lips. "Shush now. Daddy knows best."

"Knows what," I asked, annoyed. "Would you just . . ."

Freddy held up his other hand to shush me, too. "Come on," he said, standing up. "Let's go to the videotape."

Freddy walked us over to the far side of the room, where a row of iMacs sat on a long shelf that ran the length of the wall. Although it was hard to believe these boys didn't have Internet access at home, people still loved to come here and surf the Web, cruise Craigslist, or write The Great American Novel. Every station was taken.

Freddy walked over to a thirtysomething guy wearing a flannel shirt and baggy cords. Sexy in an English-professor kind of way. "Excuse me," Freddy said, "would you mind if I just used that computer for five minutes? It's really important."

The guy didn't look away from his screen. "Sorry, buddy, but . . ."

Freddy leaned over and put his soft, full lips up to the man's ear. "Please . . ." he whispered. He put a strong hand on the guy's shoulder and squeezed gently.

The guy pushed away from the computer and gave Freddy a startled, smitten look. "Um, sure. Yeah. I'll just get another cup of coffee. I'm, um, Charlie. Can I get you something, too?" He stood up eagerly.

"No, doll," Freddy said, snatching Charlie's stool and settling into it. "But thanks!" Freddy started typing and Charlie drifted away.

"How does he do that?" Cody asked me quietly.

At times like this, I thought of Freddy as The Cock Whisperer, but seeing as he and Cody were just starting to date, I thought saying so might be over-sharing. "He's just a charmer," I said.

"Would you two stop whispering and get over here?" I stepped closer and saw Freddy was on the ViewTube homepage. He stood up and maneuvered me into the stool. "You better have a seat, darling."

I did as he said and Freddy reached around to drive the mouse. He scrolled halfway down the page to "Most Popular Videos." There were links to "All Time," "This Month," "This Week," and "Today." Freddy clicked on the last category.

The page loaded and Freddy pointed with his finger to the fourth featured video.

"No fucking way," I said.

"Way," Freddy answered from behind me. I could hear the evil grin in his voice.

"Don't . . ." I began.

But it was too late.

Freddy pressed play.

37

I'm the Greatest Star

It was painful the first time I watched this scene from twenty feet away in Andrew's trailer.

Seeing it here was worse.

Someone had uploaded to the world's most popular video-sharing site an edited video of my mother and Yvonne's confrontation at my mother's beauty shop. It was cut down to five minutes, but it still had all the highlights of their exchange.

And when I say "highlights" I mean "lowlights."

The 550,673 people who'd already viewed it were treated to Yvonne sharing her innermost thoughts, like "faggots just can't control themselves," "the only people worse than the fags are the Jews," and "take my audience—a bigger bunch of morons you've never seen. I want to throw up every time I have to stand in front of those idiots and losers."

The video went through my mother's unveiling of Yvonne's bald head, and her calling Yvonne "an insufferable, homophobic, anti-Semitic poser with bad implants and a worse attitude!"

It ended on a wild-eyed Yvonne calling my mother a *"cunt"* and my mother's dismissive, "Fuck you, Kojak."

I appeared on screen for a couple of seconds, but luckily, my face was never turned toward the camera. Thank God for small favors.

I didn't realize while I was watching it, but Freddy had the volume turned up to max on the iMac's speakers, and at my mother's parting words, the room behind me erupted in applause. I turned around and saw that most of the café's patrons had been watching my mother's horrifying display. They were all talking at once.

"Did you see that?"

"Holy shit, I can't believe what came out of Yvonne's mouth!"

"What a bitch!"

"Unbelievable!"

"Well, her career's over."

"Girlfriend got *owned*."

"*Next.*"

"I loved that other woman, though."

"*Hawwwwtt!*"

"I *have* to put that up on my Facebook—did you get the address?"

"Fuck Yvonne. I want to watch more of that woman who told her off. What show is she on?"

Freddy leaned over whispered in my ear, "Shall I tell them she's your mother?"

"You do," I hissed, "and I'll kill not just you but everyone who looks likes you."

Freddy kissed the top of my head. "Come on."

I got up from the stool and my place was immediately taken by a skinny kid with a lightning bolt shaved into his crew cut. "Let's see that again," he shouted. The crowd cheered as he pressed play.

Our table was far enough away that I was able to escape my mother's voice over the speakers and the murmurings of the crowd.

I had already told Freddy about what happened the day my mother taped Yvonne's show, and he'd filled in Cody. "But what we don't know," Freddy said, "is what the hell it's doing on ViewTube."

"That makes three of us," I said. "But I think I know who does. Would you guys excuse me for a minute?"

I went outside and dialed Andrew Miller. "Did you see it?" he asked by way of greeting.

"Uh, yeah," I said.

"What did you think?"

"I don't know what to think. How did it wind up online?"

"Didn't you get my messages?"

"I haven't had a chance to listen to them yet."

Andrew explained that, as promised, Marc was able to hack into the studio's data banks and retrieve Gabe's video of my mother's fateful encounter with Yvonne. Andrew wanted to use the footage to blackmail the show's producers into giving him the freedom to leave the show, but Marc had other ideas.

"After seeing what a nightmare she was," Andrew explained, "Marc suggested we post the footage on ViewTube. Expose Yvonne for what she is."

"How does that help you?" I asked.

"Are you kidding?" Andrew asked. "I don't have to worry about working for that horror show for one more day. With that tape out, there *is* no more Yvonne. I already got an e-mail that the show was shutting down production for an 'indefinite period.' Not only am I free, but the producers are going to have to buy me out of my contract. It's going to cost them, too."

"Can't you get into trouble for leaking the tape?"

"Your friend, Marc, handled it all. He posted the video with a fake user account he created. There's nothing that leads back to me, or to him. The guy's a genius. He even had some kind of algorithm or script or something that moved the video up to ViewTube's homepage. Once it was there, it didn't need any help staying there. Did you see how many people have viewed it?"

I told him I had. "But I'm worried about my mom. Is this going to create problems for her?"

"Problems? She's going to be a national hero, man. Five minutes ago a link to the video went up on Perez Hilton. He called your mom his favorite person in the world."

"What if Yvonne takes legal action? The tape makes my mother look like a worse threat than Saddam Hussein. She actually had and used chemical weapons."

"Who cares? You think any lawyer's going to take that case?

Try to build sympathy for Yvonne after she insulted gay people, Jews, and her own viewers? You're not getting it, Kevin— Yvonne is over. Oh-vah."

I thought about what Andrew was saying. Although it all came as a shock, I had to admit he was right.

"You really think this is it?"

"Nope," Andrew said. "I think it's going to go on, Kevin. And it's just going to get better and better. Ding-fucking-dong, Kevin, the wicked witch is dead."

"Huh." I wasn't absorbing all this.

"And if it makes you feel any better," Andrew explained, "I did call your mother before I told Marc to go ahead and post the video."

"What did she say?"

"Well, after I spent a half hour trying to explain what View-Tube is, never mind the whole concept of a viral video, she seemed to get that the footage would be made public. She was thrilled. She told me to go for it."

"Wow," I said. "You did it."

"*You* did it," Andrew said. "It was your idea to find that video in the first place, and when it didn't work out with Gabe, you hooked me up with Marc. *You* made it happen, dude. You told me Yvonne's biggest mistake was fucking with you and your family, and you know what? You were right. We won, Kevin. We won."

Andrew was ebullient. For me, it was just starting to sink in that one of my plans had worked out. It was a new feeling.

"So," Andrew said, "want to come over and celebrate? You bring the champagne, I'll pop your cork, baby."

Now that, I was familiar with. "Not tonight, Andrew."

"Hey, can't blame a guy for trying. Figured I was on a roll." I could hear the shit-eating grin in his voice.

"No harm, no foul. And congratulations. I'm glad it worked out for you."

"You, too, bro. Hey, listen, how about your friend? Marc? Is he hot?"

"Very."

"Think he'd be interested in me?"

"You have his number," I reminded him.

"Maybe I could get *him* to come over," Andrew said, teasing.

A few days ago, I would have told him "no way." Marc didn't go anywhere.

"Maybe you could," I said, happily. "Maybe you could."

It was too late to call my mother, but I listened to the message she'd left earlier. "Hello, Kevin. It's your mother." As if there was any mistaking that voice.

"Didn't I tell you I was going to be a star? Well, I just got off the phone with your friend, the TV producer, Andrew—that nice boy who I think you should really consider dating because, let's face it, that policeman boyfriend of yours is never going to make up his mind and you're not getting any younger.

"Anyway, remember that little run-in I had with She Whose Name I Shall Not Speak? Well, it turns out that Andrew, who, by the way, is very attractive, has some new show; it's called *Viewing Tube* or some *fakakta* name like that. It's not on regular TV; you have to watch it on the computer. I don't know what channel.

"In any case, he's going to put what happened at my shop on his computer show and the whole world is going to see that your mother gave that terrible woman exactly what she deserved.

"Andrew told me it was all your idea, and I have to say, I'm very proud of you, baby. I told you that you have to stand up for what you believe. That potty mouth thought she was going to sue me? Once everyone hears the filth that comes out of her, the only thing she'll ever get from me is pity. I wouldn't piss in her mouth if her stomach was on fire. I wouldn't—"

My father's voice came from the distance "Are you *still* on the phone? How many people are you going to call about this? So, you're going to be on the computer, who cares? You think this is going to make you a star? What am I, living with a crazy person? You know who else is on the computer all the time?

That little blonde singer, the one who goes around without her panties all the time. So, big deal. Enough already."

"Would you please let me speak in peace," my mother yelled back. "I'm talking to—"

"You're talking to everyone. Who are you calling next? You want I should look up the president's number, too? Maybe he'd like to watch."

"Could you just . . ."

My voice mail indicator showed that the message went on for another four minutes. Figuring I'd gotten the gist of it, I disconnected.

I walked back into Tea and Strumpets feeling pretty fine. The guys who'd bothered me before were, not surprisingly, gone, and I made it to Freddy's table unmolested.

Freddy greeted me with one word. "Spill."

I told him and Cody about my phone call with Andrew.

"Holy shit," Freddy marveled. "Your mother's going to be bigger than that guy who cried about leaving Britney alone. Or that chubby hausfrau who sang on British *American Idol*. Susan Lucci."

"It was *Britain's Got Talent*," I corrected him. "And her name was Susan Boyle. There's no such thing as 'British America,' anyway."

"Not anymore." Cody put his hand over Freddy's. "But there used to be. It was the name of the original thirteen colonies that were ruled by the British in the seventeenth and eighteenth centuries, until the American Revolution forced them to recognize the United States as a sovereign nation."

Freddy and I looked at him.

"What?" Cody asked.

Freddy smirked with pride. "Nothing, baby." He took the hand that Cody had placed on his and gave it a squeeze. To me, he added, "I knew all that, by the way."

"Yeah, right," I said. I looked at Cody. "Watch *Jeopardy* much?"

"I have a mind for trivia."

Freddy wriggled his eyebrows. "And an ass for . . ."

"Freddy!" Cody yelled. He put his hand over Freddy's mouth.

I figured I'd change the subject and save Cody some embarrassment. "So, do you want to hear about my undercover operations at Jacob Locke's headquarters?"

They both did.

First, I filled Cody in on the circumstances that led me to look into Locke in the first place. After summing up my suspicions, I told them about my visits to the office. I described Jason and Lucille, the general lassitude of the campaign, and, mostly, I went on about the many moods of the mercurial Locke. I described his vanity, his open campiness, and the blatant way he cruised me.

Freddy said, "Well, darling, what did you expect? He's a man of the cloth *and* a conservative politician. If you were writing a recipe for closet homosexuals, those would be the two main ingredients."

Cody asked, "You really think he's behind what happened to Randy?"

"Randy!" I exclaimed. "I can't believe I haven't even asked how he's doing. I'm a terrible friend."

Freddy looked at me with sympathy. "Yes, but admitting you have a problem is the first step to healing, darling. I, however, asked about Randy as soon as I saw Cody, and I'm happy to report he continues to get better."

"Is he talking yet?" I asked Cody.

"Not coherently. He kind of blurts things out, like he did when you saw him the other day, but he's definitely making progress. The doctors expect a full recovery."

More good news.

"OK, but back to my question," Cody continued. "You've spent some time with him. You really think Locke could be a killer?"

"I think that man would do whatever he had to do to get ahead," I said.

"Or, to get *some* head," Freddy added.

"I mean," I continued, "how do you go out there and say

such terrible things about gay people when you're having sex with men, yourself? What kind of person would do that?"

"In Nazi Germany," Cody observed, "the Gestapo enlisted Jewish people to turn in their friends and family. They were called 'Jew Catchers.' They sent their own people to concentration camps in exchange for immunity and comfort."

"Locke is a Fag Catcher," Freddy said.

"Someone who'd do that would do anything, right?" I asked Cody.

Cody shrugged. "Who knows?"

"I don't know what's worse," Freddy said, "the fact that he'd betray his own people, that he might be a murderer, or that he wears bronzer."

"He's *so* vain," I agreed. "Everything about him is perfectly turned out. He was wearing more hairspray than the entire cast of a John Waters movie. He even does eye exercises so that he won't have to wear glasses anymore."

Cody put his elbows on the table and leaned closer to me. "What do you mean? Did you see him doing them?"

"No, it just came up in conversation. He said he had an astigmatism."

Cody turned a shade paler and shivered. He picked up his tea with both hands. They were shaking.

Freddy put his hand on the back of Cody's neck. "You OK, baby?"

Cody took a swallow of his tea. "This is just a little creepy."

"What?" I asked.

"Do you know how you treat an astigmatism?"

Freddy and I shook our heads. Cody was making us feel like the slower students today.

"Well, with an astigmatism, one eye is weaker than the other. So, your other eye works harder to make up the difference. Got it?"

We nodded.

"The problem is, the muscles in your eye are like any other. You have to use them to make them stronger. But once the good eye starts working harder, the eye with the astigmatism just gets lazy. It lets the good eye do all the work.

"So, you have to force the bad eye to work harder. And the way you do it . . ."

It was my turn to get a chill. ". . . Is by covering the good eye."

Cody blanched. I felt the blood run from my face, too.

"I don't get it," Freddy said.

"When Locke is training his weak eye to work harder . . ." Cody began.

"He covers his good eye," I continued. "What do you think he'd use for that?"

Freddy looked at me, then at Cody, then at the table. He lifted his head with a jerk. "An eye patch!"

"Got it in one," I answered.

"Like that guy who came to see Randy in the hospital. He was standing three feet away from me." Cody shivered and Freddy pulled him into his lap.

"And I think that the person driving the car that hit Randy was also wearing an eye patch," I added.

"OK, that settles it," Freddy said. "I am *so* not voting for him."

"Locke has gray hair," I said to Cody. "You said the guy at the hospital was a brunette."

"He could have been wearing a toupee," Cody said.

If he took the trouble to wear the patch to disguise himself, that made sense. "You're right."

"This is getting scary," Cody said. "What are you going to do?"

I knew, but I wasn't going to tell them. If I did, they'd try to stop me.

Only an idiot would do what I had in mind.

38

Tonight

"This is the point where Charlie's Angels get the cops involved," Freddy said as we left the café. "You need to call Tony."

"He's right," Cody said, holding on to Freddy's arm.

I really didn't have time to go into the hundred reasons why calling Tony wasn't an option. "OK," I said, meaning, "OK, I've heard you," not "OK, I'm taking your advice."

I kissed them both on the cheek and we said good night. I liked watching them walk away together, arm in arm.

A quick flash of jealousy surprised me. There's always been a spark between Freddy and me. Now, with Tony out of the picture, was I letting him get away too easily?

I'd have to figure that out later. Right now, I had a more pressing engagement.

I put my hand into my front pocket and played with what I'd slipped in there earlier this evening. The metal felt smooth and cool. Should I use it or not?

Freddy told me to go to the cops. With what? I had no evidence. Nothing tangible to suggest that the attacks on my friends were related, let alone connected to Jacob Locke. The business with the eye patch wasn't going to be enough to convince the police to open a murder investigation into a major political figure.

I needed hard proof.

My pocketed fingers traced the shape of the silver cross and the keys attached to it.

Locke's keys.

I'd lifted them from his coat when I'd gotten it for him back at the campaign office. He and Jason had joked about how Locke kept losing his keys, so I figured I could grab them with no one the wiser.

When I took them, I hadn't planned on using them. I just figured it would annoy Locke to lose them again and did it out of spite.

A childish prank, but now I was glad of my immaturity.

Did Locke really have eye patches at his office? If so, what else might I find? Don't serial killers keep mementos of their victims, or was that just on *Bones*? What about other evidence? Weapons or drugs?

I held in my hand the means to find out.

The problem was, I didn't have long to act. Jason had teased Locke about the expense of changing the locks every time Locke lost his keys. Which meant that if Locke noticed them missing anytime soon, the copy I took from him would quickly be useless.

I might have only one shot at snooping around the office.

Tonight.

If I had told Freddy and Cody what I was planning, they would have stopped me. Ditto Tony, not that he was in the picture anymore. Bastard.

The idea of breaking into Locke's office made me nervous, but, really, what was the risk? Locke was gone for the evening and I doubted he'd be going back late on a Saturday night. There was a chance Jason could still be there, but if he were, I'd just turn around and come back later.

What's the worst that could happen?

On my way to Locke's office, I stopped by a drugstore and picked up a flashlight and latex gloves.

As late it was, the streets by Times Square were still busy with theatergoers and tourists. As I approached Locke's office, I was heartened to see the lights off. Once there, I cupped my hands to my eyes and looked through the window. Best I could see, there was no one there. Unless someone was scuffling around in the dark, the place was empty.

I put on the gloves and fished out Locke's keys. I thought that maybe I should text Freddy and let him know what I was doing, just in case something happened. But that might be jinxy. I opened the door.

Sneaking into the office, I felt like a total criminal. Considering I've spent the last few years illegally getting paid for sex, you'd think I'd have that feeling more often, but no. The laws against prostitution are archaic and wrong. Break-ins and trespassing, on the other hand, you could make a reasonable case against.

The street lamps and flashing lights of Times Square made it bright enough that I didn't need the flashlight in the main office. Unfortunately, it also meant that if anyone from the street looked inside, they'd see me. After relocking the front door, I dropped to all fours.

Why is it that no matter what I do, I keep finding myself in that position?

Trying my best to stay out of sight, I crawled across the office floor till I reached the door to Locke's personal office. That was locked, too. Luckily, the key to it was also on Locke's chain.

As an interior office, Locke's space had no windows. When I closed the door behind me, I was in pitch-black. Should I turn on the lights? They'd make it easier to snoop around, but the thought made me nervous. What if there was a gap at the bottom of the door and passersby could see a sliver of light leaking out? Probably, no one would think or do anything about it, but it still made me nervous. Well, more nervous.

I was already pretty nervous, and standing here in the inky darkness wasn't doing anything to make me feel better.

I switched on my flashlight. A circle of light illuminated the wall opposite me.

Sneaking around Locke's office in the dark was creepier than I thought it would be. Every surface had a picture of him, and in each one he seemed to be staring at me, saying, "You're going to burn for this, son."

First stop, the desk. I sat in Locke's comfortable chair and opened the top drawer. Bingo. Right there. A box of black eye patches.

Aye, matey.

Nothing incriminating in any of the other drawers. Random papers, a bottle of hand lotion, a Bible, a brass letter opener, some gum. Where else could he be hiding something? I swung the flashlight around the room.

In the back was the credenza I'd observed earlier. Yahtzee. Shining the flashlight at the floor, I carefully crossed the room.

The credenza had two wide drawers. Locked. I took Locke's keychain from my pocket, but it held only the two front door keys. Crap. I put the keys down on the credenza.

Given Locke's tendency to misplace them, I doubted he carried the credenza's key on him. Which meant it was probably somewhere in the office.

Back to Locke's desk. I hadn't been looking for a key before. Maybe I'd missed it.

I sat back down in his chair and opened the top drawer again. It must have been loose in its rail, because it made a banging noise as I pulled on it.

I didn't remember that from before.

I also didn't remember the subsequent sound of footsteps and someone whistling as they got closer to where I sat.

This wasn't good.

Someone else had come in.

39

Wide-screen

OK, best-case scenario: Someone was picking something up from the outside office. They'd get whatever they needed and leave. I'd be fine.

Second-best case: It was a cleaning service. I switched off my flashlight and listened like a bat.

A few seconds later I heard a key being inserted into Locke's office door and the knob starting to turn.

Oh, *balls*.

I slipped under Locke's desk and made myself as small as possible.

Someone turned on the lights and walked in. I couldn't see who it was because of being under the desk and all.

Whoever it was, I hoped he or she wasn't planning to sit at the desk.

Luckily, the footsteps seemed to be headed away from me. I turned my head and noticed that the wide side of the desk that faced into the room had a hole cut out, probably for computer cables.

Either that, or Locke was such a perv that, out of habit, he'd drilled a glory hole there.

Speaking of pervs, yup, it was Locke in the office. He was in casual mode, wearing a grey *Washington Times* sweatshirt and a pair of new-looking jeans with a sharp crease pressed along the seam. Pressed jeans. What a dork.

He was walking toward the credenza. "There you are," he

said, picking up his keychain, which I'd left there earlier. He put it in his pocket.

His phone rang. The ringtone was "God Bless America." Told you he was a dork.

He wrestled his phone from his too-tight jeans and sat down in one of the leather chairs that faced the sofa with the flat screen over it. "Hello . . . OK. No, I'm at the office. I had an opportunity to slip out so I'd figured I'd wait here. About an hour? That's fine. No, I'll take a cab. Just call me when he gets there."

Locke hung up without saying good-bye.

I decided he was a *rude* dork.

"An hour," Locke muttered to himself. "Hmmm."

At least I knew he wasn't staying the whole night. But where would he be going at midnight on a Saturday night?

I had a feeling I knew.

Call me when he gets there.

Someone was arranging a hookup for him.

Locke walked toward his desk. I willed myself invisible. Halfway across the room, he veered left, out of my line of sight.

I didn't like not knowing what he was up to. I was also getting uncomfortable scrunched under the desk. I was cramped, nervous, and really had to pee. Which was probably due to the nervousness, but that didn't lessen the pressure on my bladder, which felt like it was about to burst like a water balloon dropped from the observation deck of the Empire State Building.

OK, I told myself, clenching my thighs together. *Don't think about bursting water balloons anymore. It's not helping.*

From the sound of things, Locke had walked to the door to lock it. It sounded like he jiggled the knob a bit to make sure it was secure.

He walked back to the far side of the room. I felt better being able to see him. He picked up a brass lamp on the end table by the sofa. He turned it over and ran his fingers along the circle of felt on the lamp's underside. At a certain place, he stopped and pinched the edge of the fabric between two fingers. I heard the zipping sound of Velcro being opened.

Something fell from the hollow cavity of the lamp and landed on the carpet. Too fast for me to see what.

What the hell was he doing?

Locke stuck the felt back into place and returned the lamp to the table. He bent over and picked up whatever had fallen out. Humming to himself, he walked to the credenza.

He brought whatever was in his hand up to the locked drawer, inserted it into the cylinder, and turned it.

So *that's* where the key was hidden. I would never have found it there. Smooth.

Locke pulled something from the drawer and put it in his front pocket. Then he grabbed something else and held it in front of him. With his back to me, I couldn't see what he'd taken.

I had a moment of panic imagining that he somehow figured out I was there and had retrieved a handgun. I held my breath, waiting for him to order me out from under the desk. Or maybe he'd just shoot me through the glory hole.

OK, that sounded dirtier than I meant it to.

Locke walked over to the DVD player. His body still blocked whatever he was doing, but I heard the familiar whir of the player's tray opening. Locke opened the DVD case he'd gotten from the credenza, inserted the DVD, and pressed "play."

He picked up two remote controls from the coffee table and sat in one of the chairs that faced the TV. He turned it on.

The menu for the DVD was displayed on the screen. *Hairy Squatter and the Horse-hung Prince.* An All Boyz Production.

OMG. He was going to watch a porno.

It was official: This was the worst stakeout ever.

Locke picked the option to "Select a Scene" and navigated through two pages of choices until he reached number twelve.

Something told me this wasn't the first time he'd seen this movie.

The scene started. An actor, whose bowl haircut and round glasses did little to make him look any younger than his mid-thirties, stood next to bearish older man. They both wore wizard's gowns. "But, Lord Dicksalot," the younger man said in a somewhat incongruous Brooklyn accent, "I don't know a spell to raise the dead!"

"Oh yeah?" answered the older man. "How about a spell to raise *this?*" He flung open his robe to reveal that wizards don't waste money on underwear.

"Lord Dicksalot! Your magic wand doth entice me!"

I had no moral problems with porn, but this dialogue was a sin.

Without his robe, Lord Dicksalot quickly fell out of character. "Then get on your knees and suck my big dick, boy."

I could see only the back of Locke's head and his upper back, but slight movements of his right shoulder suggested he was *really* starting to enjoy the movie. He stood up and reached into the pocket into which he'd placed the other item he'd taken from the credenza. I couldn't read the label from where I was, but I knew the red and black bottle. Slide Away, a sexual lubricant. Looked like Locke was about to go to town on himself.

I was glad he faced away from me.

Locke tried to twist the cap off the bottle, but it was new and sealed in shrink-wrap. He struggled for a bit, but it didn't budge. "Goddamn it," he cursed.

Locke pressed pause and started walking toward his desk. Shit. I scampered as far back as I could. As Locke walked around the desk, he was out of sight again, reappearing on the other side when he reached its front. He opened one of the middle drawers and lifted something out of it. I could see him only from the waist down, so I didn't know what he'd taken.

I could, however, see that his magic wand was just aching to be waved.

"Might as well use this, too," he muttered to himself, opening the top drawer. It just missed hitting me in the head as it slid toward him.

Locke stood there fussing with something. My legs were cramped painfully as I tried to stay as low as I could. I raised my butt off my heels for a moment to relieve the pressure when Locke suddenly slammed the top drawer closed.

The back panel of the drawer smacked me in the forehead

with the force of a baseball bat. "Ow," I cried, falling off my heels, painfully hitting the side of the desk with my right elbow. The arm went numb down to my fingers. I felt blood dripping onto my cheeks from just above my eyebrows.

"Who's there?" Locke demanded.

Stupid and dazed from the blow to my head, it seemed like a good idea to deny everything. "No one," I answered.

"Get out of there," Locke yelled. He reached under the desk and grabbed me by my hair. "Now!"

I crawled out, saying, "Ow, ow, ow, ow, ow." Locke pulled me to my feet.

"You!" Locke thundered. He glared at me menacingly. Well, as menacingly as he could glare with only one eye.

The other was covered by a black eye patch.

In his right hand, he held the heavy brass letter opener I'd seen earlier.

He yanked my head back. I was too dizzy and disoriented from the blow to my head to fight back. I was also half blinded by the blood running from my forehead. I felt like I was going to throw up, and swallowed hard.

Locke pressed the tip of the letter opener against my exposed neck.

"If you know what's good for you, boy, you better tell me what you're doing here."

40

It Had to Be You

For a guy who just a few hours earlier had been camping around the office like Harvey Fierstein starring in the Judy Garland story, Locke had a pretty strong grip. Given enough time, I was pretty sure I could get away from him. Unfortunately, time was a luxury I didn't have. Locke pushed the tip of the letter opener a little deeper into my neck.

"I'm not playing with you," he growled. "Unless you want me to carve you up like a Thanksgiving turkey, you better tell me what the hell you're doing here."

That reminded me—Thanksgiving was next week. I'd completely forgotten about it. I was considering inviting Tony to my parents', but . . .

Focus, Kevin, focus.

Thanksgiving was going to be a moot point if I didn't come up with something quick. Locke had killed at least four people. I wasn't planning on being his next victim.

What did I know about him that I could use?

"I, I . . ." *What, Kevin, think!*

I couldn't catch my breath. I didn't know if it was because of the way Locke was bending my neck back, or if it was fear constricting my lungs.

"I love you!" I squeaked through my distended throat.

"What?" Locke asked. He relaxed his grip just enough for me to straighten out my neck.

"I love you," I said, making it up as I went along. "Ever since I first saw you, I love you, I love you, I love you. . . ."

OK, maybe my resume was paper-thin and I'd never get a real job. But I'd spent the past few years of my life seducing men. That, I could do.

Locke let go of my hair and I collapsed to my knees, gasping for air.

I looked up at him pitifully. I wiped the blood from my eyes with my sleeve.

Locke's face betrayed little. He still clutched the letter opener.

I threw my arms around his legs, turning my head so my cheek pressed against his crotch.

"It's wrong," I gasped, still having trouble breathing. "I know it's wrong for one man to feel this way about another. But I can't help it."

I shook my head back and forth, as if I was using Locke's pants to wipe away my tears. Back and forth, back and forth, babbling the whole time.

"Oh, Father," I said, "I know I'm a bad, bad boy. I just can't stop thinking about touching you, loving you . . ." As I continued to cry and rub my face against Locke's jeans, he responded in the manner I expected, and soon enough the spot I was massaging with my face was a lot firmer. I made sure to make a lot of contact with his reawakened wand, breathing hotly against it at every chance.

"My son." Locke extended a hand to help me off the floor. Unfortunately, it wasn't the hand with the letter opener. Locke sat in his desk chair and pulled me into his lap. Still holding my hand, he asked me, "Why are you wearing these?"

I took off my latex gloves. "I just felt so dirty, Father. I didn't want to soil you with my perversions."

"My son," he said tenderly. Then he took the gloves from me and threw them in the trash.

I perched on the end of his knees, but he put his arm around me and pulled me closer, pressed me against his chest.

I didn't like having him at my back like this, but I didn't have much choice in the matter. Locke rested his hand on my tummy.

"My son," he said again. "You mustn't be so hard on yourself. God understands that we are men, that we have male needs."

I wriggled in his lap to keep him interested. His hand rubbed my stomach in slow circles.

You know you're having a bad day when the best you can hope for is that the guy you're trying to seduce doesn't want to kill you until *after* you've have sex with him. Not that I intended to take things that far.

"Oh, Father," I moaned, trying to make my croaking voice sound sexy instead of terrified. "The things I've thought about doing to you. About touching you, taking you in my mouth, feeling you inside me, oh, Father!" I was now openly riding his hard dick and Locke had moved his hand under my shirt to my nipple.

"It's fine," Locke groaned, his voice thick with lust. I pivoted around in his lap so I was facing him. His face was a mask of need, his mouth open and panting.

I slid off his lap, my hands running along his sides, meeting in his lap. Yuck. I wish I'd left the gloves on.

On my knees again, I reached for his belt. I opened it carefully, reverently, as if it really was my first time doing this.

My trembling hands added to the scene, but that wasn't pretending.

Locke moaned.

My plan was to get his pants down to his ankles and then make a run for it. I thought about punching him in the nuts while I was down there, but while he still held on to the letter opener, that didn't seem like such a good idea. The impact would probably make him double over, and that would just bring the dagger closer to my head.

I'd just have to take a chance on running. But then what? I still didn't have anything to take to the police. If I went to them now, Locke could just deny everything and probably get *me* arrested for breaking into his campaign office.

I slid Locke's pants down to his shoes. He was wearing white Fruit of the Looms.

All right, I thought. *He might be a serial killer, but he's still a dork.*

His hard-on throbbed menacingly beneath the thin cotton.

In this position, it'd be hard for him to run after me. It was time for me to take off. So why couldn't I will my legs to move?

I could handle myself in a fight, sure. But with my life at stake? I felt my confidence evaporate like any chance I had of happiness with Tony.

Tony? *Really?* I'm thinking about Tony at a time like this?

Focus, Kevin, focus.

I had to run for it.

What if he caught me?

If only that blow to my head wasn't so hard and I still didn't feel so goddamn *dizzy.*

I needed another option.

I needed a miracle.

Then one arrived.

41

Guilty

"Sorry to bother you, sir," I heard from the doorway. "He never showed."

Jason's voice. From where he stood, he could see only Locke from behind, sitting in his chair.

"Ahem," Locke said, "this isn't the best time." He put his hand on my head.

"Sir?"

"Just go, Jason. I'll see you tomorrow." Locke pressed down harder, holding me in place.

"All right, sir," Jason said.

I pushed Locke's hand away and jumped up. "Jason!" I screamed.

Jason was already walking away. He turned and his eyes opened wide. "Kevin?" I saw he was looking at the open gash on my forehead.

"Jason," I said, running toward him. "You have to help me. He's crazy!"

Locke stood up, his pants at his ankles, his underwear tented and damp. "What are you talking about?" he asked me. Then, to Jason, "He was here when I got here tonight. He tried to seduce me!"

"Looks like it was working." Jason chuckled. Then, remembering his position, he added, "Sir."

I grabbed Jason's arm. "He was going to kill me. Look!" I pointed at the letter opener in Locke's hand.

"This?" Locke let the weapon fall from his grasp. "I didn't even remember I had this. My mind was on . . . other things."

I bet.

"Don't believe him, Jason," I begged.

Jason put his arm around me. He took a handkerchief from his pocket and put it to my forehead. "Calm down, Kevin. I'm sure there's a logical explanation for all this."

Jason had to believe me. "I'm not the first one he's tried to kill," I told him. "There have been others. Brooklyn Roy. And Sammy White Tee. Rueben and my friend Randy, but Randy didn't die and . . ."

Locke looked at Jason. "I don't even know who those people are." He looked down for a moment and then back at Jason. "Wait, there was a boy named Roy, right? And wasn't there a Randy?"

Jason squeezed my shoulder harder and started walking me out of the room. "Kevin, it sounds like you've had a very traumatic night. Why don't we let Father Locke collect himself and talk this out . . ."

Locke interrupted him. "Wait a minute, Jason. Sammy White Tee—could that have been that young man Samuel you introduced me to? The one you told me had written the fan mail?"

Jason's eyes narrowed. "Not now, Father. Kevin, let's get out of here."

"No, let the boy talk," Locke insisted. He bent over and pulled up his pants, regaining a bit of his authority in the process. "I want to hear what he has to say."

"No, you don't," Jason insisted. "It's just a lot of nonsense and you need to . . ."

"'Nonsense!'" I shouted. "No, wait, you don't understand. Locke hired these boys, he had sex with them, and now they're all dead or . . ."

Before I had a chance to react, Jason drew his hand back and smacked me against the cheek. The unexpected impact sent me sprawling to the floor. "That's enough from you, Kevin."

Locke walked toward him in long, quick steps, his arms pumping. "What are you doing, Jason? I told you . . ."

SECOND YOU SIN   289

Jason turned to him in a fury. "You shut up, old man! Just shut up!"

Locke hadn't been hit like me, but he stumbled backward anyway.

"How *dare* you," Locke hissed. "Who do you think you are?"

"Who do I think I am?" Jason laughed. "Who do I think I am? I'm the man who made you, you old fool. I'm your creator, *Father*. I decide what you do, who you meet, what you say, and when. I'm your scheduler and your planner and your pimp. I'm the man who's been cleaning up your messes, the ones you've been stupid enough to leave behind. I'm the man you owe everything to. I'm the man who knows all your secrets, you dumb faggot. I know where the bodies are buried.

"I'm your god."

Locke blanched and looked unsteady on his feet. He fell back into his chair. "Judas," he whispered under his breath. "Blasphemer."

Jason reached behind his back and pulled a small pistol from his belt. He pointed it at me. "And now I have one more mess to clean up." He sighed. "Oh, Kevin. I had such for high hopes for you."

"No," Locke thundered from his seat. "Jason, why are you doing this?"

"Ask your little butt buddy," Jason answered, waving his pistol at me.

I glared at him.

"Cat got your tongue?" Jason asked me. "Oh, I forgot, you probably don't go much for pussy, do you?"

My mind struggled to figure out what was going on here.

Locke seemed to know at least some of the boys who'd gotten killed, but had no idea what happened to them. Meanwhile, Jason not only knew what was going on, but the gun in his hand made me think he might be the killer. But why?

And how come he didn't have an accent anymore?

"How about I get you started?" Jason said, his tone condescending. "Our friend *Father Locke* here"—Jason spat out the name as if it were venom—"has certain . . . appetites. Needs he can't control. Urges."

Locke turned even paler. His eyes filled with tears.

"When I started working with him, I heard things around the office. Rumors. People wondered about his propensity for hiring young male interns. They talked about how he'd take them on trips with him. Or meet behind closed doors for longer than seemed necessary. Such *ugly* rumors. Who would say such things?

"Still, this kind of talk wasn't going to help *me* one little bit. I hitched my wagon to Locke because I wanted to take him places. I knew from the beginning that he had political potential, and I had every intention of going along for the ride. His . . . *inconvenient* hobbies threatened to derail that train.

"Still, it was all just rumors and scuttlebutt. The vast majority of Locke's followers never heard any of it, and even if they did, those brainwashed idiots wouldn't believe a word. I figured that as long as Locke was discreet, we'd be OK.

"Then, one day, a twenty-one-year-old office assistant came to me in tears. He said that Locke was constantly making comments about his appearance, brushing against him, touching him inappropriately. Finally, he claimed that Locke told him that if he wanted to advance in Locke's ministry, he was going to have to do 'whatever it took' to get ahead.

"You remember Charlie, don't you, sir?"

Locke began to tremble. His pallor turned from white to green. He turned his head, unable to meet Jason's eyes.

"By that time, I was working as an assistant to Locke's chief of staff. I went to Locke and told him the situation. At first, Locke denied everything. But I was young back then, and not too bad-looking myself. It wasn't too hard to get him talking.

"After getting him to understand just how bad a public accusation like this would be, Locke agreed to let me pay off Charlie to keep quiet. Sure, I had to skim ten thousand dollars that we'd raised to support inner-city churches, but, hey, who cares about poor people, anyway?" He jerked his thumb over at Locke.

"Certainly not this hypocrite. Neither did Charlie. He took the money and ran.

"Once I knew Locke's secret, I had power over him. It wasn't long before I moved up to the chief of staff position myself. Locke came to trust me more and more, didn't you, Father?

"Eight months later, another young man came to me complaining about Locke's behavior. Lucas. Big blond strapping boy. Even though I'm not into guys, I had to admit you had good taste on that one, sir.

"Lucas asked if he could meet me after work. At a local bar, he poured out his heart to me. I did my best to contain the situation. I offered him the same ten thousand dollars Charlie had taken, and, when that didn't work, doubled it. Unfortunately, dear Lucas wasn't about to be bought off.

"Lucas, bless his heart, was a true believer. Although he'd come to hate Locke—sorry, sir—he liked and trusted me. He told me the only reason he'd come to me was to give me fair notice before going to the press.

"I have to say, I was impressed by his integrity. Even his thoughtfulness touched me—imagine, thinking of my welfare at such a stressful time for him.

"I walked him out to his car and commended him on his character. Then I broke his neck."

Locke doubled over and threw up into a garbage can beside his desk.

"See?" Jason said to me. "Weak. Without me pushing him, protecting him, he'd still be preaching to fat housewives on cable TV."

Locke looked up, a smear of vomit staining his shirt. "You told me Lucas went back to school," he cried.

"Because I knew you couldn't deal with the truth, old man. You'd never accept what needed to be done."

Jason turned back to me. "Soon enough, I realized I had a real problem on my hands. Locke wasn't going to give up dick, and one day I was the one who was going to get fucked. Metaphorically, of course. So, I started hiring male prostitutes."

Locke started to get up from his chair again. "What?"

"Sit down," Jason ordered, and Locke obeyed. "I figured it was worth a couple of hundred bucks to get a professional to do the job. It wasn't like the cash was coming from my pocket, after all. We had plenty of money pouring into the ministry.

"I told Locke the boys were fans, or volunteers, whatever, and arranged the meetings. Every couple of months was enough to keep the old man satisfied. The rumors about Locke died down and I counted on the fact that confidentiality was one of the perks of hiring pros.

"But after we came to New York, and I'd gone through a few boys for Locke, one of them approached me at the office. The one you called Sammy, I think. The kid was no dummy. He'd seen Locke's commercials and thought this could be his big pay-day. He told me he had pictures of his assignation with Locke, and that he'd take them to the press if we didn't pay him one hundred thousand dollars."

"So, you killed him, too," I said.

"See, I knew you were a bright boy," Jason said.

"But you realized," I continued, "that the other boys were potential problems, too."

"Exactly right. And that was part of my job. Cleaning up after Locke's messes."

Locke looked like he was going to toss his cookies again. My own stomach was queasy enough with fear that I really hoped he wouldn't.

"You killed them?" Locke asked, his voice quivering. "You killed them all?"

Jason cocked his head to the side and gave Locke the sideways grin that seemed so charming to me only hours before. Now, it was chilling.

"Just looking out for you, sir."

"Bastard!" Locke screamed. With a speed that surprised me, Locke leapt from his chair, grabbing the letter opener as he charged toward Jason. "Not in my name!"

Casually, as if using bug spray on a fly, Jason leveled his pistol at Locke and shot him. Locke crumpled to the floor, blood pooling around him.

"Oh my God!" I screamed, feeling myself becoming hysterical. "You killed him!"

"That? Please. I shot him in the shoulder. I'm surprised he even passed out, but given what a wimp he is, I guess I shouldn't be. No, as soon as I wrap things up with you, I'll call an ambulance, and he'll be good as new."

"How can you do that?" I asked. I was trying to get him off balance, force him to make a mistake. Up till now, he'd been unflappably cool and levelheaded. As I was a nervous wreck, Jason's calm put me at a distinct disadvantage. I needed him distracted.

"Won't he turn you in to the police the moment he can?" I asked.

"And say what?" Jason asked me derisively. "Tell them that I've been killing the man-whores he's been fucking? Throw away his entire career, his reputation, just to avenge some street trash he never even thought of again once he was done with them? I don't think so, Kevin. Locke owes me everything. I've been manipulating him behind the scenes for years now.

"The only thing that's going to change is that I'll be able to be more open with him about who's in charge here. It should actually make things easier for me.

"Too bad for you, though. We're going to need someone to blame for the shooting, you know." He looked at me dismissively. "I guess that's where you come in."

42

I Can Do It

"You're going to try and pin this on me?" I asked.

"Sorry," Jason said. "I really did like you. Of course, I thought you'd be useful, too. A pretty young thing like you. It was clear you worshipped Locke. Plus, you were obviously a homosexual."

Not that it was an insult to be called gay, but I thought I'd played it pretty straight. "Really?"

"Well, duh," Jason answered. "To be fair, I'm kind of an expert at reading people. I hoped that by putting you in front of Locke, giving you some time alone with him, you would be the perfect solution to my problem.

"You know, you're the real reason Locke didn't fly to DC today. I told him about you and he canceled his plans, just to meet the cute little piece of ass who'd wandered in off the street. What an idiot he is.

"Not that I minded. My hope was that Locke would be attracted to you and want to keep you around. Not only would that make it easier for me—no more trolling for hustlers, thank you very much—but I'd have you around to help *me* out, too. You really are a bright kid, Kevin. It could have been a win-win for everyone.

"When I walked in just now with you kneeling between Locke's legs, well, I thought it all worked out just right. Talk about a perfect plan! Then you had to start screaming about murder and blow the whole thing. Or, blow the *wrong* thing, I suppose." He laughed at his own joke.

"Sorry to let you down," I mumbled.

Jason shrugged as if he was dismissing a petty annoyance. "It was pretty disappointing, I can tell you that."

"You had it all worked out," I said. I was still on the floor, Jason still had the gun. I figured my best bet was to keep him talking until . . . well, I really didn't have much of a plan after that.

"I told you, Kevin, that's my job. Making sure things work out."

"But all those killings, Jason? You were a theology major. You started working for Locke because you believed in his message of peace. How could you betray all that?"

Jason threw his head back and laughed. "You believed all that shit? So did Locke. There is no 'Jason Carter.' I made him up. The school records, the family, the work history. All invented. I saw an opportunity with Locke and I went for it. I said whatever I needed to say to make Locke like me. To make him trust me."

"What about your wife and children?" I asked him.

"What wife and children?" he asked.

"The picture on your desk."

Jason laughed again. "Everyone falls for that one. That's the picture that came with the frame, Kevin."

When am I going to learn to trust my instincts?

"Even the name. Jason Carter. It's one of the first rules of the long con—use a name your target will relate to. He's Jacob, I went with Jason. I knew a narcissist like him would go for that one."

"You're good," I admitted.

"The best."

"Why'd you wear the eye patch?" I had to confirm it was him at the hospital.

"Why do you think?"

"A distraction?"

He touched a finger to his nose. "Bingo. You want to guess why I picked the last name?"

I thought about it for moment. "The initials."

Jason's smile was genuine. "You *are* smart. Those Bible-thumpers all love them some J. C."

It was kind of ironic. I had social engineered my way into Locke's life, and so had Jason.

I remembered what it was like when I was Kevin Johnson. The approval and access were seductive. My double identity was a heady, powerful secret to keep.

At the same time, though, it was a lonely place to be. People liked me, but not the *real* me. If they knew who I really was, they'd never accept me.

And everyone wants to be accepted for who they really are.

They need it.

When I was in school, I was a psychology major. In my first course, we studied the work of Abraham Maslow, whose hierarchy of needs is one of the most widely accepted tenets of modern psychology.

Maslow proposed that all human beings have the same basic needs, which he placed in a pyramid with five levels. At the bottom are the physiological needs, like food and shelter. As you work your way up, though, the needs become more psychosocial, until you reach the top. There, you find the needs to be accepted, to be valued, to be appreciated.

Without having those needs met, you can never be fulfilled.

Every week, men paid me thousands of dollars to be with me. If all they wanted was an orgasm, they could jerk off and save a lot of money.

What were those men seeking if not a person with whom they could feel accepted? Maybe even loved. For who they really were.

Even if they wanted to dress like a clown or play with feet or put me to sleep with a china cup. They all wanted to be loved.

Earlier, when I was trying to gain the upper hand with Locke, I thought that all I knew how to do was seduce men.

I sold myself short.

What I did, what I was *good* at, was understanding what a man needs and giving it to him. Sex was only a tool I used to make him feel, even if just for a moment, even if it was paid for, what he needed to feel.

Jason had been living a lie for many years, now.

I had a sense I knew what he needed.

Was I right?

I'd better be.

I was about to bet my life on it.

I looked Jason in the eye and started to stand up. He frowned. "Now, now, Kevin. Don't get up. I like it just fine where you are."

Betting that my hunch was right, I continued to stand. But as I did, I began to applaud. Jason looked confused. I was about five feet away from him.

"Sorry, buddy," I said, casually, as if we were still the best of friends, "but you deserve a standing ovation." I clapped enthusiastically. "I thought *I* was good! But that shit you've been pulling makes me look like an amateur."

Jason looked confused. "What are you talking about?"

"What's my name?"

"Look, I don't see the point of . . ."

"Please," I said. "This might be the last conversation I ever have, so cut me a little slack, OK? What's my name?"

"Your name," he said with irritation, as if indulging a particularly annoying toddler, "is Kevin."

"No, my full name."

"Kevin . . ." Jason's eyes veered to the left as he accessed his memory banks. "Kevin Johnson."

"Kevin Johnson," I repeated. I held my hand out to him. "I'm going to reach for my wallet, OK. I want to show you something."

Jason's eyes narrowed and he tightened his grip on his pistol. I took out my wallet, opened it to my driver's license, and handed it to him.

"*Kevin Connor?*" Jason asked. "I don't get it."

"Dude," I said, trying to sound casual, as if we were two friends about to share in a particularly funny joke, "Kevin Johnson doesn't exist. I made him up."

"What? But I saw the Facebook page, the article in the paper you wrote."

I wiggled my fingers in the air like a magician about to pull a rabbit out of a hat. "Abracadabra," I said. "I'm a bit of an Internet wizard." I didn't mean to claim credit for my friend Marc's work, but if things didn't work out for me here, I didn't want to send Jason after him, either.

"But why?" Jason asked.

"Same reason as you, man. I smelled opportunity the minute I saw Locke on TV. I heard rumors about him, too. Including some that linked him to one of the boys who'd been killed. I figured I'd sneak my way in here, gather some evidence, and then blackmail him. Same as Sammy.

"But after I spent some time here, working with you, I thought, 'Why settle for a few thousand dollars? Why not go after Locke for real, set myself up as his permanent boy?'

"The crazy thing is, Jason, I changed my mind because of *you*. I've really enjoyed working with you these past few days. You're super cool, you're smart, and I could see you're going places. Places I want to go, too.

"So, I was playing Locke, too. The only part I didn't like was having to lie to you, to keep up the false face.

"But now that I know about you, well, it's even better. Dude, you are my hero! I want to be your Padawan! You don't need me as another dead body on your hands. You need me as your partner!"

Jason looked skeptical. But, for the first time, he dropped the hand he held his gun in to his side. I could see he was conflicted. Should he believe me, or not?

I had two chances here. The first, best outcome would be that Jason bought my act long enough for me to escape and run to the police. The second, riskier move was for me to at least get close enough to him to try and knock the gun out of his hand. Then, it might be a fair fight.

I planned on working both options. I took a step toward him and continued to play Eve Harrington to his Margo Channing. "What a team we'd be! You'll create great plans, and I'll make them great!"

Jason looked at Locke lying across the desk, then back at me. "I've been doing pretty well on my own, Kevin Connor Johnson. Why would I need you?"

"Because you can't keep hiring boys and killing them forever, Jason. Eventually, you're going to get caught. But keep me around, and I'll make sure that Locke is satisfied on that front." I slapped my ass. "Or satisfied in the back. It's all good to me." I grinned like we were two naughty schoolboys planning a prank on the teacher.

"Huh," Jason said.

"With me around, Locke won't need any more boys. That's one less thing for you to worry about."

Jason's face was starting to relax. So was his grip on the gun. I took another step forward, turning my palms upward, as if in supplication.

"Think about it, Jason. You wouldn't be alone anymore. I'd be right there, at your side. Together, we could keep Locke in line and ride him all the way to the White House!" Another step. I was at arm's length from him now.

"You know"—Jason nodded—"you do kind of remind me of myself ten years ago. You're smart, you're devious. I bet you'd make a hell of a sidekick." He smiled broadly, his white predator's teeth brilliant and even.

I smiled back and extended my hand. "So, it's a deal?"

Jason shook his head. "You kidding? Ten years ago I was a total shit. Same as I am now. I don't even trust *myself*. Why the fuck would I trust you?"

"Because you're tired of being alone?" I offered. "Because you want someone who appreciates you and has your back? Because you need me?"

"The only thing I need you for," he said, raising his pistol toward me, "is as the dead body to pin this on."

* * *

43

Sleep in Heavenly Peace

When I was a kid, one of my favorite movies was *The Karate Kid*. The original one, with Ralph Macchio.

Remember, I was a little guy, and a bit of a girly boy. I couldn't help but relate to Macchio's character of Daniel, the skinny kid who gets picked on and beaten up by a gang of upper-class popular boys. The only way Daniel can survive is by challenging them to a karate match. The bullies had been studying martial arts for years, but Daniel was a novice. The odds of him triumphing were pathetically low.

But through his unexpected friendship with Mr. Miyagi, played to perfection by the late, great Pat Morita, Daniel discovers more than just how to fight. He learns about honor, principle, and that the best way to win a battle is to avoid it. (BTW, this is going to be relevant in a minute; hang in there.)

If those things don't work, though, he also gets the world's fastest crash course in karate. And while all the skills Mr. Miyagi taught him turn out to be useful, the most important, the crucial move that saves him in the end, is the crane kick.

Between the ages of ten and twelve, I must have practiced that kick at least once a day. Rewinding the DVD, I watched Daniel again and again.

First, he raised his arms and dropped his wrists, so that his fingers were pointing down at the floor. At the same time, he brought his left knee up as high it would go, while balancing on his right foot. Then, at the perfect moment, he switched his legs, dropping the left to the ground while bringing the right one up for an explosive kick.

I spent endless hours copying that move. I was pretty obsessed with it.

Mr. Miyagi, in the kind of pidgin English that I don't think would work today, tells Daniel, "If do right, no can defense."

As I entered my teen years, I was becoming aware of the differences between me and the other boys. I didn't want the same things they did. I didn't have the same interests. I was different.

I knew it would make me a target. I was afraid.

In an increasingly scary and unpredictable world, what I wanted, more than anything else, was one thing that, if I do right, no can defense.

Who knew it'd be more than ten years before I needed it?

In the movie, Ralph Macchio drags out the crane kick for the most dramatic tension. It works. You're at the edge of the seat as you watch Macchio's intense, vulnerable face quiver as he teeters nervously on one leg, waiting to make his move.

Years later, when I finally took martial arts lessons, I learned there really was such a maneuver, although its basis was kung fu rather than karate. I also learned the right way to do it, which is blindingly quick. With enough practice and skill, it's over before you've even noticed it begin.

Which is how it was for Jason.

"What the fu—" he said, as my body seemed to turn fluid before him. Arms up, knee high, find my balance, jump, and kick. The whole thing took place in less than a second and my aim was true.

The gun went flying out of his hand before he even processed my movements. We both watched as it flew across the room, stopping, unfortunately, upon impact with the head of the still unconscious Jacob Locke, hitting with enough momentum that we heard it thud against his skull.

Wow, I thought, *this really isn't his day.*

While I executed my crane well enough to achieve my primary objective, I didn't nail the landing. As I stumbled backward after the kick, Jason charged forward furiously. If you were drawing the animated version of our encounter, he'd have steam coming out of his nostrils. In real life, he was a blur as he raced toward me, throwing his arms around my waist, and tackling me to the ground.

"You little bitch!" he screamed as he crashed into me.

The back of my head smashed hard against the floor. If the office hadn't been so lushly carpeted, I'd probably have been knocked out. As it was, my vision went wonky and I saw stars. Jason straddled me. He probably had fifty pounds on me.

"I have to give it to you," he said, all friendly now that he had the upper hand again. "You got some moves, chief."

"Yeah," I said, my own voice sounding foreign and a million miles away. "That's why you need me at your side."

Jason slapped me hard against the cheek. The stars I saw were joined by comets and little tweety birds. I felt blood in my mouth.

"Give it up, Kevin. You can't bullshit a bullshitter."

"And you can't get away with this forever," I answered.

"Haven't you figured it out yet? I can. I have every angle covered, little man. Like this one." He reached behind and pulled something from his back pocket. He showed me the black handle before he pressed the button on its side that revealed a switchblade. "I always have a backup plan, chief."

He pressed the cold metal against my neck. His mouth was slightly open and he panted with anticipation. His eyes were wide and dilated.

Whatever else he was in this for, I realized, he liked this. He liked killing. I'd bet money that whatever neighborhood he'd grown up in had experienced a lot of missing dogs and cats.

There was no way I was going to talk him out of murdering me. He was too far gone. Was the Jason I knew even left? Had he ever even existed? I had to try to reach him.

"Please," I said to him, my eyes filling with tears. "Don't do this, Jason. Don't kill me."

Jason's mouth twisted into a shape that showed his teeth but yet was nothing like a smile. "Come on," he said. "I told you that you remind me of me. Don't go out begging like a pussy, man. These are your last words." He lowered his face to mine. "Make them memorable." A strand of spit dripped from his mouth and hit my chin.

His mouth was watering at the prospect of ending me.

I tried to say something, but all that came out was a choked sob.

Jason sat up again. He held the knife in his right hand and brought it to his left shoulder.

I bucked wildly under him. I knew he was about to slash my throat, but there was nothing I could do. I couldn't budge him. I'd been counting on a last-minute surge of adrenaline, but instead, I felt just the opposite. I was drained, exhausted. It was as if my body had already absorbed the fact that I was dead. Only my head hadn't accepted it yet.

Oh, Tony, I thought. *You're going to be so sad. I'm sorry. And Mom, and Freddy, and the world, I miss you already.*

I cursed the tears that ran down my face. I hated giving Jason that satisfaction.

I wished there was something I could say to him, some magic word that would destroy him.

He lifted the blade higher, building the momentum he needed to slash my throat.

As incredibly vivid as this all was, I felt a part of myself already drifting away, experiencing the whole thing as if in a dream. It was a kindness, really, this unreality.

"Come on," Jason taunted me. "You're the Bright Young Thing around here. You said you wanted to be my partner, my right-hand man. Isn't there one last thing you have for me, some final bit of 'help' to share? You know, so I don't wind up as fucked up and dead as you're about to be?"

My pulse was pounding so hard I could barely hear him. My eyes darted desperately around the room, landing at a place just beyond him.

"Just . . . one . . . thing . . ." I said, lifting my head to say the last word I'd ever tell him.

Jason's grin was pure evil. "That's my boy! What last wisdom do you have to share at death's door?" I think he was actually cackling.

He was having such a good time, I almost hated to spoil his fun.

"Duck," I told him.

"Du—?" he began.

And then Jacob Locke blew Jason's brains out.

44

I'm Still Here

If you've never been showered by blood and bits of brain, consider yourself lucky.

On the other hand, since the alternative to being covered in various pieces of Jason would have been for him to kill me, I was feeling pretty lucky. Almost giddy with relief.

Without his head, Jason was a lot lighter. Or maybe there was just no more conscious strength holding me down. I shifted my hips and he fell off me, landing on the carpet with a wet plop.

Locke was on his knees, mumbling. I couldn't tell if he was praying or if he'd gone mad.

I sat beside him. "I had to do it," he said. "I had to do it."

I put an arm around him. "I know."

"He was going to kill you," he said, looking at me for absolution.

"You saved my life," I told him. "You did the right thing."

"What are we going to do now?" he asked me.

"We have to call the police."

Locke began to cry. "It's all over, then, isn't it? They'll find out about my . . . indiscretions. About how Jason murdered those boys. In my name!" He grabbed my arm with surprising strength. "You know that I would never, I could never . . ." He took a deep breath. "If I'd have known what he was doing, I would have stopped him. Even if it meant losing everything. You know that, right?"

"I know," I said. I believed him. "But what I don't under-stand is why you say all that stuff about 'protecting the family' and against gay rights when you have sex with other men. What's that all about?"

"Jason made me say those things," Locke answered. "Look at my record. I never used that kind of language. But once Jason found out about my . . . needs, he started exerting more and more control. He told me I had to talk tough to appeal to 'the base.'

"He never came out and said it, but he always implied that unless I let him make the decisions, he'd expose me for what I am." He buried his face in his hands.

Was it possible that Locke was just weak and not the villain I'd thought him to be? God knows I've met a lot of conflicted men in my life. I seemed to be a magnet for them, actually. Could I have compassion for Locke, too?

"Listen," I told him. "Maybe you deserve another chance to do some good in this world. I have a plan."

By the time the police arrived, Locke and I had our stories straight.

Jason had gone to Locke to confess his sins. Specifically, that he, Jason, had been hiring male prostitutes, having sex with them, and then killing them. When Locke told him that he had to go to the police, Jason shot him, meaning to kill him, too.

That's where I came in. I had been by the office earlier to vol-unteer and left my phone. On the off chance there was someone there, I went by and found the door open. As I walked in, I heard the gunshot. I ran into Locke's office, where Jason and I scuffled.

The rest of the story was pretty much the truth. We told the police that I was able to knock the gun from Jason's hand, but that he was still able to overpower me. Locke came to and found Jason about to slash my throat. He shouted a warning, but when Jason didn't stop, Locke had no choice but to shoot him.

The weird thing is, when I was working the story out with

Locke, he insisted that he really *did* call for Jason to stop or he'd shoot.

If so, I didn't hear it. Neither did Jason, clear as I could tell.

In any case, it gave me just enough pause to wonder if maybe Locke wasn't more calculating than I believed. While everything I witnessed between him and Jason made me believe that Jason was a manipulative, psychotic freak, I couldn't deny that Locke allowed himself to be used.

If Locke *didn't* shout a warning, was it because he wanted Jason dead? And if so, why? Revenge? Or a more pragmatic decision that with Jason dead, there was one less person who knew his secrets?

Locke said that he never meant to malign gay people, that Jason had forced him into it.

About eighty percent of me believed him.

The other twenty percent bought some insurance.

I told Locke that with Jason gone, I'd keep his secrets, too. We'd pin the whole thing on Jason. I expected that once the police investigated Jason's home and belongings, there'd probably be physical evidence connecting him to the deaths of the boys we knew about.

I prayed there weren't any more.

In exchange, Locke would make good on his word. He'd withdraw from the presidential race and stay out of politics. Instead, he'd put his considerable influence over his faithful following to good use. He'd explain that he'd had an epiphany during his near-fatal encounter with Jason. He'd tell the world that he came to understand that the hateful and divisive language that he and other religious leaders used against LGBT people was ignorant and wrong. That it was intolerance like that that drove Jason to hate and fear his own God-given sexuality.

Locke would devote his life to a ministry that emphasized love, kindness, and acceptance. The main focus of his work would be to heal the divide between gay and straight people.

If not, I reminded him, Jason wasn't the only one who knew his secrets.

And then I told a fib.

I said that what led me to him was that, before he died, Sammy White Tee put a copy of his taped encounter with Locke in the mail to me. A copy I kept somewhere safe.

I told Locke that now that I knew it was Jason making him say anti-gay things, I was relieved that I'd never have to tell another soul about the tape.

I didn't exactly threaten him, but I knew Locke was smart enough to see that keeping his end of our bargain would be the best course for him.

Maybe Locke would have done the right thing on his own. Or, maybe he needed someone to control him. Hell, maybe he got off on it.

Don't ask me. I only completed the first semester of that Intro to Psychology class. I might know what works with guys, but I don't always know *why.*

I did know, however, that the person who hurt my friends would never hurt anyone again.

And, whether for the right reasons or not, Locke was going to use his considerable powers to make the world a better place.

Overall, I thought, things turned out rather well.

After I gave the police my statement, two nice officers drove me home. They offered to take me to a hospital, but I hadn't been hurt. All I wanted was to shower and crawl into bed.

The shooting in Locke's office was going to be big news. Luckily, at Locke's insistence, my name would be kept out of it.

Locke was a powerful man with a lot of influence. My participation in the evening's activities would appear only in sealed court records. I'd be left out of the public story altogether.

Whether Locke was protecting himself or me, I couldn't say.

Having washed every bit of Jason off me (I threw the clothing I'd been wearing into my building's incinerator; they'd never feel clean again), I was more than ready for bed. In fact, I just hoped I made it there—falling asleep in the shower seemed like a distinct possibility.

Then, my phone rang.

It was 2:30 in the morning. Who'd be calling? I was glad caller ID prepared me before I picked up.

"I'm OK," I said by way of greeting.

"What happened?" Tony asked. "I got a call from one of my friends at the precinct. You were involved in a shooting?"

"That was supposed to be a secret," I told him.

"Yeah, well, you had to know I'd find out, right?"

On any other night, it probably would have been some huge emotional moment for me to be hearing Tony's voice again. As it was, I was so tired and numb that I couldn't even muster up a vague sense of longing. I just wanted to sleep.

"Listen," I told him. "I asked you not to contact me until you knew where you wanted to take things with me."

"These are kind of special circumstances, Kevin. It's not every day you get involved in a murder." He paused. "OK, in your case—"

I cut him off. "I appreciate your concern, Tony. I do. But I'm fine. I'm just really tired and I'm going to bed. Thanks for calling, but don't do it again."

I turned off my phone and went to bed.

45

Here We Are at Last

The next time I opened my eyes, my bedside clock read 9:40 AM. I tried to go back to sleep, but my head was racing with images and sounds from the previous evening. Locke. Jason.

Tony.

The night before, I'd been overwhelmed by sheer physical exhaustion. In the morning, with sunlight sneaking through my blinds, the horrors of what I'd been through started to sink in.

I'd almost been killed.

I saw a man who was.

My mother was on ViewTube.

Oy.

I'm not sure if I buy the old adage that idle hands are the devil's playthings, but I was pretty certain that sitting around dwelling on what had happened wasn't going to help me. Luckily, it was Sunday. Although I'd gotten up too late to make morning services, if I hurried, I could get to church on time to colead my Sunday school class.

The kids were probably the best medicine for me, anyway.

I arrived at church ten minutes early and helped Cindy set up. The kids hugged me as they filed in, and, sure enough, each embrace chased the shadows a little further away.

When Nick and Paul arrived to drop off Aaron, they hugged me, too. As did Aaron, who excitedly introduced me to a little boy I hadn't seen there before.

"Dis is my fwiend, Rafi," he said, pushing the little boy forward.

I crouched down to meet him at eye level. "Hi, Rafi," I said. "I'm Kevin."

Rafi looked at his shoes. "Hi," he told them.

"He's a little shy," Paul whispered.

"That's OK," I said, still looking at Rafi. "I'm a little shy sometimes, too. But after a while, I really like making new friends. Aaron, why don't you show Rafi where the building blocks are?"

Aaron took him by the hand and the boys went off together to explore.

"You guys aren't auditioning a new kid to adopt, are you?" I asked.

Nick laughed. "No."

"Too bad. He's a cutie."

"He really is," Nick agreed.

"So's his daddy," Paul added.

"Hey!" Nick elbowed Paul in the ribs.

"What?" Paul shrugged. "I can't look?"

"Not," Nick said, giving him the death stare, "if you want to live."

"All righty, then," Paul said, taking him by the arm. "We better get back to the chapel. See you later, Kevin."

I turned back to the kids with a smile on my face.

A smile.

Who'd have thunk it?

As usual, the kids were great. By the end of our hour together, I realized I hadn't thought about Tony, or my mother, or Jason, or Locke the entire time. I knew I was going to have to process it eventually, but when I did, I knew it wouldn't kill me. I'd be ready.

It was hard to feel hopeless when surrounded by so much hope. Not to sound all Whitney Houston about it, but I really do think that's the magic of children. They remind us of the good that's *possible* in the world, and they inspire us to make it *real*.

Nick and Paul were the last parents to pick up their kid. By then, Cindy had already left and it was just me, Aaron, and Rafi playing with toy trains. Rafi had warmed to me pretty quickly and was sitting in my lap when Nick and Paul arrived at the door.

"Hey, guys," I said. "You taking Rafi, too?"

"Yeah," Nick said. "He's coming over for a playdate."

"Yay!" Aaron said. He and Rafi traded high fives.

"Too bad," I said, teasing. "I was hoping to meet the cute dad."

Rafi giggled at that. I ruffled his hair.

"Actually," Paul said, a big grin on his face, "his dad was hoping to see you, too."

Oh no, I thought. *If these two were planning on fixing me up with someone, I didn't even have the words to tell them how not ready I was.*

I had to try, though. "Guys," I said, "I'm really not up to . . ."

But when Paul stepped aside and Rafi's father walked into the room, my mouth stopped moving.

So did my heart.

"Daddy!" Rafi cried with glee, jumping out of my lap and into his arms.

Tony scooped Rafi up like he was weightless. "Hey, sport," he said, kissing him on the cheek. "Did you have a good time with my friend, Kevin?"

"Yeah, Daddy. He was weal nice. Just like you pwomised."

"You know Daddy always keeps his promises," Tony said, putting Rafi back down. "Are you ready to go over to Aaron's house for a while?"

"Yeah!" Rafi said. He ran over to me and gave me a quick hug. "Thanks for playing with me, Kebbin."

"Me, too," Aaron said, throwing his arms around the both of us.

I held on to them, the weight of their little bodies the only thing keeping me anchored to the floor. I didn't trust my voice enough to speak.

"OK," Nick said, "last one to the door is a sweaty sock." He and the two boys ran into the hallway.

Paul lingered for a moment. The look he gave me told me he knew exactly what Tony and I needed to talk about.

Tony must have sought them out. He planned this with them. But why?

"You guys take as long as you need," Paul said. "Pick Rafi up whenever you're ready. He'll be fine."

"Thanks," Tony said. He shook Paul's hand, and then, surprising me and, I think Paul, too, gave him a hug.

Paul left.

Tony sat on the floor facing me. "So. I think it's time we talked."

I just nodded.

"You were right. I *was* hiding something from you."

When Tony first showed up at the door, I'd been struck dumb. Then, I went numb.

Now? I could have exploded with anger.

"A *son?* You were hiding a son from me? An entire human being named Rafi?" I couldn't believe this was happening.

"His name is actually Raphael," Tony corrected me.

That made sense. I couldn't see Tony naming his son "Rafi." Tony's family was very Italian and Rafi isn't really a . . . wait a minute . . .

Who cares about the kid's name?

Focus, Kevin, focus.

"Raphael was your big secret?"

"Well, at least now you know who I took to see *Super Rangers.*"

"This isn't funny!"

"I know, I know. I've had a lot longer to imagine what it was going to be like telling you this than you've had to hear it. Sorry. But when we talk about this, and we will, whenever you're ready, I think you'll see this explains a lot."

There had been times in the past when I thought Tony had hurt me, but this was the cruelest blow of all.

"How could you not have told me you had a son, Tony?"

Usually, when I got mad at Tony, he'd get mad right back. Not today. He didn't seem defensive, or upset, or hurt.

He looked, for the first time in a long time, totally at peace. He looked . . . *relieved*. It kind of freaked me out.

"Kevin, I had a million reasons not to tell you about Rafi. At first, I didn't say anything because I thought it'd scare you away. Then, when you started talking about how you wanted to have kids, I didn't tell you because I didn't want to get your hopes up. I couldn't see two men raising a child together. Then, I didn't tell you because I hadn't told you for so long that I knew you'd be mad at me for not telling you sooner. Should I go on?"

"No," I answered, realizing that none of that mattered. There was only one question that did.

My entire world hung on the answer.

How do you know if it's love or if it's pain?

It was time to find out.

Tony saw the question in my eyes.

He leaned over and put his hands on my cheeks, brushing my bangs off my face.

"Ask me," he said.

I turned into his palm and rubbed my face against it like a cat.

"I'm afraid."

"You don't have to be. Not anymore. I promise."

You know Daddy always keeps his promises, he'd told Rafi.

How easy it was for a child to trust.

Could I be that brave?

Less than twenty-four hours ago, I had a knife at my throat and was facing death.

This was scarier.

OK, here goes nothing, I thought. *Forget about what happened before.*

"Why are you telling me about Rafi *now?*"

Tony took my hands in his and smiled like a kid in school who'd just been handed a test and realized he had all the right answers.

And you know what?

He did.